THE PERFECT VISIT

A Novel

Stuart Bennett

Longbourn Press

ISBN: 0615542700
ISBN-13: 9780615542706
Library of Congress Control Number: 2011939624
Longbourn Press, Northampton, MA

PART ONE:
APRIL 1817

It was a delightful visit; – perfect, in being much too short.

Jane Austen
Emma
Volume I, Chapter XIII

CHAPTER I

Vanessa Horwood arrived in 1817 Hampshire in a field behind a small inn. She caught her breath at the sight of an unexpected pond. It had been out of range of her time-traveller's viewfinder and if she'd landed a few feet further along she'd have been soaked.

She took careful note of where she was. Returning to this exact spot within a month would take her home. She could feel the pulse of the time-travel current, a pulse that resonated to her own body. Anyone else could walk by and never know it was there. But it wouldn't last: a month, perhaps six weeks, and it would be gone.

An April frost had hardened the mud, allowing Vanessa to reach the road with barely a splatter on her boots. She picked some crocuses on the way, stretching her long pianist's fingers to tuck them into the broad brim of her hat and push away some stray blonde curls. Her dark-blue eyes were oval and her nose aquiline. She wore no make-up.

Vanessa looked once more at her unfamiliar clothes. Her boots were really half-boots: leather, with laces and small rosettes in front of the first eyelets. Her shoemaker had used heavier material than was usual in Regency times – Vanessa was a serious walker. Her skirt was dark cream, ankle-length with multiple hems at the bottom and a warm silk shift and cotton leggings underneath. Her top, according to the 1817 *Repository of Arts*, was the latest spring fashion with a low, straight bodice, close-fitting and, Vanessa thought, quite flattering; the uncorseted

Regency fashions were kind to women who, like her, had slim hips and high busts. Over her entire outfit she wore a triple-layer pelisse, its dark green matching the trim on her dress.

The pelisse was her saving grace on this cold morning. Even though it was fashionable, elegantly cut and with a short waistline, its wool lining and high neck kept the frosty morning at bay. Its pockets held both her bank draft and a small purse with English gold and silver coins, all minted before 1817.

The glow of happiness Vanessa had felt as she said good-bye in the time-travel laboratory was gone. She wasn't happy that her top-secret mission had a mercenary motive. And she was frightened at being alone in the past, with no-one she could ask for help.

Her mission – the Project's mission – was recovering lost books and manuscripts. Only certain organic materials, including the paper and leather in books and manuscripts, could travel from the past to their own time. Stone and metal, except for objects making their return journey with a traveller, would not. This was one of time's several paradoxes. They'd told her there were bound to be others, as yet undiscovered.

The Project had recruited Vanessa in London because of her musical background. They'd thought of recovering a score in Mozart's autograph, but only too late did the recruiters learn that Vanessa spoke only English and French and would be no use in eighteenth-century Austria.

Vanessa had offered an alternative. If it worked, they would secure an immensely valuable manuscript and put Vanessa in touch with the one literary figure for whom she felt the same passion she did for her music.

But Vanessa hadn't told them her plan involved breaking one of the Project's cardinal rules. She stood at the side of the road for a moment, smiling at the thought. Then she focused on a two-storey, double-fronted brick house opposite, glad to see that even in 1817 something appeared a little askew about its architecture, as though the builders had changed their minds partway through construction and decided to make it a bit larger or smaller than originally planned. Newer bricks filled what had been a window at the left of the house, adding to its off-centeredness.

Hoofbeats drummed in the distance as a coach and six horses approached the village. Vanessa took a step back as it passed, just avoiding some splashes from the thawing road. After the coach was gone and her ears readjusted to the quiet, she heard the sound of a slightly off-key piano across the road. The tune was simple: a snippet of Bach. A moment later came a transcription of a Regency song

Vanessa knew but couldn't place. The song trailed off, unfinished, and silence returned.

It was still too early to present herself. Vanessa had spent long enough at sea to judge time by the sun and she reckoned it was nearly nine o'clock, too close to breakfast. She knew where the village church was, however, and she walked down to see it and the nearby manor house. She was back in half-an-hour with some more flowers in her hat, resolutely approaching the wide door fronting the road.

The first response to Vanessa's knock was a rustle of papers, receding footsteps, and the creak of an interior door. After a moment a servant-girl answered, giving Vanessa an inquisitive but not unfriendly look. Vanessa handed over a folded piece of paper, which she had cut from one of her own Regency scrap-albums a few days before she time-travelled. On it she had written her own introduction:

> In measured verse I'll now rehearse
> The charms of lovely Anna:
> And, first, her mind is unconfined
> Like any vast savannah.
>
> Ontario's lake may fitly speak
> Her fancy's ample bound:
> Its circuit may, on strict survey
> Five hundred miles be found.

"Will you give this to Miss Jane Austen, please, and tell her that Vanessa Horwood from Canada calls with Anna's commendation?"

The girl bobbed a curtsey. "Of course, miss. Will you come through and sit?"

Vanessa followed her through a door to the left, into a sunny drawing room. A pianoforte was in the corner, music still on the stand; opposite was a small settee flanked by three chairs. Vanessa chose one and perched gently, her heart pounding.

After a moment two women appeared and Vanessa rose. The first, strongly built, with a high forehead, a nose too long for beauty and a stern, straight mouth belied by the laugh-lines around it, had to be Martha Lloyd, Jane Austen's friend and companion. She was still holding her sewing. The second woman took a sideways step to stand beside Martha. This was Jane herself and when she met Vanessa's gaze everything else seemed to disappear. She was still tall and graceful in her early forties, her large hazel eyes luminous, skin with a few small discolorations but still clear and bright, and with curls of dark hair escaping her bonnet. Her small mouth was pursed with amusement as she held out Vanessa's slip of paper.

"What am I to make of this?"

Vanessa's wits returned. "I believe I can do better. Am I not right, Miss Lloyd, that the little sewing bag you now hold came as a parting gift:

> 'Twill serve another end:
> For when you look upon this bag,
> You'll recollect your friend.

"Indeed, Miss Horwood," said Jane, "you have the better of me. You quote my verses as though you were a family intimate, yet I cannot say there is any connection between us."

Vanessa took refuge in a well-rehearsed white lie.

"Please forgive me, Miss Austen. Your niece Anna sent the verses you are holding to a young man of my acquaintance in Ontario. He knew the affection I had for your writings and kindly sent copies, along with others of your verses, to me."

Martha spoke. "I had forgot, Jane, that I also sent Anna a copy of the poem you wrote for my sewing bag, all those years ago."

Jane turned to Martha and smiled again. "And so even our most casual effusions return to haunt us."

And then to Vanessa, "Please sit, Miss Horwood. Will you take tea?"

"I should be very pleased."

"You are uncommonly, almost indecently brown. Surely this is not the effect of a single sea-voyage?"

Vanessa smiled. She'd been a sailor all her life, but to admit it in this time would brand her as a social outcast.

"No, ma'am. In the last year I have been in the Southern Seas, as far as Australia and India."

"And now," Jane replied, "you are come from Ontario merely to embarrass me?"

Vanessa smiled again, this time a little uncomfortably.

"Would you have me state my business so soon, Miss Austen?"

Jane did not hesitate. "I find that is often the best way when strangers call at my door."

"I have four reasons for coming. May I say all of them?"

6

"Well," said Jane, "the advantage of your saying all of them now, is that when you are finished we shall be nearer our tea-time. If I have no reply, we can sip and have done."

"First," said Vanessa, "I wanted to meet the author of the four books in which I have taken the liveliest interest." Jane nodded, her face expressionless. "Second, I wanted to see your pianoforte." This raised an eyebrow. "Third, I have been asked by a gentleman to propose to you a matter of business."

A second eyebrow went up. "And there is yet a fourth reason?"

Vanessa blushed. She knew that non-interference was the primary rule of time-travel and that breaking it could have unimaginable consequences. She took a deep breath, gathered her resolve and went on.

"I believe, from looking at your complexion, that your health would be improved by drinking strong cups of liquorice tea."

Jane's laugh was musical. But when it stopped, her face was red and she was short of breath.

Vanessa was quick to apologise. "Please forgive me. I have said too much."

Martha added quietly, "Jane, I believe you should go up and rest."

Jane's colour was nearer normal now and she spoke firmly.

"Certainly not. I have, it seems, in one young woman a literary critic, a musician, a financier, and an apothecary. This is too good to miss." She turned to Vanessa. "I intend we shall proceed with the most anodyne of your personae, Miss Horwood. If you are indeed a musician, perhaps you would care to try my instrument?"

Vanessa stood. "With pleasure. But I wonder if you have the same trouble keeping it tuned as I have with mine. Would you allow me to adjust it slightly, if you have the lever?"

"Nicely put, Miss Horwood," said Martha. "Jane complained just this morning that a visit from the mechanic in Alton was overdue."

The lever was soon produced and Vanessa had just started in the middle range when tea arrived. She took a biscuit and a cup and then, dreading more questions, did her best to look busy chewing. Soon she jumped up to finish with the piano. She regretted having asked for the tuning lever, but her question had been automatic, as she had heard for herself that the instrument was flat. It would have been agony for her to play.

Within twenty minutes she had the middle range in good order – her ear was accurate enough that no fork was needed to give the true note – and she decided to leave the rest alone. She leafed through the folders on the music stand, smiling at the one in Jane's autograph which read "Juvenile Songs for Young Beginners who don't know enough to Practice." She opened a printed volume of *Favourite Sonatinas* by Pleyel. These she knew: they were simple and elegant and she rattled off a couple without pausing.

The two ladies applauded at the end. "Well done, Miss Horwood," said Martha.

Jane also smiled her encouragement. "If you are as fine an apothecary as you are a pianist, there is hope for me yet. What makes you think liquorice will do me good, when neither Mr. Curtis nor yet Mr. King Lyford in Winchester has thought of it?"

Vanessa herself had pondered this question. Most twentieth- and twenty-first-century medical writers believed that Jane Austen died of Addison's disease, a complete shutdown of her adrenal glands. If they were right – and there were dissenters – the only cure was regular doses of hydrocortisone, a modern synthetic that Vanessa could neither time-transport nor manufacture from ingredients available in 1817. But she had discovered that liquorice tea contains glycyrrhiza, which blocks the breakdown of hydrocortisone in the liver. Assuming the modern diagnosis was right, if Jane's disease were not too far advanced there was some hope that the tea would cause a natural increase of hydrocortisone in her system and give her adrenal glands enough rest for at least a partial recovery.

Vanessa knew that without intervention Jane would be dead in a matter of months. What possible harm could come from trying to extend a reclusive spinster's life in the English countryside?

But how much medical theory could Vanessa communicate? At first she tried to speak of adrenaline, only to discover that something prevented her. She could form the thought but not articulate it. After a moment, under Jane and Martha's puzzled stares, Vanessa gave the simplest possible explanation.

"You seem feverish and, if I may say so, fatigued. Two of my acquaintance in Montreal showed the same symptoms and when our apothecary prescribed liquorice tea – made strong and drank three or four times a day – they proclaimed themselves cured within a fortnight."

"Well," said Jane, "there can be no harm in it, can there, Martha?"

"None, my dear Jane," Martha answered. "I plan a walk to Alton this afternoon if the weather stays fine. I shall see if our Mr. Curtis has any of the root to hand."

Jane was starting to look tired again and her smile was forced.

"So, Miss Horwood, I am gratified you admire my writings but I believe I shall limit myself to your third attribute. What, pray, is your friend's business with me?"

Vanessa took a deep breath, searching her mind for her best Regency language. But what she had to say came without effort.

"Miss Austen, I trust you will condescend to hear this without offence. So great an admirer is my friend that he has charged me to offer you a sum of money if you would part with the manuscript of one of your novels."

Again the elegant laugh.

"What use to me is the manuscript once it is printed? I have none to speak of. I suppose that rogue Murray might still have *Emma*, though I doubt he'd part with it. Egerton's your man. He has just reprinted *Pride and Prejudice* without so much as a by-your-leave and compressed it all into two volumes to save himself a few crowns. If he's kept my scribblings, your money will have its way."

Jane was so pale after this last effort that Vanessa stood up.

"Please forgive me; I have over-tired you. I must take my leave."

"Miss Horwood." Martha stood as well. "There is by no means sufficient to entertain you in Chawton. May I ask where you go from here?"

"I confess that I too planned a walk to Alton."

"Will you not accompany me?"

"I should like nothing better," said Vanessa, "but I did not wish to impose myself."

"We shall go together then, as soon as I take Jane upstairs."

CHAPTER II

Within half-an-hour the two women were on their way. Clouds were beginning to darken the sky but Martha predicted it would stay dry long enough to keep them from catching cold.

"Young ladies are delicate plants, or so Jane says."

They retraced Vanessa's earlier walk through the handsome village with its thatched and half-timbered cottages and continued along a track which paralleled the coach road. They passed a fine village green bordered with chestnut trees and soon after were in Alton's high street.

Vanessa accompanied Martha to the apothecary's shop, determined to see that the man did not object to liquorice root. She was gratified by his approval and he provided enough for two weeks' worth of tea, which Vanessa paid for over Martha's protests.

Pointing to the now-threatening clouds, Martha decided to hurry back to Chawton, while Vanessa decided to spend the night in Alton and to shop for a change of clothes and a portmanteau. She booked a room at the old Swan Inn, purchased a seat on the post coach to London the next morning, and went to look for a bank.

She knew Jane's brother Henry had opened a branch of his bank, Austen, Gray & Vincent in Alton some years earlier, but it had been the first branch to close as the bank, and Henry, approached bankruptcy. From the records Vanessa had found, it appeared that Hoare's Bank had taken over the premises and was still operating there in 1817. She hoped so, as she had brought with her a bank draft, painstakingly acquired from a specialist dealer in her own time. It was drawn on Hoare's in the amount of two hundred pounds and Vanessa needed the money. Neither clothes nor manuscript could be bought without it.

The bank was indeed Hoare's and the elderly teller smiled benevolently when Vanessa presented her bearer's draft.

"We shall have to send this to London for confirmation, young miss, but I may tell you everything appears to be in order. I can offer an advance if you require funds in the meantime, and if you call again in two days we may conclude the matter."

Two days! Vanessa asked if matters would move more swiftly if she took the draft to London herself. The teller assured her they would not, that his courier rode that afternoon and would return the following evening. She could postpone her departure by one day and be prepared to deal with Mr. Egerton directly upon her arrival in London.

Martha's weather forecast had been accurate. When Vanessa left the bank with her ten guineas advance it had begun to rain. She dashed into the local book-shop and spent a happy hour browsing. One of her guineas went on a brand-new copy of *Emma: a Novel. In Three Volumes. By the Author of "Pride and Prejudice," &c. &c*, as sparkling as a book could be in drab sugar-paper coverings. The pages were unopened, the printed paper labels on the three spines bright and fresh.

Vanessa knew it was sacrilege to cut open the pages and could easily imagine a rare-book librarian like Ned Marston admonishing her against it. The thought of Ned made her smile. He was American, one of the Project's leaders. He'd been the first of their team to time-travel and was already planning his next trip, to Shakespeare's time.

Marston be damned. This *Emma* was new and it was hers. She was going to cut the pages and read it.

For another shilling the bookseller sold her a letter-opener and Vanessa took her book, neatly wrapped and tied with string, and dashed through the rain back to the Swan. The innkeeper sent to change the booking for her post-coach and Vanessa decided that clothes could wait. She hadn't read *Emma* in months and never in the form Jane Austen herself had seen and, presumably, approved. And *never* on the same day as drinking tea with the author.

The rest of the afternoon and evening passed in the company of Emma and her circle. Vanessa felt a tremor of happiness when the book reminded her that the line Martha Lloyd had quoted about "young ladies as delicate plants" was spoken by Emma's father.

The Perfect Visit

Vanessa took supper in her room and woke the next morning to ongoing rain. By noon the clouds had lifted and Vanessa went shopping again, adding a second dress, underclothes and shoes, and a small travelling bag to her supplies. She left them all at the dressmaker's who promised the alterations would be complete before the London coach left the next morning. Vanessa had the third and last volume of *Emma* to finish and that night she again went to sleep happy.

The next morning was sunny and as Vanessa dressed, tying a new pink ribbon around her hat, she thought of her trip to London. The coach would take her to Piccadilly Circus. Then she could find a hotel in St. James's and walk through the park to Egerton's shop in Whitehall. Assuming he still had the manuscript, an offer of a hundred pounds would surely appeal to him, leaving her plenty of money to return to the time-travel pulse in Chawton and to pay the apothecary in Alton for further supplies of liquorice for Jane.

All of this occupied Vanessa's thoughts on her walk to Hoare's Bank. But as she approached the old teller's counter her reverie was interrupted by a pair of constables.

"You are Miss Vanessa Horwood?"

"I am, sir." Vanessa looked directly at the constable who'd spoken and then at the teller. The latter dropped his eyes, discomfited.

The constable spoke again. "We have a warrant from the county magistrate requiring your immediate appearance."

"What?" Vanessa felt she'd turned to stone. Her gaze was still fixed on the teller, as though by staring at him she could make the other men disappear.

But the same constable answered again. "We have sworn statements from him" – pointing at the teller – "and his superiors. The magistrate will explain, miss."

And so Vanessa slowly retraced her steps to a small building close to the Swan Inn, where she learned that a principal of Hoare's in London had sworn an affidavit pronouncing her draft a forgery. A second affidavit from the teller confirmed that Vanessa had personally presented the draft for payment and was therefore either the forger or an accomplice to the forgery, either of which was a felony punishable by death or, in extenuating circumstances, fourteen years' transportation.

"Was the man who pronounced the draft a forgery the banker who signed it?" Vanessa demanded.

"That," said the magistrate sternly, "will be for the Judge of the Assizes and his jury to determine. The constables will accompany you to Winchester Gaol to await your trial."

"But when?" sputtered Vanessa. "What about bail?"

"Bail, miss?" The magistrate's face was lined and pale as it wrinkled in a faint smile. "Forgery is a hanging offence. There is no possibility of bail."

Vanessa's back straightened and she gave the magistrate a fierce look.

"I am innocent of this crime and the draft is a valid document. I trust I shall have the opportunity to prove it, if there is any justice in the system."

The magistrate shrugged.

"That is none of my concern. The case has been made *prima-facie* and my duty, and that of these constables, is to see you safe to Winchester."

Vanessa's earlier numbness returned. She heard the magistrate's words, felt one of the constables take her arm. But it all seemed distant, as though these things were happening to someone in a novel, someone she hardly cared about. She gave no thought to her possessions at the Swan or at the dressmaker's. Without a murmur she let herself be walked to an open wagon for the fifteen-mile drive to Winchester.

All the constables would tell her was that Winchester's new gaol was in Jewry Street — a reminder, Vanessa thought bleakly, of the society described in *The Merchant of Venice*. She felt utterly alone and without hope, as though she were on her way to have her pound of flesh cut out.

Shakespeare, she thought. Has Ned already gone there? Surely he'll come after me. If he were here right now we could easily handle the two constables and get away.

But her heart sank as she remembered something Ned and the project engineers had said, that she was on her own, they couldn't send anyone to her rescue. She'd never asked why, never doubted her ability to take care of herself. Now, slumped in her seat, she knew that even if she dared tackle the two constables she couldn't risk what effect injuring them in the year 1817 might have on the future course of events.

And what if her own imprisonment and trial affected the future? A trial meant *she'd* be making history, history that should never have happened. Was there any hope she could be acquitted before her time-travel pulse disappeared?

She tried to speak to the constables but they refused to answer. As the silence grew heavier, Vanessa began to despair.

CHAPTER III

Ned Marston shivered, although it was a warm June day in London and the big dormer windows of the converted warehouse laboratory were open to the summer breezes. He felt like there was a ghost in the room, a ghost he didn't want to acknowledge.

He looked across at Caroline Potter, who was responsible for the entire Project. Their gazes met and broke away. Vanessa was the ghost: she should have been back by now. Ned himself had travelled to Classical Greece and his return had taken less than a minute – their time – after his departure. Caroline's return from the early twentieth century had taken two seconds. Vanessa had been gone more than five minutes.

He spent ten more minutes pacing the floor before finally sitting down at a corner conference table. The adjacent window overlooked the Thames, across to the old Battersea power station. Ned stared at its four smokestacks. Nothing had burned in the power station for decades, but Ned felt his spirits enveloped by a dark, dull haze.

As if reinforcing his mood, the clouds outside had covered the sun, making the day heavier and greyer than before Vanessa's departure just a few minutes earlier. As Caroline joined him at the table a single shaft of sunlight broke through, reflecting on her hair which was a brown so dark as to be almost black. They'd made a handsome couple when they'd been together, her elegant dark beauty contrasting with Ned's sandy hair and slightly battered good looks. His amateur boxing days had skewed his nose and marked his face, but Ned had laughed when Caroline suggested cosmetic surgery.

Ned had a new beard, still a little short, filling out his face and making him look older than his mid-thirties. Caroline had told him she wasn't sure she liked it, but she knew he'd grown it in anticipation of his trip to Shakespeare's time.

Ned's shirt was clammy. He gazed across the laboratory at the time-travel machine, imagining he could hear Vanessa crying for help in the distance. Grim as it was, the thought made him smile. Vanessa was the last person in the world to cry for help.

"We have to go after her." Ned had spoken louder than he'd intended, his words booming in the warehouse. Caroline and her two fellow-inventors – lecturers from the University's engineering department – winced.

"Shh," Caroline replied. "You know we can't. In fact I heard *you* tell her we couldn't. If we re-programme the machine her return pulse will disappear. We have to wait."

"But how long?" asked Ned. "And why can't you programme a pulse that would send me there and bring both of us back?"

"The machine won't let us."

"What if my arms were around her?"

"It would probably malfunction," said Caroline. "We can't risk it."

"We may *have* to risk it," Ned replied. "But I'll wait for now. Somebody has to be here if she gets back. I have to be at the library tomorrow morning, but I'm good till then."

"Thank you," said Caroline. "I'll get someone to cover my classes tomorrow and spell you at eight o'clock."

"We'll try to be here as well," said one of the engineers. "You both know the drill for shutting the machine down if Vanessa gets back."

The other engineer shook his head. "It's an awfully big if."

Ned started to say something more but Caroline touched her finger to his lips.

"Just wait," she said. "It may all come right."

The big warehouse room was lonely after Caroline and her colleagues left. Ned stared at the time-traveller, and then walked over to check its read-outs for the twentieth time. The indicator lights flickered routinely. "Standing by" they said, "standing by for return passenger." The machine enveloped the passenger in what Ned had called a pulse, but it was more like an aura, invisible and imperceptible to anyone but the person to whose body it was keyed. The aura would remain at the passenger's point of arrival for about a month, as Ned knew from experience, and would return that person to his or her place and time of origin. But the aura didn't last forever. Would it last six weeks? Seven?

Ned put his feet up on the conference table and leaned back in his chair. There was a side office they'd converted into a bedroom where he could sleep – if he could sleep – tonight. If he slept long enough would his feelings of longing and guilt go away?

Vanessa had been in the room with them less than an hour ago but it seemed like an eternity. He could still feel the pressure of her lips when she'd kissed him goodbye. She'd been radiant as a bride in her Regency costume. Only when she'd appeared in the warehouse had Ned appreciated that she'd also behaved like a bride in not letting him see her clothes before she time-travelled. Had she thought her trip like a wedding? Uniting herself with the past she'd dreamed about all her life? If so, he knew the feeling. Those shared dreams had brought them together, closer than he'd ever felt to anyone.

The costume had suited her well. She'd shown him its practical aspect before she even said a word, in a split second hiking the skirt above her long cotton leggings and planting the sole of her boot squarely, none too gently, in the middle of Ned's chest.

"Not just a pretty face," he'd said, recovering his balance.

She'd shaken her head as she resumed her ready position. Then she'd darted forward to kiss him. Ned had started to put his arms around her but she'd pulled her body away, craning her head close to his ear and whispering.

"Thank you, Ned. I was born to do this."

Ned had known he was blushing. Of the three other people in the room only Caroline hadn't looked surprised. A moment later the two engineers started their technical countdown. Vanessa knew the procedures and had her money and clothing in order. She entered the time-traveller without hesitation. Ten seconds later she was gone.

CHAPTER IV

Winchester Gaol was a large grey building with an imposing flat front and a triangular pediment. The windows were in classical Georgian style – those on the first floor even had arched tops – but they were smaller than normal, clearly set high enough to be out of reach from the prison floors. It seemed like a place where a woman could easily disappear.

When the constables turned her over to the gaolers her fears grew. One was young and the other old. Once Vanessa was inside the door and in an empty corridor, they stopped short. The old one gaped at Vanessa and began to cackle.

"A pretty young one, isn't she? Do you know anything of gaols, miss?"

Vanessa shook her head and the old man went on. "We can make it quite pleasant" – he lingered over the last word – "if you've some money to help yourself."

Vanessa didn't know what to say. She imagined she'd be searched and her little purse would be found in any event, so she might as well speak up. "I've ten pounds, more or less."

"Hand it over then, and we'll see what we can do for you."

Vanessa gave an imploring look at the younger guard, who seemed embarrassed.

"I can deliver food, miss, and make sure your bedding's all right. Ten pounds doesn't go far, in this place." Vanessa emptied her purse and the older guard snatched the money.

"S'not ten pounds anyway," he said.

The younger one tried to interrupt, "But. . ."

"Hush your mouth," said the older, counting the money. "There's nine pounds sixteen shillings. You're the one's promised the food, Lem, so you take this five-pound note and you're responsible now. We'd better get her up to the warden."

"How long. . ." Vanessa tried to ask, as they marched her up a flight of stairs.

"Hush, miss," said the old one, in the same tone he'd used to address Lem. "And don't you go mentioning the little talk we had to the warden or you'll get no food and no favours from us."

He grew quieter with each step and by the time he finished speaking they were outside the open door of an office. A lean middle-aged man with thinning hair was bent over a stack of papers. He looked up as they entered and Vanessa saw he was wearing a clerical collar.

"Yes?" he said.

"New prisoner, sir," said the old gaoler. "Here're the papers." He handed the clergyman the same sheaf of papers the constables had carried from the magistrate's in Alton.

"Vanessa Horwood," read the clergyman. His intonation was unexpectedly pleasant and well educated. "Forgery is a serious matter, Miss Horwood. A life-and-death matter. You appear to be a young woman capable of apprehending the consequences of her actions. Would you care to say anything?"

Vanessa stared at the two gaolers and the clergyman spoke to them.

"Leave us now and close the door. I'll call for you when we've finished."

"Sir," Vanessa began, but her voice cracked.

"Sit, young lady," the clergyman said, pointing to a straight-backed chair opposite his desk. He seated himself and Vanessa perched likewise, stiff and uncomfortable. His face seemed kind, but it was deeply lined and the lines looked like sorrow. "My name is Lewcock. I am, officially, both chaplain and chief gaoler here, though I prefer to call myself warden. There aren't many of us trying to make something decent out of the prison system, but I'm proud to call myself one of them. You have perhaps heard of Sir Samuel Romilly?"

"No, sir." Vanessa managed to reply. If he was kind to her, she thought she might break down altogether. She dared not speak more.

"No," said Lewcock, "I suppose a young woman would not give a great deal of thought to the madness of our criminal justice system. Are you aware that there are still crimes where a repeatedly violent offender can, by reciting the 51st

Psalm in court with the Bible in his hands, claim the capacity of reading and, thereby, the Benefit of Clergy and absolution of his crime?"

Vanessa was completely lost. "What?"

Lewcock was intent on his subject now. "But that Benefit of Clergy is not available to anyone convicted of shoplifting goods valued at five shillings or more?"

Vanessa was more insistent now. "I don't understand."

The warden raised his eyes.

"Two women prisoners in Newgate have just had their appeals denied. They were convicted of forging a note for a far lesser amount than yours. They will hang next week. This is the system Romilly and others are trying to change." He put his hand over his eyes and bowed his head. After a moment he looked up.

"How old are you, Miss Horwood?"

"Twenty-two, sir." Vanessa replied.

"And you have family here? Someone we should notify?" He paused a moment. "Accomplices?"

Vanessa sat up straighter. "There are no accomplices, Mr. Lewcock, because there was no crime. The draft in question was purchased from a trader at the Hudson's Bay Company in Montreal." True up to a point, Vanessa realised. They *had* bought the draft from the Hudson's Bay Company in her own time. It was the only example their London agent could find. But what if the draft *originally* was a forgery?

"Montreal!" said Lewcock. "You are Canadian then?"

"Yes, sir."

"There is no chance of affidavits coming from Canada before the Summer Assizes. Have you no people in England?"

"Sir." Vanessa saw the opportunity for an answer to one question at least. "When are the Summer Assizes?"

"Mid-July."

Vanessa's heart sank: twelve weeks off. "Have I any hope of bail?"

"Your offence is too great, Miss Horwood. Even if you were gentry, which it seems you are not in spite of your appearance, the odds would be against it. Have you any ready money for counsel?"

"No, sir."

Lewcock became thoughtful. "I have a friend in London who may decide to visit when I tell her of your case. But for now you must join the women in the Debtors and Felons Gallery. Winchester Gaol is proud of its standards: you will have a wooden bed and straw of your own, and a cell with one or two other women. I suggest you leave that rather elegant pelisse with me for safekeeping, as well as anything else you would care not to lose."

To all this Vanessa had no reply. She'd already given her money away, so she shed her pelisse and handed it over. The warden's eyebrows went up at the sight of her fashionable clothes but he said no more. He called the guards; her audience was over.

CHAPTER V

Downstairs was a heavy door that opened into a cavernous room. Three walls were lined with cells; the fourth had the high windows she'd seen from outside. Below the windows some women were at needlework and others were washing clothes in iron tubs. Still others were sitting with some ragged-looking children and there were a couple of lonely figures in corners muttering to themselves. Vanessa had no time to see more; she was face-to-face with a small, tough-looking female turnkey who introduced herself as Mrs. Badger.

The older guard turned and left; Lem, the younger one, said quietly to Vanessa that he'd bring the first of her food the next morning. Mrs. Badger gave Vanessa an appraising stare and a somewhat sinister smile, showing a few brown teeth and many gaps. "She'll be lucky to keep it," she said to Lem, who winced slightly.

Mrs. Badger spoke to Vanessa. "You'll be upstairs. The ladies" – she smiled again – "will show you which cell." Then she too turned away, following Lem out of the room.

A small crowd had gathered during this conversation and once the door closed behind the guards a large blowsy woman of indeterminate age approached Vanessa.

"What's your name, dearie?" The last word was a sneer, lisped through broken teeth.

Vanessa looked at her. "Horwood."

"'orwood," said the woman. "That's all, is it?"

"That's enough for now," Vanessa said evenly.

"You've brought your garnish, 'ave you?"

"If you mean money, I've given all I had to the guards."

"It ain't the guards as get it, it's us. You'll 'ave to come upstairs for your cell, now, an' we'll discuss it." "Discuss" came out as "dithcuth," but it had the same sneer as "dearie."

Vanessa thought of answering, but decided simply to follow and see things through. Two other women flanked the large one and the one on the left said,

"I'll 'ave the skirt, Jenny, if you're not wanting it yoursel'."

Jenny was the large woman and clearly the ringleader; she only said, "Shut up, Bess."

A fourth woman joined them and with two on either side Vanessa was taken through the room. The rest of its occupants gave way either side, as Vanessa and her escort proceeded to a broad staircase and up to an iron-railed mezzanine backed by a row of cells. The two women on Vanessa's right whispered something to each other and when they reached an empty cell, one said,

"I'll take 'er, when you've done, Jenny. She'll do for me quite nicely."

Vanessa scanned the mezzanine. No help there: it was deserted. But some women from downstairs were following them up. Several in this group seemed worried; a few were younger and better dressed. One gave Vanessa a warning look and when Vanessa caught it, mouthed "careful." Vanessa gave her a quick smile in reply. Then Jenny grabbed Vanessa's arm, spun her around, and pushed her against the outside bars of the cell.

"This," murmured Vanessa, "could be a bar to further discussion."

"Wot?" said Jenny. "You shut your lip till you're spoken to."

"Sorry," said Vanessa. "Sometimes I can't help it." Her adrenalin was up now and she gave a quick look around. The onlookers were well back, though. Things weren't promising.

"Garnish, 'orwood," Jenny went on. "It's money us prisoners get for taking care of you. If you 'aven't got it, we'll have its value from wotever you 'ave. Clothes, fer instance." She pointed through the door of the cell. "Inside, and strip."

Two of her accomplices pushed Vanessa off the bars and she stumbled through the cell door. Once in, she turned to Jenny and said,

"I'm going to freeze without these."

"That's your look-out, dearie."

"What about those women out there? They've got their clothes."

The woman who'd offered to take Vanessa spoke up.

"Do as I say and I'll keep you warm, girl. Now shut your trap an' get your clothes off."

Vanessa took a deep breath. "Let's make this easy. You stay out for a moment and I'll take them off. That way nothing'll get torn, yes?"

Jenny's reply was an unpleasant bark.

"If that's the way you like it."

Vanessa sat carefully on the edge of the bedstead, unlacing her boots. She really would freeze without her skirt and petticoats. Even with the pale sunshine outside the cell felt bitterly cold. What was the warden thinking to take her only warm piece of clothing?

She considered her captors, laughing among themselves. Then she put her hat carefully on the bed, pulled off her stockings – the floor was icy on her bare feet – and unlaced her skirt and shift. Her leggings came down to her ankles and under her fashionable top she had a heavy cotton undershirt. Not quite as good as her workout sweats, but they'd do.

Vanessa stood up and moved closer to the cell door. "Who's coming first?" she called.

As Jenny moved through the cell door the ball of Vanessa's right foot hit her in the solar plexus. Jenny flew backwards into the mezzanine, hit the iron railing, and went down with a grunt. Vanessa resumed her ready stance, covering the cell door so that no more than one woman could come through at a time.

The next one was Bess, swearing. Vanessa's foot caught her in the same place, but as Bess went down a third woman moved quickly into the breach, shoving Vanessa backwards before she could recover her balance. Vanessa started to go down and the woman jumped her, her hands like talons clawing at Vanessa's face. But as Vanessa fell she twisted sideways and drove the heel of her hand into the woman's jaw. The bone cracked and the woman went limp, moaning.

Vanessa was on her feet in an instant, covering the door again, but the fourth captor backed away, raising her hands in placation. The crowd behind was immobile. Vanessa glanced at her enemy on the cell floor, who was starting to crawl.

"One more inch," Vanessa said quietly, "and I'll do the other side of your face too." The woman slumped forward and stayed.

Jenny and Bess were groaning, beginning to get up, as Vanessa called,

"If any of you women want to stop this bullying, now's the time."

She waited, holding her breath, knowing that if nobody came forward she didn't stand a chance. She caught the eye of the woman who'd mouthed the warning and slowly, holding Vanessa's gaze, that woman came forward, put her boot on Jenny's back and pushed down. Then a second woman came forward, and a third, and after a moment there were a dozen, their voices buzzing with excitement and congratulation.

One of the new arrivals bent over the woman still lying in the cell and said happily,

"Mother Norris has a broken jaw, I think." And then, to Mother Norris, "Sit up, you cow. It's naught compared to what you've done to us and would have done to her," pointing at Vanessa.

Vanessa's first ally kept her boot firmly on Jenny's back. "What now?"

It was a good question. As Vanessa thought about it she raised her hand to the side of her face. It came away bloody.

"Can someone tell me how bad this is, please?"

Her ally left Jenny to the others and came close, producing a surprisingly clean handkerchief. She wiped off the blood and smiled.

"Just a scratch. It's as well it's bleeding. There may be poison in Mother Norris's claws."

Vanessa grinned and inspected the woman more closely. Early twenties – about her own age – black-haired and freckled, an angular face with green eyes above a pert, turned-up nose. She was handsome rather than pretty.

"What's your name?"

"Megan Gallagher." She grinned back and with the smile the angles of her face softened. Suddenly she was very pretty indeed.

"You could hardly be more Irish, could you?"

"No, miss. I'd like to think you're Irish too. We can always use the likes of you against the bloody English."

"I'm Vanessa Horwood. Canadian. More later." Vanessa raised her eyes, knowing what she had to do.

She called to her dozen women. "Keep these four where they are for now. Is Mrs. Badger due back soon?" Heads shook. "Good. Let's break up their cells. Are there any others with them?" More head shakes. "And the four of them just ran the place and beat you and took whatever they wanted, yes?" Now the women looked sheepish.

Vanessa walked carefully around her group.

"I need volunteers who'll help keep them down. We'll put them as far apart as we can, one to a cell, with some of us to watch. They're not to get close to each other at any time. Sound all right?" This time Vanessa got smiles.

Meg knew everyone's name and found allies to take three of the bullies in tow. She knew without asking that she and Vanessa were going to take Jenny and she gave Vanessa a wry smile.

"We might as well take Jenny's cell too. Best in the house: linen sheets and a washbasin."

"Let's divide what's there and let the oldest women have the sheets. We need all the friends we can get."

It didn't take long to make the new arrangements and the distribution won over some prisoners who had hung back at first. That night a couple of the mad-women screamed louder, upset by the unfamiliar arrangements, but the next day was quiet and Mrs. Badger made no comment on the changes.

Vanessa was worried about Jenny and Bess, though. Both were accused of murder and expected to hang after the Summer Assizes. Bess had committed the crime, but she was known as Jenny's enforcer and assumed to be following her orders. The two would probably be in the dock on the same day and neither had much to gain by co-operating with Vanessa.

The next morning Bess jumped out of bed and mauled her two cellmates, screaming to her cohorts to break free. Vanessa and Meg barely managed to subdue Jenny, finally tearing her skirt into strips and tying her to her bedstead. But Mother Norris, in a downstairs cell not far from Bess's and still nursing a swollen jaw, made only a half-hearted effort to escape. Their other accomplice made no effort at all.

It took six of Vanessa's allies to subdue Bess. When Vanessa and Meg finally arrived, two were holding each of her arms and Bess leaned forward and spat in Meg's eye. Meg slapped her without hesitation, hard enough that Bess's eyes rolled.

Meg put her face, still wet, close to Bess's. "One more like that and I'll be after breaking your nose. I couldn't fight the four of you before, all alone, but I'm not alone now."

Bess stared past Meg, impassive, and Meg took a step back and said, seemingly to no one in particular,

"Last month two women were found dead, for no reason anyone could tell. I think Bess knows how they died but I wonder if Bess is thinking that what happened to them could happen to her."

Meg turned to Vanessa and went on. "Jenny ruled this henhouse, but that was because Jenny was strongest and liked giving orders. This one" – a shrug towards Bess – "was cruel, just for the love of it."

"I wonder if Mrs. Badger would lock her in by herself," said one of the women still holding Bess's arms.

"Could we ask?" said Vanessa.

"She'll never," snarled Bess.

"Good." Vanessa smiled. "We'll ask."

When Mrs. Badger came that morning with the bread delivery, Bess's two cellmates were produced and explained their black eyes and bruises. Mrs. Badger, mindful of the recent calm of the women's ward, listened to their request and, uncertain where the power lay, asked for Jenny, who was still upstairs tied to her bed. The battered women looked at Vanessa, hovering discreetly in the background, and Vanessa looked at Meg.

Meg stepped forward. "I think Jenny's having a little rest. Miss Horwood and I'll go see."

The two went upstairs and into their cell. Jenny had rolled onto her side, as far as her restraints allowed, her head half-buried in the straw. Vanessa leaned towards her and spoke softly.

"Listen carefully, Jenny. Mrs. Badger wants your say-so to put Bess in a cell by herself. We'll let you up to talk to her but you need to know what you have to say."

Jenny rolled over and began to curse. After a moment she glared at Vanessa.

"I'll say as I please, you bracket-faced bitch, and I'll tuck you with a spade when I've done."

"No," said Vanessa. "Whatever that means, you won't. You can talk to Mrs. Badger and make us look like we're still following your orders, or we can go back down and tell Mrs. Badger you're poorly and can't get up. And if she decides to come see you or send the surgeon, you *will* be poorly by the time they get here."

Jenny was silent and Vanessa went on.

"There's no reason you can't be in charge, Jenny. It's not hard to be fair to everyone. It might even please you."

"I'll bloody please *you*. You're likely to hang as I am. It's the pot calling the kettle black-ass." Jenny sighed. "But I might as well. And I'll be glad to see that blatchy cunt Bess behind bars." Then, more softly, "I never told her to stop the blowse's blubber, nor even to muss her up. And 'ere I am for murder."

She looked up at Vanessa. "You're a plucky one, 'orwood. I'll 'elp you run the fucking 'ospital."

Vanessa turned to Meg, who shrugged. The two of them untied Jenny, who looked ruefully at what was left of her skirt.

"You'd better 'ave saved me another. Mrs. Badger'll think summat's amiss if I'm wearing this rag."

"You're right," Vanessa agreed. "There's still a sack of your loot under Meg's bed. Help yourself."

Another minute and they were downstairs, Mrs. Badger placated, and Jenny barking orders. Vanessa listened for a moment until she was sure Jenny was all right and then whispered to Meg, "What's a bracket-faced bitch?"

Meg grinned. "About as bad as it gets. Let's say 'poxy,' and leave it at that. Have you none of our cant, me darlin'?"

Vanessa shook her head. "Not that kind. I'm really an ignorant country girl, if Canada counts as country."

"You'll learn," said Meg. "I'm in for blotting the scrip and javit, fool that I am. Fresh out of the army, he was, said if he could just get one more person to stand twenty pounds for him, he'd be after setting up a milliner's shop and we could marry. So I said I'd sign for him myself – blotted the scrip and javit. He got the money and disappeared. I could no more get twenty pounds to pay the note than a hundred and here I am for debt."

"But couldn't you be allowed to work it off?"

"The women who work here have enough money, or their families give 'em enough money, to get materials. Jenny took most of what they earned but even so they did a bit better than the rest of us. I've naught but an uncle outside Ireland and no money anywhere. So here I rot. Another year before the Relief of Debtors Act lets me loose, or so they tell me."

"What happened to you about the garnish when you came in?"

"I knew enough to keep my last two guineas sewn in my skirt, away from the guards. Jenny got 'em."

"She must have quite a lot of money. Where do you suppose it is now?"

Meg spat, then apologised.

"Ain't genteel, is it?" She went on. "Jenny has an attorney, as if he'd do her any good, and I fancy she's smuggled the money out to him."

"What would you have done if your young man had been honest?"

"Married him, I suppose. What caught me was his sweet talk about the milliner's shop. I could have set myself up as a dressmaker if I'd had a place to work."

Vanessa sighed. "Well, you won't hang, at least."

Meg gave Vanessa a sharp look.

"Three days, an' I've never asked you what you're in for. Go on, then."

"They say I forged a bank draft."

"How much?"

"Two hundred pounds."

Meg whistled. "You're right, that's a hanging one, sure."

"But I didn't do it."

"Did someone sell it to you?"

"Hudson's Bay Company in Montreal." Vanessa regretted having said so now, even though the story was, in effect, true. She wondered if the warden might try to postpone her trial to give her time to get a letter to Canada. If he did, there could be nothing positive in reply and she would hang for certain.

"You're going to need some help with this one, love," said Meg. Then she put her arms around Vanessa and held her close.

CHAPTER VI

Ned slept fitfully, checking the time-machine over and over as if it could tell him something about Vanessa's fate. Daybreak came just after four. He had always loved the early dawns of London summers, but this morning the light seemed bleak. It was the beginning of their first full day with a lost time-traveller, a traveller Ned had recruited, trained, and loved.

He splashed water in his face, dried himself, and moved to one of the laboratory's computers, searching for any mention of a Vanessa Horwood in southern England in 1817 or after. He was still at it when Caroline arrived with the two engineers, both grim-faced.

"I can't disassemble the damned machine," said the first, "in case Vanessa somehow gets back to a working pulse. But I can tell you this project is finished."

Ned was about to answer, but Caroline held up a hand for silence. "He's right, Ned. We should never have sent another traveller after the trouble you had in Greece. I'll never forgive myself for letting her go. And we're certainly not letting you go anywhere again."

"That's a knee-jerk reaction," Ned replied. "Think it through. I've shown I can get back. You've shown you can too, but the Project can't afford the risk of losing you. As soon as you convince yourselves that Vanessa's pulse is a lost cause, re-programme your machine and send me after her."

Caroline began to protest, but Ned cut her off. "You know I'm the expendable one. If I can get Vanessa to wherever the machine leaves me, we'll discover whether the pulse will carry two of us."

Caroline's voice had an edge of anger now. "Listen to me, Ned. I've already told you time-travel doesn't work that way."

"Then you can leave me with Vanessa until you figure out a way to bring us both back. If she's in trouble there's nobody there to help her. And if anyone is going to figure out a way to rescue lost time-travellers, it's the three of you."

The second engineer spoke up. "You don't *know* Vanessa's in trouble, Marston. There are any number of reasons she could have missed her return."

The other gave a forced laugh. "Maybe she likes it there."

"Don't be stupid," Caroline snapped. She looked at Ned. "You have to go to work," she said gently. "We'll discuss this later. Call me as soon as you can."

"I'll stay here today," said the first engineer. "I can check to be sure Vanessa's travel pulse is intact, and I want to run some historical database searches to see if there's an 1817 record of anything happening to her."

"I've done that," said Ned. "This afternoon I'm going to check the old newspaper microfiches at the British Library."

With that Ned headed for the door. Most of the night he'd wanted someone to talk to, to share his worries, but now others were in the laboratory all he wanted was to be alone. The Rare Book Room at London University's Senate House wasn't the solitude he had in mind, but it was familiar drudgery, so familiar as to be almost mechanical. He could be alone with his thoughts until he could get to the British Library and its newspapers.

It was three o'clock before he could get away and walk up to Euston Road. He'd ordered his microfiches that morning and they were waiting for him, a stack of plastic flimsies with a dusty reader. The reader's light bulb exploded as soon as he turned it on and another half-hour was lost finding a replacement.

The *Salisbury and Winchester Journal* had nothing from April-July 1817, nor did the next two papers Ned tried. But *The Hampshire Chronicle*, the most imperfect of all the fiches, had preserved one entry:

Alton, Wednesday April 16. This morning Miss V. Horwood, apprehended at Hoare's Bank upon presentment of a £200 note declared a forgery, was remanded by the town magistrate to Winchester Gaol for trial at the Summer Assizes. Miss Horwood, described as a young woman of prepossessing manners, attired in the latest Parisian fashion. . . .

The rest of the notice was a blur.

Ned's hands were shaking as he inserted the next three fiches, desperately searching for a notice of the summer assizes. But the quality of the images became worse and worse, with entire pages unintelligible. The librarian looked rueful when Ned asked if there were other copies available.

"We sold or pulped the originals after filming. None of the local libraries wanted them. Too bulky, they said, and not enough interest. It was one of the worst decisions the Library ever made, in my opinion."

Ned telephoned Caroline with the news. She said Ned could come to the laboratory if he wanted to talk and that no-one had any new ideas about what to do. But Ned couldn't face the laboratory again. He promised to be there in the morning and went straight home. He sat in his usual armchair, gazing at his old American furniture and remembering Vanessa's one visit to his flat, the day before she time-travelled. He'd known he was in love with her and nearly asked her not to go.

Don't think about what might have been, he told himself. After a moment his eyes came to rest on a bookcase that had been in his family more than two centuries. It would have been nearly new where – *when*, he corrected himself – she was now.

Vanessa's image stayed with him through the night. "Prepossessing manners... in the latest Parisian fashion." Again he felt the soft, fleeting pressure of her lips as she'd kissed him goodbye in the laboratory, remembered how happy she'd looked. How did she look now? If she wasn't rescued she'd be dead, of course, one way or another. Even if she'd been released from gaol and lived to be a hundred.

But the manner of her death meant more to Ned than he'd ever imagined it could. They'd discussed the dangers of time-travel, but Vanessa had been confident she was going to a comparatively safe time and place. When he'd mentioned danger she'd changed the subject, asking Ned about his plans for that summer. When Ned demurred she told him she had the offer of a small sailboat for a month and invited him to join her. Would Vanessa ever sail again?

CHAPTER VII

When Mrs. Badger finally discovered how many cellmates had changed in the Debtors and Felons Gallery, she at first threatened to bring the guards and return everyone to their original places. But Jenny insisted it was all her doing, promised peace and quiet and said Vanessa would make up a new chart and roster of inmates for the warden if Mrs. Badger would provide pen and ink.

Jenny had changed since Bess had gone to solitary confinement. Jenny, whom everyone in the ward knew was likely to hang, had slowly and painstakingly begun to read the inmates' Bible, sometimes staring out the window of her cell for hours afterwards. And instead of being the figurehead for the improvements in the women's regime, she'd actually taken them in hand herself, seeing to the equitable distribution of food and breaking up the inevitable fights and sexual bullying among some of the rougher prisoners.

Vanessa was bored almost senseless. She soon learned to tell the gaol's visiting hours by the sun and for the first week whenever Mrs. Badger came to the upper gallery Vanessa wondered if the visitor would be for her, and whether it would be Ned Marston come to her rescue.

As the second week wore on Ned was less in her daytime thoughts. She borrowed the inmates' Bible from Jenny, reading all of it herself and parts of it out loud to the children and illiterate women who cared to hear it. She repeatedly sent unanswered requests for more books to the warden, never knowing whether

Mrs. Badger had failed to convey them, or whether the warden had received and ignored them.

She found it hard to sleep at night, tossing fitfully on her cot and waking in tears. She'd stare into darkness, listening to the intermittent screams of the lunatics. Occasionally she smiled at the irony of how she'd longed to be in times and places not her own, and how she'd traded her comfortable, unappreciated life as a London University postgraduate for a Regency prison.

But most of the time her memories were painful, as she told herself how stupid she'd been to assume she could time-travel with impunity. She'd thought it would be just like her fantasies, that she'd be rich and happy in one of Jane Austen's country houses, attended by servants. Instead she was poor and hungry, surrounded by gaol-cells whose chamber-pots stank.

As her bitterness grew her thoughts returned to the man who'd made this trade-off possible: Ned Marston. The romantic visions she'd nurtured before she time-travelled and the dreams of rescue she'd entertained in the first days after her imprisonment disappeared. Now she began to blame him for leaving her stranded. He became the focus of her frustration and despair; she couldn't get her mind to let go of him.

She remembered when she'd first noticed him, a rangy man with dirty blond hair at the University gymnasium. He was ten or more years older than she, often exercising at the same times she did. She noticed he was as loyal to the boxing and fencing studios as she was to the one for *tae kwon do*. She liked the fact that he never spoke to her, although they took to nodding at each other. One day she saw an acquaintance leaving the fencing studio.

"I'm never sparring with him again," he said. "Marston is the most merciless swordsman I've ever seen. Only uses rapiers, says foils are for children. Rapiers *hurt*."

Vanessa smiled to herself. One of her *tae kwon do* opponents had recently made a similar complaint about her. A few days later she noticed Ned with what had to be a Greek or Roman short sword instead of his usual rapier. She was so curious that she decided to try to speak to him.

But he disappeared for the next month and when she saw him again he was limping. To her surprise he followed her into the *tae kwon do* studio, nodding at the instructor and taking a seat in the corner. He watched intently for an hour as the class practiced both meditative and combat moves. She grew self-conscious, even more so when at the end of the class he confronted her.

"Why are you here?" she blurted, trying not to stare at the scars around his eyes. She'd never been close enough to him to notice them.

There was something else about him that troubled her. His features were ordinary enough, handsome even, although a bit battered, and his nose slightly askew. What was it?

But his answering smile was kind enough, even sheepish.

"I was hoping this might work for my rehabilitation programme. I've done some kick-boxing, but I couldn't do the kinds of leg lifts you do even before I got hurt." He gave her an appraising look and went on. "Why *tae kwon do?*"

"For balance," she said. "I spend most of my life working with my hands. This takes me away from them."

He nodded. "I've been to your piano recitals. You're brilliant." As she stiffened at the compliment he seemed to understand he'd said the wrong thing. "Why else do you do it?"

Without thinking she told the truth. "It gets me out of the present."

"Where do you go?" he asked immediately.

This sounded as though it might become more personal than Vanessa wanted. In that instant she knew what bothered her about this man. He seemed dangerous.

"Just away," she said coldly. "Out of my head and into my body."

Ned shook his head. "Not what I meant. I think you understood the question the first time. I meant where do you go instead of the present? Where and *when?*"

He'd caught her off guard, and she answered without thinking.

"Mozart's Vienna, usually. Or the Regency, here in England."

He nodded again, completely at ease. "For me it's always Shakespeare's time. Or Classical Greece. Objects help too." For a moment he was absorbed in his own thoughts and his face softened. "For Shakespeare old books are best. Especially in their original bindings."

He stepped back and for an odd moment it seemed he was about to bow. But he caught himself.

"Nice to see you," he said. He turned and limped out of the room.

A week later he spoke to her again.

"Miss Horwood," he began, but she interrupted.

"This isn't fair," she said. "You obviously know me, but I have no idea who you are, or how you even come to be in the University gym. Are you one of the fencing instructors?"

"Do I look like one?"

"You look worse," she said. "I've seen you with boxing gloves too. You look like a thug."

He laughed. "You don't look like a concert pianist either. You're brown enough to be an Australian surfer, but they say you're Canadian."

Vanessa was angry now. She spoke slowly and deliberately.

"How. . . do. . . you. . . know?"

"I asked the registrar."

"You'd no right to do that."

"I did, in fact. I'm the rare book librarian at Senate House. Faculty privileges. My name's Ned Marston, by the way."

He held out his hand, but she didn't take it. "I suppose," she said, "you've seen my entire record."

He shook his head. "I said I was looking for an assistant in Special Collections and that your name had come up. All I got was a list of the classes you've taken."

"Well, sod off, Mr. Ned Marston. I'm not interested in being your assistant."

"I never thought you were. I want to talk to you about Mozart's Vienna."

"What about it?"

"Would you consider having lunch with Caroline Potter from the Physics Department later in the week? She'll tell the story better than I can."

"I'll think about it," Vanessa replied.

"You're still wondering if I'm trying to pick you up, aren't you? Here" – he pulled out a card and scribbled on the back – "ring Caroline directly. She'll tell you you're safe enough."

He held out the card and grinned at her. After a moment she took it, and turned away.

CHAPTER VIII

On sunny days groups of inmates were let outdoors for walks in a small courtyard, but it was a rainy spring and the grey days seemed to stretch on endlessly.

Vanessa did her best to keep count, but it wasn't long before she lost track. Too many sleepless nights had merged into days with fitful naps and irregular meals.

One night the wind blew away the clouds and Vanessa could see a full moon through the bars of her cell, the first full moon she'd seen in 1817. When she fell asleep she dreamed of the last full moon she'd seen in her own time, when Ned had walked her back from the time-travel project's warehouse in Chelsea to a flat she shared with some other postgraduate women in Fulham.

One of her flatmates was coming in as Vanessa and Ned arrived, and immediately invited Ned up for a drink.

"I know who you are," the girl said to Ned as they sat down. "I saw you last winter in the University fencing exhibition. You looked like you were going to murder your opponent."

Ned shook his head. "If you watch fencing on television, most of what you see is foils. They take a lot of skill, probably more than rapiers, but rapiers are killing swords and combats always look more dangerous."

"Never mind," Vanessa said quickly. "Ned's had a long day and I know he has to be going."

Ned took the hint and stood up. It had been a long evening, their first practicing unarmed combat, and only a few days after Vanessa had been invited into the Project to plan her trip to Mozart's Vienna. She was longing for a bath and suspected he was too. As she walked him to the door she caught his scent, a hint of fir trees. The freshness of it unsettled her. For a sudden, appalling instant she wanted to bury her face in his chest. She slammed the door in his face as he was saying goodbye.

Vanessa woke suddenly, thinking she'd heard the sound of that closing door. Ned's scent lingered in her memory. Then she caught the smell of the gaol: straw and sweat and chamber-pots. She sat up and looked out the window. The moon was nearly down, although some light still illuminated the paved courtyard.

"Shit," she whispered to herself. "Oh, shit, shit, shit."

She lay down again and tried to sleep. But she couldn't let go of the evening she'd dreamed about. After Ned had left she'd rushed upstairs only to find the way to her room blocked by a flatmate.

"You've been holding out on us, Vanessa. You're not going anywhere till you sit down and tell us exactly how you know Ned Marston and what you're doing with him."

Vanessa actually saw red for a moment, a haze around her eyes as she prepared to knock her friend downstairs. Then she perceived that the question had nothing to do with her time-travel secret, that her flatmate was looking for gossip. She let out her breath and smiled.

Their two other flatmates were in the sitting room. All four were at London University, but Vanessa was the only musician. As she sat on the sofa one of the others spoke.

"We can't believe you're dating Ned Marston. He barely talks to anybody, even when he's on the reference desk in the library. Do you know how many of us have started working with the rare book collections just so we can ask him questions?"

Vanessa snorted. "I'm not dating him. I met him at *tae kwon do* class. All we do is practice unarmed combat."

A third flatmate was quick on the uptake. "I'd practice unarmed combat with him any day of the week."

Even Vanessa laughed, but her first questioner was thoughtful.

"You've probably never heard his languages, have you, Vanessa? He came to my Elizabethans class to read for us. He did five different accents, one for every character, in a scene from *The Merry Wives of Windsor*. Then the professor got him to do ancient Greek. It's like singing, did you know that?"

Vanessa shook her head. No wonder Ned had a place in the time-travel project. With his languages and accents he could fit in wherever they sent him, and in modern London no-one would ever guess he was American.

Then a thought struck her, so hard she doubled over in her seat. *She* didn't have languages. No-one had ever asked, and she was so bloody simple that until now it had never crossed her mind that if she was going to Vienna she'd have to speak German.

She staggered up, her face pale. "I'm sorry, but I have to go to bed. Can I promise to talk some more about this tomorrow?"

All her flatmates looked apologetic. "I'm sorry, Vanessa," said the one on the sofa. "You do look tired. I should have let you go the first time."

Vanessa was out the door and into her own room by the time her friend finished speaking. With the door closed she stared at the transparent case of an animated music-box on her chest of drawers. Inside was a figure of Mozart in a formal drawing room, sitting at a pianoforte. She pushed the button and the Mozart-figure stood up and bowed. "Guten morgen, Vanessa," it said. There were six other buttons which made the figure play piano pieces, including a minuet Mozart had composed at the age of six. She'd been six years old herself when she'd received the music-box, the last present her father had given her before he died.

"Guten morgen," she said aloud. "It's the only German I know." Then she sat on her bed and began to cry.

She forgot about her bath and after a sleepless night made herself presentable and went to the laboratory. All of the others were there, with Ned about to leave for work.

After one look at Vanessa, Caroline said, "What is it?"

Ned was stuffing books into a satchel, but he stopped and faced her as well. So did the two engineers.

Vanessa stood very straight. "I'm here under false pretences."

"You're what?" said Caroline.

Vanessa glared at Ned. "How many languages do you speak?"

Ned shrugged. "Four or five, I suppose. Depends on how you count different Greek dialects."

"And you just assumed I must speak languages too."

"Well, of course," said Ned. "You're a postgraduate. You're required to have at least two. Are you telling me you don't?"

"I'm in the performance programme," Vanessa wailed. "I only need one, and it's French."

Ned's face was like iron. Caroline looked at him and began to laugh.

"And you brought her here with the bright idea she could go to Mozart's Vienna and come back with music manuscripts. But you never asked if she could speak German."

The two engineers turned away, trying to look busy. Vanessa was struggling to hold back tears and Caroline was still laughing. Suddenly Ned choked and Vanessa saw he was laughing too.

"So it's all my fault," Ned managed to say.

"Of course," Caroline replied. "It's always your fault, Neddie."

An idea came to Vanessa, so clear it was like a vision. She knew where she could go instead, the only place in her imagination where literature mattered even more than music. Caroline and Ned had stopped laughing and were staring at her.

Vanessa could feel the happiness shining in her face. "I could get a Jane Austen manuscript instead."

"No," said Caroline. "Jane Austen wrote her novels during the Napoleonic Wars. We don't send time-travellers to war zones."

"But you sent Ned to classical Athens," Vanessa protested.

"That," said Caroline, "is why we changed the policy."

Vanessa thought furiously. "Then send me *after* the wars," she said. "Jane Austen lived until 1817. . . ."

There was still enough moonlight for Vanessa to see the flaking whitewash on the ceiling of her cell. Why didn't I keep my mouth shut? I could have left the project once they knew I was useless for Mozart. The recollection haunted her.

"A Jane Austen manuscript," she said to herself. She sat up and began to cry, gulping back her sobs in an effort not to wake Meg. She could taste her tears as they ran onto her lips: bitter, the bitterest tears she'd ever known.

CHAPTER IX

The next morning stayed clear and the women were allowed into the courtyard. After a dozen tentative paces Vanessa collapsed. Two other women
helped Meg carry her to their cell, and Mrs. Badger was summoned. . . .

Vanessa was dreaming again. She was seven years old in her school auditorium, backstage and waiting her turn to perform. Her face was red with anger
as she hissed at her mother.

"I don't want to play for all those people. I don't even know them."

"Shh," whispered her mother. "They're your friends. They've come because
they want to hear you. They're going to love you."

"I don't want all that love," cried Vanessa. "There's too many of them."

"Pretend you're in that little room in your music-box, all by yourself with
Mozart. He's dressed up just for you and he's shown you how he wants you to
play the sonata. He's out there right now, waiting for you by the piano, and he'll
be watching the whole time."

"What if the audience starts clapping?"

"Don't pay any attention."

The auditorium lights went down and Vanessa grimly strode out, her eyes
focused on the piano. Without a glance at the audience she began to play.

The scene shifted. Vanessa was older now. Her mother was gone, but her
friends and fellow-finalists backstage were joking with her.

"So who's your audience going to be today?"

It was the last day at the Quebec International Pianoforte Competition, the only day the contestants could choose their own programmes. Vanessa shrugged.

"I'm playing Chopin, so it'll be Chopin. In a salon with George Sand. When the audience starts coughing I'll pretend it's his consumption."

"Anything so you don't have to be in the present. Right, Vanessa?"

Vanessa didn't answer. Her programme closed with Chopin's "Revolutionary Etude" and brought the audience to its feet. She placed second in that competition, but her hands were shaking as she stepped up to the podium to receive her prize.

There was a party afterwards, but Vanessa excused herself early. As she was leaving a young man caught up with her by the door. She'd done her best to ignore him, but he'd been to every one of her performances, sitting in the front row with his face glowing.

"I've never heard Chopin played with so much passion," he said.

"Thank you," Vanessa mumbled, eyes on the floor.

The young man swallowed hard and seized her hand. "Are you leaving early because of an engagement, or may I take you to dinner?"

"No!" she cried. She looked up as the young man recoiled, and she spoke more quietly. "I do have an engagement, but thank you for asking. Perhaps another time."

"May I have your telephone number?"

"I don't have one."

"Let me give you my card."

She took it and fled. Back in her flat she tried to play again, the improvisations that calmed her spirit after crowded concert halls. But tonight she couldn't concentrate. She knew the young man thought that because she loved her music so much she was bound to love him the same way. "Passion," he'd called it.

But her passion was for the music and the time it came from, not for the cold modern world and its audiences. She tried once more to play but her hands were shaking. As she looked down the keyboard disappeared. And then the piano itself began to dissolve. . . .

"Where's the piano?" Vanessa cried weakly.

"Hush, love," came a voice. "There's no piano. Only me. Are you awake at last?"

Vanessa tried to sit up, but couldn't. An arm reached behind her shoulders to help. Meg's face came into focus and behind her Vanessa saw the walls of her prison cell. She was back in her Regency present. She fell forward onto Meg's shoulder and began to weep.

"Don't cry, sweetling. You need your strength to get well. You had visitors yesterday you never recognised, and some medicine. They're coming back later."

Meg did her best to make Vanessa presentable before the visitors returned. She washed Vanessa's face and brushed her hair, and wrapped a blanket around her once she was sitting and propped up against the wall. Vanessa was wearing some kind of old nightgown; it was dry now, but she could smell the sweat from her fevers.

"How long have I been here?"

"Six days," Meg answered. "At first we thought you had gaol-fever and the warden was going to send you to hospital. But I've never known anyone come back alive from that place, so I said I'd look after you. Jenny emptied the next two cells along and told the others they'd answer to her if they made any noise. Yesterday you had some medicine from the doctor. And the ladies said today they're going to bring you a lamb stew."

Vanessa had a premonition. There could only be one set of ladies likely to visit, and they were the last people in the world she wanted to see her like this. But footsteps sounded in the corridor before she could say anything. Mrs. Badger opened the door and her visitors entered the cell.

Jane Austen was on Martha Lloyd's arm, looking pale but composed. Behind them came a middle-aged gentleman Vanessa didn't know, carrying a medical bag in one hand and by its smell what could only be a picnic-basket in the other. Behind him the young guard called Lem carried two stools. The two ladies sat as the gentleman came to Vanessa's side and took her pulse.

"Much better," he pronounced. "And the fever has abated."

"Excellent, Mr. King Lyford," said Jane. "You owe me a cure, and if it is not to be myself this young woman will do nicely."

"Jane!" Martha protested. "We have by no means given up hope."

Jane looked at her friend and then at the doctor, who said nothing. After a moment she cast an ironic eye on Vanessa.

"One might surmise from this exchange that they believe I have turned my own head with the happy endings of my novels. But I have seen enough of life to know the difference. And so" – Jane's voice became stern – "it appears you have, Miss Horwood, young as you are."

Vanessa looked away as Jane continued. "They say you passed your instrument at my brother Henry's former bank in Alton. Is that so?"

This time Vanessa met Jane's eyes. "I *presented* the instrument at Hoare's Bank, upon which it was drawn. It came from an unimpeachable source in Canada."

Jane laughed grimly. "Persuasive, is she not, Mr. King Lyford? I rely on you to keep her alive. She deserves her freedom if she is innocent, and if she is lying I must say she does it so well that the sooner the hangman gets her, the better off the world shall be."

"She's never a liar, miss," protested Meg. "If there were any justice in the world half or more of the women in this place would be out of it."

"And you among them, my high-spirited young lady?" Jane replied.

Meg's head went up. "It was love made me sign the note that put me here for debt," she said. "And if I ever loved again I'd probably do the same, the more fool I. But Vanessa's not like me."

Jane looked at Martha and back to Meg. "Perhaps not," said Jane. "But she is fortunate to have you as a friend. I too am fortunate in my friend, though not for much longer."

A gasp from Martha brought Jane to her feet. "As usual I have spoke too much," she said ruefully. "Come, my dear, let us leave the doctor with his patient."

"There is nothing to detain me," said the doctor. "My advice is that she eat her dinner and keep up her spirits." He turned to Meg. "If there is any recurrence of her symptoms you must have the warden send for me immediately."

Meg looked over the doctor's shoulder at the young guard. Mr. King Lyford obviously understood her meaning, as he turned and spoke to him directly. "Is that understood, young man? You will carry any word from this woman to the warden without delay."

The guard touched his forehead in salute, and with that the visitors were gone.

CHAPTER X

Slowly, slowly Vanessa began to recover some of her strength. She had a few sheets of paper left over from making the new gaol roster and one day she began to compose a version of the Cinderella story in verse. She tried it out on some of the children, who cried for more, and a comparatively pleasant week went by as she finished turning the tale into couplets.

The next time they were allowed in the courtyard Vanessa took some of the children aside and asked them to think about being in the countryside with a dog. In happier times one of them had a dog named Pompey who used to chase sheep. When the boy started to cry at the memory Vanessa began an impromptu recital:

> If Pompey will promise
> That he will be good,
> And not bark again at the sheep,
> And not run away, and behave very rude,
> I think we will give him a peep
>
> At the fields and the flowers,
> And blue sunny sky;
> To him a great pleasure will be,
> To swim in the pond, and then rub himself dry,
> And gambol around you and me.

Vanessa looked around, hoping nobody grown-up had heard how awful her verses were, but the children laughed and clapped and asked for more.

"Tomorrow," she said, "or anyway the next time we go outside." They made her promise, over and over again.

She began to practice her martial arts and to show Meg and some of the other, younger, women a few of the simpler kicks. She tried to explain their Asian origin and was confounded when she couldn't – the words simply wouldn't form in her mind. *She* knew what *tae kwon do* was, and could reflect on its origins and philosophy to herself, but as soon as she began to think in terms of communicating, the language she wanted just slipped away.

She had noticed the same phenomenon earlier, when she'd tried to explain the liquorice tea to Jane Austen or tried to describe to Meg things in Canada that (Vanessa assumed) must still have been unknown to England in 1817. This was one more piece of evidence that time itself could prevent her mis-speaking. Ned Marston had never mentioned this effect of time-travel on speech – had he known? What else had he failed to tell her?

Vanessa knew she was getting her strength back when she dreamed of Ned again that night. She'd had other dreams the week before her collapse, where Ned appeared in crowded rooms, always in the distance, always holding books or papers. Once she'd heard piano music in the background. She'd known it was Mozart, but no piece she'd ever heard before. In that dream Ned had held aloft what she knew was the autograph score for that piece – she could make out Mozart's distinctively cramped, angular musical notation. She'd pushed through the crowd, reaching for the score, but as Ned started to laugh the papers burst into flame.

This time Ned was standing in the room where Vanessa had played Jane Austen's piano. The room was empty but for the two of them and Jane herself. Jane was prone, lying across three straight-backed chairs, a pillow under her head, eyes closed. Ned was behind her, holding aloft a vial which Vanessa knew contained the cure for Jane's disease.

"I could have brought the cure myself, couldn't I?" Vanessa cried. "You knew all along. . . ."

Ned was laughing again, laughing as he dissolved and Vanessa came awake.

The dream haunted her the next day. Exercise didn't help, so she sat in a corner of the outside yard and tried to get Ned out of her mind by thinking about Caroline Potter. It was a bad choice: lunch with Caroline had been her formal introduction to the time-travel project. Ned had been almost as much a part of the interview as if he'd been there. Almost the first thing Caroline had said was that she'd gone with Ned to Vanessa's two University piano recitals. A few moments later Caroline mentioned him again.

"Ned tells us you're a fighter."

Vanessa tensed, and then shrugged. "He came to a *tae kwon do* class."

"No," Caroline replied. "He came to *your tae kwon do* class. He was impressed."

"Why?" Vanessa asked. "It's an expert class and I'm no better than most of the students." But she thought she knew what Caroline was going to say, and she was right.

"Ned told me you had good combat instincts. You followed protocol, were very gracious and all, but every time you had a chance to improvise a win, you did. Your instructor even reprimanded you over one of them." Caroline paused. "Ned liked that."

"And that's why you asked me to lunch?"

"Not exactly," said Caroline. "Ned mentioned you had studied Mozart's Vienna, that you had an affinity for it."

Vanessa smiled. "My parents started playing Mozart recordings for me when I was three. I climbed up on the piano bench and tried to imitate them. That's what started me on lessons."

"Ned thought there was more to it than that."

Vanessa became guarded. "I scarcely know Ned Marston and he seems to be presuming all sorts of things about me."

Caroline grinned at her. "He's like that. It's why I wanted to talk to you myself. For all I knew this might have been his way of trying to chat up a pretty girl."

Vanessa was annoyed. "I've spent my whole life getting rid of people who've tried to chat me up. People who think they know me because they've watched me play, people who think they can get physical with me because we've practiced *tae kwon do*. But this is the first time I've encountered a go-between."

"I'm not a go-between," said Caroline. Vanessa saw the twinkle in the woman's eyes, but her voice was serious. "I'm working on the most exciting project of my career, maybe the most exciting physics project in history, and it's one that could never have kept going without Ned Marston."

"How well do *you* know him?" Vanessa asked, curious in spite of herself.

"As well as anyone," Caroline answered. "We talked of getting married once."

"Oh," said Vanessa, embarrassed. Caroline continued.

"But I could never have married him. I need someone who lives in the present, at least most of the time. With Ned I could never be sure." She looked thoughtful. "Maybe if he'd lived in the present he'd have been no use to us."

Caroline's eyes locked on Vanessa's. "He thinks there might be a place for you in the project."

"Go on," Vanessa said.

Caroline shook her head. "That's really all I can say right now. I'm willing to follow up with you if you come to the laboratory for a longer interview. How much time can you spare from your dissertation over the next couple of months?"

"I don't know if I can answer that," said Vanessa.

Caroline's voice was stern. "You got standing ovations at both your University recitals last year, but you've refused to appear on stage ever since. There's a performance quota for your degree and you're not going to meet it. I'll need to know about that if you come for the interview."

Vanessa's eyes flashed. "I'm not sure any of this is your business."

Caroline smiled. "It is, actually. I'm one of the University preceptors. We oversee all the degree programmes and your name is on the "concerned" list for the music department."

"I told the department I wanted this year for my dissertation and that I'd go back to performing next year."

"They don't believe you. Your supervisor says it's not nerves, that your playing in public is wonderful. I can vouch for that too. But they're telling me you're lost in your research, and the only class that brings you into the present is your *tae kwon do*."

"Is this so unusual?"

"Maybe not," Caroline replied. "Especially not for our purposes. Would you like to come to the lab next week? We'll pay for your time and expenses, of course."

"I'm a student. How can I say no to free money?"

Their food was untouched on the table. Vanessa devoured hers as Caroline picked at her salad. Over coffee Caroline asked one more question.

"Have you ever had a security clearance?"

"What?"

"I can't imagine you've ever needed one, but I needed to ask. It would make my due diligence a little easier if you had."

Vanessa shook her head. "Sorry."

"May I have your permission to make enquiries?"

Vanessa leaned back in her chair. "Sure. Whatever you have to do is fine. But if it's any use to you, I've been keeping secrets all my life. Especially my own."

As Mrs. Badger called the women inside, Vanessa contemplated her biggest secret of all: time-travel. Ned is one of four people who know I'm in this time, she thought. I never breathed a word to anyone else. He should have come for me, and he didn't.

CHAPTER XI

Ned walked to the laboratory in the misty summer rain, thinking about Winchester Gaol and what it must be like – have been like (he corrected himself) – for Vanessa. He'd seen the old gaol once as a tourist; there was a pub in its ground floor now, he remembered. But the pub hadn't appealed to him and the rest of the building had been positively forbidding. He'd hurried on to the Cathedral precinct a few hundred yards away.

With the rain soaking his hair and seeping down his shirt-collar Ned contemplated one of the many paradoxes of time-travel. When he'd been to Winchester he'd never met Vanessa and so – looking at one side of the paradox – she'd never time-travelled and never been in the gaol. But the other side of the paradox was that she *had* been there, and whatever her life had become in 1817 was long since over and done with.

He thought again of the feeling he'd had immediately after Vanessa's departure, that she was somehow crying to him for help. He'd never been troubled by premonitions before, but he couldn't escape this one. The corrective voice in his head reminded him that he couldn't have had a premonition if it involved the past, and he said "shut up" out loud, attracting stares from passers-by.

He arrived at the laboratory troubled and gloomy. It didn't help that the first thing he heard was the voices of the two engineers arguing over the time-machine.

"Glad you're here, Marston," one said. "Caroline refused to take sides."

Caroline smiled grimly. "It's nothing new. You said it yesterday, Ned. Should we abandon Vanessa's pulse and re-programme the machine? We've got one yes and one no, and I'm not going to break the tie."

"You recruited Vanessa, Marston," said the engineer. "You get to decide."

"Can you send me after her?" asked Ned.

The man shrugged. "I don't see why not."

"*I* do," cried Caroline. "We are *not* going to risk losing another traveller."

Ned turned to her, watching her fight her emotions.

She took a deep breath. "Don't be a fool, Ned. Vanessa knew the risks. And if she's in gaol you'll never get to her anyway."

"Programme the pulse into her cell."

"No way," said the second engineer. "And you know why, too. You could end up materializing into a wall."

But in the end even Caroline agreed to a rescue attempt. They decided to try for a field outside Winchester as soon as Ned could be ready. Then Caroline left to visit the numismatic dealer who'd supplied Vanessa's bank draft – the cause of all her troubles, it seemed.

"I have to be the one to see the dealer," Caroline said. "I bought the draft, after all. And if Ned goes he might strangle the poor man."

Instead Ned visited their costumer, who said he could alter a Regency suit he already had in stock and have it ready that evening. Caroline called from the numismatist's to say the man swore Vanessa's bank draft was genuine, that he'd inspected it himself and that his colleague in Montreal had an impeccable reputation. She also said she'd purchased smaller-denomination pre-1817 banknotes and coins which Ned would be able to spend directly rather than negotiate at a bank.

They reconvened that night with Ned poised to time-travel.

"You should shave that beard, Ned," Caroline said.

Ned shook his head. "I don't want to look fashionable. I want to look like a sober, middle-aged man of business, like Vanessa's father or uncle."

Caroline nodded. "You're probably right. And you certainly look sober enough in that black suit."

But it was all in vain. The machine would not allow the programme to be set to the same time-destination as Vanessa's. Or even close, it turned out. At first they tried to stay within a few days, then weeks, then months. Earlier or later seemed not to matter. It was well after midnight when they gave up, with still no response from the machine at ten years either side of 1817.

"That's something you need to work on," Ned said, as mildly as he could. "Not to mention some kind of rescue sequence once a travel pulse has dissipated. It's still another reason for me to get ready for Shakespeare's time. We need the money. And *you* need to stay here and experiment."

"No." Caroline's voice was flat, but he could see the weariness and frustration in her eyes. The two engineers were sprawled in chairs, eyes closed. They'd cursed themselves into exhaustion as the evening had worn on without results.

Ned kept his voice gentle. "You're the only traveller to bring back anything we could sell, and now we're almost broke. I was making plans before any of this happened. Ten minutes in Shakespearean bookshops and I can bring back a stake for your next five years."

Caroline looked at the engineers. One of them opened his eyes.

"We're staying out of this. We've always agreed the majority would make the decisions." He looked at Ned without raising his head. "If Caroline says no, we're with her. If she says yes, you're going."

After a long pause she spoke. "I won't say no. I don't understand why we can't send two travellers to the same time, or even within ten years of the same time. There has to be a reason and I need to know what it is before we can go after Vanessa or anyone else. And we do need more money."

Ned nodded, knowing she had more to say.

"But wait one more week, okay? Vanessa might still get back. And you haven't got your Shakespearean outfit ready. You said you were having trouble finding a period sword that worked for you. Is that still true?"

"I'm getting there." He looked around the laboratory, eyes resting again on the time-machine. He felt like Vanessa's ghost was still hovering there.

"Promise me one thing," he said.

Caroline gave a wan smile and Ned went on. "If I don't make it back, keep working on a way to rescue us. Mortgage your houses. I intend to stay alive till you find me."

Caroline's eyes filled with tears, but she nodded. Ned looked over at the engineers. At first neither moved, and then both slowly raised an arm, thumbs up.

CHAPTER XII

One day, as Vanessa's group prepared for its courtyard walk, Mrs. Badger announced that Vanessa would have to stay inside. The children howled their protests and Vanessa felt a surge of resentment. There had been cold rain for days and she could finally feel a hint of this day's warmth, even through the prison walls. But she stifled her anger and stood still.

Once the others had left Mrs. Badger spoke. "You've a visitor. The warden's put 'er in the room next his office."

The news perplexed Vanessa. She'd long since given up on Ned Marston and nobody else had any notion of her existence besides the Austen household. Mrs. Badger knew Jane and Martha by sight, well enough to use their names if they called. Vanessa was still puzzling as she went upstairs.

Sure enough, the woman in the visitor's room was a stranger. Vanessa looked at her curiously. She was no beauty, but there was something striking about her. Her eyes were almost triangular, set deep beneath a high forehead which was framed by two symmetrical tufts of hair curling below an enormous white toque, not the dainty woman's variety, but what appeared to Vanessa like a classic pouched chef's hat. This was tied under the chin with a double band, which had the unfortunate effect of setting off the woman's large jowls. But her nose was elegant and her otherwise straight mouth had a small curve in the middle of the upper lip that gave her an air of both kindness and perpetual amusement. Vanessa liked the look of her.

The woman's voice had no nonsense in it. "Sit, Miss Horwood. Mr. Lewcock has told me your story and you are in grave danger."

Vanessa slowly sat in a rickety wooden chair. Her distress was obvious and the woman's voice became gentle.

"Did the warden not tell you who I am?"

"No, ma'am," Vanessa answered.

"No-one tells anyone anything in these terrible places," she said. "My name is Elizabeth Fry."

Vanessa sat up, startled. She knew *exactly* who Elizabeth Fry was. As a child Vanessa had been a member of the Elizabeth Fry Society in Montreal, which sent food and presents to prisoners, and when she was older she had gone with her schoolmates on visits. She knew that Mrs. Fry had single-handedly done more to improve conditions in women's prisons than any dozen reformers before or since.

"I. . . I thought you only visited at Newgate," Vanessa stammered.

Mrs. Fry smiled. "You have heard of my work."

"How could I not?"

"Those who most matter either have not heard or do not care," said Mrs. Fry. "But our ranks grow every day and it is past time for us to see what can be done outside London."

She scrutinised Vanessa carefully. "Mr. Lewcock says you protest your innocence and that he is inclined to believe you."

Vanessa was silent, then realised a reply was expected. "Thank you."

"Don't thank me. I did everything in my power to save two young women from the gallows only two months ago and I failed. The money involved in their crime was small and their condition was desperate. They did not deserve to die." She paused a moment. "No man, or government of men, should have the right to judicial murder." She clasped her hands together and the lines of her face deepened with sorrow.

"Mrs. Fry," Vanessa said, "I *am* innocent and I have good reason to believe the whole matter is a mistake. The draft came from an unimpeachable source in Canada and nobody has yet told me how I came to be accused."

"You have no attorney?"

"I relied on that draft for the entire expenses of my stay. I received ten guineas in advance from the teller in Alton and all of that was taken from me by the prison guards."

"Was it now?" said Mrs. Fry. "Mr. Lewcock shall hear of that."

"Oh, no," Vanessa protested, "not now."

Mrs. Fry gave a grim smile.

"Even here," she said. "Mr. Lewcock's modern prison, run on enlightened principles, and he can't put a stop to the robbery of garnish. Did you know, Miss Horwood, that at Newgate it is known as 'chummery'? Nothing could be less redolent of a chum. Nothing."

Vanessa stayed silent this time and Mrs. Fry went on.

"Those are not your own clothes, are they?"

Vanessa looked sheepishly down at the cast-offs, left over from Jenny's pile after the others had taken their pick. Meg had boiled them in a cauldron in the courtyard after Vanessa had given her own clothes to a young woman about to be released. Vanessa regretted the gift now, but at the time looking at her own clothes was too painful. All they did was remind her of her fading time-travel pulse, of her past life in a future time she never expected to see again.

Mrs. Fry went on. "No, I assumed not. Mr. Lewcock advised me you were a young woman of fashion, but I believe you are a woman of sense as well. I shall look into your case, my dear."

Vanessa dared not hope, but she asked anyway. "Is there anything I can do, anything that can be done at all?"

"The legal system at present undertakes to expose the guilty. It cares little for the presumption of innocence. We are working to change that and you are fortunate that Mr. Lewcock is one of us. I shall write to you in a fortnight and please forgive me if I end this interview now. Mr. Lewcock is going to walk me around the women's gallery, which he tells me is much improved since your arrival, though he does not know how."

Vanessa smiled, a little wanly. "I am fortunate in my friends, Mrs. Fry. Together we were able to stand up to some who were taking advantage of the weakness of most of our sex."

Mrs. Fry's answering smile was wider. "Well said, Miss Horwood. And now I have one further request, which is that you speak to no-one of this interview and that you pretend not to know me when Mr. Lewcock takes me on my tour."

Vanessa nodded acknowledgement and the visit was over.

Vanessa began counting the days again and when exactly fourteen had passed she was called to the warden's office. Without preamble Mr. Lewcock handed her an envelope.

"From Mrs. Fry," he said. "She told me she had promised to write."

Vanessa tore it open and read.

The Perfect Visit

My dear Miss Horwood,
There are distinct possibilities. Do not lose hope.
Yrs., &c.
E. Fry

"She doesn't waste words, does she?" Vanessa said ruefully.
The warden gave a distant smile. "Indeed she does not."

CHAPTER XIII

Vanessa was sleeping better now, a combination of Martha's food and the better weather which allowed more outdoor exercise. Most mornings her dreams slipped away from her before she could make them conscious, but a few let her experience happier memories from her own time. The best of all were those that took her to the open seas, sailing as a young child with her father or crewing as a teenager for her uncles and their friends.

But today was rainy and Vanessa once again had more time on her hands than she knew what to do with. As she sat in the main room between the needle-workers and the washer-women her mind once again began to wander.

It was two weeks after her lunch with Caroline. Vanessa had begun to doubt if they were still considering her as a candidate for whatever their project was, or if there was some test she hadn't passed. She wasn't sure she wanted anything to do with them, but she wanted to be the one to decide.

Ned was waiting for her after *tae kwon do*. "Do you have time to talk?"

She shrugged. "I'm talking now, so I suppose I do."

He shook his head with a smile.

"I mean really talk. Somewhere private."

"Your office?"

"No," he replied. So she offered her flat.

The Perfect Visit

It would be quiet enough with her flatmates away at classes. As they walked to the bus stop she noticed his limp was gone. He seemed healthy, even vital, full of suppressed excitement. On the bus to Fulham Vanessa had a sudden *frisson* of suspicion. Was she being set up for a sexual overture? She trusted Caroline Potter well enough, but what about Ned?

Vanessa was in a seat, with Ned hanging on one of the cords suspended from the ceiling for standing passengers. She sensed his eyes on her and looked up at him.

"You're wondering if I'm trying something on," he said.

Vanessa blushed but didn't hesitate. "Yes, I am," she declared.

He nodded. "Good." Then he turned his head, gazing out the window towards the river as the bus headed down King's Road.

Ten minutes later Vanessa was making coffee. Ned sprawled on the sofa, silent, until she brought in the tray.

"Caroline says I can talk to you," he said.

"What about?" she asked, handing him a cup and sitting in a chair opposite. She met his eyes and then looked sharply away, startled by the intensity in his face.

"Have you ever thought about time-travel?" he asked.

"You're not serious," she replied, glancing back at him. His eyes held hers and she began to shiver.

"You *are* serious," she whispered. "Have you done it?"

He nodded.

"What was it like?"

He broke their gaze, looking across the room, eyes distant. She had never seen him look so sad – perhaps never seen *anyone* look so sad.

Just as she concluded he wasn't going to answer he began to speak.

"Some of it was a dream come true. Some of it was horrible. Completely unexpected. Alien." After a moment he shrugged. "The rest came somewhere in between."

"Where did you go?"

"Greece."

"*Classical* Greece?"

He nodded.

"That's why you had that short sword," she said.

At last he smiled, returning to the present. "Well done, Vanessa. I didn't think you missed much."

"Don't patronise me!" she cried.

He raised an eyebrow. "Oh," she said, abashed. "That really was a compliment."

"You *can't* miss much if you're going to time-travel. If you do, you're dead." She could see he meant it, but she was too dazed for it to sink in.

"I don't know why I believe you," she said. "So many of my friends would think this was the perfect tease."

"And you'd fall for it?" he asked.

"Wouldn't you?" she retorted. "Wouldn't anyone? Isn't time-travel every child's favourite fantasy?"

He smiled again. There was something new in his smile this time. And in his eyes. Warmth, certainly. Kinship? When he answered his voice was soft.

"Not every child's," he said. "But ours, for certain."

For an instant she felt their minds were entirely open to each other. It made her feel giddy.

Ned came to her rescue, his smile more broad. "It's not Caroline's fantasy. And not her engineers'. Their idea of time travel is to transport, see a date on a newspaper so they know they got where they wanted, and come home. If anyone but Caroline had told me they were onto this I'd have been sure they were playing me for a sucker."

For a moment his face went hard. Then he shrugged again, lifting his hands, palms up. Self-mockery, she thought. I like that. But she wanted one straight answer.

"And so, Ned Marston, time travel is something you always wished for?"

"Yes," he said simply. "More than anything. I'm so lost in this time I can hardly breathe."

Vanessa understood perfectly. He could have been describing herself.

She gave a decisive nod. "What next?"

"Caroline," he replied. "She has the final say."

The next morning she'd sat in the laboratory at the corner conference table with Caroline, Ned, and the two engineers. Caroline apologised for the delay.

"The Canadians took their time replying, but I think it's safe to say that now you've talked to Ned you understand why we had to be so careful."

Vanessa nodded, as Caroline produced a closely-printed confidentiality agreement. "Read it carefully before you sign it."

As Vanessa read she kept glancing at Ned. He seemed more distant this morning, as though unwilling to maintain the link they'd formed yesterday. She found it hard to concentrate on the document's dense legalese, as she kept thinking about all the places – all the times – to which she might travel. Caroline had mentioned Mozart's Vienna at their lunch. Would that be it?

Ned saw the far-away look in her eyes and as soon as she signed the paper he brought her back to earth with a thump.

"Do you have any idea how dangerous time-travel can be, with no people of your own at your destination, no back-up, no safe haven?"

Vanessa looked him straight in the eye. "I can take care of myself."

"In some circumstances, maybe," he replied. "We'll try others later, before we decide for certain where, or if, you're going."

So he'd read her mind again, known she was thinking about destinations when she was supposed to have been reading the confidentiality agreement. She'd also confessed to Ned her affection for Regency England. And Ned had gone to Classical Greece. How many other time-travel missions had there already been? And where had they gone? She decided to ask.

"We've had two full-scale missions so far," said Caroline. "Mine and Ned's. As far as we can tell time-travel does no harm to the traveller's mind or body, but we want to avoid too many repeats until we can measure the longer-term effects. Mine was the first."

"Where did you go?" asked Vanessa.

Caroline smiled. "Hang on a minute and I'll tell you. But first you need to understand the principles. They sound simple enough, but it took us years to work them out. The first is that our machine will only transport to the past and back to the present. We've tried everything we can think of, but we can't make the pulse penetrate the future.

"The second principle seems to be that we can take our clothes with us if they're natural fibres, and also inorganic materials – coins, weapons, whatever – provided the inorganics were turned into objects *not later* than the time-traveller's arrival date. And we can bring back what we take with us. But we can't bring inorganic or mineral artefacts from our destination times. No works of art, no ceramics, no jewellery." She smiled. "That last one was hard for me to accept."

The other engineer picked up the story. "We had to learn most of this by trial-and-error, time-travelling back a couple of months and then years. The two of us did most of that. Scared hell out of us every time we tried to bring something back and found the pulse wouldn't function. We tried every substance we could think of. Kept tweaking the time-traveller as well. We went three times each. After that Caroline made us give up."

The first man said, "By then we were running out of money and had no idea what to do next. Then Caroline brought *him* in" – he pointed to Ned – "a complete stranger. And he said 'why don't you see if books will travel forward?'"

Caroline laughed. "He wasn't a stranger to me. And the annoying thing was that Ned was right. He'd done no research, had no scientific background; it was plain intuition. We knew we couldn't do illuminated manuscripts because of all the minerals in the paint, but I decided to go somewhere fairly recent and relatively safe to try out books."

"And?" said Vanessa.

"I went for a classic: James Joyce's *Ulysses*. I travelled to Paris on February 2nd 1922, the day it was published. Got there just before dawn and after breakfast I walked over to the Shakespeare & Company bookshop.

"We knew there were some copies of the first edition printed on hand-made paper and signed by the author, who was in the bookshop that day. I took enough money in French banknotes to pay extra for one. It would be more valuable anyway and I didn't want to deal with the possibility that the inorganic junk in machine-made paper back then would keep it from travelling. I was worried enough that metal in the printing ink might spoil things."

She smiled. "Joyce sidled up to me and asked if I'd like to meet him later, alone. I said no, but I'd like an inscription in my book. I told him my name was Sylvia." Her smile became a grin. "That was Ned's idea. Wasn't our fault that Sotheby's auctioneers figured Sylvia had to be Sylvia Beach, the Shakespeare & Co. publisher."

Vanessa straightened in her chair. "I read about that. It fetched half a million pounds."

Caroline nodded. "And paid two years of our research and development debts."

Vanessa looked around the table. "Who went next?"

"I did," said Ned, his voice flat.

"You told me," Vanessa said gently. "But you didn't tell me what happened."

"Nothing happened," said Ned brusquely. "I failed."

He leaned back in his chair, staring into space. Vanessa looked around the table.

Caroline finished the story. "Ned thought he could get a manuscript of Sappho's poems or a lost tragedy of Sophocles. But he didn't land quite where he'd planned and it didn't work out."

Vanessa nodded. Clearly this was all she was going to get. And Ned was closed up, tight as a drum.

"We're getting ahead of ourselves," he said. "We all agreed we would see about Vanessa's skills before we discussed possible projects. Especially her self-defence skills."

Caroline smiled, pointing to a large mat at the far side of the room. "I think Ned just wants to try her paces."

Vanessa bristled. "Are you sure this is necessary? He's seen me in *tae kwon do* class." She turned to Caroline. "You even told me he liked the way I fought."

The engineer spoke again. "Marston's right. We did agree about self-protection. And for what it's worth, Miss Horwood, Caroline herself took any number of bruises on that mat, from all three of us."

"All right," Vanessa said. "You told me to bring my sweats, and I'm game."

She changed in the adjacent bedroom and when she returned she saw that Ned had removed his shoes and socks. Ned explained he would come at her from behind. Vanessa nodded, and he took his position at the opposite corner, off the mat. She turned her back and waited for the sound of his footsteps.

He came at her running and at the last possible moment she hurled herself to one side, spun, and with Ned only inches away her foot connected with his thigh, knocking him sideways and upending him at the same time. She was next to him, leg poised for another strike, before he could react.

"I know a kick to the head that could break your neck in this position," she said matter-of-factly. "But it would be a shame to lose you when we're just getting to know each other."

Ned rolled to his feet and grinned at her. The man's craggy face really was handsome, especially when he smiled and his hard grey eyes softened.

"A lesson for old Marston," he said, "who thinks he's such a tough guy."

Vanessa didn't answer and he looked at her again, appraisingly.

"That was a *tae kwon do* move, yes?" When she nodded he went on. "Can you fight with your hands too?"

"Arms," she replied. "Hands only if I have to. I'm a pianist. A broken finger could be the end of me."

She could tell he understood and that he was interested.

"Let's try something else," he said.

Out of nowhere his right fist flew at her. Vanessa stepped back and her forearm knocked the fist aside. Ned nodded, resumed a ready stance, and the same fist came at her, lower this time. This time Vanessa countered with a foot. Ned's left hand was a blur, catching Vanessa's foot and dumping her backwards.

"It's not a hundred percent, your defence," he said.

Now it was Vanessa's turn to roll to her feet and smile. "Not with you," she said. "How did you learn to move so fast?"

"Boxing coach used to make us catch flies out of mid-air," he said.

"I guess it worked," Vanessa replied.

Ned shrugged. "If you like catching flies."

An argument among the other inmates roused Vanessa from her reverie. Once she and Meg had it resolved Vanessa found herself still thinking about Ned. Had he ever reached Shakespeare's time? He'd boasted that ten minutes in a bookshop there would let him come home with millions of pounds worth of first edition plays – the legendary pamphlets known as "quartos." But would he go if Vanessa never returned?

For what felt like the hundredth time she thought of her last moments in the laboratory, when she'd kissed him goodbye. What had she been thinking?

"Damn the man!" she said out loud.

"What?" asked Meg. "Who? Is this the one called Ned you were dreaming about when you were ill?"

Had she given something away in her delirium? Vanessa wondered. From her experience so far she felt certain that time itself would prevent her exposing her secret. But. . . .

"It must have been," Vanessa replied warily. "What did I say?"

"Not much," said Meg with a smile. "But you repeated the same thing a dozen times over. Something about a kiss."

Suddenly Meg was serious. "Is he the one as gave you the draft on Hoare's Bank?"

With a shock Vanessa acknowledged that it *was* Ned who'd handed her the draft. But he would never have bought a forgery, would he? Or if he had, it must have been a mistake. Mustn't it?

She shook her head. "He did give it to me, in fact. But I told you where it came from and I know he gave full value. For all the things I might blame him for, the draft isn't one of them."

"Well, my dear Miss Horwood," Meg said with mock formality. "Perhaps sometime at your convenience you'll be after telling me what it is you *do* blame him for."

Vanessa took her friend's hand. "There's nothing I wouldn't tell you, Meg. I mean it, nothing. But for now let's see if Miss Austen has sent another basket. If she has, and we leave the guards alone with it too long, there'll be nothing left for us to eat."

But Meg's question stayed with her. What *did* she blame Ned for, anyway? Was it his fault that she'd been more excited about time-travel than anything since she'd first climbed on a piano-bench? And was it his fault that she'd found herself happy in his company?

CHAPTER XIV

A few days after Elizabeth Fry's letter arrived, Mrs. Badger again called Vanessa to the visitor's room. Vanessa took for granted that it would be an emissary from Mrs. Fry or perhaps even that lady herself, and she hurried down the hall expectantly. As a result she was entirely unprepared for the sight of Martha Lloyd with a completely transformed – pale and desperately thin – Jane Austen.

Martha rose from one of the rickety chairs, keeping a hand on Jane's shoulder to prevent her friend from doing the same.

Jane gave a wan smile. "I have not been myself of late, Miss Horwood. Ever since our last visit it has troubled me that I made light of your predicament by suggesting you might deserve hanging."

Vanessa tried to smile in return as she and Martha took their seats, but she found she could not.

"Your response was natural enough, Miss Austen," Vanessa said slowly. She choked as she continued, "And I find I can say nothing that might give you comfort."

Jane's eyes, which had been so lively at their first meeting, were dull and full of death now, but they gave a sudden sparkle.

"It has crossed my mind that men may have no better conception of justice than they have of physic."

Vanessa scrutinised Jane's face. It seemed almost expressionless, the momentary sharpness in her eyes giving way to an ironic glimmer.

Vanessa finally managed a faint smile. "But your Mr. King Lyford cured me. I am more grateful than I can possibly say to you both."

"Are you, child?" said Jane softly. "If you are so certain of hanging, might it not have been better to allow yourself to be carried off by a fever?"

Vanessa sighed. "One thing I have learned, Miss Austen. And that is protestations of my innocence are entirely useless. But I have had a visit from Mrs. Elizabeth Fry, who tells me I should not lose hope."

"And so you should not," said Jane, her voice suddenly resonant. Then she paused, taking a slow breath. Much more softly she continued. "And I am told the same – but I trust your outcome will be happier than my own."

Jane slowly turned her head towards Martha. "We must go, my dear, whilst I still have strength to walk. I fear another moment in Miss Horwood's company will cause me to weep and then you would certainly have to call for a sedan chair."

The two women rose and Vanessa did the same, dropping her eyes and a curtsey. The turnkey saw the visitors out, leaving Vanessa locked up alone for a few minutes. She longed for tears, wishing she could weep for Jane, if not for herself. But a leaden weight of hopelessness descended upon her and she slowly sank back into her chair, staring at the grey light outside the barred window. Later she could not remember when the guard returned, conducting her back to the Debtors and Felons Gallery.

CHAPTER XV

Vanessa missed her poetry reading the next day and showed little interest in distributing the additional food delivered by the guards. Only gradually did she involve herself again in the affairs of the women and children. Even Jenny remarked on Vanessa's low spirits.

Vanessa knew the summer assizes were coming and she began to count the days, knowing that if she were convicted she could hang before the month was out. As the assizes came closer she found herself obsessively reliving the last few days before she time-travelled, especially her time with Ned.

It was inevitable that they would often be together as Vanessa prepared for her journey to the Regency. Ned was the only one who'd spent more than a few hours in the past, the only one who knew about the ongoing dangers time-travel posed. He helped Vanessa find books about daily life in England, directed her work with the costumers, and became the one she turned to whenever she had a question.

One of her first was about the project's purpose.

"If all we're doing is bringing back books and manuscripts to make money, what's the point? We could accidentally change history, *disastrously* change history, for no reason other than greed."

Ned shook his head. "We've all talked about that. We're terrified of changing history, but we're starting to wonder if time itself doesn't have some kind of built-in protections against it. And I know what you're thinking about greed, but even if funding this research isn't worthwhile – and I think it is – isn't there something to be said for rescuing literature that would otherwise be completely lost to us?"

Vanessa wondered what it would be like to study an original Jane Austen manuscript. Not just the scraps that she knew had survived, including a juvenile play based on another man's book, but the author's own handwritten text of one of the great novels of all time. Then she thought about Ned's failed project. If rescuing a Jane Austen manuscript was important, how much more important might it have been if Ned had come back with completely lost texts: Sappho's poems, or plays by Sophocles and Euripides?

She nodded. "I think you've persuaded me." She grinned. "And even if you haven't I wouldn't give up this chance for anything."

"Good," he replied. "Now let's run."

On some days they jogged along the Thames Embankment. Other times she taught him the rudiments of *tae kwon do* in the laboratory. In turn he showed her Elizabethan fencing manuals and some thrusts and parries with the rapier. She hadn't expected to discover something of the same ritual quality to the fencing that she'd appreciated in her own martial practices.

"You could get good at this if you chose to," he said.

Before long they began meeting at the University. At first Vanessa didn't notice him in the back of the performance studio during her tutorials, but when she caught up with him one afternoon he admitted he was taking his lunch breaks so he could hear her play. Without thinking Vanessa spoke.

"When I know my flatmates won't be home I play my own music there in the evenings. Otherwise I'm in one of the practice rooms here. It's the only way I can calm down and get to sleep." She looked at him. "Especially now."

"May I come listen?" Ned asked.

"Yes." Her immediate acceptance startled her. She'd never before wanted anyone else to hear her piano improvisations. They had always been completely private, the outpourings of her heart and soul.

Ned sensed her conflict. "Are you sure?"

Slowly she nodded. "Yes. I just surprised myself."

That night he came to the tiny practice room, sitting out of her sight in a corner behind the piano stool. At first she was self-conscious, aware of his presence close by, even catching a hint of his fir-tree scent. She concentrated on a couple of melodies she'd invented as a child, gradually expanding and improvising on them until she lost herself in the music. She played for nearly an hour, as the familiar melodies turned into new ones, unscripted and, Vanessa knew, probably irretrievable. But they were good, she knew it. When she finished she felt both relaxed and exhilarated.

Ned was quiet as they walked to the bus stop. They shared the same route as far as Chelsea and as they climbed aboard she watched his face in the interior light. There was a contentment in it she'd never seen before. Reflecting the contentment in her own face after she played? After a while he spoke.

"I think I could listen to you forever."

Vanessa lived further west than Ned so he was the first to alight. As he moved towards the exit all he said was "May I come again?" She nodded and he was gone.

She dreamed about Ned for the first time that night. The next morning she wanted to see him. She'd never been to the library when he was on duty at the reference desk and she was taken aback at the surrounding gaggle of young women.

She noticed one of her flatmates in the group and felt a burst of jealousy. Then she remembered their conversation the night Ned had first walked her home. Her sense of humour intervened: she'd been warned. She turned quickly and managed to leave the room before either the flatmate or Ned noticed her presence.

The remaining days of summer term passed quickly, all of them spent at least partly in Ned's company. Their workouts became more familiar even as their unarmed combat practice became more varied. The more they practiced, the more their physical contact brought sexual tension. One day she took him to the mat, only for him to trip her as she stepped away. As she fell he caught her, holding her by her shoulders directly above him. Their faces were only a few inches apart and the longing in his was obvious. You must know I want you too, she thought. He let his arms bend, bringing her face closer. She straightened her legs, holding herself rigid, making his arms support her entire weight in mid-air. He raised his head for their first kiss. Then he rolled to one side, landing her on the mat with a gentle thump.

"Show-off," she said.

"No more than you," he replied shortly.

For a moment she thought he would come to her, but he got to his feet, gazing – it seemed – anywhere but at her. They changed into their street clothes and left the warehouse together.

She could tell that neither of them wanted to say goodbye. She walked him back to his flat near Battersea Bridge and for the first time he invited her up for coffee. I'm ready for more than coffee, Vanessa thought. Will he think we can't go to bed so close to my departure? Will he be strong enough to stop us?

The Perfect Visit

Ned lived in a typical Georgian conversion, the second floor of a four-storey house. The door to his flat had a triple-lock and alarm system.

"How did you end up with a flat like this on a librarian's salary?" she asked.

Ned shrugged. "My mother inherited the house without ever seeing it. She divided it into flats for the income and when they got really valuable she gave this one to me and sold the rest. When my parents died I brought their furniture over from Philadelphia."

Once inside Vanessa understood the special locks. The little flat was like a museum, so charming that she began to lose herself in it. One wall displayed a glass-fronted Georgian bookcase packed with leather-bound volumes.

"All but the books were my family's," he explained. "As you said, librarians don't make enough money to buy this stuff."

"Somebody made some money, sometime," said Vanessa.

"Before the American Revolution," he replied. "It's all Philadelphia cabinetry. We were on the British side in that war, but the new government let us keep our Philadelphia townhouse and its contents. We lost everything else."

"Every piece is gorgeous," she said. "They must be very rare."

Ned smiled. "My side of the family only got a few, but they *are* rare, especially with the original receipts. I don't know how those bits of paper managed to survive, but I'm proud of my family that they did. There must have been someone in each generation with my compulsive librarian's genetic code."

Vanessa was relieved to see a couple of well-worn, overstuffed chairs among the furniture. She sprawled in one, watching while Ned went through to the little kitchen and pulled out an old, hand-cranked coffee grinder.

As they sipped she began to speak of her childhood in Canada, of the death of her musician father and how her mother and uncles encouraged her.

"I was never sure if it was me they supported, or whether they were trying to bring my father back from the grave."

Ned smiled. "Did you ever figure it out?"

"No. But I loved the music so much I didn't care. I pretended I lived in whatever time the music was written. After a while even my family became part of the audiences I tried to pretend didn't exist."

"The audiences didn't matter if you were outside their time."

Vanessa nodded. "How come you understand so well?"

He didn't smile. "I don't claim to understand," he said. "But we both have our reasons for imagining ourselves outside our own times. You were escaping – what? – your family's possessiveness?"

Vanessa nodded again.

Ned went on. "I'm not sure what I was escaping. I know I spent hours staring at this furniture. It started me on my road into the past. My parents couldn't believe I was stupid enough to go to library school. 'It's a dead profession,' they said. 'Everything you could possibly need for research is on the internet.'"

As Vanessa watched and listened she started to want him again. She wasn't sure if she could listen to another confession and was tempted to tease him. But she held back, knowing she'd have hated it if he had teased her earlier. Bridle your lust, Vanessa. At least for now. What he'd just said went to his core. Besides, there was something more she wanted to know.

"We're both misplaced in our own time. But you've actually been out of it, to ancient Greece, further in the past than anyone. You've given me advice, you've told me Greece was horrible and alien and also that it felt like a dream come true. But you haven't said anything about what it was really like."

Ned tensed, so strongly she could see the cords in his arms and neck.

"It's not what you think," he said. "Listen, Vanessa. Whatever images you have in your mind of Jane Austen's time, try to let go of them. It's not going to be like the movies and the BBC. Everyone around you will be a potential enemy. Any little thing could be the end of you."

Vanessa stood up and, coffee in one hand, moved to Ned's chair and sat on the armrest. She began to stroke his face, catching his fir-tree scent. There's something intoxicating about this man, she thought. No, she corrected herself. Not intoxicating like alcohol. Sexy, like bodies.

At first Ned flinched at her touch, but as their eyes met he relaxed.

"It must have gone very wrong," she said.

He let out his breath. "It did. Be careful, Vanessa. I don't want to lose you."

He reached out his arms and she slid onto his lap. She could feel his desire as they kissed, but he was the first to pull away.

"I'll be back almost as soon as I leave," she said softly.

"Can we pick up where we just left off?"

She smiled. "We'll have the whole summer." She hesitated, not wanting to let go of the moment. Finally she spoke again. "Do you sail?"

He shook his head. "I'm a middle-class kid from Philadelphia who got lucky with some old furniture and a flat. I don't move in sailing circles."

"I know what you mean," she said. "I was the poor relation of some rich uncles." She knew it was time for her to move, but she slid from his lap with regret. As she stood up she went on.

"If you've never sailed you might not understand. But it's one of those things whose essence hasn't changed throughout history."

He smiled. "It puts you in touch with the past and keeps you in the present, all at once."

"That's it," she said. "Like fencing, I suppose."

"Or *tae kwon do*."

"So what about it?"she asked.

"The answer is I've never sailed in my life, but I'd like to learn."

"I've been offered a little cutter in Poole Harbour for June and July. . . ." Vanessa's voice trailed off as she realised how forward the invitation must sound.

Ned's eyes met hers, understanding. "Yes, please," he said softly.

There was still a current connecting their bodies, running between them like electricity. They both laughed, a little nervously.

CHAPTER XVI

When Vanessa came back to herself in her gaol-cell she felt a dull anger. She'd never felt more alive than she had in those days with Ned. Now she was a prisoner, likely to hang. Ned might as well have been Mephistopheles, striking the devil's bargain to give Vanessa her heart's desire. And, like Faust, Vanessa's price was despair and eternal torment.

As her trial grew closer she found herself beginning to hate him. Meg had been right: she did blame him, not for any particular thing, but for *everything* that had happened since she stepped into the time-travel pulse.

Her obsession stayed with her for the next fortnight. Then Mr. Lewcock himself appeared in the women's gallery, holding a sheaf of papers. He called the inmates together and announced he had the order of trials for the Winchester Summer Assizes, which would commence in three days. The most serious offences would be heard first, with Jenny and Bess at the head of the list, followed by two women alleged to be highway robbers, and then Vanessa.

Her first indication of anything unusual came two days later, when Mrs. Badger arrived to say that Vanessa would be first to appear in court.

"Tomorrow morning," said Mrs. Badger.

"But I thought I went after the others."

"There's talk of a witness," said Mrs. Badger. "That's all I know."

Vanessa got no sleep that night. She spent some of it with Meg's hairbrush, but most of the time she tapped her fingers on their table as though it were a keyboard. She worked through two recital programmes, knowing by now that both Meg and Jenny could sleep through almost anything. She nibbled on the last of her bread and wondered how many more meals she would ever see. Then she stared through the bars of her cell, waiting for dawn to brighten its grimy windows.

She cleaned herself up as well as she could in their small basin and slowly, deliberately, put on her clothes. She had just washed her tattered leggings and undershirt, but her cast-offs from Jenny's pile were in even worse shape than when Mrs. Fry had seen them. But that, she said to herself, was the least of her worries.

Even in daylight the minutes seemed to drag on forever, until at last Mrs. Badger arrived to unlock the door.

"Warden's waiting for you," she said.

Lem was guarding the main door and didn't meet Vanessa's eyes as she walked through. Lewcock was outside, looking grave, and told her that her case would begin in an hour.

"I have brought your pelisse. It is a chilly morning and no-one will be surprised to see you in it."

Vanessa was grateful, both for its warmth and for what little remained of her vanity. She slid into it and fastened it up as far as it would go, pushing her tattered gown underneath.

Mr. Lewcock offered no further information and walked impassively beside Vanessa for the few hundred yards to the courtroom. She glanced at him several times but said nothing.

Only the clerks were present when they arrived through a side door. One started to shake his head and say that the court was not yet open to the public, but a second recognised the warden and nodded them inside. Lewcock conducted Vanessa to a bench at the front, below the judge's box, and quietly said she would be taken to the bail-box on the judge's left, that the indictment would be read and she would be asked to enter a plea.

"I assume," he said with the faintest of smiles, "you will plead 'not guilty'."

Vanessa nodded.

"There will probably be a crowd," Lewcock said. "The public love hanging cases."

Vanessa suppressed a shudder and did not reply.

A few minutes later the main doors opened and a hundred chattering people thronged the courtroom. Many were dressed as if for the theatre, with gay ribbons and other finery.

"Is it always like this?" Vanessa asked Lewcock.

The warden's face was an iron mask. "I can only pray they know no better."

Ten more minutes passed. The judge entered. "Oyez" was cried, Vanessa conducted to the dock, and the indictment read:

"Hampshire, to wit. The jurors of our Lord the King, upon their oath, present...." The crimes were stated as felonious forgery and, or in the alternative, knowingly and feloniously presenting a forged draft for the sum of two hundred pounds sterling. Vanessa already knew that either charge could see her hanged.

The clerk asked her how she pleaded and she said "Not Guilty," amazed at the clarity of her own voice.

At that moment the courthouse door opened again and across the room Vanessa could see Elizabeth Fry, in the same hat as all those weeks before, accompanied by a slightly dishevelled but still elegant older man. He was tall and lean, with sidewhiskers and the uncertain expression that comes from extreme short-sightedness. Vanessa had no idea who he was.

The prosecutor had already risen to address the jury, tilting his head up at them as well as his stooped back would allow. He turned to see the new arrivals, taking a couple of steps away from the dock and looking sharply across the room. Then he gave a decided nod and addressed the judge.

"My lord, this is the witness of whom we heard yesterday. I believe that, with your lordship's permission, we may be able to determine this proceeding by asking him to take the stand forthwith."

The judge gave his assent and the clerk swore in the witness, addressing him as "Sir Richard Colt Hoare, Baronet."

The prosecutor produced a folder from which he extracted a small document.

"Sir Richard," he said, "it is not often a court can get to the heart of a matter so expeditiously, but I shall ask you simply to examine this document and to advise me if you can identify the signature upon it."

The document was duly presented. Sir Richard held it close for an instant, and then spoke without hesitation,

"Certainly. It is my own."

"And you signed it in your capacity as an officer of Hoare's Bank."

"Indeed."

"Can you tell the Court why this was not recognised at the time the draft was presented to your bank for encashment?"

"I rarely sign drafts, haven't signed one since 1812. Some ass of a clerk in Fleet Street failed to distinguish my hand and never bothered to refer to the appropriate ledger."

Mr. Lewcock rose and the judge nodded to him.

"May I point out, my lord, that this ass of a clerk nearly caused this young woman to lose her life, which she would certainly have done on the evidence previously given to the Court."

"So noted, Mr. Lewcock," said the judge, "but I believe we need say no more. I am not required to refer to the jury in declaring this prosecution to be of no effect and the prisoner released. Sir Richard's statement and the prior affidavit of Hoare's Bank received in evidence shall be retained with prejudice in the event the prisoner wishes to bring an action."

The prosecutor was gazing up at Vanessa, who appeared unsteady on her feet. She clutched at the enclosure, caught his eye, and whispered,

"What does that mean?"

The judge swivelled his head at the interruption, realised who it was and stifled a smile.

"You may wish to consult a solicitor, young lady. The law, I am happy to say, offers some remedies for persons wrongly imprisoned upon improper testimony."

"May I step down now, sir. . . um, my lord?"

The judge's voice was firm and filled the courtroom. "This case is dismissed."

CHAPTER XVII

Sir Richard Colt Hoare and Mrs. Fry accompanied Vanessa and Rev. Lewcock from the courtroom. Sir Richard was cheerful and obviously pleased with himself, explaining how Mrs. Fry had the devil's own time tracking him down in Wiltshire.

"I was on my way to Stonehenge and Avebury when" – a gesture towards Mrs. Fry – "her rider arrived, telling me she required my presence on a matter of life or death. Now that we've saved this young woman I shall go back to my digging."

"And have you determined the original purpose of Stonehenge, Sir Richard?" Vanessa asked, as innocently as she could.

"Good God, Elizabeth! Five minutes out of the dock and she's asking an impossible question. What have you done?"

"More to the point, Sir Richard," interrupted Lewcock, "what can *you* do? The judge is surely correct that she has an action against your bank. Your clerk caused her to be imprisoned for three months and nearly hanged, through no fault of her own."

Sir Richard's face grew serious and the little group stood still on the pavement. In the distance they could hear the next case called in the courtroom; Vanessa felt certain it was Jenny's. Her moment of scholarly good-humour vanished. As her sorrows returned she heard Elizabeth Fry speaking,

". . . in common decency you should do for her what any court would."

Sir Richard shrugged. "Let us discuss the matter in a more civilised setting, my dear."

They walked to an inn a couple of hundred yards down the High Street and when Sir Richard identified himself his party was immediately taken to a private room. Vanessa was still dazed but a small voice in her head told her to keep quiet, that others now would speak for her better than she could.

Sir Richard had said something to the innkeeper as they sat and there shortly appeared a platter of scrambled eggs, rashers of bacon that to Vanessa smelled ambrosial, and a large carafe of sherry. Vanessa waited as the innkeeper served the elders first, starting of course with the baronet, and she ate sparingly, knowing from her sailing days how delicate her stomach could be after long abstinence from meat.

After a few bites and two glasses of wine Sir Richard spoke to Vanessa.

"The prosecutor gave Mr. Lewcock your draft, did he not?" Vanessa turned and the warden nodded. "Two hundred pounds?" the baronet went on.

Another nod.

"I believe I might leave instructions in Fleet Street that the young lady is to receive a further five hundred pounds upon introducing herself to my cousin there. Would that be agreeable?"

Vanessa remained quiet, looking at the warden who replied,

"That would be handsome, Sir Richard, handsome and quite just. What do you say, Mrs. Fry?"

Mrs. Fry nodded, thoughtful but less enthusiastic. "I believe that might do, Richard. But we must ask Miss Horwood."

Vanessa had just taken a bite of bacon. She dropped her eyes and mumbled her assent as best she could.

Sir Richard ordered pen and ink from the innkeeper and produced a card from an inside pocket. He dipped the pen and wrote briefly, then looked up.

"Twenty-sixth of July, is it not?" On confirmation he dipped the pen again and finished writing.

"Here is a note of introduction for you," he said. "I expect my cousin will ask you to sign a release of any other claims. No doubt Elizabeth can direct you to a solicitor if you'd care to have it read first."

Vanessa had swallowed by now.

"I have no doubt it will be in order, Sir Richard, thank you." She turned to Elizabeth as her throat began to close and her eyes filled with tears. "Thank you, too."

"Ha! Humph!" said Sir Richard. "I shall take my leave. Don't lose my card, young lady." He stood, nodded to them all, and was gone.

The warden offered Vanessa a room in his house that night. "You had better stay Sunday as well. You'll want the coach to Alton to collect on your draft and that's no use to you till Monday."

Vanessa had already considered this.

"Would you allow me, Mr. Lewcock, to return to the women's cells tonight? I should not care to leave without saying my goodbyes." She wasn't sure she wanted to spend another night in the prison but at the same time she did not think she could bear the warden's hospitality, kindly intended though it was.

"I am not certain anyone has ever made such a request," said the warden.

"It speaks well of the girl," Mrs. Fry put in. "But I think you'd better promise to let her out in the morning."

Lewcock smiled and looked at Vanessa.

"Then *you* must promise to go with me to the Cathedral for matins."

Vanessa agreed, somewhat distractedly. The date Sir Richard had declared – July 26th – was echoing in her mind. She asked about a coach to Alton on Sunday and if she could be on it if there was. The warden said he would make arrangements.

Mrs. Fry had also refused an invitation from the warden, saying she'd lost too much time already and was needed at Newgate, not to mention by her own children. A direct coach to London left that afternoon and she would be home by late evening.

Vanessa walked around Winchester in a daze, only gradually recognizing that she was actually free. As afternoon clouds began to gather she went back up the High Street, crossing over Jewry Street to the prison. She pounded on the door and waited. It was opened by Lem, the young guard, who smiled.

"The warden said you'd be along. T'ain't often someone *asks* to be put in gaol."

Vanessa smiled back. "He did say you're to let me out in the morning, didn't he?"

"First thing," said Lem.

Vanessa's arrival was greeted with a ragged chorus of cheers. At the head of the group was Meg. The Irish girl's green eyes were alight, glistening with tears as she held Vanessa at arm's length.

"They didn't get you after all," she said softly.

"No," said Vanessa, "and they're not going to keep you, either. My bank draft is good and I'll be back with the money on Monday to pay your debt."

"Sure you can't do that, love," said Meg. "I've not so very long to go and then I'll be discharged and starting over."

"Any time is too long," Vanessa answered. "But we must say no more. I'd hate for the others to know."

Meg's face lengthened. "It's true. There's others here that need help more than I."

"Don't, Meg. Don't start or I won't be able to bear it. I know this is what I have to do and I can't do more."

Meg nodded and said, "I kept you some bread. Mrs. Badger said you'd get no more as you've been officially discharged."

Vanessa laughed and then grew serious. "Is Jenny back?"

"Have y'not heard? She and Bess have been condemned and are in a holding cell next the court. The black box" – she looked at Vanessa and smiled – "that's the lawyer, love. The black box applied to the judge for leave to appeal or to beg the King for a pardon and the judge'll decide on Monday."

Meg stepped back, looking at Vanessa again. "It's just as well they're locked up. Bess might have killed you for that pelisse. It must've been lovely with those clothes you were wearing the first day."

Vanessa spent the evening circulating among the prisoners, reciting some poetry to the children and saying her farewells. Those left from her original dozen allies promised to keep up the fair distribution of food and clothing. Even a couple of the women Vanessa had thought irretrievably insane spoke to her and wished her well.

It was dark by the time Vanessa settled into her cell, carefully folding her pelisse and setting it on Jenny's bedstead.

"I had some new clothes made in Alton," she told Meg. "I wonder how long they'll keep them in the shop before they give up on me."

"Have you paid for them?"

Vanessa nodded.

"They'll be there. Our shop kept things for a year, sometimes."

But Vanessa couldn't stop worrying. What haunted her most was the possibility that there might, against all odds, be a time-travel pulse lingering in the field at Chawton. She knew she had other concerns, both immediate and long-term, but she couldn't get her mind past Chawton to deal with any of them.

CHAPTER XVIII

The warden called at the Debtors and Felons Gallery the next morning. He took Vanessa's arm and walked her up the stairs to his office, where she sat in a visitor's chair drinking lukewarm tea. The warden remained standing.

"For those of us who believe it is the duty of His Majesty's government to seek justice as well as protect its citizens from criminals, your case is an embarrassment. I do not doubt but for Mrs. Fry you would have met the same fate as the two women in Newgate and no-one would ever have been the wiser. . . ." His voice trailed off and Vanessa was touched by the emotion in the man's face. After a moment he continued.

"The government does not itself offer compensation for wrongful imprisonment but I am pleased to say I may at least pay for your place on the eleven o'clock coach to Alton, where you were, shall we say, apprehended. Sir Richard has posted a letter to the bank there and promises this time your draft will be honoured." He hesitated. "Are you wearing the same clothes as yesterday, under your pelisse?"

Vanessa smiled. "I am. But I shall keep it firmly fastened."

"Hmm," said the warden. He looked uncertain, as though he wanted to say something else, then reached across to hand her an envelope. "You should not require it but this letter will also confirm who you are and to what you are entitled."

"Mr. Lewcock," Vanessa burst out. "I need your help."

The warden nodded. "Yes?"

"I'd like to come back on Monday to pay a debt. If I pay twenty pounds to the right person, can Megan Gallagher can be discharged?"

"You might have to pay some interest," he replied, "but certainly you may." He smiled at her. "This is uncommonly generous of you. I shall take the matter in hand and have papers ready upon your return." He took pen and ink and jotted a memorandum.

Then the warden stood and smiled again, rather sadly. "I wish more of the innocent young women who come into my charge could meet such happy endings."

This was too much for Vanessa. For months she'd contended with the likelihood that she would hang or, at best, be transported to Australia in something no better than a slave-ship. When she heard "happy endings" she thought again of time-travel and the near-certain fact that her pulse could not have survived so many weeks. One freedom meant another prison: now she was the prisoner of a time not her own. Her body lurched forward on the little chair and she began to sob.

After a few moments the warden touched her arm.

"Miss Horwood," he said gently. "I am afraid we must leave soon or we shall miss the divine service."

Vanessa kept her head down, but she nodded and the warden went on,

"I must beg your kindness in one more matter. Mrs. Fry told me the guards took ten pounds from you when you arrived. Is that true?"

Vanessa nodded and tried to swallow. "Not quite ten pounds, but close."

"All the guards but the two on duty are waiting outside. Would you be willing to join me for a word with them?"

It was a task Vanessa would rather have avoided, but the warden was clearly determined. The confrontation was mercifully short. Her two were present and the older guard, under pressure, admitted she had handed over nine pounds sixteen shillings.

The warden's voice was cold as iron. "Did you give her anything in exchange?"

"She asked for fresh bread and greens and oranges, your honour," said Lem.

The warden gave him an equally stern look. "But you knew she would get bread anyway."

Vanessa spoke for the first time. "He did bring some extra bread along with the other things. Twice a week."

"For twelve weeks," said the warden. "And what did you spend for this, twice a week?"

"Four shillings a week, your honour," ventured the old guard and then, in response to the warden's glower, more softly, "Um. . . wot was it you said, Lem?"

Lem actually blushed. "Elevenpence a time – one and tenpence a week, your honour."

"I will not tolerate theft by my guards," the warden said matter-of-factly, but his eyes were blazing and the two men cringed.

"He did bring me my greens and my oranges," said Vanessa, "which I expect some might not. I am grateful for your intervention and I should be glad to have what's left of my money, but I should be sorry to see this man punished."

The warden stared at her in amazement. "You are able to say that, having been wrongly imprisoned near these three months?"

Vanessa nodded and the warden looked back at the two guards. They glanced at one another and, as though on cue, each reached into a pocket and pulled out a handful of coins. Vanessa received eight pounds, fourteen shillings in gold and silver, carefully tucking it into the purse she retrieved from her pelisse.

She left the prison without a backward glance, the warden guiding her east, then south along a narrow lane which opened onto the green surrounding the Cathedral. As they approached the entrance Vanessa noticed three elderly ladies waiting for them. They looked at her and then at the warden.

"Surely not one of your charges, Mr. Lewcock?" one asked.

"Don't be rude, Harriette," said the second with a smile. "Please join us."

The warden replied without hesitation. "You will give her breakfast after the service, my dear ladies, before she leaves for Alton?"

There was no time to answer, but one of the three gave the warden a conspiratorial nod as the group entered the chilly silence of Winchester Cathedral. As they moved forward Vanessa recognised familiar monuments and memorials on the walls and floor. She gave a sigh of relief when she saw that the one she knew best was missing: the charcoal-grey memorial stone to Jane Austen, erected by her family in praise of her piety but neglecting to mention her writing.

The sun's rays had brightened the old stained glass windows above the entrance, their abstract patterns all that could be salvaged after the medieval originals were shot to pieces by Puritan troops in 1642. The wait for the choir from Winchester College was not long and in the meantime Vanessa rather awkwardly joined the three ladies and the warden on their knees.

After a few moments she relaxed and found her own thoughts drifting upwards, towards the interlacing stonework of the Cathedral's arched ceiling and beyond. In the familiar space of the cathedral the past seemed less of a prison. For a moment Vanessa could reconcile herself to whatever fate had in store for her. Even Ned Marston seemed less of a villain.

When the choir filed down the centre aisle, the youngest boys' descant soaring above the older, deeper, voices, Vanessa was profoundly moved. As the service went on she found she could sing from memory one of the seventeenth-century hymns by George Herbert. Dull as the sermon was, she survived it by anticipating more singing, and the organ solo that accompanied their departure was one of her favourite Bach partitas, well performed.

CHAPTER XIX

After the service the warden said goodbye, but the ladies kept a firm grip on Vanessa. She cast about for an excuse to avoid breakfast but finally gave a mental shrug. The Alton coach didn't leave until eleven. She had nowhere else to go in the meantime, however much she longed to get away from Winchester, and to see what fate held in store at Chawton.

Besides, she had to admit she was ravenous again and loved the idea of eating something warm. She did her best to seem pleased by the ladies' invitation, wondered what on earth she could talk about, and followed them outside.

After a moment she realised they were walking in a direction she already knew, the only direction that could possibly distract her from her own concerns. The ladies led her through a side gate into the Cathedral Close, made a right turn to follow a sward for a couple of hundred yards, another right turn in front of a Tudor house, and exited a large gate perpendicular to the old city wall. Almost immediately they veered left through a stone archway and left again into College Street.

It was just a few steps to the double-fronted house Vanessa had thought of so often during her imprisonment, and only two more houses to that of the three spinster sisters, as they had identified themselves. Vanessa hoped she could direct the conversation to some near neighbours, sooner rather than later.

Their party was greeted by a servant girl who took their cloaks. Vanessa got a strange look when she declined to relinquish her pelisse. Harriette, the rude sister, was insistent and Vanessa, anxious now, said she'd had an accident alighting from the coach the day before and that her dress was so torn and dirty she refused to let them see it. The second sister, Matilda, declared to the servant that they would delay breakfast until Vanessa had a new dress.

"You'll not be quite *à la mode*, my dear," said Matilda, "but we never throw anything away. We trust you will find something upstairs to please you."

The servant smiled at Vanessa and was introduced as Susan. They had to climb a narrow ladder to reach the attics, one of which was Susan's bedroom. The other was an enormous storeroom, or so it seemed, with wardrobes full of dresses and poles fixed to the ceiling to hold the overflow. The attic was warm and Vanessa finally felt she could take off her pelisse without danger of freezing. When she did Susan recoiled.

"Good lord, miss," she said. "No wonder you wouldn't show that dress. There's almost nothing left of it."

"Would you burn it, please, and not mention it again?"

Susan met her eyes without flinching. "I'll help you take it off and get you into a new shift. Well, not so new, but warm enough and clean."

Susan pointedly looked away as Vanessa shed her torn and dirty clothes. She kept her tattered leggings and top and slipped regretfully (oh for a bath first, Vanessa thought) into the shift.

"You might not credit it," Susan went on, "but those three was quite the life of every party, or so I'm told. And I believe this is the wardrobe where you'll do best – Miss Matilda was always the most slender of them."

Vanessa was astonished at the number and richness of the dresses. Some were wildly ornate, others almost Greek in their classical simplicity. One dress had its bodice cut so low it was bound to reveal the breasts almost entirely and Susan giggled as she pulled it out.

"Lady Hamilton's style, miss, so they tell me. T'would suit you well, I think."

"Is there not an ordinary walking dress?" Vanessa asked. "I'll not be going to many parties."

"They've given a few to me and some to the poor, but there's one I always thought too grand."

She pulled out two hangers. One had a lightweight muslin dress, with a straight bodice decorated in red and dark green and matching trim above the hem.

"This is the under-dress," said Susan. "You can wear it on its own" – she slid it over Vanessa's shift, a near-perfect fit – "or you can put this over as well."

'This' was from the second hanger, dark-green wool with the skirt cut away at the front and swept back to end about eight inches above the hem of the underdress. Its bodice was angled at the sides and straight at the middle, just high enough to cover the muslin beneath.

"Your pelisse," said Susan, "is just the right colour for them both, and this hat" – she produced an elegant square-cut bonnet – "matches them all."

Vanessa was speechless. "Thank you, Susan. What can I ever give you in return?"

"There's no return. The clothes weren't mine to begin with. And I'd better jump to it for breakfast or the ladies'll be after me."

The main sitting room was on the middle floor and Vanessa and Susan descended together. Susan continued downstairs to the kitchen and Vanessa paused, unprepared for the conversation she heard coming through the door.

"Only a vicar's daughter, even if she does have a brother with a fine estate."

"You've not read her novels, my dear Harriette. If I had my way she'd be in the Poet's Corner at Westminster Abbey. Winchester is lucky to have her."

At this Vanessa came through the door and peremptorily said, "What is it? What are you talking about?"

"Young lady, have you been eavesdropping?" asked Harriette.

"No, but I heard something about Westminster Abbey as I came down the stairs."

Harriette gave her a sharp look but Matilda intervened.

"My dear girl, I must say my dress suits you far better than ever it did me. I declare you'll bring back the cutaway fashion in no time."

Vanessa blushed. "I should have thanked you first thing."

Matilda's answering smile was kind. "I have a notion that the works of Miss Jane Austen reached the far side of the Atlantic Ocean, did they not? And you surmised whom we were discussing?"

"I know her," Vanessa said, trying to stay calm. "Please tell me, has there been a death?"

Vanessa didn't know the third sister's name, but she spoke up.

"Jane Austen died a week ago this past Friday and was buried on Thursday in the Cathedral."

"But there was no stone," cried Vanessa.

"No stone?" said the third sister. "Oh, I see. The stone isn't ready, but how could you know?"

Vanessa had known Jane was close to death when she last visited the prison, but had somehow clung to the hope that the liquorice tea might still have had some effect. Vanessa could feel the tears on her cheeks as her only remaining hope of having done anything good in this time utterly disappeared.

"I thought," she said dejectedly, "that if Jane Austen had died I would see a memorial in the Cathedral."

"So you shall, child," said Matilda softly. "And no-one worthier."

At that moment Susan came in with the breakfast tray and Matilda said, "Now sit. There is not much time before you must go."

Vanessa moved to a chair near the fire, noticing a little carriage clock on the mantelshelf. As she sat the clock gave a gentle whir and chimed the quarter, its hands declaring the time to be 10:15. Late for a Regency breakfast, Vanessa thought. No wonder they're crabby.

Breakfast was all she had hoped: no bacon and eggs this time, but thick pieces of white toast, orange marmalade, a plum cake, and a large and aromatic pot of tea. Once they began to eat, the three sisters relaxed. Even sharp-voiced Harriette became friendly, gossipy and quite proprietary of Vanessa, remarking on her accent – "it's so *flat*, my dear; everything you say sounds the same" – but complimentary about her manners and interested in Canadian society. Of this last Vanessa knew little, but declared there were balls in the spring and that young women waited for the fashion magazines, particularly the Parisian ones, with the same breathless expectation as Englishwomen.

The sisters went on to talk of their ailments and their plans for sea bathing if the weather ever grew warmer. Vanessa asked where they planned to go and heard an animated discussion on the relative merits of Weymouth and Lyme Regis. Harriette was just beginning to compare the different cures when Matilda stood up and announced she would guide Vanessa to her coach while the others lingered over their tea.

Once outside Matilda confided that the warden had particularly asked her to look after Vanessa. The coach left from High Bridge Street, the other side of the Cathedral and only a short walk. As they crossed the Close, passing the distinctively Norman south transept, Matilda said, quite casually,

"I know your story, my dear, and I think you are an extraordinary young woman."

Vanessa froze and Matilda stopped to face her.

"The warden told me all about it. Susan and I planned your little retreat up to the attic."

Vanessa was still disoriented, thinking that Matilda knew her *whole* story, not just the part about the prison. And from that thought Vanessa's mind raced back to Chawton and on to her own family home so many years and an ocean away. Then she wondered whether, if all else failed, she could take a room at the little Chawton inn and sleep, and sleep. . . .

Matilda was asking a question. ". . . men and children alike?"

Vanessa had to guess but she got it right.

"No. There's a separate women's ward. I found a group of women who helped each other and when I showed them how we could protect each other as well, we managed to improve things. The warden does his best to treat the prisoners decently, even though some of the guards. . . ."

Vanessa took a deep breath, fighting her emotions. "Would you forgive me if I didn't speak more about it?"

"Of course, dear," said Matilda.

By now they were at the coaching inn. The other passengers were on board and the driver impatient – "another five minutes, miss, and I'd have left without you, gaoler's orders or no."

Vanessa begged the driver to let her out at Chawton and when he understood she had no luggage, he agreed. Even with a stop at Alresford it was well under two hours to the village and she alighted from the coach at the very point she had crossed the road, on that April morning a lifetime ago.

This time the field was muddy rather than flooded and Vanessa wasn't sure where the pond had been. She knew she had to make arrangements for Meg's release before she could do anything else and she wasn't sure if her new clothes would time-travel even if she could discover the pulse. But she told herself these were the least of her worries. She simply had to know – now – if she had any hope. She was still wearing her original cotton underwear but she'd time-travel naked if there was anything left to take her home.

She criss-crossed the field, imagining herself a hunting-dog trying to pick up a scent. Once she thought she sensed some kind of emanation and she remembered Ned Marston telling her that if she could feel the pulse it would pull her in the right direction. But Marston was wrong about this too, just as he'd been about everything else. There was no pull, no power at all. Only a lingering trace, reminding Vanessa of one of the perfumes she had loved to wear for special occasions.

CHAPTER XX

In spite of himself Ned was getting excited about going to Shakespeare's time. He'd returned his now-useless Regency suit to the costumers, giving instructions for a full outfit for a London gentleman, circa 1600.

Returning the Regency costume meant he was giving up on Vanessa, at least for the time being. That hurt. And he'd felt comfortable in the Regency suit, as he knew he would not in Shakespearean doublet and hose.

He completed his research, considered arrival options, and concluded that much as he'd like to bring back a copy of the 1609 Shakespeare *Sonnets* he might have a better chance to buy plays if he went a couple of years earlier. He also struggled to find a balance between making a fast and efficient journey – to fund the research necessary to rescue Vanessa – and his longing to see Shakespeare himself.

Some scholars had suggested that Shakespeare began to spend more time in Stratford-upon-Avon after the summer of 1607. Ned's final decision took this possibility into account. His time would be the spring of 1607 and the place St. Paul's Churchyard, where there was a higher concentration of booksellers than anywhere else in London.

The tailor sent Ned to look at surviving Elizabethan costumes in the Victoria and Albert Museum.

"The men were so small," Ned declared after his visit.

The tailor nodded. "You'll feel like a giant – or an aristocrat. The rich were the only ones who could afford a proper diet."

With that in mind the tailor decided on a modified version of an aristocrat's costume, one worn by Shakespeare's patron the Earl of Southampton. Ned made it clear that absolute authenticity was required, and that any metallic fittings had to be antiques, certified no later than 1605.

"Miss Horwood told us something like that as well, sir. Is this some kind of research project?"

"No," Ned replied shortly, realizing once again that sooner or later people would notice that Vanessa had disappeared. Questions would be asked, and if anyone spoke to this tailor he would doubtless link Vanessa's order to Ned's.

Then what? Ned thought.

The man was looking at Ned curiously. "Is there anything else, sir?"

"I don't think so. Do you have enough to get on with?"

The tailor finished taking Ned's measurements and produced some Elizabethan silver buttons, the price of which was more than Ned earned in six months. But he agreed to everything and said he would be back for a fitting in two days.

Ned gave up his boxing practice to concentrate on fencing. He knew a master who was an historical specialist and booked a week of private lessons. At one of their sessions the subject of protective clothing came up.

"Serious swordsmen sometimes had their midriff corsets made from leather, laced front and back to protect their ribs. And their gloves were heavy over their fore-arms, but with palms and fingers pared thin for the sword-grips."

Ned made no comment at the time, remembering he'd told the tailor he wanted no corsetry at all. But he repeated the phrases over to himself and that afternoon he went to the costumers and gave instructions.

The same fencing-master helped Ned find a replacement for his English rapier. He'd bought it as Elizabethan, but a curator at the Victoria and Albert Museum confirmed it was from the 1620s, too late for Shakespeare's time. Ned was pretty certain he could return it to the original dealer, but the fencing-master had someone prepared to swap.

"You'll get a matching dagger too, if I'm not mistaken. Have you ever worked with rapiers and daggers together?"

"No," said Ned.

The man gave a sinister grin. "You'll love it."

The weapons were 1590s Italian. Ned was mesmerised by their age and beauty. They radiated an elegant, lethal authority, with patterns delicately incised along the blades and scrolled bars either side of the square knucklebows. The rapier had a cup made up of interlocking steel circlets, a fluted pommel, and the quillons – the curved extensions to protect the hand – were shaped like ram's-horns, extending from the pommel to the cup. Ned had the costumers make a belt and sheaths for both weapons, and on his last two days of practice he carefully guarded them with leather and tried them out with the fencing-master.

Ned had never seriously handled a dagger. The instructor had to start with the basics, showing Ned how to slash right- or left-handed and the best openings for different kinds of thrusts. He placed furniture to create confined spaces where, he said, "it makes no sense to draw the rapier," and he demonstrated how to use the dagger in conjunction with wrestling and boxing moves.

"The Elizabethans never knew when they'd be in a street fight. Or where the next tavern brawl might be. Remember how Christopher Marlowe died?"

Ned knew: a dagger thrust in the eye. Whether the fight was a tavern brawl was another question entirely, but he didn't need an historical debate right now.

Ned had spent years developing his left-hand coordination for boxing. By mid-week the instructor complimented him on the way he took to using the dagger in either hand.

"If you've got enough space to fight with a rapier at all, you can keep it right-handed. But if you're in a crowd, or a little room, you have to be able to use the dagger both ways."

By the next-to-last day Ned gave as good as he got, with or without the rapier. After Ned upended the instructor for the second time, the man called a halt.

"I'm getting too old for this," he panted, pulling off his mask. "You've got the old English style, 'use as well the blow as the thrust.' You know who wrote that?"

Ned shook his head and the instructor continued. "Sir Philip Sidney. 1580. You're ready to fight with the best of them, but I don't know anyone likely to take you on."

Ned smiled. "You did."

"For money," said the instructor. "Nobody stages competitions like this any more. Even the experts get hurt. You know we almost cancelled the rapier exhibitions after you flattened that man last year."

Ned said nothing, and after a moment the instructor laughed.

"All I can say is good luck, whatever you're doing. But don't let me catch you trying this stuff around the University."

"Agreed," Ned replied. "But I don't want to give up my last session with you."

The instructor shrugged. "You paid for it," he said. "I'll see you tomorrow."

CHAPTER XXI

Ned knew he'd have to work hard to get comfortable wearing anything like authentic Elizabethan clothes, but he had no idea how difficult it would be just getting into them. He took his new outfit to the laboratory, where Caroline insisted on staying for what she called the fashion show. When Ned unwrapped his packages she began to giggle.

"Are you sure this isn't your transvestite fantasy breaking loose? I've never seen anything like it."

But she helped him into his soft shirt with the ruffled collar, laced the leather corset, slid his arms into the doublet, and helped him figure out the intricacies of all the lacings – eyelets and strings at the bottom of the doublet to tie it to the baggy half-trousers, more laces that attached a thigh-length skirt under the doublet and over the trousers, and garters that attached the trousers to silk stockings just below the knees.

By the time all the gear was on, Caroline's eyes were on fire.

"Just as well we're only friends now. There's something decidedly sexy about all this."

Their eyes locked, and Ned felt a familiar surge of lust. Caroline and he had been good together and he was a heartbeat away from putting his arms around her. But within that heartbeat Vanessa's image came to him once again, and the radiant look that had been on her face as she stepped into the time-machine.

He knew Caroline could feel his change of mood. She took refuge in motherliness, offering to cook him dinner. Ned declined, knowing that going to Caroline's flat might lead to another moment like the one just past, one harder to resist. It was an emotional complication he did not want. Instead he suggested dining at an Indian restaurant they knew, nearby on Cheyne Walk.

But first Ned had to get out of his Shakespearean gear. Caroline offered to help once again, but Ned refused.

"I'm hungry," Caroline protested. "And anyone wearing that kind of outfit would have a servant to help him get in and out. Besides, you're going directly to the bookshops and straight home again, remember?"

Ned shook his head. "Something might come up. I have to look like I know what I'm doing. It's the first rule of time travel. If I'm not mistaken, you made the rule yourself."

She laughed, and once out of the laboratory they spent most of the evening reminiscing. No talk of work or recent events, no talk of anything that might remind them of Vanessa. But Ned spoiled it on the walk home.

"What happens when people start asking where she's gone?"

He could feel Caroline tense, but she replied quietly.

"Term's over. There's nothing to link her with our project except a few letters I sent to Canada. Nobody at the University will ask any questions until September and I have a letter she wrote the day before she left, just in case. It's to the Dean of the Music School, saying she requires a leave of absence to join a crew sailing to the South Pacific. It's dated August fifteenth, almost two months from now."

"You thought of everything, didn't you?"

"Shut up," she whispered. Her shoulders were shaking and she pulled out her handkerchief to wipe her eyes. She flagged the first taxi they saw. "Walk yourself home, Ned. I didn't need an inquisitor. You're on your own."

CHAPTER XXII

Staying in Chawton was too painful to contemplate, so Vanessa started up the path to Alton. She was halfway there when it began to rain, just as it had on her first afternoon. This time she was so lost in her sorrows that she scarcely noticed it.

She told herself she had known the pulse would be gone, had reconciled herself to it after her first month in prison. But the shock she felt had nothing to do with her rational self. It was a numbness that came from within her body, a final, visceral recognition that she was stranded more than two hundred years before she was born.

The rain was only a summer shower and it ended as she came into Alton High Street. The sun was warm enough that a hint of steam could be seen rising from the rooftops. Vanessa was wet, but not quite soaked to the skin. In spite of herself she began to enjoy the way the combination of sunlight and body heat was starting to dry her clothes. It reminded her of the way the sun used to bake the sea-spray on her bathing suits, back in her sailing days.

She walked past the shuttered façade of Hoare's Bank and by the time she reached the Swan Inn she was damp rather than wet. The innkeeper recognised her and produced her copy of *Emma* immediately.

"We heard about the constables, miss," he said. "From the fact as you're here, I'd say it's all put right now." His voice had a note of question and Vanessa decided he deserved an answer.

"Yes," she said. "It was a mistake. I am most obliged to you for keeping my book all this time."

She took lodging for the night, requesting as much hot bath water as possible and dinner in her room. It was still broad daylight when she crawled under the sheets. She slept for fourteen hours, straight through.

Monday was grey, with a steady drizzle. Vanessa confirmed a place on the coach to Winchester that left the Swan at one o'clock and set out to be on the doorstep of Hoare's Bank at its nine o'clock opening. She was so determined to be prompt that she failed to notice another pedestrian heading for the same entrance. Vanessa and Martha Lloyd nearly collided at the door.

Both women dropped their eyes and began to apologise, but it was Martha who first took a step back.

"Miss Horwood," she said firmly. "This is a coincidence indeed."

Vanessa was startled into silence and Martha continued more quietly. "You were innocent after all."

Vanessa nodded, acknowledging Martha's implication. "You weren't certain, were you?"

Martha smiled. "I confess I was not. But after our first visit Jane never doubted you again."

Vanessa's face grew pale and Martha took her arm. "You are not well, my dear. I insist you come with me for tea and sit in front of a fire before you attempt anything else. And I must ask your forgiveness that our baskets of food ended so abruptly. Jane became so ill there was scarcely time for us to feed ourselves, and no time at all for charity."

A moment went by before Martha spoke again, this time fighting tears.

"That is not how I intended to explain myself. I've seen enough illness and grief to last a lifetime. I am determined to put a smile on your face before the morning is out."

There were tearooms a hundred yards away. Both women had their emotions under control by the time they arrived. Vanessa surreptitiously wiped her face with her sleeve as she entered the warm, inviting room with its smell of fresh pastries. They took a small table close to a little fireplace on the back wall.

"This was Jane's favourite place in Alton," said Martha. "It reminded her of Molland's in Bath, which was the one shop in that city for which she had any strong affection."

Vanessa's voice was unsteady, but she managed to say, "Bath" — she cleared her throat — "Bath will always be Bath."

Martha smiled sadly. "Jane's words precisely." She met Vanessa's eyes and went on. "You know, do you not, that she died ten days ago."

Vanessa nodded. "I overheard some ladies talking about the funeral."

"And you also knew that we'd moved to Winchester in May, not long before we visited you in gaol?"

Vanessa nodded and Martha went on. "Jane had felt much stronger from drinking your liquorice tea, but she had a relapse and the family felt she should be under the immediate care of Mr. King Lyford at the hospital. She was still drinking the liquorice at that time, but he insisted it could do no good and would interfere with his remedies. So Jane gave it up and" – Martha smiled – "we never told the doctor it came from you."

Martha caught her breath before she continued.

"But near the end, when it was clear to us all there was no hope, she asked for a pot, speaking most kindly of you and certain of your innocence. Her family had gone to the racetrack, leaving the two of us alone for the afternoon. Jane got up from the sofa and wrote this."

Martha fumbled in her handbag for an envelope. "She said they were foolish verses and that, as your tea was to blame, you should have them – that they might leave you with happier recollections of Winchester than those from other quarters."

Vanessa opened the envelope and unfolded its contents. Before she could begin reading, Martha spoke again.

"One more thing. I offered to make a fair copy for you, but Jane insisted on doing this herself. She said if Egerton had discarded her manuscript for *Pride and Prejudice* this might be your Canadian gentleman's only hope of an autograph."

Vanessa didn't dare try to speak. Her eyes were filling with tears, the tears for Jane she'd been unable to shed after their last meeting. Through the blur she read:

> When Winchester races first took their beginning
> It is said the good people forgot their old Saint
> Not applying at all for the leave of Saint Swithin
> And that William of Wykeham's approval was faint.
>
> The races however were fix'd and determin'd
> The company met & the Weather was charming
> The Lords & the Ladies were satinn'd & ermin'd
> And nobody saw any future alarming –

But when the old Saint was inform'd of these doings
He made but one spring from his shrine to the roof
Of the Palace which now lies so sadly in ruins
And then he address'd them all standing aloof. . . .

These races & revels & dissolute measures
With which you're debasing a neighbouring Plain
Let them stand – you shall meet with your curse in your pleasures
Set off for your course, I'll pursue with my rain. . . .

Vanessa looked up and Martha, accurately reading the strength of Vanessa's feelings, waited several minutes before speaking again.

"I haven't been to Alton since Jane died. She instructed me to leave this for you at Hoare's Bank, determined that you would be vindicated and return in due course." She smiled again, more broadly. "And so you have."

"Thank you, Miss Lloyd," Vanessa whispered.

"Call me Martha, my dear. And now," she said briskly, "here is our tea and while you were reading I waved to the girl for this plum tart, which I trust you will find agreeable. The fruit comes from Jane's brother's orchards at the Manor House."

The turmoil of Vanessa's emotions began to abate as she ate and drank. Within a few moments she was able to carry on the conversation. Martha described the stone soon to be laid in Jane's memory at Winchester Cathedral. Vanessa smiled, knowing she could recite from memory the epitaph carved on it.

As they left Martha extended an invitation to visit whenever Vanessa might be in the neighbourhood. Both promised to write, and with that they parted.

CHAPTER XXIII

"We were expecting you," declared the elderly teller at Hoare's Bank. His face was bright with welcome as he crossed the room to take Vanessa's arm.

"Will you accept my apologies on behalf of all of us here, and the bank at large?"

"It was none of your own doing, sir," replied Vanessa.

"Indeed it was not," cried the teller. "And I am informed that the clerk in Fleet Street has been discharged."

"If it was an honest mistake I am sorry to hear it."

The teller turned and bowed. "You are too generous."

He stepped behind his counter, whereupon Vanessa produced her draft, relieved finally to see the last of it. The teller suggested a note of credit and fifty pounds in cash, which she accepted.

Meg's prediction that the bespoke dress would still be waiting at its maker's proved accurate. It was too big, but Vanessa knew this was from her loss of weight in prison rather than any fault of the dressmaker. They also had her new underclothes and portmanteau.

Back at the Swan she tucked her three volumes of *Emma* into the case, smiling to herself as she carefully padded the books with her new clothes. Then she counted her blessings: a little money, two outfits, and a first edition of her favourite novel.

The morning had also found her a friend in Martha Lloyd. And Vanessa knew she already had more than a friend in Meg. But that was all. No other connections, no family (six or seven generations-removed great-grandparents did *not* signify, even if she had known who and where they were), and no prospects.

As she boarded the one o'clock coach to Winchester Vanessa was determined to make a success of her new life. Ned Marston, whether Mephistopheles or not, could go to hell.

By four o'clock Vanessa was with Meg and her creditors' solicitor in Lewcock's small office. True to his word the warden had prepared the necessary papers. Vanessa handed over her money, received the required signature, and after the solicitor left the three sat sipping the warden's inevitably-lukewarm cups of tea.

"I have some extraordinary news," Lewcock said. "The appeal of your cell-mate Jenny Cawthorn was denied today and she and her accomplice will hang on Wednesday. Her attorney came to me directly and said Jenny had left the two of you money in her will."

"A will!" Meg exclaimed.

"I am amazed as you are," said Lewcock. "Even more that the attorney has come out with it, when he could perfectly well have destroyed the will and kept the money himself."

"Well," said Meg, "it's likely to be the money she had as garnish so it's only fair it should come back round."

"It's more than that," said Lewcock. "She had somewhat in excess of five hundred pounds after attorney fees – and I am not overly soft-hearted about the attorney as he never disclosed what his fees were. But she has left fifty pounds to each of you and the remainder to improve the lot of the women in this gaol. Two hundred is for discharging as many debtors as possible and the rest is for food and, she said, for guarding the guards." He smiled ruefully. "The attorney said he had modified the language she used about the guards, but that he had communicated her intent. Out of the mouths of babes, it seems, and of uneducated felons, comes wisdom. *Quis custodiet ipsos custodes*, indeed."

"What?" said Meg.

"Who will guard the guardians," Lewcock translated. "A line from the Roman poet Juvenal."

Vanessa added, "It's better than that. Juvenal's writing about guarding women and he suggests they hire eunuchs."

"Can you speak to this matter personally, either of you?" Lewcock asked.

Meg's smile was bitter. "Some things changed after Vanessa came." She looked at Lewcock, "You're a good man, warden, but you've still some house-keeping to do."

"Well," said Lewcock, "the money is now in my care and I trust you will allow me to see Mrs. Cawthorn's wishes fulfilled."

Vanessa and Meg exchanged glances and Vanessa spoke. "I think that money might be better spent on the poor in the prison. We'll get by with what we have."

Lewcock smiled. "I anticipated you might say that and I trust you will not consider it unbecoming of me to quote St. Matthew: 'We shall always have the poor.' I believe Jenny appreciated something unusual about you two and that what she saw gave her the courage to seek her own redemption. I know the last to be true, as I have spoken to her in the gallows holding-cell."

Meg said to Vanessa. "If it's like that, then, we should never argue, love."

Vanessa nodded and Lewcock counted out the banknotes.

"It would have bought your freedom in any event, Miss Gallagher, but I was pleased to see your friend accomplish it first."

"She'll have her money back now, sure," said Meg, "and no argument."

Vanessa raised her hands in protest, but seeing the determination in Meg's eyes she tucked twenty-five pounds more in her purse. With that they said their farewells.

CHAPTER XXIV

Ned spent his last morning before time-travelling practicing with his rapier and dagger in Shakespearean clothes. He wished he dared show up wearing them for his final fencing lesson, but he knew he'd never live that down.

After a long series of solitary thrusts and parries he began drawing and sheathing the weapons, first separately, then together, over and over. He began to feel like an idiot, like some imitation Old West cowboy practicing quick draws with a six-shooter.

When he returned from his fencing lesson he thought of putting on his costume one more time. But he refused to allow himself. He was as ready to time-travel as he'd ever be. It was time to rest.

He sprawled in his usual armchair, staring through the glass front of the bookcase at his little collection. Looking at his books usually calmed him down, but ever since Vanessa had visited everything in his flat reminded him of her. He could feel her touch as she'd sat on his lap in this same chair. He smiled, remembering how she'd suddenly stood up when they'd started to talk about sailing. A month in a sailboat with Vanessa had seemed the most desirable prospect in the world. Now she was gone, without a trace, unreachable.

The phone rang. It was Caroline, apologising for her outburst after last night's dinner. She promised to bring a taxi for him first thing next morning.

Ned spent a restless night. By daybreak he'd trimmed his beard, breakfasted, and put on his Shakespearean outfit. Caroline arrived just as he was struggling all over again with the laces attaching trousers to doublet. He'd drunk an entire pot of coffee and his bladder was paying the price.

Caroline had an ancient leather purse full of pre-1607 English coins.

"I had to spend a lot more than I ever imagined for these," she confessed. "The gold ones especially. The dealer said examples in fine condition were very rare, and most of their dates are so close to your arrival that I knew they'd look suspicious if they *weren't* fine."

"I still don't understand how these coins can be in two places at once. Isn't that what has to happen when I take them back in time?"

"Don't ask," said Caroline. "I think when we time-transport there's some kind of exchange at the atomic level, that as you and the coins go back in time an equal amount of matter will come forward. But neither of the engineers agrees with me."

"Or with each other?"

Caroline laughed. "That too."

There was little else for them to do. Ned put on a long raincoat to hide his outfit and they took Caroline's taxi to the warehouse. The two engineers checked the machine's programme. Then they shook Ned's hand.

"See you in a minute, Marston," one said.

They stood back and Caroline stepped forward, putting her arms around him. They were both self-conscious, but she stayed close, putting her lips to his ear.

"There's one more thing," she whispered. "I wanted you to have as much money as I could find. There's more than you could possibly need for buying pamphlets."

Caroline's breath caught and for a moment Ned thought she was going to cry. But she drew herself away, glancing at the two engineers intent on their preparations.

"I have a feeling about this trip. At first I wanted to stop you from going, but I knew that would be wrong. Something good is going to happen. I'm not sure it's what any of us expects but" – she looked straight into Ned's eyes – "it *is* going to be good, my love. And I know we'll meet again. Maybe not in any way we can think of now, but we will."

She went up on tiptoe to kiss him, and Ned climbed into the time-traveller, ready to go back four hundred years with her lipstick on his mouth.

The Perfect Visit

After Ned disappeared Caroline turned and headed for the warehouse door.

"Aren't you going to wait for him?" one of the engineers called.

"I don't think he's coming back," she said.

"Christ," said the other. "Now she tells us."

PART TWO:
1607 AND 1817

Thus the whirligig of time brings in his revenges.

William Shakespeare
Twelfth-Night
Act V, Scene 1

CHAPTER I

The sky was cloudless as Ned materialised in an alley at the west end of St. Paul's Churchyard. The sun was low on the eastern horizon and there was only the slightest bite in the breeze. It was early on a spring morning, just as they'd planned.

Ned stuck out his tongue, feeling part of the beard that he'd trimmed that morning in best Shakespearean style. Then he tasted Caroline's lipstick, smiled, and rubbed at it with his glove. Her kiss had been gentle, almost maternal, a far cry from the passion he'd felt from Vanessa. But what had Caroline meant when she'd said their next meeting might be 'not any way we can think of now'?

He shook his head and started to look around. The first thing he saw was the cathedral, utterly unlike the iconic domed St. Paul's Ned had always taken for granted. This earlier church reminded him of Winchester, built as a roman cross, with a short tower instead of a dome or steeple.

Winchester reminded him once again of Vanessa. He should be there, not here. Let it go, he thought. It's time to buy some books.

There were small crowds of people scattered around the churchyard, some selling food, some setting up market-stands for all manner of other goods. Most of the shops around the perimeter were still locked up, but a few were beginning to open. Ned could hear the chatter of the apprentice-boys pulling at the shutters. He eyed the groups of browsers nearest him, noticing without surprise that he was a head taller than most of the men. He tugged at his doublet, uncomfortably.

He had time to reconnoitre, to choose the bookshops where he might try his luck. He knew that booksellers in this time traded their stock. He might find almost anything anywhere, but St. Paul's had the highest concentration not only of booksellers generally, but of booksellers holding copyrights in plays. Including Shakespeare's plays.

But the works he saw in the few unshuttered windows were entirely religious. Disappointed, he decided to browse the open-air market and come back later.

A nearby vendor was shaking his head. "Bright too early, 'tis. Rain by afternoon, mark my words."

His companion noticed Ned. "Out of bed so early, my lord?"

A toothless old woman with a lisp called from a fruit-stall. "Maybe never abed at all. Try a Spanish orange, m'lud. T'will wake you up proper."

Ned decided to buy an orange, a first taste of his new world.

He smiled at the old woman, pulled out a silver sixpence and received his orange and a penny change. The fruit was delicious, its juice dribbling into Ned's beard.

He drifted towards a couple of nearby tables covered with pamphlets, peering at the titles from a distance as he finished his orange. Most were pure theology, but a couple had long sub-titles referring to Catholics and the Gunpowder Plot. If his 1607 arrival date was accurate, the Plot was a year-and-a-half old. Time, Ned hoped, for London to have calmed down.

On his right two clergymen were arguing with the pamphlet-seller. Ned stayed to listen.

"'Tis the Reverend Jewell's *Seven Sermons* indeed," one said. "How come you to this? T'was printed no more than a month since, at twice your price."

Craning his neck Ned could see the title page, dated 1607 at the bottom. He gave a mental sigh of relief. But the pamphlet-seller caught Ned's eye.

"Are you waiting to ask some misbegotten question as well, my lord?"

"I'm no lord. Just a visitor from the country, looking for plays."

"Plays!" The bookseller's snort was indignant. "You might go to that upstart at St. Austin's Gate. He's printed *The Whore of Babylon*."

Ned nodded to the man, trying to look as though he knew where St. Austin's Gate was. He ambled away, scanning St. Paul's Churchyard once more. More of the shop-shutters were now open and everywhere he looked the windows were full of books. There had to be *someone* selling Shakespeare. St. Paul's was, after all, the centre of the book trade in this time.

One shop, close to the north door of the cathedral, had a sign over the door showing a cannon and some volumes of poetry in the window. Ned pulled off his hat and gloves and walked inside.

The bookseller behind the counter was not young. Wisps of white hair peeked from under his flat-topped cap; his beard was patchy and his long coat a little shabby. But the lines of his face were strong and his eyes were bright. The shop was shelved with books of different heights bound in dark calf and pale vellum. The page-edges faced outwards and except for some words inked sideways along some of them there was no telling what their titles were. Underneath the shelves were cupboards, which Ned knew would contain unbound books and pamphlets.

"Plays," the man smiled at Ned's question. "I've a few." He opened a cupboard and pulled out a small stack. Halfway through Ned's heart skipped a beat. He was looking at *The Tragicall Historie of Hamlet Prince of Denmarke. By William Shake-speare,* printed in 1603. His first glimpse inside showed Ned this was the mangled version known as the "bad quarto":

> To be, or not to be, I there's the point,
> To Die, to sleepe, is that all? I all:
> No, to sleepe, to dreame, I mary there it goes. . .
> The vndiscouered country, at whose sight
> The happy smile, and the accursed damn'd.

Ned tried to look casual as he set the pamphlet aside. It was famous in his own time, having survived in a single example. A few more like this and he'd be ready to go.

He started to reach for another but his hands were shaking. He rested them on the counter and asked the price of *Hamlet*. The bookseller raised his eyebrows.

"The usual price, sir." Then he picked it up. "Ah, 'tis the bastard copy, or so Master Ling asserts. He would exchange it for a fair one if you cared to take it to him. I'll not charge the full sixpence, as I should for the latest printings."

Ned saw his chance. "Might you have any more of the old ones?"

"To what end, sir?"

"My own amusement," Ned replied.

The bookseller turned back to his cupboard, reaching well inside and producing another pile, all in the same small square-ish format as *Hamlet* – quartos.

"These are mostly my own printings. You may choose what you will at fivepence each, or a dozen for four shillings."

Ned began to flip through the stack, dust rising as he did so. There was Thomas Kyd's *Spanish Tragedy*, 1592, and *The moste famous Chronicle Historye of Leire Kinge of England and his Three Daughters,* 1594, surely a source for Shakespeare. Ned let his breath out slowly as he came to *The Most Lamentable Romaine Tragedie of Titus Andronicus*, 1594. Like most plays of the 1590s, no author was given, but this was Shakespeare himself, the earliest known edition of any of his works.

All of these had some variation of the name Edward White in the imprint, "to be solde. . . at the signe of the Gunne." Ned looked up, as nonchalantly as he could.

"Master White, are you not?"

The bookseller nodded. "Anything take your fancy?"

"I've three more so far," Ned said. "May I continue?" A pleased smile was Ned's reply, and he realised how limited the market must be for these outdated printings.

"Have you others by Master Shakespeare?"

White glanced at the pamphlets Ned had put aside and then riffled through the stack himself. He shook his head.

"Naught else." Ned swallowed his disappointment as White continued. "You might find some at Matthew Law's t'other side of the churchyard, but the man you want is my quondam partner Nicholas Ling in Fleet Street. He's been buying up Shakespeare's copy from the other booksellers, I don't know why – aye, and Ben Jonson's too. His boy is here now and can take you to his shop at St. Dunstan's if you've the time."

Ned was torn. If Matthew Law had a half-dozen Shakespeares Ned could return to his own time in an hour or less. But if Law had only a couple Ned would still need to go to Ling's shop, and he'd be without a guide. He nodded his acceptance at a boy in the corner of the room and then tried his luck transacting business.

"I've not made the dozen, but can you give me a price for these four?"

White didn't hesitate. "One and eightpence the lot."

Fivepence each, just as the man had said. Ned plucked a silver crown from inside his doublet. White gave him his change, wrapped the pamphlets in a folio sheet covered with old writing and nodded to Ling's apprentice.

CHAPTER II

The boy's name was Thomas Crane. He was eleven or twelve, quick to chatter, with eyes bright as a bird's. Within a couple of minutes Ned knew how recently the boy had started his apprenticeship and that Ling had taken him because he wrote a fair hand and was good with numbers. He wasn't shy with his questions either, asking Ned if he was any relation to John Marston the playwright.

"You look a bit like him, sir, but taller, and you haven't his villainous red hair."

Ned smiled, wondering when red locks had finally ceased to be a liability in Christian societies. He asked Thomas if the poets spent much time in Ling's shop.

"Oh yes, sir. Especially Master Shakespeare. My master has a full cupboard of Shakespeare's works, both printed and manuscript. Master Shakespeare laughs and says it is his 'monument without a tomb.'" The boy stopped and struck a pose as he quoted the last few words. Ned was charmed.

Thomas had one more package to deliver so he led Ned a couple hundred yards north to Paternoster Row, then west to Amen Corner and the booksellers' headquarters at Stationers' Hall. Afterwards they took a shortcut down Cock Alley to Ludgate Street.

Half-timbered, cantilevered houses lined either side of the alley and the two picked their way through slops thrown earlier from the windows. Cats and dogs, some wary rats, and a couple of brave birds picked through the garbage and excrement, most of which would be devoured, one way or another, in a couple of hours. The sun was still in the east, and the alley was shadowed.

Five or six people had gathered at the far end of the alley where it joined the main thoroughfare. Some others were turning back the way they had come. Ned heard a muffled scream. A girl of perhaps twenty was struggling with two men wearing the dishevelled livery of a nobleman. One had his hand over her mouth. The girl bit down and the man pulled his hand free with a curse, tearing her bodice as he did.

"Get off, you pragging whoresons," she spat at them, but the second man moved in from behind and grabbed her arms.

"We've a fighting kite, that's sure." His voice was slurred and his red beard patchy over a pockmarked face; his clothes were the dirtier of the two. "We'll have you betimes, my mistress, like it or not."

Thomas tugged Ned's sleeve. "We know her," he whispered. "That's Mistress Judith."

Ned was already stepping forward. The girl gave him an imploring look. She was no beauty – her forehead was too high and her cheeks too large and round – but there was something of Vanessa's spirit in her blazing eyes and expressive mouth. Under what was left of her dress her figure was luscious. Ripe, Ned thought, but not for their plucking.

"Do you know these men, mistress?" Ned called.

Her wit was quick. "I choose better than these, when I choose at all." Then she blushed. "Which I do not, my lord."

The man with the bitten finger sneered. "Off with you, master knucklehead. This is none of yours."

Judith spoke again, quietly. "'Tis rape, sir."

Ned stood still. "Gentlemen," he said calmly. "The girl declines your invitations. Save them for another."

Bitten finger drew his sword. "Be off, sirrah, or I'll scour thee."

Part of Ned felt like a fool, unable to walk a half-mile without getting into a fight. He knew he shouldn't risk his mission – or his life – but he'd grown up boxing and fencing, both unpopular sports in his own time. Now he was in a world where his skills mattered and his blood was racing. And besides, he told himself, it was clear enough the girl was honest and in desperate need of a champion.

He pulled his rapier and out of the corner of one eye he saw red-beard let go of Judith and do the same.

"Two yoke-devils," she called scornfully, "afraid to fight one-on-one like gentlemen."

Ned drew his dagger with his left hand, thinking that at least he had two blades to match their two rapiers. He moved in warily, hoping to get at the first man before red-beard got into position. His opponent tried a feint, but clumsily, whether from drink or lack of skill Ned couldn't tell. With half-an-eye on red beard, Ned went in low, then whipped his blade up over his enemy's, thrusting down towards the forearm in a move known as an *imbrocatta*. He caught the man's glove, the rapier's point cutting through the leather and along the top of the hand. The man grunted with pain, dropping his weapon and sinking to the ground, clutching his wound.

Ned kicked the blade aside and whirled to confront red-beard, whose sword was already coming at him from the outside. Ned knocked it away with his dagger, and the man was so off-balance that he staggered forward. As Ned leaped aside, red-beard fell face-first into a pile of slops. Ned put his foot on the man's outstretched sword-arm.

"Let go," Ned said. No response. Ned's blood was up and he had little patience. "Let go your sword or I'll cut it loose."

The hand opened and Ned picked up the rapier. Then he moved to the second man who was ruefully nursing his cut, rapier forgotten. Ned picked up that blade as well and said to Thomas, "Shall we leave their swords close by, so they can pick them up when they're sober?"

Judith moved closer, clutching at her torn dress. "I know an inn just along in Blackfriars, sir."

Ned told the two men where their weapons would be and followed Judith and Thomas to the end of the alley. Blackfriars was close by, to the southwest. He sent Thomas to the innkeeper with the swords, not wishing to be seen there himself or to leave the girl alone.

Ned could see her staring at him and wondered what she thought. He must be taller than most men she knew. What would she make of his accent? Did his clothes pass muster? Did she know many men with crooked noses and boxing scars along their cheekbones?

She blushed as she became aware of Ned's gaze, dropping her own eyes and – still holding the bodice of her dress – curtseying.

"I am Judith Shakespeare, sir, and I am in your debt."

Ned felt dizzy, and put out an arm to lean against the building.

"Are you well, sir?" the girl asked. Ned stared down at her, realizing that the high forehead and round cheeks he'd dismissed so lightly were those of her father. Add a beard, take away the blush, and she'd look like Shakespeare's portrait in the First Folio.

"I . . . I have admired your father's plays, mistress," Ned stammered.

"I shall tell him. He, too, is in your debt."

Then Thomas reappeared, strutting a little at his own importance, and the three walked over to Ludgate Hill where Judith knew a shop that would mend her dress. When she smiled and thanked him again, her face lit up so prettily that it was Ned's turn to blush.

Judith spoke to the boy.

"You're taking him to Master Ling's shop, Thomas?" When the boy nodded she turned once more to Ned. "If you are friend to Master Ling, we shall meet again."

She went into the dressmaker's before Ned could reply and, still thunderstruck, he followed Thomas to the bottom of Ludgate Hill, across the bridge over the foul-smelling Fleet Ditch, and into Fleet Street.

The road bustled with traffic and there were constant comings-and-goings from the side courts and alleys that led away at all angles. Thomas gave a sudden tug at Ned's sleeve, pulling him out of the way of a horse-drawn cart full of building materials. New shops were everywhere. London's trade had increasingly moved west, with King James's arrival four years earlier providing a boost not only for industry and art, but also for the lawyers who were concentrated in the four Inns of Court, two of which were next to Fleet Street.

It was only a few steps more to the sprawling church of St. Dunstan-in-the-West. The front of the church projected some distance into Fleet Street and where the road narrowed there was a traffic jam and shouting. Before they reached the thick of it Thomas led Ned to a narrow walkway that opened into the comparatively peaceful expanse of the churchyard.

The church was large but from the outside unimpressive. The shops were attached to the longest wall of the church and a crenellated parapet ran along their tops. Each shop had its own display window and what appeared to be living quarters above.

The earlier sunshine had vanished. Ned remembered the trader's prediction that morning: "Bright too early," the first words he'd heard in Shakespeare's time. As the rain started to fall Thomas made a run for Nicholas Ling's still-open door. Ned followed him through and looked around. The arrangement was much the same as in the shop at St. Paul's, although with more books on the shelves and some elaborate gilded bindings in calf, goatskin and velvet on display.

The boy stood at the entrance to a back room, calling in his excited treble, "Master Nicholas, Master Nicholas."

A deep voice replied, "A moment, Thomas," and a dark-bearded, barrel-chested man emerged. His greying hair was long, cut straight below his ears, and he had narrow, almond eyes above high cheekbones. His beard was straight and closely trimmed, and he wore the uniform of a prosperous merchant, a modestly-ruffled silk shirt beneath a knee-length surcoat. The coat had a single row of silver buttons running up the middle and some discreet embroidered facings either side.

Thomas was tugging at those facings and the man's face was kind as he gave the boy his attention.

"Master Nicholas," the boy repeated.

"I am he, Thomas. What have you to tell?"

"Master Ned came to talk to you about your plays and on our way we saw Mistress Judith and two bullies. They'd torn her clothes and she was screaming. . . ."

"Who is Master Ned?" Ling interrupted, and the boy was silent, pointing at the figure in the doorway.

"Edward Marston, sir, at your service."

Ling half-smiled. "No relation of our strutting playwright, I hope."

Thomas was wound up again. "John Marston's no relation. He told me."

"Quiet, Thomas," Ling said. "We'll hear the rest from Master Marston."

"The girl was terrified," said Ned, "and the men were drunk. They drew as soon as I told them to give way." Ned shrugged and it suddenly became a shudder. He pulled himself together and repeated, "They were drunk. And I was lucky."

This was too much for Thomas. "He cut one of them and left 'em both in the mud."

"We know only one Mistress Judith," Ling said quietly. "Did Thomas tell you who she was?"

"Master Shakespeare's daughter!" Thomas said excitedly.

"Yes," said Ling. "Down from Stratford to keep house for her father and, he says, help him move home to the country for good. But what brings you here?"

Thomas interrupted again. "Master White sent him!"

Ling turned to his boy and said mildly, "Thomas, run across to the Devil and get yourself a pie. Afterwards tell Toby to give you two more out of the oven to bring back for Master Marston and me. And tell Toby if Will Shakespeare comes to the tavern this afternoon, I want to know."

Thomas nodded, cast his bright eyes towards Ned one more time and dashed out the door.

Ned picked up where they'd left off. "I've ridden from the country myself to buy all the Shakespeare plays I can find. Master White told me you were the man to see."

"In truth I am," replied Ling. Then he looked at Ned's package. "But y'have purchased something from White?"

Ned unwrapped the paper cover, setting his four pamphlets on the table, and Nicholas nodded sagely. *"Titus Andronicus,* 1594. Even I have only one of this, although there are later impressions." He glanced at the other pamphlets and Ned could see the man's disappointment. "And the bastard text of *Hamlet.*"

Ling looked up. "I had hoped, sir, you might have found a copy of *Love's Labours Won.*"

Ned knew the title: a play Shakespeare was reported to have written, but no edition of the text had survived.

Ling continued. "The actors dictated their parts to White's man in 1596. White printed it but never sent copies to me. He says he sold all he had during the season it played. It must be somewhere, but even Shakespeare has none, nor the manuscript neither."

He opened a cupboard. "I've new printings of *Romeo and Juliet* and *Love's Labours Lost.* And you should have the corrected *Hamlet* as well."

Ned smiled. "I shall have them with pleasure, sir, but have you any of the earlier editions?"

Ling became thoughtful. "I've some put by for my own use – more copies than I need of several and I'll sell 'em if you care to have 'em." He gave Ned an appraising look. "But they'll cost more than the usual sixpence."

"Agreed, Master Ling," Ned said immediately. But he had one more question. The encounter with Judith had shaken what little resolve he had to hurry home. A few more hours here would make no difference when he returned. Ned knew he couldn't leave if there was a chance of meeting Shakespeare himself.

"You said you were to be told if Master Shakespeare came to the tavern."

"Aye, sir," said Nicholas. "I've business with the man."

"Might I join you?"

Ling could see the longing in Ned's eyes and replied in the gentle voice Ned had heard him use with his apprentice.

"Aye, sir," Nicholas repeated. "That you might."

CHAPTER III

The warden asked them to supper, but Vanessa and Meg declined, leaving Winchester Gaol without a backward look. They headed for the coaching inn and shared a room for the night, much of it spent talking. Meg had never before asked Vanessa what she might do if acquitted.

"I had hopes, love, but knowing how much the English judges love hanging I'd have been daft to have rated your chances."

Now she floated the question and each discovered that the other had neither family nor commitments waiting upon their returns.

"All my family in Ireland wants is for me to send money," Meg said ruefully.

Vanessa responded with vague, albeit true, references to a dead father and other, unspecified, family difficulties in Canada. And all the while they dared not say what they both most hoped, which was that they could join forces and face their new lives together.

Meg finally found courage to speak as their only candle guttered.

"I believe," Meg said, "that God meant you to be the sister I never had."

"I'll try," Vanessa whispered.

"Trying isn't in it," Meg said with a smile, but in the flickering candlelight her gaze was intense. "You needn't do any more than stay alive."

"Meg," Vanessa began, intending to tell the full story of where – and when – she was from. She could feel something blocking her speech, but was determined to overcome it. She tried a dozen different ways to tell her story and each one failed. In the end Vanessa sat on the edge of the bed, sobbing helplessly.

Meg couldn't know why Vanessa looked so shocked, but she knew what to do. She held her friend close and as the candle sputtered out the two settled down to sleep side-by-side, deeply and dreamlessly until the innkeeper's knock woke them just before dawn.

They had asked to be called in time for the early coach to London. It was an express, left at six o'clock, and stopped in Alresford, Alton, Farnham, and Guildford before travelling the longer distance to London's Charing Cross. Even with four stops they covered the fifty miles in just over seven hours.

Meg had an uncle who was hostler at the Bell Inn near St. Paul's. Charing Cross was as close to the Bell as their coach would get. Hungry as they were, the inn at the terminus had a mouldy smell that boded ill for diners. Meg couldn't wait on another matter, however, and claimed a passenger's right to use the privy.

Vanessa stayed with her small piece of luggage. She must have appeared as lost as she felt, for a portly and solicitous man with mutton-chop whiskers, a patterned green waistcoat, and a long gold watch-chain approached her.

"Young lady, I beg your pardon."

Vanessa turned warily and the man bowed.

"I can see you are new to London and a young woman of fashion. You may wish to find lodgings of better quality and less expense than this or any other inn can provide. May I present my card?"

"That won't be necessary, sir," Vanessa replied.

Another bow. "Then at least let me show you the way."

He moved closer to Vanessa and suddenly staggered past her, barely saving himself a fall in the muddy road. Meg had planted a kick in the small of his back and as he straightened indignantly to face her, she spat.

"Give over, you black-balled waggoner. What d'you take us for?"

The man attempted to recover his dignity. "I took *her* for a young lady of quality."

"A prospect, more like. We're none of your gullible boobies – be off with you or we'll call the constables."

Without another word he stalked into the inn.

"Did he get close enough to touch you?" Meg asked.

Vanessa shook her head and Meg went on. "Chances are he's a pickpocket too. Or a ring-dropper. His kind always have more than one calling."

Vanessa was interested. "What's a ring-dropper? And a waggoner?"

"Let's get away from here. We'll talk of it later."

They saved money by walking to St. Paul's, taking turns carrying Vanessa's case. The first half-mile along the Strand was the worst, with staggering drunks, pimps parading their bruised and glassy-eyed women, amputees with their begging-cups out, and mounds of filth spilling out of the gutters onto the pavement.

"It's worse than this, even, past the City and by the docks," Meg said, "but it's better for a time after we pass St. Clement's. The law-courts and the lawyers' inns are down there and their be-wigged lordships don't want to have to look at all the people they've pulled down by their injustices."

Vanessa was surprised at the passion in Meg's voice, but said nothing. After fifteen minutes they passed Middle Temple Lane and a hundred yards further was Hoare's Bank. An ancient church projected into the street nearly opposite and Vanessa gazed across at it, drawn to look inside.

Meg smiled at her. "It's an ancient one, that. St. Dunstan's-in-the-West. They say the shops alongside are some of the oldest in London."

She was willing to go along with Vanessa. As they crossed the wide stone threshold they could smell the incense lingering in the musty air and sense what felt like the ghosts of all eternity coming and going in the candlelight.

"There's something about this place," Vanessa whispered.

After a few minutes Meg took her arm and led her out. A shaft of sunlight had broken through the thick clouds.

"Will you see the bankers now?"

Vanessa shook her head. "Let's go to your uncle and get settled. We need his advice."

Meg smiled. "He'll have little to offer. We'll have to make plans of our own, love."

Vanessa was delighted with the Bell Inn. Its Elizabethan timbers and cantilevered upper storeys lifted her spirits up and away from the bleak scenes they had witnessed along the Strand. And Liam Gallagher, Meg's uncle, welcomed them both, smiling approvingly at Vanessa when Meg told the story of their release from Winchester Gaol. He was able to get them a tiny garret room with a bed just big enough to fit them both, for four shillings a week.

"The room's not even half what they charge downstairs – with the beds no better," he said. "And starting tomorrow you'll eat with us."

Meg gave him a kiss. "It's the lap of luxury next to what we've been used to, uncle." She turned to Vanessa. "And I'll find a job with a dressmaker, so we won't have to pay for it out of our savings."

"What's she going to do, then?" the uncle asked, nodding at Vanessa.

"Good question," said Vanessa. "Give piano lessons, I suppose."

The food at the Bell was excellent and Vanessa and Meg ate their fill.

"Just this once, to celebrate," Meg said. "And I'm paying."

"No you're not," replied Vanessa.

"I am, truly," Meg insisted. "But you can buy us a bumper of Madeira. I do love it so."

"For us both then. Just this once."

They drank each other's health and ordered a pint of ale sent through to Meg's uncle. Then Vanessa smiled.

"I know we've a lot to talk about, but tell me about waggoners and ring-droppers first. I feel such an innocent."

"Your father told you never to talk to strangers, did he not?"

"That wasn't such a problem in Montreal, but yes, he did."

"They're the worst of all London," said Meg. "The waggoners meet coaches in from the country and pick up young girls come looking for work. Usually they're younger and less fashionable than the likes of you, love; he must have been desperate to have gambled you were alone. He'd have been all smiles walking you up to his house and from the outside it would have been the picture of respectability. Inside they'd have given you a meal and a drink and it would all have been full of the poppy. You'd have woken up without your clothes or your money, drugged and raped. And before you'd have known it they'd have poured another drought down your throat and raped you again. Once you were cowed enough they'd start selling you."

"My God," said Vanessa.

"If I hadn't heard the line about the lodgings," Meg said, "I'd have assumed he was trying to sell you something. Which is what the ring-droppers do, of course – they all have the same smooth style. He'll drop a gold-painted ring and say 'Oh, look what we've found.' He'll insist that because you were with him you should share the value of it and then he'll say the nearest goldsmith's too far away, or it's closed for dinner, or whatever. Then he'll show you a mark inside that he'll say is a hallmark and he'll tell you sweet as ever can be that as you're such a nice young lady he'll let you have it for half-a-crown and you can take the profit."

Vanessa laughed. "I don't think even I would have fallen for that one."

Meg didn't smile. "You'd be amazed at the number who do."

Vanessa shot her a look. "Oh dear, Meg. You weren't one of them, were you?"

Now Meg smiled back. "No, love, not me."

CHAPTER IV

As soon as Nicholas Ling agreed to introduce Shakespeare Ned began to feel guilty about breaking his promise to return directly to his own time. But Ling had suggested there were more and earlier plays in his private store, surely a prospect worth waiting for. The plays Ned had so far weren't nearly enough to justify the trip. Or so he told himself.

Thomas returned from the Devil tavern a moment later.

"Toby says the pies are in the oven and he'll send them along with his boy soon as they're ready." The boy grinned. "He'll leave yours in the oven longest because you like them overcooked."

This brought a sideways glance from Ling. "And so should you, Master Marston, if you value your health. Have you time to join us in our meal?"

Ned nodded, gulped, and committed himself. "I've need of lodging as well, if I may ask your counsel."

"You've need of more than lodging, sir, if I do not mistake. This is your first time in London?"

"Am I so obvious?"

Ling's smile was more open this time. "In truth you need a guide as well as a place to stay. I'll do nicely enough for both." Out of the corner of his eye Ned saw Thomas looking at them, astonished.

Ned bowed. "Thank you, Master Ling. I trust you will allow me to pay for this hospitality."

"Doubt it not, sir." Ling replied.

While they waited for their dinner, Ling sent Thomas upstairs with Ned to a garret room, two flights up a narrow staircase. In the same breath Ling told Thomas to show Ned the plays in the Shakespeare cupboard.

The garret had a small window and bedstead that smelled of fresh straw.

"My room's just opposite," Thomas said, proudly opening the door into a tiny airless closet, some matting just visible on the floor. "Hardly any of the boys my age have their own rooms." He closed the door. "And now I'm to show you the old plays. Master Ling says if there are three copies or more, you may take one."

They went down one flight. On one side was Ling's bedroom, on the other a storeroom overflowing with books. The Shakespeare cupboard was not large but it was well away from the window, safe from rain and damp. The top shelf included *The Taming of the Shrew*, *Love's Labours Lost*, and *Romeo and Juliet,* all from the 1590s. There were several copies of what looked like first editions and also the same plays "newly corrected." Ned held his breath and took a copy of each.

The next shelf down had fewer multiples but Ned got three plays printed in 1600: *A Midsommer Nights Dreame*, *The Cronicle History of Henry the Fift*, and *The Most Excellent Historie of the Merchant of Venice*. The lower shelves were all manuscripts, some of them Shakespeare's own.

Ned wasn't sure how much time had passed before Thomas interrupted him, shifting his weight from one leg to another, obviously desperate for the privy. Ned gathered up his plays, knowing he had more than he could ever have hoped for, and aware that he now had no excuse not to pay his bill and head for home.

As he descended the stairs Ned thought of the old adage, "on the horns of a dilemma." Was it as old as this time? And was he betraying Vanessa if he stayed long enough to meet Shakespeare?

Ling was behind the counter, his face impassive as Ned handed over his small stack.

"Nine," Ling counted out loud. And then, pointing to the corrected editions Ned had picked earlier, "Twelve with these three."

By now Thomas had returned from his errand with the pail. Nicholas glanced at the boy and turned to Ned, smiling mischievously.

"You gave Master White five pence each for his four?"

Ned nodded.

"These twelve will cost you five pounds," Ling announced. Ned heard Thomas gasp, whereupon Nicholas's grin softened. "But we'll include your bed and board for a fortnight as well."

A few moments later the tray of pies arrived, still steaming. Nicholas passed one to Thomas.

"We'll to the back room, boy. Mind the shop, if you please."

Over dinner Ling gestured to a sheaf of papers on a side table.

"When you have finished your dinner you may care to look at this. Came in today from a young spark who fancies himself a poet. He's circulated his own and other verses, but now he's got gambling debts and knows I'll pay more for the manuscript than anyone else."

"Doesn't he want them printed anyway?" asked Ned.

"No *gentleman* cares to see his works in print. 'Tis the end of their grace when anyone can buy verses for a shilling or two."

Ned wiped the grease off his hands and reached for the manuscript. The first poem began,

> I wonder by my troth, what thou, and I
> Did, till we lov'd. Were we not wean'd till then?
> But suck'd on countrey pleasures, childishly?
> Or snorted we i'the seaven sleepers den?

"My God," Ned whispered. "John Donne."

"Jack Donne, he calls himself." Ling said. "Lodges not far from here in the Strand; some nights you'll see him at the Devil with the other wags. Other poems in there are by Will Shakespeare himself – and he'd curse to see them so – and Ben Jonson, Kit Marlowe of blessed memory, and the rest. I must show this to Will and tell him 'tis past time he saw his sonnets into print."

CHAPTER V

The pies were delicious and Ned was grateful for seconds. After the meal he went to the privy and took coins from his money-belt. Caroline had said that the silver coins had been proportionately less expensive than gold, so Ned lightened his load of silver crowns and made up the balance with two gold angels.

Ling thereupon sharpened the horns of Ned's dilemma.

"Master Toby sends word that Will Shakespeare has arrived and that George Chapman invites us to see Paul's boys tonight. By the dial 'tis half past three and the boys begin at five. We've no time to waste."

Ned knew he should decline the invitation, should take his plays and return to his time-travel pulse. But he couldn't do it.

"We'll see Shakespeare before the theatre?"

Ling gave him a sympathetic look. "Yes, my friend, we'll see Shakespeare."

Ned was tense with anticipation and worry as they crossed Fleet Street. It was wet from the afternoon rain, but the sun was peeking through the clouds as they walked the hundred yards to the Devil. Its sign showed St. Dunstan tweaking the Devil's nose with blacksmith's pincers, but the saint was largely forgotten in the pleasures of the tavern, a favourite of the poets and dramatists.

Ned had eyes for only one man and recognised him immediately, comfortably sprawled on a corner bench, back against the wall, a large pot of ale in front of him. His cheeks were brighter than Ned would have guessed, bespeaking the

133

fondness for drink that some accounts had reported, but otherwise he was the image of his portrait, and of his daughter as well. However much he had drunk he showed no lack of coordination when he stood to greet them.

"Master Nicholas," Shakespeare said. "I am glad of you. My play will be on tomorrow at Middle Temple Hall and I want you there." He turned a startlingly intense gaze on Ned and went on. "And your friend too. Master Ned, I believe."

Ned's hat was off already and he made a short leg.

"Edward Marston, Master Shakespeare, at your service."

Shakespeare sat back on his bench and waved them to the one opposite, calling for the landlord to bring more ale.

"And so you have been, my friend, and friend you are. Call me Will, Ned Marston. I have heard from my daughter of your morning's exercise."

Ned shrugged as Shakespeare turned to Ling. "I was confounded to hear he was a Marston, but I can see the likeness to our scribbling friend." He faced Ned once more. "A cousin at the least. You must know him."

Ned had heard old recordings of the Welsh poet Dylan Thomas. Shakespeare's voice had something of the same quality: melodious, deep, and slightly husky. It seemed to come from a well inside him, bubbling up like a spring, filling the room with its resonance.

"Only by reputation," Ned finally replied.

"Well," said Shakespeare. "Chapman tells me you'll have more than reputation soon enough. John Marston is certain to be at the theatre this evening. His *Antonio and Mellida* is the text for Paul's boys."

Ned couldn't resist. "'An aery of children, little eyases, that cry out on the top of the question, and are most tyrannically clapped for't.'"

Will's eyes narrowed. "That's my line, sir. Are you so fond of Melopomene that you've taken my *Hamlet* to heart?"

Ned felt like he was floating and didn't want to come down. "Aye, sir," he replied, grinning like a fool, "and not only your tragic muse but your comic and lyric as well."

Will did not look pleased. "My *Lucrece* and *Adonis* are a boy's ramblings, Ned. I should not care to be remembered for 'em."

"He does not mean those, Will," said Nicholas. "He's been reading these" – he held up the afternoon's sheaf of manuscript – "which came from a young spark with debts to pay." Ling handed the papers to Shakespeare.

Will's eyes were entirely alert now. He started at the beginning – "Jack Donne's, I know these" – flipped through the pages muttering other names and then flung it on the table. "Too many of mine here, Nicholas. Is there no stopping it?"

"I think not, Will. Tom Thorpe has a manuscript too but 'tis a poor thing. He says he'll print it if he doesn't get a better one."

"Plague take the man," Shakespeare said. He raised his voice, which effortlessly carried across the buzz of tavern-talk. "Ben," he roared. Ned held his breath.

Ben Jonson had a shock of curly brown hair, round cheeks like Will's and a high forehead, but his nose was broader, his mouth more slack, and his eyes set just a little too close together. At first he seemed like nothing more than the bricklayer he'd been for a time, but when he spoke his inflection was fair and his face became lively.

"Master Shakespeare." His smile was ironic. "Heav'n forfend I should fail to answer thy summons."

"Sit," Shakespeare said. He looked up, caught the boy Toby's eye, and in a moment another pot of ale was on the table. "I've a favour to ask of you."

"Sir," Jonson's eyes were wary.

"I want you to tell Thorpe to belay printing my poems till I'm home in Stratford for good. Nicholas will give him better copy next year, if we're spared."

"Why should he listen?" Jonson asked.

"Tell him you'll give him no more plays to print if he doesn't."

"And who's to print 'em if not Thorpe? The stationers aren't lining up to beg, Will."

At that moment a lean man appeared at their table and Ned was introduced to George Chapman.

"Time to go, Nicholas. The boys will be sharp upon their hour." As Ned rose Chapman gestured to the other men at the table.

"He's not unlike our playwright, is he, gentlemen?" Ned was getting a little tired of this and simply raised a hand in farewell.

"Come to my play at the Middle Temple tomorrow, Ned," Shakespeare called. "We've more to discuss."

Ned took a step closer and leaned over the table. "Will," he said softly, as intent as he'd ever been in his life. "Your sonnets are the glory of the English language. Don't let them be lost to the world."

CHAPTER VI

Ned and Nicholas shortened their strides to match George Chapman's on the walk to the boys' theatre at St. Paul's. His walk was stiff and measured, from arthritis, Ned guessed. Chapman had large, sharp eyes above a long hooked nose. His lean face was animated and he was chatty and quick-witted. He'd clapped his hat over his thinning top, but the grey hair on the sides of his head was thick and curly and his beard was full.

"Master Marston will meet his namesake tonight, Nicholas. It's a revival of *Antonio and Mellida*. John's lucky to have it."

"That he is, George," Nicholas replied. "I'd hoped it would be your new play instead, fine work indeed."

Chapman stopped and gave a graceful nod, his small mouth pursed like a schoolmaster's.

"A handsome compliment from one so discerning. My *Bussy d'Ambois* is in rehearsal and I'll see you've an invitation next week."

They took their seats at the little theatre five minutes before music signalled the start of the play. The set and props were minimal but the boys' costumes were elaborate. The performance was ritualised and declamatory, all grand gestures and swoons. And the play itself was, to put it mildly, overblown. At first Ned was amused at all the fustian, but speeches like the heroine Mellida's response to a disagreeable suitor soon wore thin:

137

My thoughts are as black as your beard; my fortunes
as ill-proportioned as your legs; and all the powers
of my mind as leaden as your wit, and as dusty as
your face is swarthy.

The fetid air of the theatre didn't help matters. Ned was yawning halfway through the first act and well before the end of the play he was fast asleep.

He woke to a discreet tug on his sleeve from Nicholas. Ned's body jerked forward and Chapman, on his other side, looked amused.

"Time to go, Ned," said Nicholas. "The play's over and I've told George we'll take supper with him at the Bell."

The Bell Inn was a stone's throw from the little theatre and another favourite with the players and poets. With the booksellers too, as Ned found when he saw Master White devouring a chop and Nicholas greeting him and half-a-dozen others at the same table. Chapman took Ned's arm, however, and turned him towards a small, redheaded man moving through the crowd in their direction.

"You must meet your namesake, Master Ned," Chapman said. Ned saw a vaguely-familiar face, with high cheekbones and a long, straight nose, marred only by a pair of quick, almost shifty, green eyes. The man's beard was more blond than red, and his eyebrows so pale as to be nearly invisible. He was more than dapper: he was dressed as a dandy, with silver lace on his grey doublet, dagger and rapier hilts filigreed in gold, and bright but rather incongruous yellow hose.

"So, George," the man said. "This is your friend who sleeps through my play."

"Ah," said Chapman. "You mustn't blame him, John. He's had a long day."

"Yes," said the man. "Shakespeare's hero. I have heard of this. Why bring him at all, if sleep was what he needed?"

"Give over, John. Remember your manners and greet another Marston," Chapman said. "This is Master Edward, from Shropshire."

John preened, the fashionable slashes in the front of his doublet swelling open. "My own family is from Shropshire. Who, pray, is your father?"

At that moment Nicholas intervened. "Master John. 'Twas an admirable revival and the boys in fine fettle. You must have been pleased."

"Not so pleased to watch your lackey sleep through it. Your counterfeit friend, who claims my name and county."

"I've no reason to believe him counterfeit," said Nicholas.

"Which means you know not whether he is genuine," crowed the other. "My father left the county an unmarried man, with no brothers and a father dead. If this one claims my name he is a whore's son."

Ned had been called bastard enough in his own time that he didn't react, but Chapman recoiled and Nicholas froze. All eyes turned to Ned, but before he could answer Nicholas recovered, firmly taking Ned's arm and marching him to the door.

"We'll find a link-man by the church to see us home," Nicholas said. He held on to Ned's arm, guiding him through the darkness towards the west entrance of St. Paul's where a small cluster of burly men sat around a brazier. Nicholas negotiated with one, who picked up a torch and a cudgel and walked ahead of them, keeping to the main thoroughfare of Ludgate Hill and Fleet Street.

Ned finally asked, "What was that all about?"

"Surely you know it was a challenge, Ned. You were supposed to answer 'Thou liest' and then you would have sent a letter. . ."

"My God." It was a serious matter, but somewhere from the recesses of Ned's memory came the voice of Sir Toby from Shakespeare's *Twelfth Night*.

"Go," he quoted, "write it in a martial hand; be curst and brief. . . eloquent, and full of invention. . . if thou thou'st him thrice, it shall not be amiss."

Nicholas craned his head towards Ned in the waning light, his dark eyes sparkling. "That's Will again, isn't it? I'm becoming fond of you, Ned Marston."

Ned clapped his hand on Ling's shoulder, nodding acknowledgment. "But what shall I do, truly?"

"Nothing," said Nicholas. "Let me think on it."

But Ned knew he hadn't needed to ask the question. He should return to Ling's shop, take his plays, and let the link-man escort him back to St. Paul's and the time-traveller. But Shakespeare had invited him to his play and said they had more to discuss. He wasn't ready to run away just yet.

CHAPTER VII

M eg found a job on their fourth day in London. She'd been tireless entering shops to offer her services and one day a Mrs. Thomas in Chancery Lane responded.

Meg laughed as she told Vanessa the story.

"She looked me up and down and said 'Are you pregnant?' 'No, ma'am,' I replied, 'and no plans to become so neither.' 'You'll pardon the question, Miss,' said Mrs. T., 'but I've only this morning discharged my assistant who was starting to show.'"

"What work will you do?" asked Vanessa.

"Don't know yet. Mrs. T. is, as she declares, a 'modiste.' Her shop sign says 'articles in the Linen, Woollen, Haberdashery, and Hosiery.' My first job is to alter the clothes her last assistant wore so's they'll fit me, and she's docking my wages two shillings a week for a year. After that I'll own them."

Vanessa knew that her own best hope was to offer piano lessons. She offered her services at schools and a couple of conservatories, none of which cared to employ a colonial without references.

After a week she decided that she had no choice but self-employment. She checked a merchant's directory for piano manufacturers and dealers and got lucky on her third try. One Thomas Tomkisson had a room with an instrument that he rented by the day to instructors. He had one day per week free. His premises were in Dean Street off Holborn, an easy walk from the Bell. Vanessa paid the rent for a month and commissioned newspaper advertisements and handbills.

She only had three responses to her advertisements, but one of the other instructors had scheduling problems and passed another two pupils her way. On her first appearance Vanessa discovered that the pianoforte was out of tune. But it wasn't a bad instrument and she had it in good order within an hour, before the first of her pupils was due to appear. If they all showed up and paid she stood to earn, after her overhead for the room and instrument, about six shillings.

The first three lessons came hard upon each other and demanded different treatments. One girl was petulant and under-practiced but had natural flair and a good ear; the others were hardworking but without much talent. Vanessa did her best to be agreeable and all the parents engaged her for a six-month series.

A fourth student, after dinner, was a society lady wanting to brush up her skills. She and Vanessa got along well, shared some tastes in opera and keyboard music, and she invited Vanessa to teach three times a week at her house near Gray's Inn.

The last lesson was scheduled for late afternoon and Vanessa understood this was to be a beginner. The girl turned out to be seven and her mother, though pleasant enough, was clearly at a loss how to deal with her daughter's gift.

"She sings all the time, our Fanny. And whenever she hears a new song, even if it's just a snatch coming out a window, she can sing it sweetly as if she'd known it all her life."

"And what makes you believe the girl is suited to the piano, Mrs. Dickens?" Vanessa inquired.

"Ask her," said her mother.

Vanessa looked at the girl, who was staring hungrily at the pianoforte. "Do you want to learn to play, Fanny?"

The girl was dark-haired and dark-eyed, radiating quick intelligence. Her reply was heartfelt.

"Oh, yes, miss. More than anything."

Sounds of a scuffle behind her made Vanessa whirl around. A little boy, very like the girl but a couple of years younger, was tugging at their mother's skirts and saying, quietly but earnestly,

"I do so want to stay and listen. And I *do* promise to be quiet."

"Who is this?" asked Vanessa. "Another musician?"

"My apologies, miss. He wanted to see where his sister was going."

"And how old are you?" Vanessa asked.

The boy blushed and met her eyes only for an instant before dropping his own. In that instant Vanessa thought she'd never seen such sad eyes, all the sadness of the world in one so young. And a presentiment of who this was stole upon her.

"Five," said the boy, dashing behind his mother's skirt to hide.

"Come on, Charlie," his sister called. "How old are you really?"

The boy's face popped out and for a moment it was luminous. "Five years, five months, and twenty-four days." Then he hid again.

"Well, Charlie, if your mother's going to stay and you really will be quiet, please honour us with your company. But this is Fanny's hour and we've work to do."

Mother and boy sat in a corner and Vanessa turned to Fanny.

"Do you know your gamut?"

She nodded, producing a little coloured chapbook called *The Gamut and Time-Table in Verse*. "I know it all by heart."

Vanessa continued. "Have you ever played the pianoforte?"

A shake of the head.

"I'm going to play, starting with middle C, here" – Vanessa struck the key – "and you follow me up one octave and back down with your voice. Do you understand?"

Bright eyes and another nod.

Vanessa played the scale and the girl followed. Then Vanessa sat her at the piano to play the same progression from a music-sheet, followed by some simple chords. After fifteen minutes Vanessa asked Fanny if she could pick out the tune to a song she already knew, without printed music. Fanny thought for a moment and began to play and sing, first one note at a time with her right hand and then slowly, carefully, adding some chords.

> Oh Shennydore, I long to hear you,
> Away, you rolling river.
> O Shennydore, I long to hear you,
> Away, I'm bound away. . . .

On the bench beside her Vanessa sat stock-still, shivering at the haunting ballad she had no idea was so old or had travelled so far. When Fanny had finished her last "across the wide Mizzourye," Vanessa asked her how she came to know it.

"Some black men in the docks were singing it, miss, winding the capstan on their ship to pull in the anchor. They sang it over and over."

Vanessa asked if Fanny would like to hear her play the same song on the piano. The girl's eyes were shining.

"Yes, please, miss."

It was a song Vanessa had always loved and she longed to add some twentieth- and twenty-first century jazz riffs to it. She could hear them in her mind but what emerged from her hands and the instrument was formal and quite stately: the main melody carried in the right hand, set off with harmonizing chords and a little contrapuntal embellishment in the left.

When Fanny sat down to try again she was able to carry the melody just as Vanessa had done. She added some of the same chords, stumbling here and there, but introducing a couple of changes not in Vanessa's version.

Only when Mrs. Dickens and Charles became restless did Vanessa stop to look at the time. They were well over their hour and she began to apologise.

"Never in life, Miss Horwood. I perceive my daughter has a genuine talent."

"Indeed she has, Mrs. Dickens."

"Humph," came a little voice from behind the mother's skirts.

Vanessa stepped to one side and caught young Charles puffing out his cheeks, about to give another snort. She ruffled his head and said, "And so have you, young master."

CHAPTER VIII

Ned spent a restless night in his pallet. It was no more than five feet long and there were fleas in the straw. By daybreak he was cursing himself for not leaving when he'd had the chance. He resolved to wait till Ling and his boy were up and then make his excuses and go. But he fell back to sleep and woke late, stiff from the pallet and sore from his flea-bites.

The fire in Ling's back room had gone down, but there were some lukewarm eggs scrambled in a pan, and scones and a pot of ginger brew on the table. There'd been no supper the night before, after their precipitate exit from the Bell. Ned was ravenous.

He was scooping his breakfast straight out of the pan, longing for a cup of coffee but knowing it would be another fifty years before it was introduced to England. He had egg on his fingers and in his beard as Nicholas walked in.

"I hope these are for me," Ned said, embarrassed.

"They are now," said Ling with a smile. "Sit."

Ned noticed a shadow behind the bookseller as a second presence entered the room.

It was Shakespeare. "Nicholas came to me this morning with news of your namesake. If he treats all who come to his theatre as he did you, soon enough the boys will have no audience at all."

Ned swallowed the last of the eggs, joining the other two at the table. Shakespeare reached for a scone.

"Have you slept so late?" he asked Ned.

"'Tis gone eleven o'clock," Nicholas explained. He looked at Shakespeare. "Master Ned seems less troubled by mortal insults than most of us." His gaze returned to Ned and his face became serious. "I've been to Ben Jonson and also George Chapman. Both are probably as close to John Marston as anyone can be and neither understands why he took so against you."

Ned shrugged. "I might be touchy about someone sleeping through my play."

"It's not that," Will put in. "Ben and I both believe the answer lies in how you look."

"What?" Ned's eyebrows went up and he leaned back in his chair, which groaned under his weight.

"There is a likeness," Will said. "Can you not see it yourself?" Ned shook his head and Shakespeare continued. "You're taller, handsomer." He paused. "You know what they call John's hair, do you not?" Ned shook his head. "Judas-coloured. Judas is supposed to have had red hair and so has John. Pale eyes and pale skin, as though God never finished colouring him. Ben thinks John looked at you and saw what he wished for himself. And he hated you for it."

Ned was taken aback. "Are playwrights so vain?"

"All men have some form of vanity. Think about your own sometime." Shakespeare's thoughts went elsewhere, his eyes drifting away. Abruptly they returned to Ned.

"Judith tells me y'are no mean swordsman."

"I cannot claim so much. Her two bravos were drunk and falling over themselves." Suddenly another line from *Hamlet* came to him. "But I have been in continual practice."

Will's eyes narrowed as he recognised the quotation, then he laughed. "I am none myself, sir." He stood up. "But I've enough broils digested for you in my play this evening, aye, and instruments of war as well. Y'are coming, both of you?"

Nicholas nodded, and Shakespeare continued. "I must away now and see to my actors." With that he popped the last piece of scone into his mouth, turned and was gone.

Nicholas gave Ned a rueful smile. "We'll stay in the shop till then. Let us sort through your plays and decide how you want them bound."

Ned hadn't considered binding them before. He knew that a bookbinder would take at least a day with them, a day Ned knew he shouldn't risk. But he'd paid for a fortnight's lodging and in any event Nicholas would expect him to want his plays bound. Should he refuse the offer and simply confess he wanted to run away from John Marston's insult? Ned couldn't bring himself to that, at least not yet.

The two men spent a happy hour looking at Ned's pile of quartos, of which there were sixteen now. Nicholas had stories to tell about most of them and Ned hung on every word, especially Ling's explanation of how actors had been paid to dictate the texts of the earliest editions of *Taming of the Shrew* and *Romeo and Juliet*.

"We know which actors took the money," said Nicholas. "Their own parts are always the most accurately given. Will discovered that one of his company had done the same with *Hamlet* even as the printer was still setting the type. The printer said he'd produce an accurate copy if Will supplied the manuscript, *gratis*. You can imagine what Will said to that. I went to the man – I'll not say his name – and offered to buy the entire edition if he'd include the copyright. And all of us, White and Law and the others, agreed to put it to the Stationers Company that it should allow no more copyright entries for plays without permission of the authors."

Ling smiled and continued. "With that Will gave me the manuscript and I printed a correct text. I leave you to compare 'em. Now, sir, I must to the bookbinder's. Give me your instructions for these and I'll have 'em done on the morrow."

One more day, Ned thought. No more – and the plays will be more valuable in bindings of the period. They'd have to figure out some way to age them when he got back to his own time.

At Ling's suggestion Ned gave directions to bind the three printed in 1600 together in calf and to keep the others separate, in vellum wrappers. Nicholas said the binder's bill for the lot wouldn't be more than four shillings.

Ned minded the shop with Thomas while Nicholas was away and then it was time to set out. They crossed over Fleet Street towards the Devil, saw a crowd of rowdies outside, and went the longer way around, down Fleet Street through the Pillars of Hercules, past Temple Churchyard along to Middle Temple Lane, where they turned left towards the river. The Hall was on their right, an imposing building of grey stone, with candlelight shining through its tall windows even though the afternoon sun was still bright.

The crowd was largely, though not entirely, lawyers. Nicholas spoke to one of the liveried men guarding the entrance to the main dining room and they were passed through with a promise of seats at one of the three high tables, along with other members of the Stationers' Company.

As they entered they were handed half-pint pewter mugs. Ned sniffed at the potent smell: sherry or, as he knew it was called in this time, sack.

"How can I drink this and stay awake?"

Nicholas laughed. "You'll learn to love it." But his face turned grim as John Marston swaggered up. "How come you here, John?" he asked.

"You forget, Master Ling, that I am a Middle Templar, trained to the law."

John turned to Ned and pushed out his chest. "Y'have not answered me, sirrah."

But Ned was spared once more. A friendly hand clapped him on the shoulder and Will Shakespeare's rich and gentle voice interrupted.

"So, Master Ned. I see you've met our Judas-coloured friend."

"So yourself, Will," said John Marston, deflated and petulant. "Is there no part for you in your own play, then?"

"You'll see soon enough," said Shakespeare. "Y'have left your boys behind to see how men make theatre?"

John Marston sniffed. "Better to see you here than among the cut-purses at the Globe. And I'm told you've more than men tonight. Is't true y'have brought Mistress Cleveland's whores to play the ladies?"

Shakespeare's smile held but his face stiffened.

"It's as close to 'em as you'll ever get, I don't doubt." Will waited an instant for the remark to hit home and then added, "But I must see to my company."

As Will retreated Ling took Ned's arm and marched him towards their table.

"Do they hate each other then?" asked Ned as they threaded their way through the crowd.

"John is jealous, of Will's talent and the favour the lords show him. All the playwrights are jealous, except Ben and George Chapman. They take refuge in Latin and Greek where Will cannot go."

"What about the whores?"

"John has the truth of it and fired his shot. But Will turned the ball back. Last winter John struck a girl in a Covent Garden brothel and now none of the good houses will let him in.

"You can't put women onstage at the common theatres, Ned – they wouldn't be safe from the pit. The boys playing ladies help the mob remember the difference between stage and reality. But the lawyers and gentry love to see the real thing."

"And who is Mistress Cleveland?" Ned asked as they took their seats.

"She'll be here somewhere, dressed as a man and none too smartly for all her wealth."

"And what of the women in the play?"

"Her best," said Nicholas. "The most beautiful, the sweetest voices. She'll charge twenty crowns to take one of 'em after the play and she'll have more takers than women, I'll warrant. 'Sweet Helen,'" he quoted, albeit from another man's play. "'Make me immortal with a kiss. . . .'"

"That reminds me," said Ned. "What's the play today?" He thought he knew and Nicholas confirmed.

"Sweet Helen it is, Ned. *Troilus and Cressida.*"

They finished their main course and moved on to a heavy pudding and more sack. After the toasts to the King, the House, and absent friends, the diners quieted and swivelled on their benches to look across the hall. A handful of musicians played an interlude and there was a collective gasp from the audience as a striking, tall, beautifully-dressed and unquestionably female chorus emerged, her full breasts entirely uncovered, face heavily painted and jewels sparkling on her arms and neck.

> In Troy, there lies the scene: from Isles of Greece
> The Princes orgillous, their high blood chaf'd. . . .

The play ran nearly three hours but almost nobody moved. Ned was struck by the difference between the acting here and that of the boys the night before. Shakespeare was right: this was theatre for grown-ups. Troilus was dashing, Cressida as obviously female as the chorus, who also played Helen of Troy. Cressida's gown was only slightly less revealing, but where Helen was all allure and air-headedness, Cressida brought a heart-tugging innocence to her role that belied her real-life status as a lady-of-pleasure.

Even knowing the play's sad ending Ned was jealous of Troilus as Cressida turned her wide eyes upon him at their first assignation:

> Hard to seem won; but I was won, my lord,
> With the first glance that ever. . . See, we fools!
> Why have I blabbed? Who shall be true to us
> When we are so unsecret to ourselves?

Ajax was hulking and stupid, Thersites persuasively loathsome with the audience grunting approval at every blow he took. But best of all was Ulysses, performed by Shakespeare himself.

Ned had always perceived Ulysses as a dry philosopher – Polonius in *Hamlet* but without the humour. No doubt all of Ulysses's philosophising was for the special, highly-educated audience Ned had joined here. But Shakespeare's portrayal made Ulysses vital and magnetic, the focal point of the play. Ned occasionally heard whispers or the chink of a glass during the other actors' scenes, but when Ulysses appeared the only noise was a slight rustling – the sound of near-two hundred men sitting up straighter on their benches. When Ulysses presented his soliloquy at the end of Act III, Shakespeare's rich voice effortlessly filled the room:

> Time hath, my lord, a wallet at his back,
> Wherein he puts alms for oblivion:
> A great-sized monster of ingratitudes.
> Those scraps are good deeds past, which are devoured
> As fast as they are made, forgot as soon
> As done. . . .

Halfway through this speech Ned heard a slight intake of breath and when he turned he saw tears on Nicholas's cheeks, glistening in the candlelight. For a moment Ned's mind wandered as he thought about his rescue of Judith the day before, his own "good deed past." Had it somehow affected history, or would it be 'devoured. . . forgot as soon as done'?

The applause afterwards was long and loud. Nicholas and Ned were slow to leave, enjoying the praise of play and players alike. Ned shared a few words with Master White the bookseller and then watched Mistress Cleveland in her man's doublet, striking bargains with the lawyers for the costumed actresses.

Ned felt a tug at his arm. Nicholas spoke urgently.

"John Marston left before the end, Ned. He was drunk and muttering threats against you."

"Surely there are too many people in the hall for there to be any trouble."

As they both looked around Ned realised how much the crowd had thinned.

"Most of these will go home by barge," Nicholas said, "and it's near dark. I could send you south of the river with Will, I suppose, but we're close to home. Stay here until I come back with the link-men."

150

Nicholas might be over-reacting, and Ned knew he could take care of himself. But this was Nicholas's world and if he was so intent upon a plan, Ned felt he should honour it. He said as much and Nicholas nodded his approval.

"I'll be off now."

Ten minutes came and went and Ned was the last person in the Hall. Shakespeare and the players had gone their separate ways, Will clapping Ned on the back with a promise they'd meet on the morrow. The attendants cleared the last remains of the meal and one of the liveried men approached.

"Time to empty the Hall, sir," he said.

Ned nodded and stepped outside to a covered porch. It was full darkness now and he could barely see the trees twenty yards uphill. There was still some dim candlelight from the Hall illuminating part of Middle Temple Lane, however, and more light would likely come from Temple Church just a few hundred yards further on. With the Hall empty, he was no safer on its porch than anywhere else.

He started up the lane, peering into shadows. The lane itself went directly to Fleet Street but that way was pitch dark, whereas some light could be seen coming from Pump Court to the right. Probably the Church, Ned thought, and he made the turn.

A sharp push from behind sent Ned reeling along the narrow passageway. It widened a few yards ahead and as it did Ned staggered to the right, backing into a recessed corner of one of the barristers' dwelling houses.

Two men were ahead of him. The third, who'd pushed him, was out of sight —Ned could hear him running in the opposite direction, perhaps taking a message to his master. As Ned drew his dagger and rapier he could tell even in the gloom that neither man he could see was drunk and that both seemed to know what they were about. Each carried a cudgel. The one on the left was familiar: the red-bearded, pockmarked face of the morning before.

"Remember me?" he sneered. "We'll scour you this time, Master Lick-Spittle."

If red-beard was talking, he wasn't fighting, so Ned ignored him and without a word dashed forward and to his right, slashing at the cudgel-arm of the furthest man. He scored a hit and the man dropped his weapon with a curse. But he'd been a decoy: as Ned started to turn towards red-beard another cudgel from behind slammed onto the cuff of his shoulder. Ned's dagger-hand went numb and he dropped his knife just as red-beard kicked Ned's legs out from under him.

As he went down Ned heard a cry of "Ho, the watch there, ho!" and then a boot connected with the side of his face. In a fog of pain Ned heard red-beard saying,

"A present from your namesake, sirrah."

Ned was dimly aware of running feet, the thud of another cudgel – not on him – and the uneven sound of feet moving away. Then Nicholas was at his side, gently lifting his head, his voice full of worry.

"Can you hear me?"

Ned raised a hand to the side of his face, felt a trickle of blood under his beard, and Nicholas helped him sit up.

"You wounded one of them, I think," Nicholas said. "And my man here broke the arm of the red-headed one. He won't be bothering anyone for a while."

"Good," Ned said, and then spat a little blood. The kick had knocked his cheek into his teeth, but as Ned ran his tongue around the inside of his mouth he acknowledged that, sore as they were, neither cheekbone nor any teeth were broken. He moved his left arm and it still worked. "Let's see if I can stand up."

Nicholas supported Ned's right arm as they passed the entrance to Temple Church and slowly moved towards Fleet Street. By the time they reached the main crossing, Ned could walk on his own. Once in the shop he sat still while Nicholas bathed his cuts (the kettle had boiled first, Ned was glad to see) and he drank a cup of hot ginger brew without vomiting. Afterwards Nicholas gave Ned an old nightshirt and Ned slowly climbed the stairs to his room. He pulled off his clothes, checked his bruises right and left, counted himself lucky and fell into bed.

CHAPTER IX

Ned hurt all over when he woke. The straw pallet seemed to have formed lumps under his worst bruises and even the feathers in his pillow were painful on his swollen face. Served him right, he thought. He should never have stayed after he'd bought all his plays. He'd broken his promise and, worse, betrayed Vanessa. He was lucky to be alive.

He dragged himself out of bed, thankful for Nicholas's nightshirt, and saw freshly laundered ruffles and a pair of stockings on the chair by the window. These must have been Ling's too and Ned was glad shirts of that time were cut so long: this one came down just far enough. He looked at his body before putting it on. Some new flea-bites, black-and blue along the right leg and left arm, but when he stretched, his movements, though painful, were unimpeded.

Ned left his leather corset on the bed and wrestled his way into the rest of his clothes. Ling's stockings were short and loose around his calves, but Ned wasn't complaining. He staggered downstairs and got sympathetic looks from both the bookseller and his boy.

Nicholas sent Thomas into the shop and brought a rather cloudy mirror to show Ned the purple blotch under his beard.

"Could have been much worse," Nicholas said, shaking his head. "They were just getting started when we arrived."

"They might have killed me."

"Not killed," Nicholas replied. "Hired bravos like those know just how far they can go. Murdering a gentleman brings the law down but it's harder to make a case for a few broken bones, even when they'll never mend properly."

Ned shivered and felt sick. He fell heavily into a chair by the little table and Nicholas poured him another mug of the hot ginger brew.

"Drink and eat, Ned. You've taken no harm a little time won't heal."

Ned felt better for the warmth in his belly. "They were John Marston's men, weren't they? Were you close enough to hear one of them say 'A present from your namesake?'"

"Ned." Ling's voice was low. "You've no reason to stay here. I'll have your books at the end of the day and you can go home to Shropshire."

"But Will promised another visit." Ned heard his own voice, sounding like a petulant child's.

"Give me your word," Nicholas said. "Stay here at the shop, or in the churchyard at least, all day today and we'll speak of this tomorrow morning."

Ned agreed. He longed for a hot bath but remembered reading somewhere that Queen Elizabeth used to bathe once a year whether she needed to or not, and that commoners had to make do with less frequency. He knew he couldn't leave before his books came back from the binder, and he also knew something that would take his mind off his bruises. He asked Nicholas if he could go back to the upstairs storeroom.

Although the Shakespeare cupboard had pride of place, on his previous visit Ned had seen open shelves of bound books and other trunks and cupboards begging to be looked at.

For two hours Ned forgot his injuries, lost in the world of literature. He knew from his rare-book training that at least eighty percent of books printed in Shakespeare's time were on religious or legal subjects, but there were none in this room.

Ned couldn't believe so much English literature existed in 1607. Most of the two bookcases were devoted to bound poetry and plays: multiple editions – going back to William Caxton – of gothic-letter folios of Chaucer's *Canterbury Tales*, quartos of Spenser's *Faerie Queene,* and works by Samuel Daniel, Michael Drayton, George Gascoigne, and others. One shelf was devoted to small anthologies of Elizabethan lyric poets, another to collections of letters. A cupboard had unbound pamphlet poems and a trunk was full of plays and dramatic interludes, including an edition of *Everyman* printed in the 1530s. Another trunk had ballads, most printed on single sheets, including *Robin Hood, The Children of the Wood*, and other stories which later found their way into nursery rhymes and which Ned would never have believed were so old.

Ned skimmed through some texts, sought out familiar passages in Chaucer and Spenser, and was finally, painfully, called back to his physical self by his aching jaw and the rumblings of his stomach. As he gave the room a last, parting look, he guessed that probably half the texts he'd just seen, especially the ephemeral interludes and poems, would disappear over the next few centuries. How much of what would survive could be attributed to the hoardings of this one determined bookseller?

Ned's injuries seemed more painful going downstairs than they had coming up. Maybe, he thought ruefully, this was his body's revenge for the transcendent happiness he'd felt going through at Nicholas's literary hoard.

Ned began to smell food before he reached the ground floor. Thomas joined them and Nicholas smiled at Ned's enthusiasm for the storeroom. But over dinner Nicholas fell silent and became increasingly preoccupied.

Afterwards Ned surprised himself by feeling sleepy and Nicholas ordered him back to bed. When Ned woke he decided to try his injured leg with a walk in the churchyard. It eased as he rounded the perimeter and on a whim he headed for Fleet Street. Two minutes later he was face-to-face with John Marston.

"Well met, sirrah," said John with a sneer. "I see y'have learned the price of cowardice."

"You might ask your bullies if their night's hire was worth it, Master Marston."

John answered with more arrogance. "I paid well for their injuries. And someone is about to pay for your insult to my family, since y'have shown yourself without honour."

Ned looked at John's out-thrust chin, realizing he could take the man then and there. Ned's fists clenched: two punches would see John into the muddy roadway.

John sensed Ned's anger and cringed. Then, furious at showing weakness, John hissed, "You dare not strike me, villain."

"Never ask what I dare, sir," Ned retorted, meeting the other's eyes. "And riddle me no riddles. What do you intend?"

John recovered his composure and smirked. "It is no riddle. I am on my way to the Devil where Will Shakespeare is drinking. I shall ask him how it pleases him to have his daughter the whore of a bastard and if it pleases him to think of that same bastard begetting more bastards upon her."

Ned didn't think much more could shock him in this time and place but he was wrong. He nearly gasped.

"It is another mortal insult."

"No more than mine to you, bastard."

Ned had hunched forward from the impact of John's declaration as though winded from a blow. He straightened and took a slow, deep breath.

"What do you want?"

"My family's honour, sirrah. You may fight me or hie thee hence to Shropshire – or wherever it is you come from."

"And if I fight, or depart, what of Shakespeare?"

"I have no quarrel with Shakespeare once you are dead or gone."

Ned's reply was reflexive, quick as a counterpunch. "Tomorrow, then. Send your man to Ling with the time and place."

For an instant fear glimmered in John's eyes. Then he sneered once more.

"Done, sir. But when your acquaintance have spoke of my swordsmanship you may yet choose to fly Ling's nest."

Abruptly John turned and retraced his steps away from the Devil. Ned sighed as he watched his namesake go. Obviously he had just saved Shakespeare a duel. Will would have had to challenge the statement John had threatened to make. If John were the swordsman he claimed to be, Shakespeare wouldn't have stood a chance.

Ned, however, had spent his life fencing and now, against all the rules of time-travel, he'd just succumbed to his desire to confront his enemy. But this would be life or death, not marks on a scoreboard.

And what if John was his *ancestor* and Ned killed him? Would Ned disappear then and there, his own existence rendered impossible? What other consequences might there be? Surely Ned's own death wouldn't matter to history. . . or would it? His mind went around in circles until gradually he became aware of the sound of St. Dunstan's church-bells.

He wasn't getting anywhere trying to think so he decided to go to evensong.

St. Dunstan's had seemed an undistinguished pile, its five hundred year-old structure pierced at random to create additional chapels, choir-spaces, and a chapter-house. But when Ned went inside the architectural incongruities disappeared. The stained glass was beautiful, the church's crossbeams and ceiling timbers painted with gilt stars and moons, and the ceiling itself a deep blue. Candles were everywhere. Ned had never seen so many, lining the walls of the nave and the front of the reredos.

As the parishioners took their places in the pews Ned was startled by the touch of a hand on his arm, guiding him to a seat. It was Judith Shakespeare, her face bright with welcome.

"Sit with me, Master Ned," she whispered.

"Is it proper?" Ned whispered back.

"Those who know me know who you are. A few tongues will wag but I do not care."

She slid into a pew without another word. Ned sat on the aisle, trying to get his boots under the pew in front. Judith had gone on her knees to pray so Ned knelt too, his right leg stiff, bending his head but raising his eyes to watch the candles. Each flame had its own life, and Ned grew calm as his gaze drifted from one candle to another, their waxen lights flickering up towards divinity. He could almost smell the centuries of prayer in the thick walls of the church.

Infinite space, he thought, reminding himself that there were physicists who argued that if you went far enough in space you'd end up back where you started. How far is far enough? If space is infinite, there's no end to it, and no beginning. World without end, amen.

And what about time? Surely time goes forward and back forever, or if time started with a bang, that bang must have preceded time, which came to the same thing. Could there also be a *sideways* infinity to time? Parallel sequences of events stretching on and on, each making room for another as travellers like him created new parallels, new wrinkles in time's fabric? Vanessa had created a new wrinkle too, he thought, and with that recollection came another surge of guilt.

Judith plucked his sleeve and Ned saw that the congregation was standing. He scrambled to his feet as the boy-choir came in, their treble voices raised in elegant polyphony. There were only twenty or so singers but at least five musical lines were sung simultaneously. Ned knew some of the old service from childhood. He followed the confession and absolution, and gradually began to join in the prayers and the Creed, stumbling when the texts differed from the ones he remembered.

As the congregation departed Judith pulled a small book from her shoulder bag.

"My father said you loved the lyric muse as well as the dramatic, Master Ned. He charged me to give this to you."

The book was bound in dark-red velvet, beautifully made but completely undecorated. Ned opened it. The writing was in an italic hand, a relief from the crabbed secretarial script Ned had seen in Ling's manuscripts. Each letter was perfectly shaped, with flourishes to the capitals. Here and there were corrections in a much more difficult handwriting, which Ned assumed was Shakespeare's own.

He shivered as he read the page his random opening revealed:

> Weary with toil, I haste me to my bed,
> The dear repose for limbs with travel tired,
> But then begins a journey in my head
> To work my mind when body's work's expired.

"Your father's sonnets," Ned said simply. Then he turned to the first page, where there was an inscription: "For Master Marston, from one who loves him well. Their authour W.S."

Ned looked at Judith, entirely unable to speak. They left the church together with Judith accompanying Ned around the corner to Ling's shop. The door was open, Thomas behind the counter, and they stepped inside.

Thomas smiled at them, pointing at a package neatly wrapped in a piece of decorated vellum, apparently an old antiphonal leaf. "Your books are back from the binder, Master Ned. And you. . . ." He trailed off and a deeper voice completed the sentence for him.

"You have a visitor." It was Will Shakespeare, who stepped through the kitchen door with an actor's perfect timing. Even in his weariness Ned had to appreciate the master's dramatic touch.

"I see Judith has given you my book," said Will, his mobile face alive with friendship. "And I've an offer for you as well. Come with us to Stratford, Ned. I need a man at New Place, and. . ." Shakespeare paused and gave a wry smile. "And Judith speaks well of you."

Ned looked at Judith, who blushed, and then he met Shakespeare's eyes. Ned felt himself nearly lost. If not for John Marston, Ned's visit to Shakespeare's London would have been unalloyed happiness. He felt himself on the brink of throwing over his own time entirely and accepting Will's offer. How could he refuse? To be so close to genius, to be part of the family whose history had posed an eternal puzzle after the playwright's death. Could he deliver his books to Caroline back home, doing his duty by her and Vanessa, and then return to this time?

Nicholas had joined them in the shop but remained silent. Shakespeare saved the moment, crossing the room to grip Ned's good arm.

"Put the man to bed, Nicholas – he's near dead on his feet. I'll call on the morrow for his answer."

158

Shakespeare took Judith's hand. As they left she looked back over her shoulder at Ned, but neither spoke.

Ned was still in pain but Shakespeare was wrong. Ned wasn't dead on his feet. His mind was on fire with the prospect of Stratford-upon-Avon, fuelled by visions of its ancient buildings as he remembered them from his visits to the town and its modern theatre. There had to be a way for him to stay, or at least to come back to Shakespeare's time. He remembered Judith's expression as she'd departed and was certain he knew what Shakespeare had meant with his cryptic "Judith speaks well of you."

But Ned had promises to keep. The thought of Vanessa steadied him, reminding him how much was at stake and where his heart belonged. He also knew that joining Shakespeare in Stratford would never satisfy John Marston. The man's jealousy would only increase if Ned was happily settled.

Ned looked at Nicholas again, and then around the bookshop. This time and place seemed an image of happiness, an image fragile as glass and now starting to shatter. He wanted more time here, and felt a mounting rage at John Marston who had single-handedly destroyed that possibility. Ned had held back this afternoon, but maybe a beating instead of a swordfight would teach John better manners.

Nicholas's hand on his shoulder brought him back to the present. "Y'are unwell, Ned. Rest a while and sup with us."

Ned saw the concern in the old man's eyes. "I must to the Bell, Nicholas. I've business with John Marston."

"No, my friend. John has already spoke of his challenge – the news is all over town. He's bragged that when y'have heard of his skill as a swordsman you will run in spite of accepting him." Nicholas paused. "And run you must, Ned."

Ned's pride nearly cried out as Nicholas continued.

"I do not doubt you could fight the man. But unless you kill him he will never stop tormenting Will. If you run John will have his victory and in a fortnight you will be forgotten."

Nicholas was right, and Ned knew it was time to let go of his arrogance. He imagined his little flat in modern London, and Caroline, the University library, friends and students. A vision of Vanessa appeared, dressed for Regency England as she stepped into the time-traveller, never to return.

He thought again of Shakespeare and Stratford and fought back tears. With all the resolve he could muster Ned pushed Shakespeare to the back of his mind, knowing the man's image would haunt him forever.

He picked up his books from the counter, securing Shakespeare's manuscript under his doublet. But Nicholas hadn't quite finished.

"I say you will be forgotten, Ned, but not by me. When I saw the look on your face as you came down from my storeroom, I could scarcely speak for knowing I had found a successor for my business. If not for John I'd have made you another offer, trying to overmatch Will's."

Ned couldn't find his voice to answer. Instead he embraced the old man. It was an awkward hug, as Ned had his books in one hand and his rapier and dagger in his sword-belt. His chin touched the top of Nicholas's head. Ned's tears came again, in full force this time, and he left the shop before Nicholas and his boy could see them.

The walk to St. Paul's was painful. It was full darkness by the time Ned reached the turning to his alley and began to feel the tug of the time-travel pulse. He nearly missed the sound of running footsteps behind him.

Ned whirled to confront two of the ruffians from last evening's encounter. One had a bandage around his sword-arm, but both held rapiers and daggers and were poised to strike.

Ned dared not drop his package of books. He kept it in his left hand and drew his rapier, backing towards the time-travel pulse as fast as he dared.

"Stand and fight, coward," called one swordsman, rushing forward.

The challenge was too much for Ned. All his anger at leaving Shakespeare and running away from John Marston returned. As he stood his ground the sound that escaped his mouth was like nothing before in his life. Part howl of grief, part roar of rage, Ned's cry accompanied a savage rapier blow that knocked his opponent's sword out of his hand, leaving the man's arm hanging useless at his side. Ned whirled to take on the second swordsman, but his rational mind told him he had a moment's respite and that he must use it.

He ran for the pulse as fast as his injured leg would allow, but his limp betrayed his weakness and his second assailant was close behind. The pulse grew stronger as Ned approached but he knew he wasn't going to make it. He turned to face his pursuer, who was running too fast to stop. He impaled himself on Ned's rapier with such force that his outthrust dagger connected with Ned's sword-arm, opening a cut just below the shoulder before the dying man's nerveless hands dropped both knife and sword. The impact of the collision pushed both men backwards into the time-travel pulse, their two bodies disappearing together.

CHAPTER X

One day a week teaching piano students left Vanessa with a lot of free time. Reluctantly she started to revisit her sheaf of manuscript poems from Winchester, poems she'd been embarrassed to recite but which had brought so much pleasure to the imprisoned children. Without telling Meg she began to revise and make fair copies of the ones she found least excruciating.

Within a couple of weeks Vanessa had enough material for two or three pamphlets – what the booksellers referred to as chapbooks – and a start on a longer collection. She decided that before she went any further she should test the market.

A half dozen shops specialising in children's books were within a mile of her piano studio. One of the closest was on Skinner Street, but when Vanessa went in she saw the harried proprietress arguing with a pair of bill-collectors, trying to distract them while an older man, presumably her husband, descended the stairs and made a dash for the back door.

Vanessa left the shop quietly and continued along to Holborn Hill, where another shop window was decorated with prints and a sign declaring the availability of "Works of Merit Soon as Published." The shop's owner leafed through Vanessa's manuscript. Her spirits rose as he smiled approvingly.

"A charming work for younger children, Miss Horwood. We should be delighted if you were to engage us to publish it."

"Thank you, Mr. Darton. I had imagined a chapbook, perhaps, with a coloured frontispiece."

"Of course, ma'am. I should say an edition of a thousand copies, priced sixpence. Allowing for the engraver, I should think it would be complete within a month. And you say you have more manuscripts similar?"

Vanessa nodded.

"In that case," said Mr. Darton, "we may begin as I should expect to continue. If you will give me your deposit of five pounds, I shall apply it towards the expense of printing and in due course I shall provide you an accounting and a half share of the profits."

For a moment Vanessa was too astonished to answer. "But I expected you to *buy* the manuscript."

Mr. Darton smiled. "Oh, no, young lady. You must understand we have dozens of authors offering us manuscripts every week. An unknown, untested poet like you – well, I believe an outright purchase of copy is a risk few booksellers will undertake in these difficult times."

Vanessa did her best to hide her disappointment, gathering up her pages and saying as politely as possible that she would consider his most generous proposal. Another bookseller, Mr. Harris on the south side of St. Paul's Churchyard, offered similar terms and Vanessa considered giving up. But she remembered another shop near the Bank of England. There was time for one more try before admitting defeat.

She walked north, then east along Cheapside to Old Broad Street. Dean and Munday's bookshop was close by in Threadneedle Street and Vanessa took heart when she discovered that the partners were women. Mrs. Munday was as approving of the manuscript as the other booksellers and told Vanessa she would like to show it to Mrs. Dean. Vanessa wasn't sure she wanted to leave it behind, but when she began to explain, Mrs. Munday smiled.

"I quite understand, my dear. You are concerned we might take a copy of your poems and publish them without so much as a by-your-leave. That is not, however, what I intend. Mrs. Dean is upstairs – ah! – she arrives even as we speak."

The two women were like peas in a pod, Vanessa thought, but they clearly knew their business. The shop was not as grand as Mr. Darton's or Mr. Harris's, but the single assistant seemed to have a steady stream of customers, most buying sixpenny chapbooks similar to what Vanessa hoped her own manuscript would become.

She looked up as the two women began muttering to each other.

"D,P,X,S?" said the first.

"Y,P, I should suggest," said Mrs. Dean. "Along with her agreement that we shall have first refusal of her next three manuscripts."

"Excellent," replied Mrs. Munday. Then she turned to Vanessa.

"I imagine you wondered what we were about, Miss Horwood. My partner and I sometimes speak about money in code, so as not to embarrass our listeners. You will be pleased to know that I suggested one pound ten shillings for your copy but that Mrs. Dean insisted we should offer two pounds, if you are agreeable to promising us additional manuscripts."

Vanessa sighed with relief. Two pounds in hand was better than an indeterminate share of future profits. But she wanted to be certain.

"Um. . . would I receive any royalties if the edition is successful?"

"Oh, no, Miss Horwood," said Mrs. Munday. "I am surprised you should ask, after Mrs. Dean's generous offer. Two pounds is to purchase the copyright."

"I accept," said Vanessa with a smile. "And thank you, ladies. I trust it will be a great success, and that we shall have many more."

CHAPTER XI

B y the spring of 1818 Martha Lloyd and Vanessa had met twice for meals and theatre in London. Meg joined them the second time and she and Martha made plans to attend Vanessa's next recital together.

It came that June, Vanessa's most important performance so far, at the new Argyll Rooms on Regent Street. By chance she had met one of the Rooms' principals, a music professor. He'd been in Tomkisson's piano shop and overheard her demonstrating some complicated sections in a Beethoven sonata to one of her pupils. An invitation to audition came soon after and she was engaged to play Haydn and Beethoven trios.

After the performance Vanessa joined Martha and Meg, who were accompanied by two familiar-looking gentlemen. Even before their introductions Vanessa made the connection: they were Austens. The one in the clerical collar had to be Henry, whose memoir of his sister had just been published in *Northanger Abbey and Persuasion*. The other, younger, handsomer, and worn by sun and exercise rather than time and trouble, was in naval uniform – it *had* to be a naval uniform because that was the only service in which two of Jane's brothers had made their careers.

"My dear Vanessa," cried Martha. "I thought I had the measure of your talent, but I declare I have never heard you play with such spirit."

"Indeed," Henry concurred. "But, Martha, you are ahead of yourself, surely."

Martha blushed, and Vanessa noticed her friend's eyes not on Henry, who'd given the remonstrance, but on the other brother, who smiled first at Martha and then turned to Vanessa.

"Your servant, ma'am," he said with a bow. He turned to Martha with a wider grin. "After a performance like that I am not surprised you forgot your manners. If only Jane could have heard it."

Martha was also smiling by now, but still embarrassed.

"May I present Captain Francis Austen and Mr. Henry Austen? You know, of course, whose brothers they are."

"Lord, Vanessa," Meg put in as Vanessa curtsied. "How I wished you were there to speak with them at the interval. I have never heard such learned talk of books and music. It quite wore me out."

"Indeed it did not, Miss Horwood," Francis demurred. "Your friend claimed no knowledge of literature, but she was quite the expert on the music you play. And I conceive you are both regular visitors to the opera?"

Vanessa murmured a "yes," but the combination of the night's performance and the unexpected introduction to Jane's favourite brothers had thrown her emotions into turmoil. In her own time she'd once seen a daguerreotype of Francis in old age and remarked the similarity of his features to the only known likeness of Jane, but meeting the man in person was a shock.

He was only a year older than his sister and where the Jane last seen by Vanessa had been emaciated and dying, Francis in his mid-forties was Jane revitalised – and masculine. Disconcertingly so, Vanessa admitted, as Francis's gaze lingered on her. His energy reminded her of Ned Marston, a reminder she did not want. She blushed and turned away.

Francis diplomatically turned to Martha with another bow. "I deeply regret I am unable to join you tomorrow. But you were quite right, Martha, to invite them both."

"I answered for you, love," said Meg excitedly. "I knew you would never say no to Miss Lloyd, nor to the Austens."

Henry stepped forward, his solemn features and clerical collar giving Meg pause.

"I was asked to convey the invitation from my brother Edward." He smiled. "You may wonder, Miss Horwood, quite how many of us Austens there are, but you have nearly reached the end. One more sister, who must remain with our mother in Hampshire, and yet another brother, who is away at sea. All others, saving Frank here, will be present tomorrow."

Vanessa knew who all the Austens were, of course. Edward was the rich brother who'd been adopted by a family in Kent and inherited their property. But she let Henry continue.

"Edward is in town with his family for a fortnight and taken a house near my former property in Sloane Street. Martha has spoken of you so many times that Edward expresses the determination of us all to become better acquainted. He requests that you and your friend favour us with your presence at Sunday dinner tomorrow."

"My wife is expecting another child," Francis put in. "Any moment now. Had I not been required at the Admiralty I should never have left Hampshire." He looked once more at Martha. "I missed far too many of my children's birthings during the War."

Vanessa curtsied to both men and turned to Henry. "Of course Megan is quite correct," she said primly. "I should never decline an invitation from Miss Lloyd or the Austens."

Henry bowed and turned to his brother, as Vanessa impulsively kissed Martha's cheek. "Thank you, Martha," she said softly. "It will give us the liveliest pleasure."

"I am especially anxious for you to meet Fanny Knight," Martha replied. "Jane told me you put her much in mind of Fanny, who was always – though Jane rarely confessed so much – her favourite niece."

Vanessa and Meg walked to Sloane Street the next morning. They gave themselves two hours, idling their way through side roads to Covent Garden, then across St. Martin's Lane towards Queen Charlotte's house and along to Knightsbridge. Edward Austen Knight's house was on the west side of Sloane Street, opposite a square. It was smaller than Vanessa had expected, but she remembered the litigation in which Edward had been embroiled over his Chawton estates and the twenty thousand pounds he'd lost when Henry's bank collapsed. No doubt Edward was seeking economies.

There were a dozen strangers in the parlour. Edward's daughter Fanny acted as hostess and immediately came forward to welcome Vanessa and Meg. Like any lover of Jane Austen, Vanessa searched Fanny's face for some clue to the character of a woman who would later repay her literary aunt's affection by writing that she was "very much below par as to good society and its ways."

But all she saw was a slender, elegant and, Vanessa thought, extremely attractive young woman about her own age. Fanny managed her hostess's duties effortlessly and had arranged the dining-table seating in advance. She placed Vanessa at one end next to Henry with, on her other side, a handsome, military-looking man in his thirties. Next to that man went Meg.

"Robert Carpenter," he said, introducing himself with a bow and, in turn, holding their chairs. He had brown hair with long sidewhiskers, penetrating eyes, ruddy cheeks and a ready smile. He seated Meg first, but as he turned to hold Vanessa's chair he seemed unable to tear his eyes away from the Irishwoman. Vanessa nearly sat on thin air.

"Pray forgive me, madam," he cried. "I have entirely forgot myself."

Vanessa was amused to see Meg blushing.

"By no means, sir," Vanessa replied with a smile. "There is no harm done. Are you a friend of Mr. Knight's?"

"By association, ma'am. I served with Frank – Captain Austen, I should say – at Santo Domingo and after." He seated himself and immediately turned to Meg.

"I was in the *Hermes* when we captured an American schooner off the Azores in the year twelve. Captain Austen promoted me commander to take in the prize and I was made post soon after. I . . . ." He cut himself off. "I am quite certain, Miss Gallagher, that I have spoke too much. Ladies take little interest in ancient history."

"On the contrary, Captain Carpenter," Meg protested. "I had two brothers of my own in the navy during the War."

"Older brothers, I do not doubt," said the Captain. "I served with some splendid Irishmen, but I do not collect any named Gallagher."

Meg's smile had an edge this time. "You might not collect these Gallaghers in any event, sir. One was a gunner on the *Guerriere*, killed in action against the Americans in the year you made post. The other had just been rated able when he lost a leg off Toulon."

She looked straight into the Captain's eyes as she continued. "Another month and he'd have been a free man."

The Captain nodded, unfazed. "Pressed, like most seamen. Where is he now?"

"In Ireland, with what's left of my family."

Martha spoke from across the table. "Jane told me her brothers thought it a disgrace for a Christian country to so abandon its injured soldiers and sailors."

"Indeed it is, Miss Lloyd," Captain Carpenter declared fervently. "I intend to employ only disabled servicemen when I open my cotton factory in Lancashire next year." He turned to Meg. "It will be a taut ship, Miss Gallagher, but a happy one, I trust, and I should be glad of your brother's company if he might care to apply."

Meg was fighting back tears. "You astonish me, sir," she gulped. "I had not expected such kindness. My family does not accept charity. . . ."

"Say no more, ma'am. With your permission I shall call on you. . . deliver a copy of my recruiting broadside, what?"

After supper Meg delivered another surprise: she was a card-player. "The priests said it was a sin, but my parents loved it. And with an Irish family there's always more than enough for a whist-table."

Captain Carpenter wasted no time volunteering himself as Meg's partner and two tables of four quickly assembled. Vanessa found herself with a group of non-players that included Henry Austen, Fanny Knight and three or four others. They alternated between charades and rebuses. It was Vanessa's first experience of Regency party-games and she was pleased that she managed a few successes. Even Henry's long face began to grow animated as the evening proceeded, and he positively hooted with pleasure when Vanessa broke a tie by solving the final rebus. Fanny had posed the question:

"What English word starts out with one syllable but, by taking away its first two letters, becomes a word of two syllables?"

The answer came to Vanessa at once, but she fidgeted over it, wondering if she might be making a mistake in pronunciation. Finally she ventured:

"Plague? – And ag-ue?"

"Indeed," said Fanny.

"Oh, brava," cried Henry, looking as though he might embrace her. Then Fanny looked at her, almost shyly.

"Might we, Miss Horwood, impose upon you so far as to ask that you play the pianoforte? I believe this house has a fine instrument, accurately tuned."

"But will you not play for us first, Miss Knight?" Vanessa replied.

"Yes, do, Fanny," called her father from one of the card-tables.

"Perhaps I shall," said Fanny with a smile. "As I shan't dare to try my poor skill after we hear Miss Horwood."

She sat at the piano and began to play, one of the shorter sequences from Clementi's *Gradus ad Parnassum*. Vanessa paid close attention: some of her recent acquaintances knew Clementi personally and had suggested she might audition for performances with his Philharmonic Society. Fanny played competently enough, though without enough technique to keep consistent tempi in the faster sections, and the music was well-suited to the rather thin tone of what had to be at least a twenty year-old instrument.

By the time Fanny finished Vanessa had thought of a piece that would neither overshadow Fanny nor overtax the piano. It was a Haydn sonata, and by leaving out the final movement she was finished in ten minutes. Meg's card-table had stopped to listen but the other played straight through. Vanessa knew she need perform no more that evening.

Captain Carpenter insisted his way home took him past St. Paul's and the Bell, and that Vanessa and Meg must allow him the pleasure of their company in his cabriolet.

"The pleasure of *your* company, he means," Vanessa whispered.

When they reached Charing Cross, progressing along the Strand towards Fleet Street, the captain began asking more questions, to which Meg gave entirely candid answers, omitting only their stay in Winchester Gaol. She made a particular point of telling him that she was engaged at Mrs. Thomas's shop in Chancery Lane.

Vanessa knew enough about Regency society to appreciate that Meg was, in effect, issuing a challenge, expecting the captain to lose interest in anyone so meanly employed.

But he asked her to point out the shop as they passed, declaring he had been postponing a number of purchases for want of a suitable place to make them.

After they'd said their goodbyes and were back in the Bell Vanessa began to tease her friend.

"You've found an admirer."

"Maybe I have," said Meg grimly. "But Martha told me he's married, even though he's not lived with his wife for years."

"Oh, love," cried Vanessa. "That makes things so hard, doesn't it?"

"It makes things impossible," said Meg.

CHAPTER XII

C aptain Carpenter called at Meg's shop the next day, delighting her employer with the amount of money he spent. He invited Meg and Vanessa to a late dinner after the shop closed. Vanessa was there when Meg looked him in the eye and declared that she knew he was a married man.

"Our mean employment does not make us demi-reps, sir. I shall be no man's concubine."

Meg's voice cracked as she spoke. Vanessa could see tears in her eyes.

Captain Carpenter blushed bright red. "You must forgive me, Miss Gallagher. It was no part of my intention to withhold the fact of my marriage from you for any length of time, merely that I found it damnably awkward to find the means of telling you about it."

He raised his head and smiled. "I do not plan to compromise you, ma'am. I should be grateful for your company on any terms you allow, and for Miss Horwood or anyone else you name to accompany us as chaperone at all times." He shook his head. "Do you not feel it, Miss Gallagher? Some connection between us?"

Now it was Meg's turn to blush. "I should never confess so much, sir, but I do. And it is handsome of you to speak as you have."

"I must return to Liverpool tomorrow, but I trust you will allow me to call upon you when I return."

Meg nodded, and the conversation became more general, turning to Meg's dressmaking and Vanessa's music.

For most of the next six months the Captain was a regular caller at Meg's shop and at the Bell. He was the also the main source of Meg and Vanessa's night life, showing them what he called the "haut ton."

"I confess I enjoy the fodder," he said. "And I enjoy a good farce as much as the next man. But I leave the judgment of our musical outings to you ladies."

"And I to Vanessa," said Meg.

Vanessa smiled, but she knew there was trouble ahead. How long would Meg allow herself to be chaperoned this way? And what of Vanessa's own life? Fanny Dickens was the only bright spark in her teaching career. The society lady was pleasant enough when Vanessa went to her home for lessons but, unlike Robert Carpenter, she made it quite clear to Vanessa that piano teachers were part of a class far beneath her own and that there would be no outside contact of any kind.

In her own time, as a modern Canadian studying at London University, Vanessa had found the vestiges of the British class system amusing, largely because as a foreigner she herself was outside it. But in 1818 Canada was a colony. Many of the people she met in London assumed her family were transported convicts and treated Vanessa like a servant.

Even Robert's friends, when he provided companions for Vanessa for dining or theatre, were sometimes patronising about her nationality. Others assumed she would be an easy conquest. Vanessa didn't blame Robert for this; it was a simple matter to reject such men and she wanted nothing to do with romance anyway. Watching Meg fall in love was enough, most of the time anyway.

One Saturday night in early 1819 the two were dressing to meet Robert for an opera when Meg turned to Vanessa, eyes bright.

"He's taken a flat in Mayfair, love. I'm going to go home with him tonight."

"Are you sure?"

"Sure that I want to be a fallen woman?" Meg cried. "Of course I'm not. But I love him, and that's enough."

Vanessa winced as an image of Ned Marston came to her mind. Get out, an inner voice hissed. You betrayed me. She threw her arms around her friend, holding her close to escape Ned's presence

"Love isn't always enough," she whispered. "But I hope it will be, for you both."

The Perfect Visit

After her recital in the Argyll Rooms Vanessa answered every advertisement she saw for piano accompanists. Few led to anything more than one engagement but even so she discovered that such playing gave her a little more status than teaching. But none of her subsequent jobs equalled the serendipity of that first one.

A group of string players based in Manchester asked her to join them whenever they visited London and advised her she would do better in the provinces both as a player and a teacher. A young violinist hired her to accompany his sonatas at a half-dozen different London venues, paying her better than she had any reason to expect. When he afterwards suggested she come with him to Birmingham and Liverpool, she demurred, whereupon he proposed marriage. She refused point-blank, furious, and lost her best employer.

That spring Meg confessed that Robert had offered to set her up as a dressmaker in Bond Street. She'd declined.

"It would change how we are, love. I'd be a kept woman, taking his money in exchange for my virtue."

Vanessa smiled. "So instead you give him your virtue for nothing."

"Don't say that," Meg replied, eyes flashing. "I give what I choose. It's nothing that will see me back in Winchester gaol, ever again."

"I know, sweetling," Vanessa replied. "And I wouldn't change how you are for anything."

But Meg confessed her work for the modiste was tiresome and repetitive, sewing borders on handkerchiefs and table-cloths, repairing tears in mittens and gloves, decorating hats and, most often of all, running errands. Only occasionally was she allowed to do the dressmaking she liked best. She made about as much money as Vanessa did teaching, but there were no opportunities beyond shop-assistant open to her anywhere in London.

Nor could Vanessa extend her list of piano pupils.

"Too many unmarried women looking for work," Meg commiserated. "All the sons killed in the War and the daughters with nowhere to go."

Vanessa grimaced. "And all those daughters play the piano, don't they?"

"Not like you, love."

"But that doesn't matter. All they have to do is teach children. And some of them will hire on as governesses so their employers' daughters can go husband-hunting."

"Are you sure you were right to turn down that violinist?"

Vanessa winced. The young man had reminded her of the worst kind of simpering admirer she'd had in her own time. Better poverty as a single woman than marriage to a man like that. Or so she'd thought at the time.

"It's water under the bridge, Meg. And I don't notice you husband-hunting either."

Meg laughed. "My hunting days are over and it's a jezebel I've become. Or worse. Did you know Robert's wife left him eight years ago, even before he became a post captain? And yet I'm an adulteress all the same."

Vanessa could see the pain in her friend's eyes. "It's the law that's wicked, love, not you. It will all come right, someday."

Both friends spent time in the evenings helping the Gallaghers with their baby daughter. Mrs. Gallagher was soon pregnant again and in the summer of 1819 Meg took time off from her shop to take over some of the shopping and cooking.

As their third autumn approached Vanessa began to despair. She had not touched her account at Hoare's, but neither had she been able to add to it. And Tomkisson was getting fretful about her shortage of pupils, complaining that the other teachers who rented his room and instrument had more, and that more of their students bought his pianos.

One afternoon in late September, Vanessa arrived at Tomkisson's only to discover that two of her three lessons had cancelled. It was a raw day, with rain and wind from the northeast and Vanessa could feel herself coming down with a cold. When Tomkisson resumed his litany of complaint, Vanessa cut him off with a glacial stare.

"Find another, sir."

"What?" said Tomkisson.

"Find another teacher," Vanessa said. "I've done with it."

"But you cannot, Miss Horwood," he spluttered. "I was only trying to encourage you."

"You have done nothing of the kind."

"But you have a fine talent and your students are fond of you."

"I shall visit Fanny Dickens and recommend her to another of your teachers. As to the other students, I shall write to them. There is no love lost."

She wished him good day, gathered up her music and left without a backward glance. The only thing that spoiled her moment of departure was a bout of sneezing. Meg took one look at her that night and put her to bed with a warming pan and a hot toddy.

Two mornings later, Vanessa went downstairs and across the courtyard to visit the Gallaghers. It had rained without ceasing and that morning the storm seemed even more violent. A sudden squall blew water into her face and she shivered as she came into the Gallaghers' rooms above the stables. The toddler Molly smiled up at Vanessa.

"Cold and wet."

"Yes I am, Molly," replied Vanessa.

Vanessa spoke to Molly's mother. "Isn't there anywhere in this country one can go to get warm?"

"Why, Bath, love," said Mrs. Gallagher.

Just then her husband stumped in. "Aye," said Liam. "Bath's the place."

The next day Vanessa took fifty pounds from her savings and Meg replied to an advertisement for a milliner's assistant in Bath, in a shop off Milsom Street. Three days later Meg had a conditional offer of employment. They were on their way.

PART THREE: SEPTEMBER 1833

Seldom, very seldom does complete truth belong to any
human disclosure; seldom can it happen that something
is not a little disguised, or a little mistaken.

Jane Austen
Emma
Volume III, Chapter XIII

CHAPTER I

Fourteen years in Bath, Vanessa thought. Sixteen years stranded. Another few years and I'll have spent half my life in this time.

She shook her head at the thought, only to notice another passenger – a young man – about to speak to her. Quickly she dropped her eyes. The latest novel by Lady Blessington was open on her lap for no reason other than to keep conversation at bay.

Vanessa didn't often have time to ruminate. This morning, travelling by herself on the early coach from Bath to London, offered a rare opportunity. What had she accomplished in sixteen years? Some piano recitals, a few more children's publications, a couple of suitors, but no real friendships since her first year.

She smiled to herself. Meg, Martha Lloyd, and the Austens were all friendships of a lifetime. But what was she to make of her latest and grandest suitor, Lord James Hamilton? Was he a lifetime proposition?

He was the reason she was on this coach. Protest as he might that it was Vanessa's talent that had secured her engagement at London's Academy of Music, she knew he had called in a favour. Piano teachers from the provinces didn't otherwise receive such invitations.

It was the *Royal* Academy of Music now, she reminded herself, its charter from King George IV only three years old. It was her grandest venue since the Argyll Rooms in Regent Street fifteen years earlier, or – she smiled at the thought – Wigmore Hall nearly two hundred years in the future. There would be a rehearsal this evening and another rehearsal tomorrow, September 10th 1833, with high tea before the performance.

Vanessa's piano students in Bath were used to shifting schedules, but she worried that missing more afternoons as the accompanist at the Assembly Rooms might cause her to lose her place there. She also hated to miss her gymnastics in Westgate Buildings. They had been a feature of her life for most of her time in Bath, ever since the instructor had become a customer at Meg's millinery shop more than a dozen years ago.

Vanessa smiled as she thought of their first session. Meg hadn't been sure she could take time from work for exercise, but Vanessa had insisted.

"Our rooms are much too small for us to do anything like our practice in gaol, and if we don't keep up the stretching and kicking we'll end up old and fat before our time."

"Don't say it," Meg protested. "When I last saw my mother I thought she must weigh thirteen stone at least. And she's scarce five feet tall."

"Right," said Vanessa. "Off we go."

They arrived in Westgate Buildings early, well before the millinery shop opened. The mistress was Mrs. Giorgio, pleasant-looking in a big-boned and slightly horsy way. She had a selection of hoops and bars, whalebone corsetry to straighten bowed backs, and scarves – from Meg's shop – to wave rhythmically in the air.

"Of course I also teach dancing along with callisthenics and Grecian exercise," said Mrs. Giorgio. "But I stress to my pupils that they must avoid the violent twists and turns so deleterious to the spine and inconsistent with feminine grace."

She grinned. "This comforts the mothers and grandmothers."

When Vanessa mentioned that she played the piano, Mrs. Giorgio offered her a job then and there. She also agreed to allow Vanessa and Meg the freedom of the studio in the early morning, and any evening when classes were not held. When she saw Vanessa's *tae kwon do* practice Mrs. Giorgio also suggested that Vanessa might help with the callisthenics, "although I've never seen movements like those before."

After their session the three women chatted easily. When Meg asked about Mr. Giorgio their new acquaintance started to laugh.

"There's no Mr. Giorgio," she declared. "My name is Polly Smith. But who would pay for Grecian exercise from a teacher with a name like that?"

She went on to confess that she lived with a female friend above the studio and after a few more questions about Vanessa and Meg's arrangements she discreetly enquired whether their living together meant they were also of the Sapphic persuasion, as she and her housemate were.

Vanessa blushed furiously when Meg laughed and replied.

"If ever I were that way inclined, miss, I can tell you Vanessa would be my very first choice. But for her bosom you might almost dress her as a boy."

"My thought precisely," said the woman. "But we are embarrassing her, are we not?"

"It doesn't matter," said Vanessa, smiling through her discomfiture. "I admire anyone who can keep a lover, of any sex. I doubt I shall ever have the patience for it."

"Never believe it, sweetling," Meg cried. "You'll know when you find him, just as I did with Robert."

From then on Vanessa played the piano and helped teach exercise classes four mornings a week. Over time she secured some private piano pupils and, much later, afternoon employment playing for dancing classes at the Assembly Rooms. She learned the latest dance steps along with her employers, passing them on to Meg. Combined with the country walks available within a few minutes of Bath, Mrs. Giorgio's studio gave Vanessa a nearly complete sense of physical fulfilment.

Except for one thing, she said to herself ruefully, as the coach slowed for the inn at Chippenham. Sex.

She stretched her legs and used the privy, and when the coach resumed its eastward journey her musings picked up where they'd left off. Her suitor Lord Jamie had made no amorous overtures in the three months she'd so far known him. She supposed that was a good sign: everything she'd ever read suggested that British aristocrats in this time never married anyone they could sleep with first. But did she want to marry him?

Martha Lloyd had surprised Vanessa by asking that very question on a visit to Bath a few weeks earlier.

"Surely it is past time you married, my dear. Even" – she smiled – "if it is not the love match Jane would have written for you."

Martha herself had then gone on to raise the subject of sex, to Vanessa's astonishment.

"Can you imagine," Martha said, "what it is like to cease to be a virgin at the age of sixty-two? I had no idea Frank would even consider I should perform the marriage act." She blushed and Vanessa had to hide a smile. "I suppose if he *had* mentioned it I should have been horrified, but it was the happiest moment of my entire life. You should ensure, my dear, that you do not wait so long."

Frank's – Francis Austen's – first wife had died in childbirth in 1823. He'd waited more than a decent interval to propose to Martha: Vanessa had been present at the wedding in Hampshire in 1828. It had been a small party, consisting mostly of Austens and a few of Frank's fellow naval officers.

It was a happy day, a mix of young and old Austens and some new people Vanessa thought might have become friends had they lived closer than a hundred miles from Bath. The high point of her day was a hug and a kiss from Martha after the ceremony, when she had whispered,

"Every one of Jane's novels ended with a wedding, and I feel like one of her heroines. Like Elizabeth Bennet."

"Oh no, love," Vanessa replied quickly, with a glance at Frank, resplendent in his dress uniform. "You're Anne Elliot with Captain Wentworth, in the most wonderful ending of them all."

Martha had blushed, looking like a girl for all her years.

Vanessa had danced with some of the younger officers afterwards, and she'd gone to her bedroom at the inn feeling as though she might – at last – be adapting to this time.

The coach hit a bump and Vanessa came back to herself. Thinking about the Austens always gave Vanessa a sense of belonging. But after the wedding Martha and Frank had gone to sea and then settled near Portsmouth. More than a year passed before they visited Bath as a married couple. By then they looked as though they'd been bonded for a lifetime – as perhaps they had, given the lifelong closeness of the Austen family's connection with Martha's. And even though Martha was now past sixty-five – nine years older than her husband – Vanessa was certain that marriage had made her look younger.

Vanessa smiled once more at Martha's confession about her wedding night. Vanessa knew that, even if the vagaries of time would allow it, she could never tell Martha that she too had lost her virginity, sharing a tiny cabin with a distant cousin while sailing in the South Pacific at the age of eighteen.

The swaying of the coach reminded her of the motion of that yacht half a world and more than a lifetime away. She thought of hot days and swimming. Slowly she drifted off to sleep, not waking again until the inn at Reading. It was at least three more hours to London and she knew she had a busy evening's rehearsal ahead of her. She hoped she'd have time to go to the Bell Inn first, where she'd stayed only once since she and Meg had left London. Would she even get a glimpse of Meg's uncle Liam and his family? She shook her head, dismayed at how much she had to do during the next twenty-four hours. She was glad she'd managed a nap.

The Perfect Visit

The coach arrived in good time and Vanessa enjoyed a brisk walk to the Bell, where it turned out Liam and his wife had left for the evening. Vanessa knew she should save money by finding an omnibus to go to the Academy, but it would soon be getting dark. She'd use the danger of unaccompanied night-walking an excuse to take a cabriolet. That way she could have a luxurious hour in her room before leaving for the rehearsal. She'd take the omnibus tomorrow.

When she went downstairs there was some kind of commotion in the public bar. The landlord's boys were occupied, unable to fetch her a carriage. But when she went outside there was one discharging a passenger. She arrived at the Academy with time to spare.

Vanessa was pleased with her fellow-performers, advanced students on the cello and violin. She was especially happy with the young cellist, who had chosen a programme of recently-published compositions by Franz Schubert. They would make up the first half of the evening, with the violinist joining them for Mozart trios after the interval.

The musicians were surprised she was staying as far away as the Bell and insisted she spend the next night, after their performance, in a guest-room at the Academy. Vanessa agreed – she was too tired to argue – and in the cabriolet back to the Bell she was relieved she had. If she was this tired after rehearsal, she was bound to be exhausted after the performance.

CHAPTER II

Ned Marston was trapped, entangled with a dead body in a time-travel pulse. Its force-field prevented any movement but Ned could feel blood coagulating on his skin. He hoped that most of it was the dead man's, but he knew some was his own, from the dagger cut he'd taken in the closing seconds of their fight.

Ned had known something was wrong as soon as the time-travel pulse enveloped the two of them, beginning its return journey from Shakespeare's London. At first the oscillations seemed regular, but after a few seconds they slowed and the intervals became uneven. With two bodies in a pulse configured for only one, the time-traveller was labouring. Slowly, almost painfully, the oscillations subsided.

As they slowed Ned began to see his surroundings. They changed more and more slowly and he began to doubt he would ever get home. At least he could feel his precious Shakespearean books close to his body and the even more precious manuscript under his doublet. They had successfully time-travelled with him, along with the dead man. But where – and when – was he?

When the pulses finally stopped, Ned was still in the alley he'd left in Shakespeare's time, with some of the same cantilevered houses looming overhead. But now the alley was cobbled and the smells were more of smoke than ordure. Ned had no time to think, however, because as soon as the force-field disappeared the full weight of the dead man collapsed against him, knocking him backwards. Ned crawled out from under the body, gritted his teeth and pulled his rapier from the corpse. Then he looked down at his doublet, soaked with blood just below the bulge of his Shakespeare manuscript.

Luckily night had fallen and nobody was nearby. In a flash of criminality, Ned knew he had to destroy any evidence that linked him to this corpse from Shakespeare's London.

He didn't have much time. Nor had he the strength to move the body, but he could strip it. The man's doublet hung open and was, astonishingly, unbloodied. Ned pulled off his own and put on the dead man's, his bare flesh flinching at the touch. He moved his money to his new pockets and tied the bloody clothes around his rapier and dagger. Then he headed for the river, leaving the naked corpse behind.

As he emerged from the alley Ned could make out a familiar dome just ahead. The St. Paul's Church he had come to know in 1607 had vanished and instead Wren's masterpiece towered over the churchyard. To the north a gaslight illuminated the galleried front of the old Bell Inn, more weather-beaten than Ned remembered it.

He headed south, keeping to the shadows as best he could, and in less than ten minutes his incriminating package had vanished into the dirty waters of the Thames. He decided to go back to the Bell. At first he told himself that perhaps his Shakespearean clothes wouldn't seem quite so out of place there, but as he realised the foolishness of that notion he comforted himself that at least the inn would be familiar.

And he needed something familiar. His arm was still bleeding from the dead man's dagger-cut and, as his adrenaline waned, the horror of having killed a man struck him. As he retraced his steps the shock, combined with Ned's own injuries and loss of blood, overwhelmed him. What was left of his strength began to fail.

It was all he could do to get back to the Bell. A couple of men leaving the inn looked at him with a combination of amusement and disgust. Ned thought of asking for help, but the first man he approached recoiled from Ned's tattered outfit and the blood dripping from his arm. The dress of that man told Ned how far he was from home, both from Shakespeare's time and his own. The man's clothing was unquestionably nineteenth-century. Quite when Ned wasn't sure, probably earlier rather than later.

With a final effort Ned stumbled inside to the bar.

"Landlord," he croaked. "My name is Marston. I've one of Shakespeare's gold sovereigns for your best bed and all the hot water you can bring. And you can see I've need of a doctor. Now, please."

So saying, Ned produced a sovereign and snapped it down. The landlord, wide-eyed and speechless, picked it up and bit it.

"Well, sir?" Ned demanded.

"On our way," said the landlord. He roared for help and three boys appeared in a matter of seconds. Two helped Ned to an upstairs room, while the third followed with a tub of hot water. Once inside, Ned reminded the boys of his need of a doctor, dismissed them, stacked his books on the table, and pulled off his doublet.

He turned to the basin and began to wash, but as he worked soap around his wound Ned felt dizzy. He towelled off the worst of the blood and dirt and took a weary couple of steps back to the bed, propping himself against one of the bedposts to wait for the doctor. He couldn't think; his head slumped forward and his body was numb. In the gloom of a single candle Ned's unfocused eyes traced a spider's web in a corner of the room.

CHAPTER III

A loud knock at the door ended Ned's reverie. He was still bare-chested and he shivered as he staggered from the bed to answer.

The landlord was carrying a lamp and was followed by a man with a satchel. The doctor took the lamp, waved the landlord away and closed the door.

"Walcot, sir, physician." As he approached he held up the lamp for a closer look at Ned, taking in his bruises and the more recent cut on his upper arm.

"Constables have been in the public rooms downstairs," said the doctor. "Asking about a corpse not far from here. A naked corpse, sir, pierced by a blade of considerable size. The landlord believes they should speak to you but agrees to await my direction."

The doctor's gaze was calculating but Ned met it. Tired as he was, his mind was racing.

"I was attacked, Doctor, returning from a costume party. I took the cut you see here, but escaped. I heard the two of them shouting at each other, but I was running for my life and did not see what happened after."

"You are Canadian, sir? American? Attending a costume party?" The doctor was suspicious now.

"American, Doctor." Without thinking Ned had let himself speak in the accent most familiar to him. Now he was glad of it.

The doctor began to swab and bandage Ned's arm. "And your bruises, sir? They are recent but not new."

"I take my exercise in the boxing ring, doctor. I have some skill or I should not have escaped tonight's footpads."

Dr. Walcot gave a decisive nod and the suspicion in his blue eyes faded.

"I see no reason to doubt your story," he said, crossing to the table on which Ned had set his books. "And I believe I may spare you a visit from the constables. In exchange may I ask you to speak of this?"

He held up Ned's package. "I am something of an antiquarian, sir, and if the contents are of an age with the antiphonal leaf used as packaging, it should be of considerable interest."

Ned thought quickly. "Books and pamphlets, doctor, from what is left of my grandfather's collections in Philadelphia. Some go back to my family's time in Shropshire two centuries ago and more."

"May I see?" Walcot's medical solicitousness had disappeared and a greedy look appeared in his eyes.

Ned was running out of invention and longing to be rid of this inquisitive medic. But the doctor had been kind enough and had promised to save him from an encounter with the police. Perhaps something was to be gained from knowing him. Ned gestured at the books and nodded.

Walcot carefully unfolded the wrapping and his eyes opened wide as he leafed through the quartos. He set them down slowly and carefully and Ned heard a sharp intake of breath as the doctor opened the manuscript of Shakespeare's sonnets. He read the opening page aloud: "For Master Marston, from one who loves him well. Their authour W.S."

"This Master Marston. . . your relation?" he asked.

Ned nodded.

"These must be the finest Shakespeares outside Pimlico."

"Pimlico?" asked Ned.

"Richard Heber's house."

"I am not current with these matters. Do you mean the famous book-collector?"

"The greatest collector of all, and the greatest Shakespearean."

"I know," said Ned. "The man who said a gentleman should have three copies of every book."

"Just so," said the doctor. "One for show, one for use, and one for borrowers. Now, sir, we must discuss these volumes further."

"Dr. Walcot," Ned interrupted wearily. "You must forgive me. I have not told you the rest of my story. I returned to my usual lodgings tonight to find my money and trunk gone and the landlord bare-facedly denying he had ever seen me before. I am in the only clothes I have, with nothing but Elizabethan coins in my pockets. The books are with me because I carry them wherever I go."

The doctor flushed.

"This is a disaster indeed, sir – though with such books to your name you need never be indigent. And you say you have Elizabethan coins as well?"

A moment later Walcot stood holding the contents of Ned's pockets.

"More than thirty pounds in gold and silver," he said. "Not all Elizabethan but not a coin minted after 1606. I should hate to see such artefacts spent as ready cash, Mr. Marston."

"I imagine I have no choice," said Ned. "I cannot be seen in public as I am."

The doctor started to speak, and then stopped. Finally he came to some resolution with himself and began again.

"Mr. Marston." Ned looked up, and waited. "This may be highly improper, but would you allow me to act for you in the matter of these coins? I should like to purchase some for my own collection, although others may be too valuable for my purse. But I know a man will advise me and I shall see you right. . . ." He trailed off.

This time Ned's smile was genuine. "I am entirely in your hands."

"I shall also enquire about your books. But I know full well they are entirely beyond my means."

"I could not ask for greater kindness, sir."

Walcot handed Ned fifteen pounds in current gold and silver – "only a deposit, sir; there will be more to follow" – and wrote out a receipt for the coins. When Ned mentioned that the landlord had another of his Shakespearean sovereigns, Walcot promised to retrieve it.

"A pound will buy you three nights in this room or a week upstairs, I believe. Without meals." The doctor smiled. "I might add that the food is excellent here."

He was almost at the door when Ned called him back.

"Would your influence run to getting me that upstairs room for a week? I should like to economise. Indeed I believe I must."

Walcot gave a sympathetic nod. "Leave it to me."

"And – please forgive so many questions – I am going to need a visit from a tailor."

Walcot grinned. "I know a good one. If I send him here in the morning he can make you respectable by noon."

Ned smiled back. "I believe you've become my guardian angel."

"I have plans for you, sir," said Walcot. "I am counting on you and your books coming with me to the Society of Antiquaries at your earliest convenience."

"We'll discuss that another day, if you don't mind."

"Dine with me tomorrow, then."

"Thank you," Ned started to say, but his voice broke.

Walcot clapped him gently on his good shoulder.

"One o'clock. Dolly's Chop-House in Paternoster Row."

The doctor let himself out and within five minutes a young maidservant appeared with a supper-tray. Ned followed her up a narrow staircase to a small garret room. Another, younger maid was inside, holding a small portmanteau. She left, as the first maid set Ned's supper-tray on the table.

"Could you answer a foolish question?" he asked. She gave a cautious smile and he continued. "What day is it?"

"Why, Monday, sir."

"And the day of the month, and year?"

Her face grew more perplexed. "Ninth of September, sir. Eighteen thirty-three."

Ned's heart leaped. Sixteen years after Vanessa's arrival, he thought. If she was still alive she could be here in London. And if she'd been transported to Australia he could go after her. But what if she'd hanged? He had to find out.

The maid was openly staring at him now. "Thank you, miss," Ned croaked.

She curtsied. "A pleasure, sir. You'll be staying some time, then?"

"Longer than I'd ever dreamed."

CHAPTER IV

When Vanessa reached the Bell Inn after her rehearsal it was too late to speak to the Gallaghers. Mr. Chumley, the Bell's landlord, had gone to bed, and the night clerk told her they'd moved her portmanteau into one of the grander bedrooms on the first floor.

"I trust you won't mind, ma'am," he said. "There's no extra charge – after you left we had someone in as wanted the top room for a week."

Without a word Vanessa took her key and went upstairs. Tired as she was she found it hard to sleep, and when she finally did she was troubled with bad dreams. She got up, paced the room, and flung open the window to see if anything outside had disturbed her. But all was peaceful. Her room overlooked the inn's courtyard; a little light from outside showed a long-legged spider and its web in a corner. She shook her head, drank some water, drew the curtains, and went back to bed.

Another dream came: Ned Marston, oddly dressed and covered with blood. She woke up sweating. Was he lost too? Those were Shakespearean clothes – Elizabethan clothes – in her dream. Had he been killed on his time-travels?

"God *damn* Ned Marston," she said softly. He wasn't the kind of man who gets killed. Right now he was probably back in the time-travel laboratory with his next guinea-pig, setting her up for a one-way trip to nowhere.

She got out of bed and looked out the window again. She told herself she wasn't being fair, that Ned and the others were bound to have tried to rescue her and any other lost time-travellers. But if their machine was all they said it was, why couldn't they have come for her years ago?

The sky was just beginning to show pink amidst rising plumes of coal-smoke. She fell back into bed, worrying that her nerves would be so shattered that she'd bungle her performance that night. The next thing she knew was a knock at the door and a girl – almost the image of Meg – holding her breakfast tray. Vanessa nearly hugged the girl before she realised that the gesture would inevitably lead to a long visit with her parents. It was time she could not spare. Twenty minutes later she left the inn. She'd paid for her room in advance, so she didn't stop to say goodbye to the landlord. He was busy anyway, speaking to two men carrying tailor's samples.

CHAPTER V

Tired as he was, Ned couldn't get his mind off Vanessa. Even if she'd been transported for seven or fourteen years she might have returned here, to England if not London. He gave a wry smile, remembering that in one of their first conversations he'd told her she looked like an Australian surfer. No surfing for transported convicts, he thought.

The cabbage and beef on Ned's supper-tray were a comfort. His bruises ached and although the bleeding in his arm had stopped, the wound still throbbed under its new bandage. He leaned back in his armchair, part of his mind numb, the rest struggling to come to terms with his new time and place.

How had he come to be in 1833 anyway? Something had gone seriously amiss with the time-traveller. It had to have been the result of the second, dead body. It had been spring in Shakespeare's time and now it was autumn. The season was different, the year was different, and yet there was no sense or symmetry to the changes. He was about halfway back to his own time, and that was all.

Shouldn't he have gone halfway from St. Paul's to Chelsea too? But he hadn't, and he hadn't felt any kind of continuing time-travel pulse here either, the way he had when he arrived in Shakespeare's time. He knew he was stranded, that there was nothing left to take him the rest of the way home.

He gave a wan smile. Another research project for Caroline and her engineers. But unless they somehow found him they'd never know, never have the data to formulate a new theory.

The Perfect Visit

Ned's lamp sputtered out and he stared into darkness. Would he ever be rescued? How could anyone ever know to look for him in 1833? And what if Vanessa had been rescued years earlier? If she hadn't, would their permanent presence in the past change the course of history? Had his killing the cutthroat in Shakespeare's time *already* changed it?

Visions of death began to haunt him. The image of the naked corpse in the alley metamorphosed into one of Vanessa, wearing a beautiful Regency gown but also dead, suspended in a gibbet. He staggered up from his chair, nearly upsetting what was left of his dinner, pulled off what was left of his clothes and fell into bed. He was asleep almost immediately.

Ned woke to grey light outside and sounds of activity in the inn. The chamber-pot was on the dresser. He lifted it to the floor and began his new life in London by missing his aim.

The idea of getting back into his battered doublet and hose was more than Ned could bear. He crawled back under the covers and after a few minutes there came a knock. The younger of the two maids came in. Her tray was smaller but Ned smelled something divine.

"Coffee!" he cried, propping himself up on one elbow.

The girl laughed. "You sound as though you've been on a desert island, sir. The tailor's boy came to tell you they'll be along at nine o'clock. It's half after eight now."

"Can you have someone bring some scissors, and hot water and a razor?" She nodded. "And can you tell me your name, and the other maid's and the landlord's? I was in a bad way last night."

"You was that, sir, so Molly told me. She's my sister. I'm Nell. The landlord's Mr. Chumley."

"Is he your father?"

"Oh, no, sir. Our father's Liam Gallagher, the hostler."

Next to the coffee was a bowl of hot porridge and a hard breadroll with a wedge of butter and some marmalade. Ned stayed in bed to eat and by the time he had finished he began to feel almost human. The pain in his cuts and bruises was starting to subside – was there something rehabilitative about time-travel?

"Time heals all wounds," he said aloud. "Ugh."

If yesterday's time-travel had helped him heal, it was the only good thing he could say about it. Both of his missions were failures, and now the time-travel project, along with its efforts to rescue Vanessa, would have to end for want of

196

money. Nor, with him lost, could he imagine that Caroline would allow anyone else to time-travel, ever.

And that was that, Ned concluded. It was time to accommodate himself to this brave new world, the world (he paused to think about it) of King William the Fourth.

The first thing was to find news of Vanessa. But where? How? Would the British Library have a newspaper archive in 1833? *Was* there a British Library?

He might have obsessed all morning if a knock at the door hadn't signalled Nell's return with the razor. It was some relief to see that the bruise on the side of his face had largely disappeared. When the tailor arrived soon after, a still-troubled but newly-beardless Ned shook hands in what remained of his Shakespearean clothes.

The tailor explained that Dr. Walcot had given him an idea of Ned's size and that he'd brought a selection of styles.

"There are just enough stitches to hold the pieces together, sir, so let us fit them on. We can run the seams at the shop and have a suit ready for you in two hours."

Ned was relieved to wear trousers again, close-fitting as they were, and he chose one pair each in cream and dark grey, black and brown cut-away jackets, and waistcoats in pale grey and dark red. One of the assistants had samples of shoes. Ned chose half boots called Wellingtons.

"I suggest," said the tailor, "that we prepare one suit straightaway. Tomorrow if you'd care to call at the shop in Threadneedle Street we can provide you with the remainder of your order, an overcoat and hat, perhaps an additional cravat, and any other *accoutrements* you might wish."

Ned smiled at the thought of his tailor's working in the eponymous Threadneedle Street.

"I am most grateful to you, sir. Before we go further, I must tell you I am waiting for a remittance. I do not wish to trouble you with an application for credit. Can you tell me the cost of these articles so far, in ready money?"

"Well, sir," replied the tailor, slightly taken aback. "We should have been pleased to offer credit as you've come to us through Dr. Walcot. The boots are two guineas and I believe we can supply you with what you have here and a suitable overcoat and hat at the shop, for" —he ticked his fingers, counting – "eleven pounds, ten and sixpence."

"I should like to have two extra shirts and a second set of underclothes. But these need not be completed by tomorrow."

"Shall we say twelve pounds even, sir?"

"With pleasure."

The tailor bowed and Ned continued. "You appreciate, I trust, that I am not fit to leave this room in my present state."

"I do, sir. My assistant will return within two hours."

By noon Ned had one of his suits and was as close to a gentleman as he was ever likely to get. He went downstairs and found the landlord behind the bar, polishing glasses.

"Mr. Chumley, I believe," said Ned.

Chumley did not smile. "Mr. Marston. Pleased to see you looking more yoursel'. You gave us a stir last night."

"For that I apologise. And I thank you for your many courtesies."

"Doctor called this morning and left you this." He handed over an envelope, which Ned opened as the landlord continued to speak. It contained a banknote for five pounds, contained in a sheet of paper which read, 'On account.'

"Said you'd be staying the week at least. You're paid up for six more nights, room, breakfast and one other meal each day. Thirty-seven shillings and sixpence a week."

"Pardon me," said Ned. "You've had only my gold sovereign."

"Oh," said Chumley and this time he did smile. "Doctor took it off me and gave me a pound. Then 'e told me 'e was payin' for your week. Nice touch that – should really 'ave got the difference from you, not 'im."

"Well," said Ned, "thank you, I suppose. Now I wonder if you could recommend a bank to me, where I could leave my books in safe deposit."

"'Oare's," came the reply. "In Fleet Street."

"Have you a satchel I might borrow for the afternoon to carry them?"

A nod. "And finally," said Ned, "have you someone who could meet me at Dolly's Chop-House at two-thirty and walk with me to Fleet Street?"

"I believe I take your meaning," said the landlord. "But so as we're certain, why don't you tell me just what kind of someone you're thinking of?"

"A large someone," said Ned. "The kind of someone you use to throw difficult customers outside."

"Gallagher," said the landlord. "'e'll be in for 'is pint any time now."

Chumley disappeared through a door between tall racks of bottles. A moment later he returned with a well-worn leather bag, its flap and shoulder strap showing signs of several repairs. "I'll want it back this ev'nin'."

"Will Gallagher be in this room?"

"Naw," said Chumley. "'e'll be out back. But I'll 'ave 'im 'ere soon as you're ready ter go."

Ned went upstairs to put his manuscript and books in the satchel. He returned in five minutes and saw the landlord talking to a big man with curly black hair. When Chumley saw Ned he nodded and once again went through the door behind the bar. The big man turned. Ned could see something of the two chambermaids in his features. And more: an expression of laughter around the eyes that struck him as peculiarly Irish, some chipped teeth in a well-shaped and intelligent mouth, and a powerful body bespeaking the easy authority of a man who spends much of his life with large animals.

"May I buy you a drink, Mr. Gallagher?"

"I've a pot back with my dinner, sir, an' the wife'll skin me if I'm with you so long."

"Let's make it quick then. I want to walk this satchel down to Fleet Street after I've had my dinner and I want to be sure it gets there safe and sound."

Gallagher smiled. "I think I can manage that." His eyes narrowed. "Any reason to think someone's after it?"

Ned shook his head. "Just being careful."

Gallagher nodded. "Am I enough for you, then, or shall I be after bringing one of the lads as well?"

It was Ned's turn to smile. "I think you'll do. It's broad daylight after all."

Gallagher shook his head and his voice was serious.

"There's more evil done in the city in broad daylight than in all the nights that ever were, sir. Mark my word for it."

Ned nodded. "I believe you. Can you be free at half past two and meet me at Dolly's Chop-House around the corner?"

"That I can," said Gallagher.

"And may I pay you something or will the landlord charge me for your time?"

"I'm my own man, sir, an' I'll see you safe because I choose to. But I'll not quibble over taking your money."

"Done," said Ned. "And I am impressed with your two daughters."

Gallagher's face grew dark. Ned realised how dangerous the man could be.

"Every young spark as sees 'em's been impressed, as you say. I've broken more than a couple of heads of those as been too impressed."

Ned threw up his hands in protest. "Not what I meant, Gallagher. I'm of an age with you, old enough to be their father."

"It's the older ones are worst," he growled. "The Bond Street lot come here thinking all they have to say is the word an' my girls'll go into keeping."

"Do I look like one of them?"

"You do at that," said Gallagher. "But I heard something different about you last night. American, are you?"

Ned nodded and Gallagher looked around to be sure they weren't overheard.

"Any man whose country serves out the bloody English is a friend of mine."

CHAPTER VI

Dolly's was only a few hundred yards from the Bell, east along Paternoster Row and across from Rivington's bookshop, publishers to the Society for Promoting Christian Knowledge. The chophouse clearly attracted a higher class of patron than the Bell. As Ned was shown to a table he took in the handsome dark wall panelling, starched white tablecloths, and the scattering of well-dressed diners.

He tucked his satchel under his chair and a moment later Walcot arrived, accompanied by a lean young man with round spectacles, long sidewhiskers, elegant arched eyebrows, and wavy brown hair brushed straight back at the top. The man's face looked meant for cheerfulness, but there were deep lines around his mouth and his eyes were grim.

Ned stood up, almost tripping over his satchel.

"I hope you'll forgive my bringing a guest, Marston," Walcot began, "but I don't doubt you'll be pleased with him. Madden, I give you Mr. Edward Marston."

Ned bowed and Madden did likewise. "Sir Frederic," Walcot blurted, correcting himself. "I've forgot my manners." He smiled at Ned. "Made a Knight Bachelor this very year. He's the youngest keeper at the British Museum and the finest palaeographer in the country."

Madden threw up his hands. "Enough, Walcot. And I am *assistant* keeper, not keeper. But these are trifling things compared to the news you give me about Mr. Marston."

At this point the waiter appeared and all three of them ordered lamb cutlets.

"And claret," said Walcot. "French-bottled, none of your own casks, if you please."

"We have the Langoa-Barton, 1828, if it is not too young for you, sir."

"Estate belongs to that damned Irishman, don't you know, Walcot?" said Madden.

"Well," said Walcot, "I've had it before and it's sweet as a daisy." He smiled at Ned. "And I think Madden will choke it down, Irish or no." He turned to the waiter. "Two bottles."

As the waiter retreated Ned was ready to ask if the British Museum had an archive of newspapers. But Sir Frederic Madden was clearly agitated, and Walcot was trying to suppress another smile.

"Go ahead, Madden. There's no reason to be shy."

Before anyone else could speak the waiter returned with the wine. It was so good that it made Ned feel he could bear Sir Frederic's testiness and more. He leaned back in his chair contentedly, hoping it would have the same effect on the others. They both took mouthfuls. Walcot smiled, and even Madden allowed it to be very fine.

"As I was about to say," Walcot continued. "Marston's rescued the books from America. He's already told me he plans to sell them."

"Hmph," said Madden. "They'd no business being in America in the first place. Damned ungrateful humbugging rebels."

Walcot's smile grew wider. "And, as I was about to say, Marston is American himself."

Madden's eyes flashed as he looked across the table, clearly unrepentant. "Be that as it may, sir, Walcot tells me you have what purports to be a manuscript of Shakespeare's sonnets."

Ned took another swallow of wine, remembering his promise of forbearance.

"*Purports*," he said evenly, "is not how I would put it, sir. It has been in our family since Shakespeare's time."

Walcot read the danger signals in this exchange.

"I believe, Marston, that Sir Frederic refers to the Shakespearean forgeries imposed on the world by Mr. Ireland some years ago."

"We are not so credulous now as we were then," said Madden, staring purposefully at Ned. "I have made a particular study of Shakespeare's autograph and of the orthography of his name. I have but one or two more examples to trace before putting my findings into print."

"I am glad to hear it, sir," Ned replied. "Dr. Walcot may have told you that my manuscript is a fair copy in an italic hand, but there is an inscription by Shakespeare and a number of changes to the text in his autograph."

"That remains to be seen," said Madden frostily.

Fortunately for all, at that moment a group of waiters appeared with their meal. Ned took this as his opportunity to ask about a newspaper archive.

"There is no such thing, sir," Madden replied. "But I allow there should be. Nearly every town has its own journal by now."

"How would you advise me to look for a news item from, say, Hampshire a dozen or more years ago?"

"You must go to Hampshire, sir." Madden's tone suggested he had said all he intended. Ned looked at Dr. Walcot, who changed the subject, asking Madden about the upcoming meeting of the Society of Antiquaries.

They finished dinner without further incident and as the waiters cleared the plates Sir Frederic turned once again to Ned.

"So, Mr. Marston, do you intend to produce this Shakespearean marvel for our inspection?"

Ned hadn't expected to be put on the spot so soon and his response surprised not only the others, but himself.

"I intend," he said, "to offer it to Mr. Heber."

"Heber!" exploded Madden, and then in a calmer voice, "Heber is unwell and cannot keep track of the books he already has. Moreover, Heber does not take the same interest in manuscripts he does in printed books. I should reconsider, sir."

Ned was about to answer when Walcot held up a restraining hand.

"It is a fair suggestion and I am sure no-one can fault Marston for contacting the greatest collector in the country. If there is anything I can do to assist, please do not hesitate to ask."

It took Madden some effort but after a moment he spoke quietly. "Heber and I are fellow members of the Athenaeum Club. I shall write him a letter of introduction, Mr. Marston. It will save you a deal of bother."

"That is handsome of you, Sir Frederic," said Ned. "Now may I trouble one of you gentlemen for the time?"

Madden pulled out his watch. "Near half-past two, sir."

"Just so," said Ned. "Dr. Walcot, will you allow me to pay my share of that excellent dinner?"

"Certainly not," said Walcot.

"Then I shall say farewell until I hear from you again."

"Indeed, Marston, and that soon."

Ned leaned over and picked up his satchel. As Madden gaped at it Ned left the restaurant without a backward look.

Liam Gallagher was outside the chophouse, leaning casually against an iron railing. A north wind was blowing and the sky had turned grey. Ned, who had yet to collect his new overcoat, shivered and asked if it looked like rain. Gallagher scanned the horizon with an expert eye and replied that he believed it would hold off till evening.

"Long enough for our business, if I don't mistake."

It was a short walk from Paternoster Row to Ludgate Hill. Gallagher asked a few questions about America, commenting that things were so difficult for his family in Ireland that some were planning to emigrate. Ned wasn't sure what to say but did his best to be encouraging.

For most of the walk Ned wrestled with the prospect of selling the Shakespeare manuscript. He could feel his stomach tighten with the pain of losing it, but he knew — he *knew* it was his only truly valuable asset in this time. Shakespeare quartos were worth something, of course, but Ned remembered the famous auctions of the 1830s, Richard Heber's among them, and no Shakespeare quarto, even one thought to be unique, had made as much as a hundred pounds. If he was going to search for Vanessa in Hampshire, let alone Australia, he had to raise money first.

In fifteen minutes they were at Hoare's Bank. Ned stopped at the entrance.

"I should be in no danger once I'm inside."

Gallagher grinned. "Different kind of danger, sir. I wouldn't trust those bankers with a shillin', even if I had one."

Ned laughed, and reached into his pocket. "Well you have now. Except you must take half-a-crown so I can ask for your help again."

Gallagher took the coin and touched his cap. "You'll have it, Mr. Marston, an' you can call on my lads at the stables as well, any time. They'll know you for asking."

Ned nodded and turned into the bank. Inside it was a straightforward matter to rent a strongbox in the vault. He filled out the appropriate papers, paid his sovereign, checked the double lock, and emptied the satchel of its books.

Outside the sky was no darker than an hour before and Ned decided to continue west along Fleet Street to St. Dunstan's. He'd gone no more than a hundred yards when he saw that nothing was as he'd remembered. Where the inn called the Devil had been was now a bland Georgian façade. Across the street, where St. Dunstan's Church had thrust itself into the roadway and caused such chaos with the traffic, was a neat new pavement, backed by a shiny neo-gothic church.

Ned couldn't take his eyes off this new church. As he crossed the street for a closer look he was nearly run down by a horse-drawn omnibus, its driver roaring and swearing as it lumbered past. But that was nothing to Ned; the new stone church had disappeared in a blur of tears. Everything connected with Nicholas Ling's and Will Shakespeare's lives was gone. Ned had nothing to replace those memories, nowhere to go in this cold, bustling, 1833 London. Vanessa was certain to have hanged, and he had no hope of returning either to Shakespeare's or his own time. As the full extent of his losses struck Ned, he stood on the pavement and wept.

CHAPTER VII

Tuesday morning, September 10th 1833, was fair and Vanessa decided to walk at least part of the way to the Academy of Music. Portmanteau in hand, she set off in the direction of Holborn. Ten minutes and a couple of enquiries took her to an omnibus stop where for sixpence she boarded a conveyance that took her all the way to the Marylebone Road. It was slow, noisy, and chaotic, but after the second stop she managed to find a seat.

Settling in, she tried to tell herself that it was pre-performance nerves that had given her bad dreams the night before. But she knew nerves weren't the problem. She'd long ago gotten over her uneasiness about playing in public. In her own time she'd given herself imaginary audiences from the past. Now she was *in* the past and had the very audiences she'd wanted. Nothing about them troubled her.

Not entirely true, she corrected herself. Even now she still got an occasional, unwelcome admirer, usually young and always male. At first she imagined Lord James Hamilton would be another of those, but Meg's lover Robert Carpenter, who'd arranged the dinner party where she and Jamie first met, had reassured her beforehand.

"Never doubt that he's a music-lover, my dear, but he is so full of himself that you need not fear he will be overly attentive."

Vanessa had smiled. It was kind of Robert to match-make, and Meg had long since let him know how difficult his task would be. There'd been other dinner-parties with Robert's friends, some of whom had shown interest in Vanessa. But most had been Robert's contemporaries, a dozen or more years older than she. Vanessa had become so fond of Robert that she measured his friends against him. None of them came close.

She came to herself with a start, realising that the busman had just called something about the Academy of Music. She'd missed her stop, and had to walk several hundred yards back, retracing the omnibus route.

She was still in time for her ten o'clock rehearsal, and somehow cheered by the bustle of life she'd seen around her in the last hour. As she checked the tuning of her piano-forte she thought again of Lord Jamie. He'd been uncertain whether he could attend the recital that night. Vanessa allowed herself to hope he wouldn't. If he did there would be a supper-party afterwards and she wasn't sure she could bear it. She was more tired than she wanted to admit, and she couldn't shake last night's dream about a blood-soaked Ned Marston.

"Bloody in more ways than one," she whispered to herself.

The recital went better than she expected, although the audience – many of them professional musicians – seemed reserved at first. Even Schubert's ravishing *Andante* for cello and piano, which closed the first half, failed to move them.

But the addition of the violinist after the interval seemed to change the audience's mood, or perhaps it was the shift to Mozart's music. Vanessa set the pace for the trios, as Mozart himself had done a generation earlier when he played the piano parts for Viennese audiences. At the end the audience applauded so insistently that they reprised the allegro movement of the C-Major trio that ended the programme.

Vanessa took the Wednesday morning express to Bath. Frank – by now an admiral – and Martha Austen were in town and Robert had arranged dinner at the York Hotel, followed by a visit to the Assembly Rooms where, thankfully, Vanessa would not have to perform. When she arrived at the Bath terminus she indulged herself in a sedan chair up the hill to her and Meg's newly-rented cottage in Lansdown. She was home by five o'clock, where she found Meg both angry and amused.

"Our landlord Mr. Beckford came round just now to offer me a tour of the Etruscan Library in his Tower," she said. "I told him there was no point going without you, that you were the only one of us who cared for books, but he insisted."

"He's had his eye on you, love. From the day we first met him."

"So you said. I never believed it, but you must be right. Or else he was drunk enough not to care. Halfway along the library he slid his hand straight down my dress. I was after kicking him the way you taught me, but I let him off with a slap to the face."

"No!" said Vanessa, wide-eyed.

"None of it seemed to bother him. He only asked if I'd care to see the rest of the books. I told him not without you and walked out."

"And that was that?"

"He truly must have been drunk. He said he didn't fancy you at all, that you were too brown and he liked my peaches-and-cream and bigger bubbies."

Vanessa snorted. "You'd better not tell Robert."

"No," said Meg. Her expression became sad. "Robert's asked if I'd go to Australia with him, where we could live as man and wife."

"My God, love, you've had a busy couple of days. What did you say?"

"I said no. I said it was sin enough that I'd been his concubine all these years and that I'd not add to God's insult by letting him become a bigamist."

"He does love you."

"I know, sweetling. But I'm happy enough as I am. I might give you up for a husband, but never for anything less."

Vanessa took her arm, and together they hurried down the hill to Robert's hotel. She usually felt the odd one out in a dinner party of five, but Martha was so glad to see her that the meal sped by in a glow of contentment. Meg and Robert excused themselves afterwards, leaving only three for the concert at the Assembly Rooms. Frank Austen suppressed a frown at Robert's abrupt departure. Vanessa wondered if Robert had confided in his old friend. She doubted it, knowing the Admiral's staunch religious principles. Was it obvious to everyone that Robert was seizing one of his rare opportunities for an evening in bed with his mistress? For Meg's sake Vanessa hoped not.

CHAPTER VIII

Ned wiped his eyes, gulped hard, and decided to get away from this new St. Dunstan's Church as fast as he could. He was cold and wanted his overcoat; he'd need it before he could go to Hampshire to try to pick up Vanessa's trail. And he needed a watch. His tailor would know where to find one. But he'd need money for a watch, he told himself. And for everything else. What am I going to do about money?

He passed the south side of St. Paul's, hesitating at the shop-window of Harris's Juvenile Library and nearly losing his resolve for the tailor as he gazed at its sparkling display of brightly-coloured books. But he pressed on, cutting north and then east, following Cheapside to the Bank of England. Past the bank he turned into Threadneedle Street, where he found yet another children's bookshop.

This one declared its owners as Dean and Munday. A shiver ran up his spine as he stared in the window. The shop display contained a quartet of small books "by Miss Horwood." They were *Baby Tales*; *Little Emma and her Father*; *The Lily, or, Little William and his Mamma*, and, more substantially, a part leather-bound *Original Poetry for Young Minds*. His heart pounding, Ned went inside to buy the lot.

Halfway to the counter he realised he might not have enough money even for a cheap watch until he concluded his business with Dr. Walcot. A couple of shillings might make all the difference. He'd take one of the books, no more.

It came down to *Little Emma* or *Little William*, both priced sixpence. Ned chose the latter, beginning to feel like a fool as he handed over his money. Vanessa had gone missing in 1817, and Horwood was not-so-uncommon an English name, after all. What connection could there be? But he asked the shop assistant if she knew anything of the author.

"We've dozens of authors, sir. It's Mrs. Dean as keeps track, or else her bookkeeper."

Ned looked across to the bookkeeper, an elderly woman with her face buried in a ledger, and thought wryly that the Vanessa he knew would approve of this all-female establishment. Mrs. Dean proved to be unavailable, but a shilling to the bookkeeper brought forth a card with an address in Bath though not, Ned was sorry to see, the author's first name.

Should he take the next coach there? An instant's reflection was all it took to decide against it. The odds against this Miss Horwood being Vanessa were too long. He had to start his search where she'd last been heard of: Winchester. And before he could do that he had to finish his errands and hope that Dr. Walcot had some more money for him.

But he lingered a few more minutes in the bookshop, scanning the shelves with practised eyes before retracing his steps to the door. It was only a few more yards to the tailor's, where Ned learned that ten more minutes would see his overcoat finished. With his new coat and hat he felt quite the dandy as he enquired where he might go for a pocket watch.

The assistant he asked had helped with Ned's fitting at the Bell.

"Begging your pardon, sir, but if its economy you require I should go to Hooper's in Cheapside. You can get a second-hand watch and a pinchbeck fob for shillings instead of pounds."

Ned smiled gratefully. "I'll take that advice."

The young man gave him a conspiratorial smile and said, "Only problem as you'll have, sir, is persuading Hooper you need a bargain, you look so flash in your new clothes."

Hooper's was just the ticket and twenty minutes later Ned had a watch guaranteed time-worthy, with a long chain that crossed over his waistcoat just like Sir Frederic Madden's. For good measure he also bought a glass tie-pin which could, at a considerable distance, be mistaken for a ruby. He was back at the Bell by six.

The Perfect Visit

After supper Ned read himself to sleep with *The Lily; or Little William and his Mamma*. It didn't take long. "Little William" was the subject of the coloured frontispiece, a smug little boy with a mortarboard hat, fat cheeks, and a ruffled collar. The poetry was terrible. Ned's eyes felt leaden as he scanned some lines about a dog named Pompey:

> If Pompey will promise
> That he will be good,
> And not bark again at the sheep,
> And not run away, and behave very rude,
> I think we will give him a peep
>
> At the fields and the flowers,
> And blue sunny sky. . . .

CHAPTER IX

The next thing Ned knew was Nell's knock at the door. He jumped out of bed, threw on his overcoat and called for her to come in.

"I'll say this for you, sir," the girl said cheerfully. "You've no trouble with your sleep. It's half after eight again and I've a letter for you." Behind her Molly had a basin of hot water, soap, and a razor, which she set on a table in front of the looking-glass.

Nell pulled the curtains open and set the breakfast tray by the window; both girls bobbed curtseys and were gone. He opened an elegant embossed envelope and pulled out a single page.

> Sir,
>
> Sr. Fredr. Madden informs me you have an item of interest.
>
> I shd. be pleased for you to bring it to the Athenaeum, Pall Mall, on the 13th inst., at eleven o'clock.
>
> Yrs. &c.
>
> R. Heber

That was sufficiently to the point, Ned decided. There was no return address but just to be safe Ned decided to send a confirmation to Heber care of the Athenaeum Club. For a moment he pondered what to write but the language seemed to come naturally enough. He mirrored the tone of Heber's short letter and Chumley promised it would reach the Athenaeum via the penny post by the end of the day.

Dr. Walcot arrived shortly after noon and accepted Ned's invitation to an early dinner.

"It was a nice touch, Marston, tantalizing poor Madden with the thought of your Shakespeare manuscript and then lifting it – at least I assume that was it – from under your chair after dinner."

"I cannot say I found him charming, Doctor."

"No indeed. Charm is not Madden's strong suit. But you will never meet a better scholar and I count no man a truer friend."

"Well," said Ned, "I have no choice but to sell the manuscript. I've made an appointment to see Heber at his club on the 13th."

"Friday the thirteenth!" declared Walcot. "Pleased to hear you're not super-stitious, Marston. Perhaps you and your manuscript will join me at the Society of Antiquaries that evening?"

Ned winced: he hadn't connected Friday to the thirteenth day of the month. But he'd written to Heber and it was too late to back out now.

"If you don't mind," Ned replied, "I'll let you know after I see Mr. Heber."

Walcot gave an understanding nod and Ned continued.

"The books are the only real assets my family has left and I have no skills I might use to seek employment. I knew my family were not good businessmen, but I never imagined we were so close to bankruptcy."

"It's the way of the world, my friend. Times have not been good in this country either, the last fifteen years or so. You would be amazed how many of our ancient families have had to sell their estates to men newly rich from indus-try, especially in the northern counties."

"Is not Mr. Heber one of those northern families?"

"Indeed he is. And some say he too is seriously encumbered. But if he is taken with your manuscript he would have no trouble paying whatever price you ask. I should warn you that he will share Madden's scepticism. Those Shakespeare forgeries of the 1790s were a lesson scholars and collectors will never forget."

The doctor produced a leather wallet. "Now, sir, I shall speak of your ancient coins and offer you some cheer. I have been to see London's pre-eminent dealer who gave me a list of prices for the collection you entrusted to me. I purchased some myself, at ten percent over what he was prepared to pay, and accepted his offer for the remainder. You had several extreme rarities, I am happy to say, and I have brought you both his and my own cheques."

Ned was relieved to see they amounted to nearly two hundred pounds. It wasn't enough to support him in the long term, but would allow him to act according to his plan, even if he had to go to Australia. He remembered what Caroline had said about how expensive the coins had been when she'd bought them. They must have cost tens of thousands of pounds to have been worth nearly two hundred in 1833.

"I am more grateful than I can possibly say, Doctor. If Mr. Heber is interested in the manuscript there may be hope for me yet."

Pleased as Ned was to have his immediate financial worries resolved, he had something else on his mind.

"Before I see Heber, or anyone else, I must find a bathhouse. I had thought to ask the landlord but I'd prefer your advice."

"Baths," replied Walcot. "On the whole I deprecate them. But those in Newgate Street are decent enough in spite of the name: Bagnio Court. Go early for fresh water and keep the key when they lock up your clothes. If you have a warm bath, wait until your perspiration has entirely ceased before you venture outdoors."

"Thank you."

Walcot laughed. "You sound more grateful for the baths than for anything else."

Ned grinned back. "Maybe I am."

CHAPTER X

Chumley had a post-coach timetable at the front desk and Ned saw there was regular service from Charing Cross to Southampton via Winchester, with an express leaving later that afternoon. It would arrive after dark, but Chumley said Ned would have no problem taking a room at the coaching inn for the night.

"You may 'ave to share it, though."

"I'll manage," said Ned.

He had just enough time to get to Bagnio Court first, a fresh shirt and underwear tucked in his overcoat. The baths were crowded and the water, as Walcot had warned, less than fresh, but Ned followed the rest of the doctor's instructions to the letter. His hair was still a little damp but he was finally clean, with two hundred years of God-knew-what encrustations scrubbed away.

The coach made a few stops on the way to Winchester. One of them was Alton, close to what Ned knew was Vanessa's point of arrival at Chawton. But it was dark by the time they got there and he had no way of telling one village from another.

The Winchester coaching inn had one private room left. As he settled in he could feel Vanessa's ghost returning, as palpably as it had in the laboratory the morning after she time-travelled. Had Vanessa been in this inn? If so, was it before or after her arrest? Could she have left Winchester alive? He finally managed to sleep, but the next morning he woke with the sun, tense with anticipation.

The innkeeper told Ned that the Winchester gaoler was new, the previous one having retired a year earlier. No sooner was Ned admitted to the gaoler's office than the man began a lecture on his duty to keep inmates' records private.

"I have no way of determining your interest, sir. For all I know you are a criminal yourself, seeking an accomplice, or revenge."

"But surely," Ned protested, "you can tell me if Miss Horwood was convicted and hanged. That would have been in the newspapers, would it not?"

"In that case, sir, you may enquire of the newspapers. The offices of the *Hampshire Chronicle* are no great distance."

Ned swallowed his anger, stood, and bowed. A guard accompanied him back to the prison gate. When no-one was near the man whispered.

"I 'eard your question, sir, an' I know about Miz 'orwood. I was 'ere at the time, might've lost my place but for 'er kindness."

The guard paused and Ned fumbled in his pocket for money. He pulled out a shilling but the man shook his head.

"Wasn't waitin' for money, sir. Was tryin' to get the measure of you. You don't strike me as a criminal, but then neither do some of those as 'ang."

Ned waited for more and the man obliged. "Miz 'orwood never 'anged, sir."

Ned caught his breath. "You're certain?"

"Sure as life. I saw 'er to this same gate the morning she was set free. Whole charge a mistake, as we was told. The old warden might tell you more. Did this one tell you 'ow to find 'im?"

Ned shook his head and the guard smiled, showing several broken teeth.

"Reverend Lewcock. 'e's got a church now, St. Anne's in Alton. An' I can take your money for that, sir."

Ned grinned and handed over the shilling. A moment later he was outside the gate, half-running for the coaching inn. His meeting with Richard Heber was tomorrow morning in London which meant that, come what may, he had to return at latest on this evening's coach. All coaches stopped in Alton, however, so he had a few hours leeway.

But the innkeeper said it was two hours till the next one and Ned knew he couldn't wait. He was spending money he should save, but this was his only lead. There was little chance the old warden would have current news of Vanessa, or if he did that he'd share it, but Ned had to know, now. He hired a trap to take him the fifteen miles to Alton.

The driver knew St. Anne's Church, but no-one was there when Ned went inside. A handsome brick house was behind the cemetery, surely the rectory.

Ned gave a sigh of relief when a tall, spare man in a clerical collar answered the door, brushing a wisp of white hair from his spectacles.

"Reverend Lewcock?" Ned began, but the clergyman raised an arm.

"You are agitated, young man. As you bear no resemblance to any of my parishioners I expect this is a matter from my previous employment."

Ned took a deep breath. "Yes, sir. My name is Edward Marston."

"You speak and dress well enough, although you have the face of a pugilist. Would you care to take a glass with me, whilst I explain why I cannot help you?"

Ned began to protest, but the clergyman drew himself up.

"The matter is not open to discussion, sir. You interest me, but interest is not enough to compromise the safety of my charges, past and present."

"I accept what you say, sir," Ned replied. "And I am grateful to speak to you on whatever terms you choose. But you should know I have come a considerable distance to ask a simple question."

"About Miss Horwood, perhaps?"

Ned recoiled, nearly falling backwards off the stoop. "How could you know?"

"Your accent, sir. It is Canadian, I believe, like hers."

"American, in fact. But you have a good ear."

"There is more to it than simply your accent. Something in your demeanour. Are you a relation?"

"No." Ned had an inspiration. "But her relations in Canada asked me to enquire."

Reverend Lewcock stepped aside and beckoned Ned into a large, low-ceilinged and dark room. It had an uneven stone floor and a smell of damp. At the near end an ancient dining-table was set for one.

"Perhaps I might offer more than a glass, Mr. Marston. I shall shortly commence my afternoon meal and I should take it as a kindness if you would join me. No more than bread and cheese, I'm afraid."

A stooped old woman shuffled through an archway and took instructions to provide for the visitor. Lewcock turned away from the table and escorted Ned through a door at the opposite end of the room. This, Ned saw, was the place his host actually lived, a snug study with overstuffed chairs and a small fire.

A dog was on a rug in front of the hearth. It looked up, opening its mouth to bark. Then it changed its mind and walked slowly over to Ned, pushing its grey muzzle between his legs. Ned reached down to scratch between its ears.

"He is usually a better guard against strangers," observed Lewcock. "I am not certain I have ever seen him so tame."

Ned smiled. "Animals and small children usually like me, Mr. Lewcock. It is grown people who give trouble."

Lewcock laughed, the lines in his face taking some time to move out of their accustomed furrows. "Well said, sir. And so they do me."

A decanter was on a side table. As his host poured Ned looked around the room. Bookshelves lined three walls, drawing him like a magnet.

"I should not have taken you for a scholar, Mr. Marston," Lewcock said, handing over a glass. The sherry was as sweet and thick as the sack of Shakespeare's time. Ned savoured the familiar, cloying taste.

"Nor am I," he replied. "But I have worked with books and can see this is an exceptional collection." One wall was dark calf and vellum, the spines unlettered but for a few with faint manuscript. Another wall mixed lighter and darker leather, most bearing gilt titles but only a few with decorated spines. On either side of the fireplace were rows of more modern books, paper and cloth bindings with printed labels.

Ned approached the modern sections: books on jurisprudence and prison reform. One book was present in three copies: Joseph Gurney's account of a trip to English and Scottish prisons in the company of Elizabeth Fry. Ned turned to another wall and recognised more names on the labels of eighteenth-century books.

"You are wondering," said Lewcock, "what the purpose of all these are. What they have in common."

Ned smiled, appreciating the man's pride of ownership. "I believe I can speak to that. I am guessing, of course, as to your sixteenth and seventeenth-century books, but based on these" – he pointed to the later ones – "I should say you begin with books by those who share your own knowledge of modern prisons. You are clearly a reformer yourself or you would not have the works of so many others, and I believe your earlier works are also largely by reforming philosophers and jurists: Voltaire, Lord Kames, Blackstone, Beccaria, Howard."

"You astonish me, sir," said Lewcock. "And the others?"

"There are too many books before 1700 for them not to be largely theological. Perhaps pertaining to the punishment of sinners?"

Lewcock's eyebrows rose. "Exactly so, Mr. Marston. And who spoke to you of this? Surely you do not glean so much from two minutes scanning."

Ned shrugged, turning his palms wide. "I'm afraid so, sir. I hope I do not offend you."

Ned liked this old cleric and, anxious as he was for news, he was worried that he'd made a mistake by indulging his interest in the man's books instead of directly asking more about Vanessa. Most collectors were flattered by attention, but Lewcock's face was inscrutable.

To Ned's relief the clergyman smiled again, more broadly this time.

"It is a fine parlour-trick, Mr. Marston. I shall see if I can learn to practice it myself, in the far grander libraries of my local gentry. In any case you have certainly earned your dinner. Come along, sir."

Ned followed his host back into the entry hall, where the table was now set for two. Bread and cheese were on the sideboard, along with a large bottle.

"Cider, sir," said Lewcock. "From my own apples."

Ned nodded. Lewcock poured, sliced the bread and cheese, added some pickled onions to each plate and the two men sat down.

"Wonderful cider, sir," Ned said after a moment.

"I had no time for such pursuits in Winchester, Mr. Marston. Although St. Anne's is an active church and there are many calls upon my time, I confess it is a rustic idyll compared to my former employment."

Ned said nothing, holding the man's gaze.

"But I am teasing you, sir," said Lewcock. "Let me get to the point. If you are looking for Miss Horwood I cannot help you. Nor would I if I could. Engaging as you are, I cannot ascertain your motive for seeking her. If, however, her relations and you are unaware of her history I may tell you she was in the gravest danger imaginable. Thanks to the efforts of my friend Elizabeth Fry the truth was revealed in time to save her from the gallows."

"This was in 1817," said Ned, "if I am not mistaken."

"Indeed, sir. She did not reveal her destination when she left my charge, but she was accompanied by a young Irishwoman whose name. . . I must confess I have forgot her name, Mr. Marston. But I had some indirect news of Miss Horwood from one of my fellow-clergy who performed the marriage service for Captain Austen, as he then was, about five years ago. My colleague sat with her at dinner and was quite taken. Evidently my name came up and she asked him to convey her kind regard. Another colleague, the captain's brother Henry Austen, was also present at the wedding and brought similar greetings. She makes a distinct impression, it seems."

Ned's heart was pounding. So Vanessa had found Jane Austen. More than found her, if Vanessa was still seeing family members ten years later.

"Is there anything else you can tell me, sir?" he asked.

Lewcock gave a faint smile. "I can understand why a young man like you might be anxious on her account, but I truly have no information concerning her present whereabouts."

He looked thoughtfully at Ned before continuing. "You might," he said slowly, "write to Admiral Austen. Rear-Admiral Francis Austen. His wife and Miss Horwood are intimate, I am told. A letter should reach him through the Admiralty with dispatch, I should imagine, if he is not at sea. Henry Austen is normally closer to hand, but I believe he is travelling at present. He has the curacy at Bentley, four miles up the road."

"I am more grateful to you than I can possibly say."

"I wish her well, sir. A young woman of considerable spirit, and the victim of a gross injustice. But it could have been worse."

Lewcock had finished his meal. Ned bolted the last of his and rose to his feet.

"Will you forgive me if I say farewell? I must return to London today and I am uncertain how far it is to the coaching inn."

Lewcock wiped his mouth. "Five minutes walk, sir." Then he shook out his napkin and accompanied Ned outdoors.

On the arbour above the garden gate a few roses were at the end of their bloom. As the clergyman gave Ned directions a gust of wind brought a cascade of petals onto their clothes. Lewcock absent-mindedly brushed them away, but Ned gathered his up in a handkerchief and put them in his pocket.

Ned had missed an earlier coach in Winchester and now learned he'd just missed another. It would be another two hours wait until the next one, the last of the day. He thought of Henry Austen's village of Bentley, surely an easy enough walk. Even if the curate wasn't there Ned could leave a message at the church.

But he shook his head, realizing he dared not miss this last coach to London. The penny post would do well enough, and if there was no reply from either Austen Ned would simply come back to Hampshire. Those two men were his only hope.

The afternoon was breezy and pleasant and Ned decided to walk around Alton. Scudding clouds cast intermittent shadows as he passed a row of handsome brick buildings, one of which was the Hoare's Bank that must have been the scene of Vanessa's arrest, as reported in the newspaper microfiche Ned had found in the British Library.

The street opened onto a large green and at the far end Ned could see a crowd of people and hear faint sounds of music. Drawing closer he saw that the crowd was a mix of townspeople and farm-workers, with many children among them. At the centre was a gypsy troupe performing circus tricks. There were costumed stilt-walkers, fire-eaters, and jugglers. Some exotically-dressed young women were dancing to the music – mothers pulled children away from the sight – and some young men were roping off a rectangle.

"It's the boxing," Ned heard a voice say. "Come on, lads."

Ned followed, intrigued, and heard a call for all comers. A large bare-chested man with a round face, flattened nose, and eyes like slits held his arms up. He looked overweight but Ned could see the ridges of muscle under the fat. If the man could move well he'd be dangerous. Some of the farm-boys didn't see the threat and were making jokes about the boxer's corpulence.

"I've no fear," one said. As Ned wondered how much of the man's courage came from a bottle he pulled off his shirt and stepped up.

"What's the stake?"

"Your ten shillings to his sovereign," said an older man who was obviously in charge. He raised his voice to the crowd. "Come along and wager on your own brave lad, gentlemen. I'll give two to one odds in favour of my man here."

The farm-boy was a strapping specimen, taller than the boxer, much younger, and altogether in better shape. The spectators wanted some sport and stepped up to place bets.

In the first two rounds the boxer toyed with the amateur, not wanting to end the bout too quickly, but at the beginning of the third Ned saw the book-maker nod, and the boy was on the ropes in seconds, his nose streaming with blood. He staggered up to try again, raising his fists gamely, but the professional went under his guard with two midriff blows that made the boy collapse forward, vomiting whatever it was that had given him his courage. His friends helped him out of the ring as some of the gypsies cleared the mess.

Two more men in the audience tried their skill with similar results. The bookmaker offered better odds to the challengers each time, but took fewer and fewer wagers. Then someone outside the circle of farm-workers stepped up, appraising the crowd with eyes that seemed to Ned a little too canny for the circumstances. By now the bookmaker was giving six to one odds. The three-round victor gave a contemptuous look at the new man.

"Give 'im six to one for a knockout," he suggested. "Four to one I'll have 'im on his back inside two minutes."

The new challenger seemed to be weaving on his feet, but Ned wasn't persuaded the man was drunk, although his speech was slurred enough.

"All I do is stay on my feet for two minutes and I win?"

"You won't," said his opponent.

Both spoke loudly enough for all present to hear, and the challenger brandished a sovereign of his own money, bragging that he knew a few tricks of his own. Nobody seemed to believe him, and fifteen or twenty people approached to wager on the three-time victor.

Ned decided he smelled a rat. The challenger had come out of nowhere and was smaller and older than any of the brawny farm-boys whose attempts had failed so dismally. Ned stepped forward for a closer look at the new man and saw the network of facial scars and broken veins that signalled another career boxer. Then he approached the bookmaker.

"Ten pounds on the challenger," Ned said quietly, pulling out a banknote. "For a knockout."

"Can't take it," said the man. "It's too much."

"I don't think so," said Ned. "You just took ten from one of the townspeople over there, betting on your favourite."

"You don't belong here," said the bookmaker, slowly shaking his head. "Who sent you?"

Ned didn't answer. It was obvious enough this was a confidence game, with the gypsies as a front. Did the bookmaker think Ned was from another gambling syndicate, poaching on his territory?

I suppose, Ned thought, I don't look quite the gentleman I'd hoped. He wondered what other swindles would be offered later, after nightfall.

Ned took a step closer and finally the bookmaker nodded, accepting Ned's banknote.

"I'll stay right here with you," Ned said. "This won't take long, will it?"

The challenger took a few punches that looked authentic enough, as the bookmaker accepted a few more bets on the favourite. But Ned could see that the match was choreographed. Gradually the momentum shifted, with the favourite showing that he couldn't keep up with the faster arms of his opponent. A flurry of punches – most of them pulled, Ned could tell – brought the bout to an end after about ten minutes, with the favourite spitting blood as he slumped to the turf. A sheep's bladder in his mouth, Ned was certain. They've taken care to make it look good, not to be caught out for a rigged match.

The bookmaker turned away but Ned caught his arm. "Let's settle now, shall we, before your friends come round?"

The man pulled out a wallet and extracted three new twenty-pound notes.

Ned shook his head. "I want my ten pounds back, and the notes you took from the townspeople. And you can give me as much silver and gold as you please. But I won't take those."

"You're a fuckin' ding boy, you are. I could have the law on you for calling me counterfeit."

Ned grinned. "If you get the law to say those aren't counterfeit, I'll take them."

"Bugger you. Here're your bloody banknotes and some gold to stuff your codpiece. You can tell your mates if any of 'em come on my turf again we'll have a reception waiting."

Ned took the money, realizing the man was taking longer than necessary to hand it over. It was well over an hour since Ned had left the coaching inn and he knew that in such fine weather the London express would be sharp on its schedule. He pushed the banknotes into his jacket and was about to pocket the sovereigns when he felt a hand on his arm.

Without looking Ned spun, closing his hand around the sovereigns and smashing the side of his fist into his assailant's jaw. As the blow fell Ned realised it was the victor of the last boxing match, the source of Ned's funds. The man went down without a cry, hitting the ground hard.

But others were closing in and Ned took off at a run. His leg that had taken the bully-blow in Shakespeare's time cramped and he nearly slipped on the grass. But he steadied, and had just enough head-start on his pursuers to reach the edge of town before the fastest one caught up with him.

Ned whirled and saw the man had drawn a knife.

"Do you really want to cut me, right here in town where everyone can see?"

"Give us the money, then."

Ned's grin was wolfish. "Come and get it." He went into his ready position as the man thrust forward. Ned chopped his wrist and the knife fell. As the man dived for it Ned's boot caught him on the side of the head, knocking him sideways onto the grass. Two of his cohorts had arrived by now and Ned's first instinct was to go after them as well. But they backed off, hands in the air.

Ned backed away too, across the main road into the High Street. The coaching inn was only a hundred yards away. After a few more backward paces Ned could see that his assailants had given up. He turned and walked the rest of the way normally, not meeting the stares of some passers-by. His sore leg was shaking when he reached the inn and the whiskey he ordered to calm his nerves had little effect.

The coach left on schedule. Once they were underway Ned reached into his jacket to retrieve his banknotes. He also got a handful of rose petals, souvenir of the rector's arbour. They took his mind off what he knew had been a dangerous piece of foolishness. He was glad to have won the money, however, and surely some of the banknotes had to be genuine. He'd take them to Hoare's in Fleet Street to be certain, and they could check the coins at the same time.

But I've still been a fool, he told himself. Then he put the rose-petals to his nose and thought of Vanessa. And now I'm a sentimental fool.

CHAPTER XI

Friday September 13th brought the return of dreary autumn weather, with a cold wind from the northeast and a leaden sky. Ned was up early for once, thinking of Walcot's invitation to the Society of Antiquaries. He decided he didn't need to delay his acceptance. He could post a letter that Walcot would receive by mid-afternoon, and another letter to Francis Austen care of the Admiralty. For good measure he wrote a third to Henry Austen at Bentley Church.

Ned walked down to Hoare's, where the cashiers approved his gambling acquisitions of gold sovereigns and banknotes. He collected his Shakespeare manuscript from the vault and hailed a cabriolet heading west along the Strand. After Charing Cross he was surrounded by chaos. One new terrace of houses in Cockspur Street rose up from the rubble; all else was in the process of demolition or construction. But when he crossed Waterloo Place civilisation returned, with imposing new buildings on all sides.

The Athenaeum Club was on the left. It was only three or four years old, a large square building in neo-classical style with a Doric portico framing the entrance and, above, a replica of the long frieze from the Parthenon. The entrance hall was equally classical, with an arched ceiling, Corinthian columns, copies of ancient statues, and a tiled floor. Ned stared until a porter touched his arm and asked his business.

Clearly the name of Richard Heber was one to be conjured with. The porter became deferential. Ned held onto his manuscript as the porter took Ned's overcoat and hat and ushered him into a large and well-furnished reception room.

It was still a few minutes shy of eleven when Heber arrived. He looked emaciated and frail, but under his bald head and thick spectacles he was all impatience and bustling energy.

"So, sir, so," he began. "There is no business to be talked of in the common rooms and I have taken a small one by the Library. I see you have your package. Come along, Mr. Marston, this way."

Heber led them upstairs, through an enormous, three-tiered library – "finest of any club in London" – and into an austere little conference room with a mahogany table and straight-backed chairs. He sat and waved Ned to a chair opposite. Before Ned was seated Heber began talking again.

"Never thought to hear from Madden about an acquisition. That man believes everything should be in the public eye. Which means under his thumb, if you take my meaning, sir."

Ned smiled. There was something charming about the man's energy. A quote from the poet Thomas Campbell drifted into his head. "Heber, fiercest and strongest of the bibliomaniacs."

"Hmm?" said Heber sharply. "What's that?"

Ned hadn't appreciated that he'd spoken aloud.

"Bibliomania, sir. I was asking if Madden was one of the bibliomaniacs."

"Ha!" said Heber. "You've heard of that, have you?"

Ned smiled again. "Hasn't everyone?" He began to unwrap his package, untying the string carefully so he could use it again.

"You say this is an heirloom, sir?"

"Yes."

"And you are one of the Shropshire Marstons?"

Ned nodded, warily.

"I know that county, sir. Was sheriff only ten years or so ago. I've two or three Marston families as tenants, but I can't say I ever met yours."

Ned smiled. "No, sir, you would not. My grandfather went to Philadelphia in 1770, fought on the King's side in the War of Independence, and died young. My father was a child when they emigrated, and I was born there."

"Hmm," said Heber. "Yankee. That explains your accent – flat, sir, no cadence to it."

By now Ned had removed the velvet-bound manuscript from its wrapping-paper. Heber was leaning over the table, hovering hungrily.

Ned said simply, "I shall let this speak for itself," and handed it over.

Now it was Ned's turn to hover above the table, but Heber handled the little book like an eggshell, with Ned nodding approval.

"Master Marston," Heber read, "from one who loves him well. Their authour W.S."

Heber looked up. "Are you descended from that caterwauling playwright, sir? *The Malcontent. Antonio & Mellida.* Weak things indeed."

Ned left the question hanging as Heber leafed gently through the manuscript pages. He was clearly lost in the poetry, muttering passages to himself and commenting on the fine italic hand.

"Quite different to the inscription, of course. But there are corrections – emendations – in that same hand. Main text doubtless a copyist, hmm? Afterwards corrected?"

He closed the volume and held it gently in one hand, the other drumming on the table.

"Wish Malone were alive. Ever since that damned rogue Ireland plagued us with his Shakespeare forgeries we've had to look askance at anything to do with the Swan of Avon."

"Well, Mr. Heber," Ned replied, "you know its source and I believe there is no question about its age and authenticity."

"Pah, sir!" said Heber. "The binding and paper are perfectly right, no doubt about it. It is the text I question. Anyone practiced in the secretary and italic hands could write this. And if you'll forgive me, sir, anyone could assert his name was Marston and that the volume came down through his family."

"Mr. Heber." Ned could feel the flush on his face but he kept his voice even. "If that is your opinion I shall waste no more of your time."

He stood up but Heber waved him back.

"Sit, sir, sit. I intended no offence but these are difficult matters. There is much to commend about your volume including, if I may say so, your own manner. Let us collect some opinions and discuss it further."

"Opinions?" asked Ned.

"Aye, sir. Young Madden is a fine judge of such things and I believe we might also visit Messrs. Collier and Dyce, if you would be so kind."

"To the same end?"

"Yes," said Heber. "Collier and Dyce are the best scholars of the early drama since – well, I'm not sure we've had better. Collier's finishing a supplement to his edition of the *Old Plays* and has spent some time with my quartos. I believe he is correcting sheets in Chancery Lane this week."

Ned didn't know if he wanted to spend days chasing all over London with Heber. Nor was he at all certain he wanted to engage John Payne Collier. In library school Ned had read about the man's dubious reputation as a Shakespearean dealer and forger. He didn't want to lose his best chance to sell the manuscript, but he wanted to be able to travel as soon as he heard from the Austens.

"May I venture an alternative, sir?"

"By all means, Mr. Marston."

"Sir Frederic Madden will be at the Society of Antiquaries tonight, where I have been invited by my friend Dr. Walcot. If you and these other gentlemen are members, perhaps we might accomplish all we need at once."

"Capital, sir, capital!" Heber was clearly delighted at the prospect. "But you must not let them tempt you with offers."

Ned smiled, but before he could answer Heber asked, "By the way, sir, what is the price?"

"Mr. Heber," Ned replied formally. "I know my price but you have called the authenticity of the manuscript into question. I do not propose to disclose the amount until the question is settled, but if you will provide me with paper and ink and an envelope and sealing-wax, I shall write down the price, seal it up, and if we reach a satisfactory resolution you may open it."

"Sounds like a damned quibble to me."

Ned looked Heber straight in the eye and said evenly,

"The quibble, sir, was not of my making."

Writing materials were duly produced and the envelope was signed, sealed, and impressed with the insignia of the Athenaeum Club. Ned offered it to Heber.

"I am content to leave it in your safekeeping, sir" – Ned's smile had a forbidding edge – "but if the seal is broken our negotiations are finished."

Heber bowed and waited in silence as Ned wrapped up the manuscript, afterwards walking him to the porter's alcove where they shook hands.

"Until this evening, sir," said Heber calmly.

But the man's eyes were on fire.

CHAPTER XII

Late that afternoon Dr. Walcot finished his rounds and collected Ned at the Bell. The morning's leaden sky had given way to rain. Walcot was standing by the fireplace, shaking water from his coat, when Ned came downstairs.

"We shall take a cabriolet down to the Strand together," said Walcot. "There is a first-rate hotel will give us tea worthy of the Duchess of Bedford herself – or would you prefer the Cigar Divan?"

"No cigars, Doctor, I beg, but tea would be welcome. And then we are off to the Antiquaries?"

"We are indeed: the entire Society is a-buzz with you. Madden has mentioned your manuscript to old Mr. Perkins, author of *Illustrations of Shakespeare*, who is determined to make his doddery way into our company. And of course Collier and Dyce will be there, each trying to out-do the other."

Ned wanted to know these men's reputations in their own time. "Tell me more about them."

"Both brilliant. Dyce is enormous, sometimes gives the impression of a trained bear, dancing. Perfect manners, quite the gallant, and rich. He has a fine little book collection, pays for his own publications: all things to which Collier at present can only aspire."

"So how does Collier out-do Dyce?"

"Collier's the more accomplished scholar. But Dyce can publish whatever he will, so he anticipates Collier's projects with his own. The two compliment each other in barbed little footnotes, praising each other's genius in general terms, even as they point out the other's specific misquotations and lapses."

Ned smiled, thinking of similar academic squabbles from his own time, and noting that the doctor had given no hint that Collier was considered anything but respectable.

"Are they authorities on Shakespeare's autograph?"

"They believe themselves so. But they will be looking to Madden for the conclusive opinion."

Ned patted his overcoat for the dozenth time, feeling for its precious package.

"You'll be going home to Knightsbridge after the meeting, I assume."

Walcot nodded.

"Then I shall make other arrangements for my return."

Ned stopped by the stables on their way out and Gallagher promised to meet him at Somerset House at nine o'clock.

Tea in the Strand was everything Ned could wish, with six different kinds of sandwiches and a sponge cake. The waiter announced their new aromatic brew, "at the express request of his lordship the Prime Minister." Walcot nodded and Ned dared not admit that he didn't know who the Prime Minister was. But he knew after his first sip: Earl Grey. He was fond of the blend and recognising it gave him an absurd pleasure.

When they left the hotel the rain had stopped and the clouds were breaking up. A last burst of sunlight coloured the evening sky deep red. It was a short walk to Somerset House, which Ned had no idea would be so imposing: a huge Georgian pile, some twenty or so windows wide, with a central classical portico.

"Is this all the Society of Antiquaries?" Ned asked, trying to keep his mouth from dropping open.

"Oh, no," Walcot replied, laughing. "The great exhibition room is taken up by the Royal Academy of Arts, with pictures hung floor to ceiling. But we get by, as you'll see."

Walcot led Ned through the porter's lobby and up a flight of stairs. Double doors opened onto a large salon, with a vast table framed by ordinary chairs on three sides and a solitary, throne-like armchair on the fourth. Bits and pieces of manuscripts, coins, pottery, and other, unidentifiable, flotsam were spread out on the table and groups of antiquaries, some of the older ones wearing now-unfashionable wigs, were waving their arms and squabbling over definitions and identifications. It was pandemonium, but of an amiable kind.

They approached Sir Frederic Madden, who bowed rather stiffly to Ned.

"So, Mr. Marston, am I to believe I shall finally get sight of this vaunted manuscript of yours?"

Ned bowed back. "It will be an honour, sir. But should we not wait until all interested parties are present?"

"Of course we should," put in Walcot. "Come along, Madden. Let's gather them up and find places at the table."

Across the room Ned saw Richard Heber in company with two tall men, one of them towering above all others. From Walcot's description Ned knew this was Alexander Dyce. The other, about Ned's size though a good deal older, had to be John Payne Collier. Once they found a place for Heber to sit at the exhibition table, Ned handed him the Shakespeare package. Heber unwrapped it with the same care he had shown that morning, obviously unwilling to let the volume out of his hands. He carefully opened the velvet covers to show the leaf with Shakespeare's inscription.

Madden whipped out a large magnifying glass and peered at it. "Clearly the correct ink for the period and a different ink to that of the italic scribe."

"Carry on, Mr. Heber," said Dyce, "you told us there were pages with corrections in the same hand."

"Patience, gentlemen," said Heber. "Ah, here is a fine example." He read aloud:

> Shall I compare thee to a Summer's day?
> Thou art more lovely and more temperate:
> Rough winds do shake the darling buds of May,
> And Summer's lease hath all too short a date.

He looked up at Dyce and Collier. "The familiar text, yes? And so it is here. But only with the corrections."

"So I see," said Dyce, leaning his bulk over Heber's shoulder. "The italic has 'sweeter' for 'more lovely' in the second line, which does not properly scan, and 'estate' instead of 'a date' in the fourth."

Collier had been leaning over the table, intent on the manuscript. Now he straightened and waved a dismissive hand.

"I am not impressed," he said. "Any of these *soi-disant* earlier stages of the text are within the grasp of an impostor."

Dyce brought his huge head around and stared at Collier. "That judgment came hellish quick, my friend."

"I do not wish to see Mr. Heber imposed upon," replied Collier loftily.

"Nor does any man here," said Madden, taking off his spectacles and applying the magnifier once again. "The corrections are the same ink, same orthography as the inscription, presumably done in anticipation of the presentation."

Heber went through the manuscript one page at a time. There were another five sonnets with more than two corrections, and word substitutions in several others. When they had finished, Madden reapplied his spectacles and looked up.

After a long silence Walcot said,

"Well, gentlemen, Shakespeare or no?"

Heber turned and peered up at Collier and Dyce. "My question precisely."

Collier, still tense, snapped, "I have nothing more to say." He glanced towards the doorway, nodded to the other experts, and moved away to speak to a man who had just entered the room.

Dyce slowly smiled at Collier's retreating back.

"I would normally be guided by my learned colleague, but I must say I find nothing objectionable about the manuscript. Indeed, the secretary hand of the inscription and corrections appears entirely consistent with what little else survives of Shakespeare's autograph."

"Well said, Dyce," came a quavering voice. "Will you allow an old, old man a little closer proximity?"

"Why, Mr. Perkins." Dyce stepped aside, bowing, and the old man produced a jeweller's lens of his own. After a moment he spoke.

"Finest example of his autograph we're ever likely to see, gentlemen."

"I concur, Mr. Perkins," said Madden. "I confess I had my doubts, but the handwriting is unimpeachable."

Ned let out his breath slowly, so softly that only Walcot appeared to hear him. Heber stood up, reaching into his pocket.

"Ha, sir. You will see I have this morning's envelope, the seal quite untouched. Perhaps you will allow me to open it now?"

"Please do, Mr. Heber," replied Ned.

Heber broke the seal with a smile but his face went hard when he read the price.

"Three thousand pounds, sir! It is nothing short of extortion."

It was the same tone Heber had used that morning when he complained of Ned's quibbling. Ned's response was equally firm.

"There is no extortion, sir. The manuscript is mine to price and you need only say no."

"What folly leads you to believe anyone would pay this amount for such a small thing?" Heber sounded almost plaintive.

"The finest poetry ever written in English, in a manuscript corrected by Shakespeare's own hand? May I remind you that the Marquess of Blandford paid over two thousand pounds for a *printed* Boccaccio in the Roxburghe auction?"

"Times have changed, Mr. Marston," said Dyce. "The identical copy of Boccaccio fetched only nine hundred-odd pounds when it was reoffered in 1819 and no-one would suggest the market has since improved."

Ned stood up, looking around at variously puzzled and hostile faces. Madden's was bright red – not much hope of an offer from the British Museum. Only Walcot's was friendly; Collier by now had disappeared altogether. Ned caught the Doctor's eye, smiled, and addressed the group.

"Gentlemen, I am grateful to all of you for your time and your expert analysis. This evening should remind us all that what drops out of public view can be forgotten and mistaken later."

He picked up the manuscript and began rewrapping it. "I expect someday my countrymen will be grateful that this went back to America."

Ned bent over the table to tie the brown paper up with string. Afterwards he gazed once more around the room. The crowd was a little thinner and there were spaces at the table where some of the groups had broken up to join the Shakespeare audience. Dyce, Madden, and Perkins were saying their farewells to Heber, who was still standing, pale with anger. Dyce caught Ned's eye and bowed, as did Perkins. Madden turned on his heel and strode from the room.

Dr. Walcot took Heber's arm, encouraging him to sit.

"You are not well, sir," Walcot said. "We must bring you a cordial."

"Pah, Doctor," replied Heber. "It is nothing. Or I should say nothing but the man's insolence."

"I do not find him insolent, Mr. Heber. I have never felt so close to Shakespeare as in the presence of that manuscript. There is magic in it."

"Pah!" said Heber again, but he resumed his seat, breathing heavily. Ned pulled out his watch; it was just a few minutes short of nine o'clock. He caught Walcot's eye, pointed at the watch and then at the door. Walcot raised a hand in silent farewell.

CHAPTER XIII

L iam Gallagher was waiting outside. "A grand building, sir, is it not?"

"Grand indeed, Gallagher. But I shall lose no sleep if I never see it again."

Ned looked at the sky, fleecy clouds around a sliver of new moon. The clear weather had brought a chill to the air and Ned was glad of his overcoat. He had already buttoned the manuscript into its inner pocket and the two men headed companionably east along the Strand, past St. Clement's Church and Temple Bar and into Fleet Street.

Ned had wanted money in the bank before he started his search for Vanessa, something to offer her if she was still alive. Now all he had was Walcot's hundred-odd pounds, some ill-gotten gains from betting, and what was left of his wits. But he was ready to get out of London, and was hoping – even praying – for an early reply from Admiral Austen.

They crossed Fleet Bridge. As the Belle Sauvage Inn loomed out of the darkness on their left, they heard the sound of rapid footsteps. Four men emerged from the shadow of the inn, their hats pushed down low. One in each pair carried a cudgel.

There was no hope of a safe haven so Ned turned to face them. One of the men with cudgels spoke to Gallagher.

"What brings you 'ere, mate?"

"Sure it's the evening air, brother," said Gallagher conversationally.

"We've business with the gentleman. Why don't you stow yer gab and go along for the evening air somewheres else."

Ned had thought of speaking but anger overwhelmed him. The humiliation he still felt at running away from Shakespeare's time combined with his resentment at the way he'd been treated this evening. And now someone was after his manuscript, someone who both knew that he had it and knew it was genuine. The only possible person was John Payne Collier, who had disappeared before the discussion ended. Collier, whom Walcot had said was too poor to collect as seriously as he might wish.

With all the force he could muster Ned kicked the speaker in the groin. The man crumpled forward with a gasp and Ned caught his cudgel before it hit the pavement, swinging it hard around at the next in line. It glanced off the man's left arm but he'd already started to swing his own club at Ned.

Gallagher intercepted that blow and both cudgels flew into the road. The other two men had circled either side and Gallagher called "Back to back, Marston."

Ned took his position and the three men still standing began to look wary. One put up his fists and Gallagher called "Come on, then."

"All we're after is the book in 'is pocket. Throw it 'ere an' there'll be no harm done."

Ned's overcoat was constricting and he threw his shoulders back to loosen it as best he could. As he did so he thought protectively of the little manuscript buttoned inside. Then he met the eyes of the man closest to him.

"Let's see what you've got."

The man laughed. Clearly he didn't think Ned posed much of a threat but as he came forward Ned ambushed him with a quick left hook, connecting with the side of his nose. Ned felt the jolt of pain in his knuckles that signalled a good punch.

Gallagher was in the thick of it, clearly giving as good as he got and humming a tune to himself. Ned recognised the music, "Là ci darem la mano," the aria from Mozart's *Don Giovanni*. He almost laughed out loud: "Give me your hand," Gallagher was asking. But he had no time for the joke. The third man was crossing the road, going after the cudgels.

Gallagher saw it too and muttered, "There's no sport in the bastards." He ducked the first of a one-two sequence of punches from his antagonist, but took the second on the chin. He shook his head, a little dazed, and then brought forth a tremendous right cross, slamming into his opponent's jaw and lifting him sideways off his feet.

Ned could hear the unmistakable crunch as the man's jaw broke, but in the same instant he took a hard jab in the solar plexus that doubled him over. He ducked to one side, gasping as he barely avoided a follow-up punch from his opponent. From the corner of his eye Ned could see Gallagher leap across the road, catching the third man as he started to lift a cudgel out of the gutter. In one quick move Gallagher had it out of his hand and swung it to the back of the man's head, laying him out flat. Then he advanced on Ned's opponent, who turned tail, running as fast as his legs would carry him back across Fleet Bridge.

Ned, still trying to catch his breath, surveyed the scene. One man was stretched out on the far pavement, barely moving. The one with the broken jaw had sat up and the leader who'd caught Ned's kick was still on the ground, rocking back and forth with pain.

"This is the one we want," Gallagher said, jerking the last to his feet.

The man groaned as his body straightened and Gallagher said,

"You're probably after wishing the constables would come save you, but they won't. My friend has some questions, an' you'd do well to answer."

The leader spat and Gallagher casually backhanded him across the mouth, splitting the man's upper lip.

"I've nothing to tell," he said.

"Your partner asked me for my book," Ned said. "That's something."

The man tried to shrug but the movement made him wince.

"Got a call to an upstairs room at the Belle," he said. "Man behind a screen threw out a sovereign. Said there'd be five more for each of us if we brought back a red book from a tall gentleman dressed like you, who'd be along within five minutes."

"Almost missed your chance, didn't you?" said Gallagher.

"Aye," he answered. "And 'e never said the gent'd 'ave a fucking Irish bruiser keeping him company."

"You never saw your employer then," said Ned.

The man hesitated an instant too long before shaking his head.

This time Ned hit him. "What did he look like?"

The man shook his head.

"About my size?" Ned demanded. "Grey hair, round face?"

Gallagher moved in again and at the last minute the man gave a quick nod.

So it was Collier, no doubt about it.

"He might still be there," said Gallagher, "waiting for the book."

"He might be there," Ned replied. "Or he might be somewhere else altogether. I don't think we'll get any more out of this one. Honour code of thieves, I suppose. And whoever it was will deny everything anyway."

"It has to be one of your Antiquaries, doesn't it?"

Ned nodded. "I know who it is and to hell with it." He looked at the leader. "Did he tell you my name?"

"No." The ringleader had pulled himself together and become sullen. "But it was a scurvy 'un to kick me that way."

"And right and proper for four men to come after me, thinking I was alone? What kind of a town is this?"

"London-town," said Gallagher. He turned away contemptuously and Ned followed. As they walked up Ave-Mary Lane towards the Bell Inn, Gallagher tossed the cudgel aside. Ned remembered why he'd laughed.

"How do you come to sing Mozart in the middle of a street fight?"

Gallagher lit up. "*Don Giovanni*," he said happily. "My niece an' her friend took the missus and me to Drury-Lane. Must have been fifteen years ago, when they were still in London. Never heard anything like it in my life."

As they entered the Bell's courtyard Ned glanced inside his coat, realizing he'd split the lining along one sleeve. But the manuscript was safe and the rest of his new wardrobe undamaged. Apart from an angry spot on one cheekbone, a sore belly and some swollen knuckles, so was his body. He touched his cheek gently and caught Gallagher grinning at him.

"Not so bad a night out, was it?"

Ned smiled back. "Not bad at all. But you'll have to let me make it worth your while."

"Not a penny, sir. Haven't had such a fine time since I was a lad in Dublin."

CHAPTER XIV

Ned woke in the night from the pain in his knuckles and when Saturday dawned he saw that both his hands were still swollen. He cursed to himself, remembering the buckets of ice water in which he used to soak his hands after boxing – and that was when he used gloves. He splashed his face from the basin and, realizing how cold its water was, he immersed his hands for a few minutes.

As the cold water eased the pain Ned discovered he felt happier. At first he couldn't understand why. He still had no real news of Vanessa and his best hope for hatching a nest egg had become a dismal failure.

He slowly concluded it was the fight that had changed his mood. 'Not a bad night,' Gallagher had said. It had helped Ned accept that he intended to survive in this time, one way or another.

When Nell came with his breakfast tray he asked if there was anything in the post. There wasn't, so he had a day free to explore possibilities. Last night he'd been ready to leave London, but this morning he appreciated that Vanessa could easily be here too. She might be settled, even married with children. He had to make contingency plans, whether he found her or not.

Tying his cravat with swollen hands took longer than usual. When he'd finished dressing he took an omnibus to Hoare's Bank to redeposit the Shakespeare manuscript and withdraw some money. Afterwards he walked along the Strand, thinking about John Payne Collier.

Collier had been the only one to challenge the manuscript's authenticity. Had he hoped to discredit it and then buy it on the cheap? Were his hired thugs a last-minute improvisation, or had he learned from Heber where Ned lodged and planned them in advance?

Ned shrugged. None of it really mattered now that he couldn't sell the manuscript. Somehow he was going to have to find a way to make a living in this time. He'd already made enemies that precluded finding work as a librarian. Still, he thought, there were rare-book dealers in 1833 London who might need assistants. He knew where some of their shops were. It was time to go exploring.

Which one first? A sudden squall of wind and sleet almost blinded him and he began to sneeze. He saw another pedestrian holding a newspaper over his head. The man caught Ned's eye and muttered, "And this only September." Ned sneezed again, flushed, and abandoned his plans.

He was shivering by the time he reached the Bell's courtyard, where Gallagher had taken cover in the stables.

"Isn't there anywhere in this country one can go to get warm?" Ned called.

"Aye, Bath, Marston. Bath's the place."

Ned decided to go, whether or not he received a letter from the Austens, provided he survived whatever disease he'd just caught. Bath couldn't be more expensive than London, and he could put to rest any lingering doubts he had about the Miss Horwood who was supposed to live there.

As he stepped into the Inn another bout of sneezing took him. He pulled out his handkerchief and covered his face. A letter was waiting for him at the bar. Ned tore it open, splashing water from his sleeves onto the envelope. The writing paper had a Pimlico address and the note read:

Sir,

Against my own judgment I am resolved to pay yr. price for the Shakspere ms. I shall meet you at Messrs. Coutts, Bankers, The Strand, on Monday 16th inst., at ten o'clock.

Please advise

Yr. most obd't serv't

R. Heber

Ned folded the note with a smile, wrote a reply and went to bed. He stayed there with a warming pan and a streaming cold through Sunday, but concluded his transaction with Heber on schedule. On Wednesday morning he had a letter from Mrs. Francis Austen and that afternoon, stuffy-nosed but improving, he climbed aboard the coach for Bath.

PART FOUR: SEPTEMBER 1833 (CONTINUED)

You must learn some of my philosophy. Think only of the past as its remembrance gives you pleasure.

Jane Austen
Pride and Prejudice
Volume III, Chapter XVI

CHAPTER I

The outside air was crisp with the onset of autumn, but the mid-September sky was blue and the patrons at Molland's tearooms in Bath's fashionable Milsom Street were high-spirited and elegant. Vanessa watched them as she waited for her tea to be measured: gossiping young women, lovers flirting, and old ladies planning their card parties at the Assembly Rooms. Fourteen years in Bath meant familiar faces in almost any crowd and Vanessa nodded as a couple of her piano pupils smiled at her.

As the shop assistant added tea-leaves to the scale Vanessa felt a touch on her arm. She spun around – old habits were slow to die – and saw a man about her own age. His grey eyes were familiar, penetrating eyes in a handsome, albeit somewhat battered, face. He wore what Meg would have called a modish suit, probably bespoke, she thought.

"Miss Horwood, I believe." He bowed.

As she recognised him she also saw her nightmare vision of the same man in Shakespearean costume. She nearly staggered.

"Ned Marston." Her whisper was almost a hiss, as the sense of betrayal she'd carried so long flooded her consciousness.

"Will you take a cup of tea, madam?" She could tell he was oblivious to her feelings. His eyes were dancing with pleasure.

Behind the counter the girl continued to measure the tea. Vanessa struggled to regain her composure and as she did she felt a glimmer of hope. She turned back to Ned, speaking carefully.

"I have had my tea, sir, and am about to walk up to Lansdown. Would you care to join me? The hill is a fine constitutional."

"I have just come from there, ma'am. From your Gamekeeper's Cottage at Beckford's Tower. But there was no-one at home."

Vanessa felt a surge of resentment. "May I ask, sir, by what means you discovered my residence there?"

Ned became serious. "From your friend Mrs. Austen. Did she not tell you of my enquiry?"

"No, sir. Doubtless she intends to mention it when I see her tomorrow. Now you may walk up the hill again and explain yourself, if you would be so kind."

"It would give me the liveliest pleasure."

Vanessa paid for her canister of tea and led the way out, setting a good pace up Milsom Street. They avoided a couple of carriages crossing George Street and went up the steps and along the handsome paved alley that led towards the Assembly Rooms. Still without speaking Vanessa turned left into Bennett Street and on to the Circus. They paused in the centre and Ned gawked at the imposing circle of uniform, honey-coloured Georgian houses. Vanessa faced him.

"I think we can finally talk," she said.

Ned nodded and she blurted, "Is this a rescue?"

"I can't rescue anyone, not even myself."

Vanessa ignored the implication. "What celebrity manuscript are you chasing today?"

Ned shook his head. "No more celebrities, Vanessa. No more manuscripts."

"Then what the bloody hell *are* you doing here?"

"I'm here for the duration – as trapped as you are. Stranded."

"You'd better go get stranded somewhere else. I don't want you here."

Ned shook his head. "It hasn't been easy for you, has it?"

She looked up into his eyes, which were gentle and full of sympathy.

"My God, Vanessa," he went on. "I'm so glad I found you."

The anger she'd felt since Winchester Gaol overwhelmed her.

"Are you?" she managed to reply. "Well, here." And with a flick of her wrist she emptied the tea canister into his face.

His hands came up reflexively but too late. Then he started to laugh, brushing the tea-leaves from his shoulders and hair.

In a fury Vanessa turned and strode away across the Circus. She could hear him laughing behind her, and then the sound of his footsteps coming after.

CHAPTER II

Vanessa knew Ned was following as she made her way down Brock Street towards the Royal Crescent. She wondered if he was going to make a scene.

"Perfect," she said to herself bitterly. The surge of homesickness she'd felt as she recognised him was a reminder that she'd never fully accepted the life she'd so painfully constructed for herself in Bath. Now she had no choice but to return to it.

Anger boiled within her again, rage at the loss of her own time, rage at the man who had imprisoned her in this one. She had tried to tell herself that Marston had been out of her life for sixteen years and that she'd gotten over the betrayal. What, she asked herself again, is *doing* here?

Ned was still brushing tea-leaves from his jacket as he caught up with her. She could hardly bear to look at him, thought she'd never be able to look at him again without thinking of all she'd lost.

"Go away," she said. "I told you to get stranded somewhere else."

Ned shook his head. "I want to help."

"Fuck off, Marston."

A group of pedestrians was approaching. "Oh, God," cried Vanessa. "One of my students."

She pulled herself together and made small talk for a few minutes, deliberately ignoring Ned, at whom her fourteen year-old girl pupil openly gaped.

When the group finally moved on Ned followed Vanessa west as she continued along Brock Street.

If Marston wasn't here to take her back, he had no reason to be in Bath. He couldn't be thinking she still cared about him, could he? There had to be a way to get rid of him. But how?

They were side-by-side when they reached Margaret's Buildings. Ned took her arm, pulling her to a halt.

"It's too much," he said. "This is the most beautiful town I've ever seen."

Vanessa relaxed a little.

"You've never been here?"

Ned shook his head. She withdrew her arm, sensing his uncertainty. She didn't want the contact, didn't want to be close enough to him to sense any of his feelings. Being close to him reminded her of her own time, and home. Things she couldn't have and didn't want to think about.

She stepped back, looking him up and down.

"I shall give you a tour, Mr. Marston. A *very* short tour, before you leave Bath." She began to walk again.

A few moments later Ned stopped again, in an open field with a view of the Royal Crescent on his right and the city on his left. Vanessa kept her voice light as she insisted there were other crescents and views still more perfect. They paused to take in the scenery, the nearby groups keeping their speech formal. They made small talk about Ned's journey from London and his plan to take the Bath waters. When he mentioned his lodgings in Queen Square, Vanessa grimaced.

"Do you not know about Queen Square, Mr. Marston?"

Ned shook his head.

She gave a reminiscent smile. "'None of your Queens Squares for us,' said the Miss Musgroves."

"I'm not sure I'm any the wiser," said Ned.

"Jane Austen," Vanessa answered. *"Persuasion."*

"You found her, did you not?" She could feel Ned's excitement but refused to meet his eyes. She began to walk again and Ned had to lengthen his stride to keep up.

There were still people all around and Ned's voice remained formal.

"Where should I lodge if not Queen Square?"

"Lansdown Crescent," said Vanessa immediately. "Or Macaulay Buildings the other side. You *descend* to take the Bath-waters, and go back uphill for the air."

"Oh," said Ned. Vanessa knew he had no idea where either place was, and she didn't care.

They passed the western end of Royal Crescent and crossed onto the Common, which was entirely deserted. They walked another fifty yards before Ned spoke.

"Vanessa, you have to know we did everything we could think of to come after you."

"You told me before I left there was nothing you could do if I got stranded."

"That's what they told me when I went to Greece. But when you didn't come back I made them programme the machine to send me to 1817. The screen went blank. We tried again and again, ten years either side. Nothing."

"Then what are you doing here now?"

"I told you I was trapped. It was an accident. I was never supposed to be here." He stopped, smiling to himself. "Or maybe I was, after all."

For an instant, in spite of herself, Vanessa began to warm to him.

Then he said, "I had a Shakespeare manuscript with me," and her anger returned. He'd been smiling about the manuscript, not her. She could tell Ned was flustered, knew he longed for some encouragement, but she refused to give it.

He rushed on. "I sold it to Richard Heber, the greatest book-collector of this time."

Vanessa's eyes were glacial, her back ramrod-straight. "Now you're starting to sound like the mercenary I remember."

"No," said Ned. She could hear the desperation in his voice, see how pale his face was. "The point is I got three thousand pounds for it. We're both stuck in this time and we should share it."

"Are you trying to buy my friendship?" Vanessa's voice was dangerous.

"No!" Ned cried. "You and I are probably all we're ever going to have of the twenty-first century. I'm saying that whatever you might think of me we should try to look after each other."

Along with rage and grief, Ned's unexpected presence had brought Vanessa a flood of memories, memories of everything she most missed in her own time. Ned himself was part of them. She couldn't untangle the man she had begun to love from the man she felt had betrayed her, the man she had grown to hate over her sixteen years of isolation.

She tried to think of Martha Lloyd and the Austens, and of Meg. Especially Meg. But she couldn't make them supplant her sudden, desperate longing for home. The conflict was more than she could bear.

She took a step back, tugging at her skirt, ready to deliver one of her *tae kwon do* kicks. But Ned – damn the man! – faced her openly, bewildered and defenceless, his arms hanging at his sides.

She moved closer, looking into his eyes. "You can't *really* care, can you, Marston? After all these years?"

"It's not so long for me, Vanessa. I always cared, from the first moment I saw you."

"Do you know I'm practically engaged?"

Ned took a step back. "No," he replied. If his face was pale before, now it was ashen.

Vanessa gave a sharp, sarcastic laugh. "An earl's son."

"Do you love him?"

Vanessa choked, her eyes filling with tears. "You stupid, *bloody* man. Can't you see that I don't want love?"

She began to cover her face with her hands, and then she threw herself at him, pummelling the front of his shoulders.

"Shit!" she cried as she hit him. "Oh, shit, shit, shit."

At first Ned didn't move; then he tried to hold her wrists. As he reached for her she threw her arms around him, buried her face in his chest and began to sob. Ned's arms were still outstretched but she felt them slowly, slowly fold around her back.

After a moment she spoke.

"Let. . . go . . . of . . . me."

Ned backed away, holding his hands out in supplication. Vanessa tried to glower at him. But she knew her cheeks were puffy and streaked with tears, and that what she'd intended as a basilisk stare was completely ineffectual. Ned smiled.

"Damn you, Marston," she snarled, turning away up the hill. She walked about ten yards before she looked back.

"Call on us." It was a command, not a request. "At the cottage. Four o'clock tomorrow."

Ned gave her a military salute as Vanessa stalked away.

CHAPTER III

Ned finished his salute, dropping his arm back to his side. He stood on the Common watching Vanessa's retreating back. He felt entirely drained of energy, unable to move.

At the back of his mind an imaginary voice taunted him, reminding him how much he had staked on finding Vanessa, how much he had counted on her still wanting him. Now she'd made it clear: she didn't want him at all.

He managed to silence that voice as he retraced his steps along the Royal Crescent and back to the Circus. Then he headed down Gay Street to Queen Square.

A new interior voice began to chatter, this one offering distractions. Vanessa was right about the air in Bath, the voice said. It got closer and even a little fetid as he neared Queen Square. Was the location of his room really so bad? Surely it was all right for now, and he was paying for it a day at a time. Besides, the voice continued, it was close to the baths.

Reluctantly he came back to reality. This one day might be all he needed. As he entered his lodging-house he thought again of the way Vanessa had kissed him good-bye before she'd time-travelled. For Ned less than a fortnight had passed since that moment. But for her it had been sixteen years. She was his own age now, and for all those sixteen years she'd felt betrayed. How could he blame her for hating him? He was the symbol, the embodiment of everything that had gone wrong for her.

Physically she'd hardly changed from the girl he'd helped send to Jane Austen's time. He knew the dress she was wearing wasn't altogether fashionable, but she looked terrific in its classic contours and low, square bodice. Her blonde curls had been in disarray and she'd worn no make-up, but she was beautiful, more beautiful than he'd remembered her. He couldn't get her image out of his mind.

How could he have been so stupid as to offer to share the proceeds of the Shakespeare manuscript? It had to have sounded like an attempt to buy her friendship, just as she'd said. And she obviously didn't need the money. She was engaged. To an earl's son.

But she'd invited, no commanded, him to appear at her cottage tomorrow. Was she giving him a chance to redeem himself? Or planning to clarify her marching orders? Part of him was ready to leave Bath now, to avoid another confrontation. But he'd accepted her invitation with his parting salute. He owed her this last visit, and she could make of it whatever she wanted.

Ned knew his self-recriminations would never end if he stayed in his lodgings. He thought of visiting the baths. But he remembered the dirt and grease in the afternoon water at Bagnio Court. If he waited till morning the water would be fresh. So he asked his landlord for directions to the bookshops. Bookshops always diverted him. Maybe they'd even let him escape the memory of Vanessa, if only for a few minutes.

The sky had clouded over but it was only a short walk back to the bottom of Milsom Street, near Molland's tearooms. He'd come almost full circle since his walk with Vanessa. As he picked his way through a cluster of carriages rain began to fall and the horses became skittish. Ned barely avoided their hooves as he climbed the kerb to the paving stones of Bond Street. A handsome bookshop on his left bore a plaque declaring it as "Mr. Barrett's." Ned ducked inside.

An overdressed young shop assistant asked if he might be of service and Ned inquired whether they had any books by Jane Austen.

"We have them all, sir," sniffed the assistant. "The last came in this week. We can offer matched sets bound in linen at five shillings the volume."

"May I see?"

The books were in a corner with others of similar size: compact, quite elegant, but the type painfully small.

"I don't think so," Ned said. "Have you none in the original format?"

"None for sale," the young man said. "They are seldom fine enough for our purposes." He paused, taking a pinch of snuff. "We send them down to

Gibbons's second-hand department. We might have one in" – he paused for another pinch, sneezed and went on – "the subscription section."

"Ah," said Ned. "The lending library. Perhaps I had better go see Gibbons."

The rain was still coming down but across the street Ned could see umbrellas in a shop window. He made a dash and bought one. He already had his directions to Gibbons and, armoured against the rain, he promenaded the few hundred yards to a row of shops adjacent to Pulteney Bridge, for the moment quite pleased with himself.

Mr. Gibbons was less pompous than the young man at Barrett's. He wore dusty and slightly dishevelled clothes and had notes on his shirt-cuffs. His spectacles were pushed well down his nose. Salt-and-pepper hair sprouted voluminously on his head and face and even down his neck, where it curled out of his shirt collar. A stack of books was on the counter and he was listing prices as a middle-aged woman anxiously looked on.

"Excellent," said Gibbons. "The last is the best by far: North's Plutarch in the Vautrollier 1579 edition. I can give twelve shillings for it, making my offer for the lot what I hope is a comforting two pounds ten."

"Mr. Gibbons," the woman's voice was plaintive. "I know my husband gave six guineas for that one book. Can there be no improvement in the prices at all?"

"Madam," said Gibbons. "I fear not. Times are poor and I shall be fortunate to get two pounds for it nowadays."

Ned couldn't stand it. "Forgive me, sir, and madam." He bowed to each. "I should be very pleased to buy North's Plutarch. If I gave you, sir, the six guineas just mentioned, could you not protect your profit by giving the lady three of them?"

"Why that is handsome of you, sir." She gave him a broad smile. "Surely, Mr. Gibbons, you cannot gainsay so generous an offer."

"No, indeed I cannot," said Gibbons, trying to remain composed. Ned counted out six sovereigns and six shillings and took possession of the Plutarch, a large folio in a handsome blindstamped binding. Gibbons duly handed three of each coin to the lady, did a sum on his shirt-cuff, and began to count out some more money.

"Two pounds ten, less twelve shillings, madam. Here you are then, another one pound, eighteen."

The lady curtsied.

"Thank you, Mr. Gibbons. Thank you, sir." She left the shop, oblivious of the rain.

"Well, sir," growled Gibbons. "Your interference has cost me a good ten pounds. I've half a mind to give you your six guineas and take back the book."

"Too late for that, Mr. Gibbons. If you were out to cheat the lady, you dug your own grave and walked straight in."

"Hmpf," said Gibbons. "A man can't make a decent profit any more, without some busybody telling him how to run his business."

Ned grinned at him. "Next time make a better offer."

Gibbons shrugged and smiled back.

"*Touché*, sir. Now what had you in mind when you first darkened my door?"

"Jane Austen," said Ned. "That popinjay up at Barrett's only has little clothbound books with tiny type. I want the three-deckers."

"I've only one, *Northanger Abbey and Persuasion*, and it's four volumes not three. A Canadian lady has a standing order for Jane Austen and we're still waiting for *Pride and Prejudice* to turn up."

"Miss Horwood?" asked Ned.

"The very same, sir."

Gibbons stepped back into a storeroom and emerged with the four books, elegantly bound in marbled paper and dark-red leather with gold tooling. He blew dust off their tops before setting them down.

"I won't punish you for taking my Plutarch either. This came out fifteen years ago at twenty-four shillings the set, in boards. I'll sell it at that price, saving you the ten shillings extra you'd have paid for the half binding."

"Done," said Ned. "It's the very one I wanted."

Ned dined at a nearby inn before returning to his room. His book purchases had distracted him, at least for the time being. He began to page through his Plutarch, thinking how Vanessa's fierce beauty earlier that day reminded him of the Amazon warrior Hippolyta. Plutarch had written a life of Theseus, whom Hippolyta had married. Ned was hoping for a description of her. No such luck.

With Vanessa still in mind he turned to his Jane Austen purchase, skipping the first two volumes to start at the beginning of *Persuasion*. He sprawled on his bed, reading without pause for two hours, captivated by the novel's heroine, Anne Elliot, and longing to discover how her story ended. His lamp guttered before he could find out.

The next morning Ned rose soon after sunrise. He'd had a restless night, dreaming of Jane Austen heroines and Amazon princesses. There was no point staying in bed. He went for another walk around town and by eight o'clock was at the Hot Baths. The man in charge was called the serjeant and he asked if this was Ned's first visit. When Ned said yes, he recommended the open pool followed by a private vapour-bath.

"The vapour will cleanse the pores of the sulphurous infusions of the water, sir, and clear the lungs of any impurities such as those of us who inhabit cities cannot avoid. And there is no further charge should you care to use the open bath as well."

Ned paid his four shillings, pleased to see that the place was scrupulously clean, as were the flannels and towels included in the charges. He changed into his flannels and walked carefully across slippery flagstones to a large pool that was the open bath. With the new supply of hot water bubbling up from the sulphurous hot springs below, a pleasant steam rose from the pool's surface. Ned stretched his body and sank to the level of his chin, beginning to feel fully warm and relaxed for the first time in, he thought wryly, centuries. He made a mental note to save money next time and stick to the open bath. And to come often.

The "vapour" turned out to be a steam bath, as cleansing as the serjeant had promised. Contented and armed with the information he needed for future bathing, Ned decided on another luxury: a real breakfast. He had not yet visited the York Hotel, said to be the largest and finest inn outside London. His eggs and bacon were served on silver platters along with fried tomatoes and mushrooms; his coffeepot had its own plate-warmer.

After breakfast Ned took another walk around town, this time under a cloudless sky, finally making his way back to Queen Square and *Persuasion*. He finished the novel well before he needed to leave for Vanessa's cottage and spent an hour pacing his room, imagining a dozen different versions of their impending conversation, none of them pleasant.

Finally he set off towards Lansdown, scarcely noticing the houses on either side in his rapid climb of the steep hill. He arrived both winded and twenty minutes early. Feeling like a fool, he continued up the road to a point overlooking the Tower and its pleasure-gardens. When he returned the gatehouse was unoccupied so Ned walked through. The closer he got to Beckford's folly the more impressive it was, soaring over a hundred feet high and completely dominating the surrounding landscape. Beyond it Ned could see a handsome cottage of Bath stone, partway down a slope and set off by fruit-trees and shrubbery.

As he got closer he could hear piano music drifting out the window. The instrument's tone sounded a little thin for such a powerful piece, but the playing was very accomplished. It was Chopin, the "Revolutionary" etude.

He waited until the final stentorian chords faded, and then knocked on the door.

CHAPTER IV

Vanessa answered, flushed from her performance. Her piano was halfway between the door and the fireplace, a rectangular instrument in an elaborately carved mahogany case. In a small fireplace grate was a smouldering mix of wood and coal and by the hearth a tabby-cat was asleep, its paws curled up by its ears. It was as far from the piano as it could get and still be close to the fire.

Vanessa was on edge, regretting her invitation. She'd lived through so much since she'd been stranded, and only recently had her life truly taken a turn for the better. Marston could not be allowed to interfere.

Ned was looking across the room, alternating between Meg and the cat. Vanessa followed his gaze.

"Katrina is not a musical cat, I fear."

Then Meg rose, holding her needlework, and Vanessa offered a more formal introduction.

"Mr. Marston. May I present my dear friend Miss Megan Gallagher?"

Meg curtsied. "Mr. Marston." Her smile was open and friendly but it changed to an "o" of astonishment when Ned blurted,

"The hostler's family? From the Bell Inn?"

Vanessa watched in silence as Meg and Ned worked through the intricacies of their respective connections with the Bell.

"Can you believe, sir, that Vanessa was there this past fortnight, and not a word did she say to my uncle?"

"The past fortnight?" Ned asked. His face was intent, as though working out a puzzle. After a moment he turned to Vanessa.

"May I ask when you were there, exactly?"

"The night of the ninth, not that it's any of your business. I had a recital on the tenth."

Ned gave a decisive nod, as though the puzzle, whatever it was, had been solved. Meg spoke next.

"Vanessa told me of your arrival in Bath. I trust you heard her playing as you approached the cottage."

"Chopin, if I do not mistake."

Meg stared at Vanessa. "How could he know? You said this was the very latest, just off the Bristol packet?"

Vanessa hid her nerves behind sarcasm. "Mr. Marston must be a connoisseur."

Ned bowed, hiding a smile. Chopin's Revolutionary etude was a staple of the twenty-first century piano repertory, but he would not complain if, for once, a little knowledge from his own time allowed him to appear learned in this one.

"A penny for your thoughts, Mr. Marston," said Meg.

Ned came out of his reverie with a start. "I was thinking that with a cottage like this and two beautiful women in it, there should be two earls as suitors rather than one." Ned tried to smile, but Vanessa could see the effort behind it.

Meg frowned. "You are another Canadian, Mr. Marston?" she asked.

"American," Ned replied, clearly at a loss.

"Then you did not suffer twenty years of war as we did. At present there are at least two or three spinsters our age, in every English town, for every marriageable bachelor." She dropped her eyes. "For a time Vanessa and I did our best to swear off men."

"Not true," Vanessa put in. She turned to Ned with her first smile of the evening. "Megan has defied the odds and has a suitor quite devoted."

Meg blushed. "He's married and no bloody suitor at all. It's yours who matters, love." She looked at Ned. "Vanessa has the next-best thing to an earl, Mr. Marston. An earl's son. Lord James Hamilton, the most eligible bachelor in Bath."

Vanessa's face darkened. "I spent sixteen years in this country with every shopkeeper looking down his nose at me because I'm colonial and poor. Then Robert introduces me to a young man who sees me play the piano and decides he's in love with me."

"Can you blame the young man, Mr. Marston?" Meg asked with a mischievous smile.

"Will I meet this paragon?" Ned asked.

"No," Vanessa said grimly. "He is presently in Scotland with his family. I intend you will be gone by the time he returns."

She looked away, through the archway into the kitchen. When her eyes came back to Ned she could see the pain in his face.

"Is it too soon to wish you happiness?" he asked.

Meg beamed. "I think not, Mr. Marston. The whole town is speaking of their engagement. And Lord Jamie truly is a paragon. Rich as they come. And he loves music."

"Music," Ned repeated. "Speaking of music, I have not heard your piano close to, Miss Horwood. If we haven't put you off entirely, would you play again, another of the Chopin etudes?"

"Oh, yes," said Meg. "The sad one, love. You know the one I mean."

Vanessa knew Ned was trying to direct the conversation away from Jamie. She supposed she should be grateful.

She did her best to smile as she returned to the piano.

"I expect Mr. Marston knows this one too. It's the third one in the book, in E Major."

As her right hand started on the plaintive melody, her left caressing the keys with their lilting accompaniment, she caught a glimpse of Ned, intent on the music. She began to relax, and by the time she reached the complex middle section she was lost in her playing.

Both she and the cat were startled when Ned applauded at the end. Meg joined in, as Katrina jumped away from the fireplace at the unfamiliar noise. The cat gave the room at large an accusing glare, then padded over to Ned, sniffed at his trousers and jumped onto his lap.

Vanessa watched from the piano bench as Ned scratched under Katrina's chin and the cat settled, first turning around twice, then lying with her face over one of his legs and her tail trailing over the other. Ned's hands were strong and square, with a couple of fingers slightly askew, she supposed from boxing injuries. But they were gentle as they stroked along the cat's spine.

She looked down, discomfited, at her own long, tapering fingers. Pianist's fingers. Ned's hands reflected his personality. He was little more than a thug, really, in spite of his library degree. She should never have let herself fall in love with him. The sooner he left Bath, the better.

The cat gave a loud purr, and Meg smiled. "Katrina seems to like your visitor."

"She doesn't know him very well," said Vanessa.

"Do you know Mr. Marston so well yourself that you're after tormenting him?"

"Ned knew my family in Montreal," Vanessa lied, knowing he wouldn't dare deny it and that it would explain their previous acquaintance.

"You never said this was the Ned you spoke of so often," Meg cried. "He *must* have known your family well, for you to treat him like this after so many years."

Vanessa gave Ned an appraising stare. She could tell he was pleased at Meg's reference to him as "spoke of so often." Vanessa needed the rest of his story soon, to be sure he posed no danger. She knew from her own experience there was nothing he could *say* that would betray her. But his presence alone was a threat. She made a plan and then smiled, as innocently as she could.

"Mr. Marston, Megan and I are dining with friends before the theatre this evening. Will you join us?"

Meg started forward in astonishment. But Ned spoke first.

"Surely this is too short notice?"

Meg recovered quickly. "No indeed, Mr. Marston. Robert has booked a table for five at the York Hotel and there will surely be room for a sixth. You are most welcome."

"Then it's settled," said Vanessa. "We'll put on our walking boots and rejoin you in a moment."

The two women went upstairs, leaving Ned with the cat in his lap. Once the bedroom door was closed Meg whirled on Vanessa.

"You said you wanted him gone from Bath."

"I know I did, and I do. But I haven't had all his news and, well, I suppose I want to hear more of home." True as far as it goes, Vanessa thought, but Meg isn't going to be satisfied. She tried another tack.

"Besides, I think Robert and the Austens would like him, don't you?"

Meg's face glowed. "Ach, they would at that. They're men's men, the three of them. And there's something else about your Ned. . . ."

"He's not my Ned," Vanessa snapped.

"I didn't mean it that way, love."

CHAPTER V

The cat shifted on Ned's lap, but showed no sign of leaving. Ned was dumbfounded as Vanessa and Meg climbed the stairs. Clearly Vanessa didn't want to be rid of him just yet, but why? Did she want more of his news? Could she have guessed the significance of her being at the Bell Inn on September 9th, the night he'd arrived? Or did she just want him to promise to get out of town, and to say where he was going so she could avoid him?

As the three walked down Lansdown Hill Meg asked a few more questions about her uncle in London, but Vanessa remained silent. They arrived at the same York Hotel where Ned had breakfasted that morning. In the lobby were two middle-aged men seated at a table, deep in conversation. One of them, in uniform, spoke animatedly as an older woman next to him concentrated on her needlework. All rose for Vanessa's introductions and Robert Carpenter, the one in civilian clothes, pumped Ned's hand, grinning.

"So," said Robert. "A Canadian friend of Vanessa's family. First we've heard of a family in all these years."

Ned darted a glance at Vanessa. "American, sir. From Philadelphia."

He bowed to Martha, who nodded in response. Then he turned to Frank Austen, humbled. Ned knew that this was not only an important man in his own right, but perhaps his sister Jane's favourite brother.

Good-looking, Ned thought as they shook hands. Shorter than he'd imagined. A serious, intelligent face. If Jane had a feminine version of those features she'd have been prettier than her sister Cassandra's sketch – the only likeness Ned had seen – suggested.

They walked towards the hotel dining-room where Robert detoured to speak to the headwaiter. The man nodded, bowed to the ladies, and ushered the six of them to a private chamber upstairs. When they were seated Robert spoke to Ned.

"I've already ordered for the ladies, Mr. Marston. And instructed the waiter to bring more of the Admiral's and my own fodder for you. Hope you won't mind."

Ned saw Vanessa's eyes flicker with amusement. He knew she could tell that he wanted to know more, but didn't think it polite to ask. Meg came to his rescue.

"Salt beef and biscuit, Mr. Marston. Royal Navy fare."

"Are you both still in the Navy, gentlemen?" asked Ned.

Robert shook his head. "Admiral Austen got his flag three years ago and bids fair to end his days as Admiral of the Fleet. But I've been out near twenty years. The Admiralty made me post in the year twelve and I retired from the service after the war."

"A Post Captain," Ned said, still sounding uncertain.

Frank spoke next. "Carpenter and his frigate *Corinth* emptied the seas of French prizes."

"Sweetest sailor you ever saw," Robert interjected.

"Whilst I," Frank continued, "his senior officer, did convoy duty in the frozen Baltic." He smiled at Robert, affectionately but not without irony. "Carpenter retired rich after the war. So did his flag-officer. I returned to Hampshire on half pay."

"I cannot deny it, Marston," said Robert. "I set up my cotton factory with Bonaparte's money. But I did spend *some* time on the French blockade, Austen."

"Captain Wentworth," declared Ned.

"What's that?" Robert replied. But Vanessa and Frank Austen smiled.

"My sister's last novel," said Frank. "Wentworth was a frigate captain like you, Carpenter, turned ashore rich."

"Perhaps like you as well, Frank," Vanessa interjected. "If I do not take too great a liberty saying so, Wentworth was also a man who followed his heart and married for love."

Frank glanced at his wife, who blushed and dropped her eyes. Then a troupe of waiters arrived, uncovering dishes. One began to carve a roast beef; another divided a salmon for the ladies.

"We'll have spotted dick afterwards," Robert said, his face bright with anticipation.

Meg laughed. "His pudding alone marks him for a Navy man, does it not, Mr. Marston?"

Robert spoke before Ned could reply. "Indeed it does, my dear. But before we begin let us lift our glasses to Marston's arrival, and to us all becoming better acquainted."

The claret was dark and aromatic, reminding Ned of the wine he'd drunk with Dr. Walcot and Sir Frederic Madden not so long ago. Robert told them to eat with dispatch, that they would lose their seats if they were late for the theatre. By the time Ned finished dinner, claret, and the heavy suet pudding with two glasses of madeira, he felt bloated and sleepy.

Robert was pulling back Meg's chair when Vanessa asked a question.

"Have you booked this room for the evening, Robert?"

"No, my dear. Why should you ask?"

"If you had, I thought I might stay and speak to Mr. Marston."

Robert and Meg exchanged glances.

"I shall ask the concierge," said Robert. "They see enough of my money that I cannot believe they would deny me, unless the room is particularly bespoke."

He returned a moment later. "It is yours until ten o'clock."

Vanessa rose and kissed his cheek. "I shall meet you after the theatre, or perhaps even" – she gave Ned a sideways look – "at the interval."

The others stood and the four theatre-goers prepared to depart. As a parting gesture Robert poured the last of the madeira into Vanessa and Ned's glasses.

Ned waved at his. "I'm half asleep already," he protested.

But as he spoke he realised he wasn't. He'd been sluggish five minutes earlier, but the prospect of being alone with Vanessa brought him wide awake.

"Won't your friends miss you at the theatre?" he asked.

Martha Austen turned back. "It is a new farce by an author Vanessa despises. You have given her a blessing, Mr. Marston."

CHAPTER VI

Vanessa exchanged farewell kisses with Martha and Meg. As four pairs of footsteps receded in the hall she pulled the door closed.

"It is altogether improper to be an unmarried woman dining alone in a private room with a man, but the staff here is famously discreet. As Meg and Robert can attest. And now we can speak freely."

"I like them all," Ned said. "Have you known them long?"

"Meg since my first day at Winchester Gaol." She watched Ned closely, expecting a shocked response that never came. Finally he replied.

"I found a *Hampshire Chronicle* notice in the British Library files." He gave a wry smile. "I told you yesterday I wanted to come after you in 1817. I tried to get the engineers to time-transport me to your cell."

Vanessa snorted. "Wouldn't have done much good if they had. In fact it would have made things worse, much worse. I was in the Women's Debtors and Felons Gallery.

"But I don't want to talk about that. I met Martha even before Meg. She was Martha Lloyd then, Jane's best friend. We stayed in touch after I got out of gaol and she married Frank five years ago. Meg and Robert have been together more than fifteen, but Robert has a wife in London. She left him soon after they were married, but she's never given him grounds for divorce."

Ned nodded. "I saw how he and Meg looked at each other. It's nice to see them so attracted after all those years."

Vanessa smiled. "Yes, they are. But Robert hates what he calls making her dishonest. He's suggested selling his factory and taking her to Australia."

"Would you go with them?"

Vanessa shook her head. "No." She stood up, realising it was time to talk about Jamie. She turned her back on Ned before continuing.

"My romance – I suppose that's what it is – is more straightforward. Jamie really is one of the most eligible men in Bath. He promotes my music all over town and tells anyone who'll listen that we'll soon be married. I think the reason the Assembly Rooms are full for my recitals nowadays is because half the audience comes for him. Friends, relations, and hangers-on."

She knew Ned was probably expecting a stronger declaration of love for her noble suitor, but she didn't care. She began to pace the room, pausing at the window to look out at the city lights before facing him again.

"I'm sorry I treated you so badly yesterday."

"I understood how you felt," Ned replied. "You couldn't have known we were trying to come back for you." He looked away, hesitating. "For what it's worth, I can't blame anyone but myself for being stranded."

"What happened?"

"It's a long story, but I think I finally understand most of it. You gave me the part I was missing earlier tonight."

He paused. "Do you go from Bath to the Bell Inn often?"

Vanessa shook her head. "Meg and I lived at the Bell after we got out of gaol. But after we moved to Bath in 1819 I only went back a couple of times. I think the last was in 1823, until I went for the recital at the beginning of last week."

Ned nodded. "That has to be it. I told you we tried to time-transport ten years either side of 1817."

He paused again. "Go on," Vanessa said.

He smiled in reply – a forced smile, she thought.

"Okay," he said. "You'll understand why this isn't easy in a minute. . . . I let someone else get stuck in my travel pulse with me. The machine malfunctioned. It couldn't handle the second body, had no instructions for it. I think what happened is that it reverted to your signal, sought you out at the closest geographical point to where I was when I left 1607. I still don't understand why I didn't go to 1817, but the same rule must have applied as when the engineers tried to send me after you. The machine could only look for you in London more than ten years after your arrival, and once it found you it dumped me there too."

Vanessa shook her head. "What about the person with you? He – or she – would have been travelling to the future, which I thought was impossible."

Ned refused to meet her eyes. She had a premonition of what was coming next.

"Live people can't travel to the future," he said. "This one was dead."

Even though she'd felt it coming, Ned's statement shocked her. She stared at him, holding her breath.

His face was pale. "He wasn't dead from the time-travelling. He was dead before the pulse took him."

He stood up, put his hands on the dining-table, and leaned towards her.

"I should probably leave now. You won't want anything more to do with me when I tell you I was the one who killed him."

"You *killed* him," Vanessa almost whispered. "My God, Ned, you broke the cardinal rule of time-travel."

Ned had started for the door as Vanessa spoke. Now he turned back.

"Don't you think I know that?" His voice was as low as hers but it was full of misery, close to breaking. "Our own time, and *this* time, could be completely changed and it would be my fault."

He looked so desperate that Vanessa relented. "Don't go," she said. "What are you going to do now?"

"I don't know," he said. "I'm as trapped as you are. I thought I could work with books in London, but I spoiled that. Then I thought I might feel more at home in Philadelphia. . . ." His voice trailed off.

In spite of herself Vanessa was starting to feel sorry for him, remembering her own first months as a stranded time-traveller. At least Meg had been with her. Meg had kept her sane.

"Philadelphia makes sense," she said gently.

"But I'd hardly know the place," he replied. "And I didn't want to leave England without trying to find you."

"Even though you knew you couldn't do anything to help."

Ned shook his head. "I was stupid to think I could. But I wanted to see if you were alive." He looked down, and then gave her a shy glance as he continued in a small voice. "And I wanted to see if you still felt the same way about me."

Vanessa could feel her face go hard with denial.

Ned quickly added, "And the Gallaghers said I could get warm in Bath."

This was something to which she could respond. "The Gallaghers told me that too. But it'll be cold enough here in a couple of months."

Ned was still by the door, but he'd stopped looking like he was about to run away.

She suppressed a smile. "Maybe you should go to Florida for the winter."

Ned brightened. "That's not a bad line for a Regency gentlewoman."

She smiled for real this time. "Sometimes I can't help myself," she replied, resuming her seat. "I think you'd better tell me the rest of your story."

Ned came back to his chair, opposite hers. He stared out the window as he described his first book purchases, the fight with Judith Shakespeare's ruffians, and Nicholas Ling's shop. His voice tightened as he recounted his growing friendship with Shakespeare, John Marston's jealous rage, and finally the gift of the manuscript sonnets. Her eyes were on him as he tried to say more but he choked, covering his face with one hand.

Only when Ned stopped speaking did Vanessa realise she'd been holding her breath, spellbound. After a moment she said softly,

"You didn't want to leave, did you?"

Ned shook his head. He was hoarse when he replied.

"I had no choice. John would have goaded Shakespeare into fighting and Shakespeare wouldn't have stood a chance. And I think if John had killed me, Will might have challenged him anyway. I couldn't take the risk."

"No," she agreed. "You couldn't. It's odd how different things were for us. When I first saw you at Molland's I felt certain you were there to take me home and I knew I wanted to go, more than anything. That's why I was so furious with you."

She dropped her eyes, needing another introspective moment. Her longing to return to her own time felt like a betrayal of her friends, not to mention Lord Jamie. But Ned himself didn't feel like a threat anymore, or like part of that betrayal. She looked at him, allowing herself to feel the sympathy in his return gaze. But it turned out to be more than she could bear. She turned away, asking another leading question as she did so.

"What happened after you decided to keep the peace for Shakespeare?"

"John Marston's bullies caught up with me as I reached the time-traveller. I couldn't run fast enough to escape."

"But you tried?"

"Oh yes," Ned said. "But the same men had beaten me up the night before. I had a bad leg."

Vanessa shook her head, bemused. "And with all the beatings you'd still have stayed, if it hadn't been for your namesake."

"Maybe an ancestor as well as a namesake." He met Vanessa's eyes with an intensity that made her flinch. "But no," he said. "I didn't want to leave, but I would never have stayed. I had to try to find you. . . ."

His voice trailed off. Vanessa watched as he struggled to find more neutral ground for their conversation.

"You seem so settled here," he said. "How did you do it?"

"It was Meg," she said simply. "And for the last couple of months there's been Jamie." She looked straight at him. "I'm not going to let you spoil that."

Ned gave a wan smile. "I've spoiled enough already. I'll do anything you want."

"Even leave?"

"Just say the word."

Vanessa sighed with relief. "Thank you. Is there anything else I should tell you?"

"I could ask questions all night," said Ned. "Especially about Jane Austen. But since we're supposed to be old acquaintances I'd better ask what you've said about your past. Don't you get questions about your family?"

"Oh, yes," she said. "I tell them my parents are dead and my uncles sent me to England. The less you say, the better."

Ned nodded. "I told people in London that my grandfather left Shropshire for Philadelphia before the American Revolution. It's true, too, except he was my six or seven times great-grandfather."

"You really would do better back in America, you know. Your money would buy a lot of land."

"I don't know what I'd do with land," he said. "I'm a bookman." He hesitated. "Have you ever looked at American printings from the 1830s?"

She raised an eyebrow, expecting some kind of joke, but he was serious.

"I know it sounds trivial, but it means a lot to me. Those books are junk. Cheap paper, cheap bindings. I can't live in a country where people think that's all books need to be."

Vanessa would have laughed, but the conviction in his voice prevented her. Ned was a maze of contradictions. He'd horrified her when he admitted killing a man. Then he'd brought her close to tears as he told the rest of his story. Now he sounded like an old maid, fussing over the aesthetics of American book production. Nonplussed, she waited for him to finish.

"Do you suppose I could set up a bookshop?" he asked.

This was completely unexpected. "Here?"

Ned looked anxious. "I don't know. Maybe. I can't help thinking Gibbons could use some competition. When I walked into his shop yesterday he was practically stealing books from an old woman down on her luck."

Vanessa liked Ned for that. Honesty mattered to her too, and she'd wondered about Gibbons. But she shook her head.

"I don't know anything about bookshops. But surely if *you're* lost the time-travel people will do all they can to find you. You're more important than I am."

Ned bristled. "No, I'm not. The only reason I went to Shakespeare's time was to raise money so we could keep trying to search for you. I don't know what will happen now. I told Caroline they should mortgage their houses, but even if they do there may be no way to rescue us."

Vanessa shook her head. "If it's true that your time-travel pulse somehow went looking for me, there has to be more to this than they've figured out so far."

Ned nodded. "That seems right. If I can come from 1607 to you, then we both ought to be able to go the other two hundred years, back to our own time."

"Except for one thing," Vanessa said. "You had an active pulse in 1607."

"Yes," Ned replied. "It malfunctioned, but it was active. We don't have anything like that now."

"We're stuck," she said. Then she gave a mischievous smile. "And even if you *are* more important than I am, they'll never look for you in this time. What if they just find me?"

"I hope you'll tell them that I'm here too."

"What if they find me before you get here? – got here – whatever."

Ned recoiled. "They could, couldn't they? And you'd never know I came."

"But then if I weren't here, you *wouldn't* come, would you?"

"This is too much for me," Ned said. "Let's talk about something else."

At that moment there was a knock at the door. It was the concierge, telling them it was time to go.

"Walk with me, Mr. Marston," Vanessa said formally. "I doubt the play is finished and I should be glad of your company."

The busy nighttime streets and pavements kept their talk superficial. Vanessa pointed out shops and landmarks. As they approached the theatre she could feel Ned becoming edgy. His voice became an urgent whisper.

"May I see you again?"

His tension was contagious.

"Why?" she asked sharply. "You have to leave soon, you know."

"I know. Maybe just once or twice? To hear more about what you've done. To talk about things we can't say to anyone else in this time."

Vanessa took a deep breath, knowing she wanted that too. She let her shoulders drop.

"I can do that," she sighed. "At least until Jamie comes back. And then you have to go."

Vanessa was wrong about the theatre. The play had ended ten minutes earlier and her friends were waiting outside, with discontented looks that confirmed her suspicion that the new play would be dull. Ned accompanied them back to the York Hotel, where Robert called a carriage for Vanessa and Meg. As he took Meg's arm to help her up Vanessa spoke to Ned.

"Megan and I shall attend the ball at the Assembly Rooms tomorrow evening, Mr. Marston. Eligible gentlemen are much in demand and we shall expect to see you there. Eight o'clock."

"Good," said Robert, turning from Vanessa and clapping Ned on the shoulder. "A fine invitation, and the answer to the question you are about to ask is yes – I shall certainly be there as well. And so will the Austens, though I anticipate we shall spend much of our time at the card-tables."

Ned handed Vanessa into the carriage, bowed, and started to turn away, but as Vanessa settled herself Robert called Ned back.

"Stay a moment, sir. I have another invitation for you." He turned, looking up at Vanessa. "Megan was concerned you might have given Marston marching orders. She wanted to forestall them by asking him to breakfast with us tomorrow. But perhaps your invitation supplants this other."

"I should not wish to impose, Captain," said Ned.

Good, Marston, Vanessa thought. At least you have some manners.

But Meg spoiled her hopes. "Vanessa's invitation does *not* supplant this one, Mr. Marston. Join us here at ten o'clock."

Robert bowed and Ned, who seemed dazed at all the social whirl, followed suit. As the carriage pulled away Meg turned to Vanessa, eyes bright.

"How was your evening? Did you get the rest of the news about your family?"

"Shh," Vanessa replied. "I'll tell you tomorrow."

"I want to hear now. You seemed so annoyed with him. I was afraid you'd send him away."

"You can see I didn't," Vanessa replied. "Not yet, anyway. The ball should distract him well enough. He'll be surrounded by husband-hunters. But why did you have to invite him to breakfast as well?"

"So I can get to know him better."

"I don't *want* you to know him better. He's too dangerous."

Meg's teeth showed in the dark as she smiled. "That's what I like about him, love. I've never in my entire life met anyone who reminded me so much of you."

CHAPTER VII

It was raining the next morning as the two women once again walked down Lansdown Hill to the York Hotel. They shed their wet coats in the lobby and joined the men in the dining room, where Robert had taken a small alcove.

Ned and Robert were already engrossed in conversation, looking for all the world like old friends. They stood and bowed. No sooner were they seated than Robert spoke to Meg.

"I have taken the liberty, my dear, of suggesting that Marston invite you to dance at the Assembly Rooms tonight."

Vanessa knew this would prompt a laugh from Meg.

"Of course you would. It gives you more time for your whist."

"And," Robert riposted, "it spares *you* having me tread all over your feet."

"You are not so bad as that," Meg protested.

"I am," Ned put in. "Your feet don't stand a chance with me as your partner."

"Is that true, Mr. Marston?" asked Meg. "Perhaps Vanessa and I should come to the hotel beforehand to show you some of the dances."

Vanessa didn't want Ned receiving so much solicitude.

"You go, Meg," she said shortly. "I'll meet you at the Assembly Rooms afterwards."

The waiters arrived with coffee and tea, and a platter of Bath buns with curds and jams. Meg clapped her hands with pleasure. By the time they finished the sun had come out.

"Let's walk," said Vanessa, pointing to the window.

She could see Meg and Robert reach an unspoken agreement.

"No, love," Meg said softly. "Be off with Mr. Marston, the two of you."

Vanessa still wasn't sure why Meg was so insistent on giving her time alone with Ned, but she decided not to argue. Jamie would be furious if he found out, but the disobedient girl in her said 'go anyway.' Besides, she told herself, she was longing to be outdoors.

She led Ned in the direction of Gibbons's bookshop and Pulteney Bridge, setting a brisk pace to avoid more conversation. But Ned was undaunted. As they settled into their stride he began to ask more about Robert and Meg.

"I barely know either of them," he said, "but after two meetings they could almost be my closest friends in the world."

Vanessa glanced at him, touched by the longing in his voice.

"They are mine," she replied.

She could tell Ned was waiting for more, but there was nothing to add. Soon they reached the bridge and some stone steps leading down to the river.

"The path goes south and then west," Vanessa said, pausing at the top of the steps. "We can either cut back at the bend or go all the way round to the quay." Her rebellious mood was back and she failed to hide a smirk. "I can point out a few sights if you aren't squeamish."

"Squeamish?" asked Ned.

But Vanessa had anticipated his question and started down the steps to avoid answering. At the bottom she pointed back at Pulteney Bridge. It made a beautiful sight with its elegant shops overlooking the barges moving along the river. She let him stare for a moment.

As they resumed walking she deliberately chose a neutral topic.

"You said you'd visited Gibbons's bookshop on Thursday. Did you buy anything?"

"*Northanger Abbey and Persuasion,* and a really handsome Plutarch. North's translation, 1579."

Ned sounded so enthusiastic that Vanessa couldn't resist a tease.

"Do you ever *read* those things?"

"As a matter of fact," he said, "I've been reading Plutarch's life of Theseus."

Now she wasn't teasing. "What does he say about Ariadne?"

"He gives several possibilities," said Ned. "One is that she went crazy with the maenads on Naxos. The second is that she died there and the third is that she never left Crete at all."

"Humph," said Vanessa, annoyed. "Even the ancients were making excuses for Theseus, the betrayer."

"That version's a twentieth-century invention."

"I think not, sir," she replied formally. A group of walkers was within earshot and Vanessa's speech had changed to fit the period. Her tone was firm and precise, but there was a cutting edge to it.

"There are some capital paintings of Emma Hamilton – no relation to Lord James – as the abandoned Ariadne, and a splendid cantata by Haydn written to an Italian text called *Arianna a Naxos*. Emma herself sang the part, accompanied by Haydn, when the Hamiltons and Lord Nelson stopped in Vienna on their way home from Naples in 1800. Both these treatments derive from the view that Ariadne was seduced and abandoned."

The walkers had passed them now and disappeared around a bend. Vanessa let fly.

"So take that!"

"Well how about this?" Ned retorted. "Theseus was doing the right thing by letting Ariadne go with him. She helped him escape the labyrinth and she probably would have been killed if she'd stayed in Knossos. What could Theseus do when he discovered she was a nut-case at the first island they landed on, covered in blood and shrieking on a mountaintop with a bunch of crazy women?"

Vanessa stopped and faced him. This was their third meeting in Bath and he'd managed to upset her at each one.

"That's how women are," she said icily. "Men have to take it or leave it."

"Oh, for God's sake," Ned snorted. "Feminism comes to Regency Bath."

"It was here all along," she replied.

Ned looked at her sharply, as though sensing danger. Her voice was quieter now, but just as fierce.

"You have to search for it, because men run all the important publishing houses and are selective about what they print. Look at Mary Wollstonecraft, whose *Vindication of the Rights of Woman* only came out forty years ago because of one radical bookseller. And Catharine Macaulay, a better English historian than David Hume.

"You've been a librarian: you know that at least half the English novels published between 1780 and 1830 were written by women, but most of them were published anonymously. Men have never liked to acknowledge women's intellect. That's why Catharine Macaulay's history had a tiny edition and Hume's was reprinted again and again."

Vanessa clenched her fists as she continued. "And look at Meg, running her business and taking a lover instead of accepting one of the dozen proposals she's had from idiot traders without a tenth her wit. Did you know she sends thirty shillings a week to her family in Ireland? It's half what she earns after her expenses."

"Vanessa," Ned said slowly. "Stop type-casting me."

She met his eyes, surprised out of her passion. She took a slow, deep breath.

"You're right. I am."

"You've worked up a lot to say over the last sixteen years."

Her answering smile was grim.

"You bet I have."

Their path had curved to the west and another party of walkers was approaching from the opposite direction. Vanessa took Ned's arm.

"Apart from the barge traffic there's little business on the river itself, Mr. Marston, but you can see on the right" – she pointed – "the City Infirmary and Dispensary for the Sick Poor. You can get a cowpox vaccination *gratis*, if you like."

The other party was close now and clearly eavesdropping: three middle-aged ladies in black and two lean and long-faced gentlemen. Vanessa could tell Ned was trying not to laugh.

"And there is the Black Alms for paupers, so named because they give you a new black coat every two years. And there" – she pointed again and this time her smile was wicked – "is Avon Street, home to fallen women."

The other party was upon them now and they stopped dead as Vanessa began to declaim,

> The loveliest forms of nature in the street,
> > The fair, the black, the lasting brown!
> And whilst their charms enraptured I surveyed,
> > This pretty legend on their lips I read –
> 'Kisses, O gentle shepherd, kisses, and more, for a crown.'

Ned's laughter exploded as the five walkers hurried past, pausing to look quickly over their shoulders once they'd reached a safe distance.

Vanessa did her best to stay impassive, but her shoulders were shaking.

"They're tourists," she choked. "I wouldn't have dared if they'd been locals. I think they're scared we'll come after them."

"You might quote another poem."

She gave him a conspiratorial smile, her earlier anger forgotten.

"If we have to speak Regency whenever we get close to anyone else, at least we can choose what to say."

"I think you're showing off," Ned said.

Vanessa's eyes flashed. "I'm just getting started."

A few yards further along was another set of stone steps. They climbed up from the river, crossing a busy thoroughfare and passing a particularly fine row of houses on Kingsmead Terrace. They zigzagged through some shorter streets, past the baths Ned had attended the day before, and arrived back at the York Hotel in time for Vanessa to walk home with Meg.

"The concierge has promised a room to ourselves at seven o'clock," Meg said with a smile. "Robert will offer advice, and I shall show you a few of the dances."

Ned bowed. "I cannot tell you how grateful I am, Miss Gallagher."

"Call me Meg," she encouraged. "The steps are simple enough. And when we reach the Assembly Rooms I'll take you for the first two dances and show you what to expect. I daren't start you off with Vanessa, but you must promise to dance with her before the evening is over."

Vanessa straightened her shoulders. "Mr. Marston doesn't have to promise anything."

"Well, that's true enough," said Meg. "And when he sees you in your dancing gown he'll know why you've no shortage of partners."

After saying goodbye Vanessa and Meg started up the hill. Meg was first to speak.

"You really must dance with him, love."

"Must I? Yes, I suppose I must."

"And Lord Jamie will hear of it, even if he is still in Scotland."

Vanessa smiled. "That will do Jamie no harm."

CHAPTER VIII

Ned tried to remember what he knew of English country dancing. It wasn't much. He envisioned lines of men and women stepping forward in turn, bowing to each other, crossing on diagonal lines and raising their arms, gradually swinging their way through the assembly. The more he thought about it, the worse he felt.

He arrived at the York Hotel promptly at seven to find Meg and Robert in a small room off the lobby. Meg was elegant in a dress of burgundy velvet, simply cut but with some gold embroidery at the hem and bodice. Robert managed to look comfortable in spite of his formal jacket. He was sprawled in an upholstered chair, nursing a large glass of sherry.

"Have you no evening costume, Marston?"

"None to hand, Captain."

"Hmm. My cutaway would not fit you, sir. So I shall trust you once more and leave Megan with you unchaperoned."

"Where are you going, love?" asked Meg.

"If Marston has dressed for the afternoon, why then so shall I."

Before Ned could object Robert strode from the room, and when Ned turned back to Meg she had her arms curved over her head, her heels almost touching, and toes pointed in opposite directions.

She gave up her pose and curtseyed.

"Robert and I were discussing where to begin your lesson, and wondering how much you already know."

Ned shook his head and tried to describe the dance he'd been imagining earlier.

Meg smiled. "The Roger de Coverley. Most difficult of all. But it's the finishing dance and you'll only have to do it once. In fact," she gave Ned a sympathetic look, "you won't have to do it at all if you'd rather not. Robert and I will sit it out with you."

She resumed her dancing pose. "Now, sir. This is the opening position for the reels. They're the easiest. You scarcely touch your partner and are in no danger of stepping on her feet."

She pranced around him in a circle. "Like this. Keep your eyes on your partner. Stay close and tell her you'll change direction when she does."

Ned nodded and Meg continued. "Try to make yourself the last in any of the allemandes. That way you can watch the others and copy them. Here" – she took his arm – "is the way to swing your partner round and if it's a chase instead of a swing, put your hands on your own waist for the procession. Be a mirror to your partner and you won't go far wrong. And if you do" – she gave him her smile again – "you won't be alone."

Ten minutes later Robert returned, resuming his seat and thumping the beat on the arm as Meg and Ned practised. After half an hour Ned was pronounced ready for action and the three walked companionably uphill to the Assembly Rooms. Robert clapped Ned on the shoulder as they approached the entrance on Bennett Street.

"I expect you to do your duty, sir. We have given you all the target practice you could wish, and now you must take aim at the enemy."

Meg laughed. "And a battle it will be, when Mr. Marston sees all the unmarried women cutting each other for the first introduction."

At a call from behind of "Captain Carpenter" they turned. Vanessa was on the pavement behind them, dancing slippers in one hand and walking boots just visible under the hem of her dress. She was wearing a green pelisse, somewhat the worse for wear but obviously much loved.

When they gave up their coats at the cloakroom Ned was struck once again by Vanessa's beauty. She wore another low-cut, uncorseted and out-of-fashion Regency gown, ideally suited to her slender figure and high bust. She had rouged her cheeks and lips, setting off her blue eyes and light-brown skin. And now her blonde hair was in ringlets, her forehead with a single row of drooping curls over a silver ribbon. For a moment Ned wondered if Vanessa imagined herself a Jane Austen heroine. If so, she certainly looked the part.

There were seventy or eighty people at the Assembly Rooms, along with a flautist and string quartet to play the dance tunes.

"Now, sir and ladies," said Robert. "I shall take a hand or two of whist and if the play is any good you may get a half-dozen dances before I join you."

Meg wagged a finger at him. "I expect you back after a single rubber."

Robert smiled. "If Frank and Martha are not yet partnered I may stay for two. But no more." He bowed, turning to follow an older couple disappearing into a side room.

Meg spoke softly to Vanessa. "Remember you promised to dance with Ned, love. It would be cruel to make a wallflower of him."

Ned saw the malice in Vanessa's answering smile. "You know a dozen girls will be plucking your sleeve all night to ask who the handsome newcomer is. Mr. Marston will have no shortage of partners."

Ned mustered his courage. "Captain Carpenter has granted me four dances with Meg. Promise me the fifth and sixth and if I'm too much of an embarrassment I'll not bother you the rest of the evening."

Vanessa nodded and turned away. A pale young man was hovering nearby and as soon as Vanessa was alone he pounced. She gave him a rather strained smile, took his arm, and joined the dancers.

The music was a Scotch reel. Ned knew he was in trouble from the very beginning. He painstakingly attempted to copy Meg and then tried modelling himself on Vanessa's partner. Neither worked. He was out of time with the music and heaved a sigh of relief when it finally ended.

Meg said the second dance would be slower. After a moment the music picked up, a simple tune that repeated itself as the dancers lined up.

"Oh, dear," said Meg. "It's 'The Pleasures of the Town,' an allemande. It *is* slower, but you may find it a bit difficult. Let's step back and watch the first go-round. There are supposed to be three couples in each group to match the triple meter. There's usually a group that's a couple short, and we can come in when the music repeats."

She talked Ned through the first round. They spotted a group with only two couples and Ned watched as the pairs paraded down and back, parted, passed around their partners, turned and bowed. But his eyes kept returning to Vanessa. Her head was up, her colour high, and she was clearly delighting in the exercise. Her young man seemed dull by comparison.

Meg brought Ned into the allemande for the second round, which he managed clumsily but without any glaring mistakes. By the fifth round he was actually getting the hang of it. Meg's cheeks were bright pink and as she lifted her skirt her promenade became a high-spirited prance. Afterwards she complimented Ned with such enthusiasm that a few of the older ladies began to whisper.

The next dance was another triple and this time Ned was more confident. He took pleasure in the music, the other dancers, and his own movements. But the fourth dance was new and Meg decided not to push their luck. They sat it out, with Meg threatening to introduce Ned to some of the young women hovering nearby. Vanessa had changed partners and was now dancing with one of the musicians.

"Can the players just walk away from their instruments like that?" Ned asked.

"They take turns."

"Humph," said Ned. "I hope she's told them she has to dance the next two with me."

"Why, Ned. Are you jealous?"

The music ended and Robert emerged from the far door. As Ned walked Meg across the room she spoke kindly.

"The next two dances are bound to be triples. You did well with them so look happy and enjoy yourself."

She took Robert's arm and gave Ned a parting smile.

"Vanessa says that to be fond of dancing is a certain step towards falling in love."

As Ned approached, Vanessa's partner protested. She held up a hand to silence him and turned to Ned with a curtsey.

The music started up again and Vanessa said, "Another allemande. You'll be fine." Which meant, Ned realised, she must have been watching him as well.

He appreciated at once that Vanessa's dancing was on a higher level than her friend's. Her movements seemed both spontaneous and perfectly defined and she was always precisely on the beat. Her knowledge of the music was so exact that she was able to help Ned anticipate each sequence.

After three dances he was ready for a break.

"Would you care for refreshment, Miss Horwood?" She nodded and they steered for the punch bowl. Ned found a quiet corner where he asked about the young men in the music box. Vanessa shrugged.

"Some of them are half my age. I'm a comfortable dance partner for them because they know me so well. We often play together and are fond of each other."

"And 'to be fond of dancing is a certain step towards falling in love?'"

"That's a line from *Pride and Prejudice*. Almost anything good I have to say comes from Jane Austen's books."

She stood up. "But I'm not going to explain myself to you. Let's dance."

Vanessa's expertise saw them through the next two numbers. At the end of the second another young musician approached them.

Ned looked at Vanessa. "Am I allowed any more?"

Vanessa's response was wary. "Are you serious?"

"Entirely so, madam."

"Two dances with this puppy and then two more with you."

Ned eased his way towards the spectators' chairs and found Meg accompanied by a handsome young woman in a bright, almost gaudy, yellow dress. Meg gave Ned a sympathetic look.

"May I present Miss Amanda Torrington, Mr. Marston?"

Miss Torrington had a mane of chestnut hair and flashing hazel eyes that met Ned's own with unusual directness. She began to speak even as she curtsied.

"Miss Gallagher tells us you are newly-arrived in Bath, sir. Will you stay long?"

"Not long, but I should say I have made no plans to depart." Ned smiled, hoping he'd managed the right balance of decorum and gallantry. He knew what he had to say next.

"Would you care to dance, ma'am?"

The next two dances were allemandes. Miss Torrington was effusive in her praise.

"If all Americans dance like you, Mr. Marston, my countrymen should be ashamed."

The musicians began another tune and she took his arm. "Now, sir, I've a companion anxious to meet you. This way, please."

Miss Torrington had a firm grip on Ned's arm when Vanessa appeared. "Allow me, Mr. Marston," she murmured. She turned to his companion.

"He's mine for the next two." Vanessa's tone brooked no argument.

"Miss Horwood," came the indignant rejoinder. "This is most uncivil. . . a newcomer to Bath, Mr. Marston must be in want of further acquaintance, surely."

Ned intervened. "Miss Torrington, I cannot properly express my gratitude, but Miss Horwood promised more dances at my earlier request. My stay in Bath is short and . . . ."

"I am pleased to hear it, sir," said a new, male voice behind them.

Vanessa spun around. "Jamie," she breathed.

The man was in his late twenties, stocky and blond, with pale blue eyes in a broad and pleasant face. His smile was open and his tone was bantering, but there was a hint of concern in it as he continued.

"Is this what I must expect whenever I leave you alone, my dear?"

Vanessa's eyes flashed, but Ned saw her catch herself. She curtsied and smiled back.

"Mr. Marston, may I present Lord James Hamilton?"

Lord Jamie bowed, casting an appraising eye on Ned.

"We have not met, sir. Yet I believed I knew Vanessa's entire acquaintance in Bath."

Ned's mind was racing. This was Vanessa's suitor: younger than she, quite handsome, and from the way he looked at Vanessa obviously in love. Ned bowed.

"I am recently arrived, Lord James, a friend of Miss Horwood's family visiting from America."

Both Meg and Miss Torrington had vanished during these introductions. Ned was relieved when he saw the former approaching with Robert Carpenter.

"Lord James," Carpenter said with a bow. "Megan tells me the ladies have had enough dancing and we are to escort Miss Horwood home."

"I protest! Vanessa has never yet failed to dance with me at the Assembly Rooms and I claim my right of one at the least."

He gave Vanessa a proprietary look and a courtly bow. Once again Ned could see the man's charm, but Vanessa hesitated a moment before giving an answering curtsey.

"Very well, sir. But the evening is late, and one is all you get."

As the dancers took to the floor Meg stepped between Ned and Robert, taking an arm from each. When they were safely in a corner Ned spoke softly.

"Am I in the way?"

"Don't be daft, Ned. Lord Jamie is Vanessa's suitor, but he does not own her."

"Yet I saw the look in his eyes," Robert added thoughtfully. "He is more determined than I had credited."

They watched the dancers to the end of the next number, occasionally catching glimpses of Vanessa and Lord Jamie at the far end of the room. When the music started up again Robert smiled at Meg and patted her hand.

"Come along, my dear, and let us join the last dance. I know you love the Roger de Coverley."

Meg took Robert's arm and across the room Ned saw Vanessa shake her head. Lord Jamie said something more and after a moment she let him lead her to the dance floor. This time the dancers at the far end began to give way. Soon Vanessa and Lord Jamie were in the centre position, not far from Meg and Robert.

At first Ned thought the shift had something to do with Lord Jamie's rank, as indeed perhaps it did. But when he saw the two dancing – heads up, arms extended, their movements in perfect unison – Ned could see they were a couple that would take centre stage in any gathering. He was a perfect match for her on the dance floor, and he could see Vanessa's face flush with pleasure as she concentrated on her movements and her partner.

At the end Lord Jamie took Vanessa's hands in what was clearly another entreaty. After a moment she nodded her acceptance.

With Vanessa on his arm he crossed the floor to Robert.

"Captain Carpenter. Miss Horwood has consented to join my party for supper at the White-Hart Hotel. I beg that you and Miss Gallagher will join us and allow my carriage to take the ladies home after." He nodded at Ned. "And your friend is welcome as well."

Vanessa's face was still bright from the dancing, but she remained quiet.

Robert raised his eyebrows at Meg.

"How may we resist?" she answered with a smile.

Robert bowed his acceptance. "And you, Marston?"

Ned took his cue from Robert and also bowed. "I am obliged to you, Lord James, for such kindness to a stranger. I shall be pleased to join you."

Ned accompanied Meg and Robert outside. Why am I doing this? he thought. Watching Vanessa happy with her Scottish lord was the last thing he needed. But it was too late to back out now.

As they left the ballroom Ned glanced back to see Vanessa and Lord Jamie surrounded by a small group of fashionable young people. The rest of the supper-party. Vanessa's new world.

As they headed down the alley to George Street Ned spoke to Robert.

"I cannot understand Vanessa's protestations about Lord James. She was practically glowing with happiness."

"It is hard to fathom," said Robert. "Megan tells me she knows a score of young women who would happily commit murder to be the object of his affections. But Vanessa does sometimes complain."

"We have been spinsters together these last sixteen years," said Meg . "Old habits die hard."

CHAPTER IX

Vanessa took a deep breath of fresh air as she and Jamie brought up the rear of the supper-party. They started down the pavement towards the hotel, arm-in-arm. She could sense his uneasiness and smiled up at him.

"You returned sooner than you planned."

Jamie's eyes were troubled. "I missed you. I imagined you at the ball tonight and I couldn't bear it. But the roads were bad and the coach was slow. And when I arrived you were dancing with a stranger."

"He's not a stranger. He's a friend of my family. I haven't seen him since I was a child." Her words brought back the image of Ned, lecturing her in the time-travel laboratory all those years ago. She *had* been a child then, a child in the future.

Jamie was still looking at her and she decided to elaborate. And to give herself a bolt-hole in case she needed one.

"Mr. Marston tells me I have a small inheritance. My family asks that I return to Canada."

"No!" cried Jamie. "All he must take back is your news."

"What?" asked Vanessa.

"You must not go, my dear. You know it is past time we set the date for our wedding. Let Mr. Marston take our announcement to your family. Surely they will understand."

Vanessa was silent. Jamie's proposal was not new. They had known each other two months and all Bath assumed them to be engaged. Everyone treated her with deference now. Shopkeepers offered credit, society matrons who used to pass her in silence stopped and curtsied, and she had more applications for piano lessons than she could possibly accommodate.

Ned's arrival had reminded her how precarious her position had been and how much Jamie's courtship had affected her life. For the first time since she'd arrived in Regency England Vanessa had begun to feel safe.

Jamie's voice broke in on her reflections. "Vanessa. . . ? You haven't answered."

"Soon, Jamie. We'll talk about it soon."

"Next week," he replied, a little too smugly for Vanessa's taste. "We should make the announcement at Blackthorne Park."

Vanessa had been looking forward to a house party at Blackthorne Park on Monday. It would be her first trip with Jamie outside Bath and when he'd written with the invitation a week ago she'd thought it a perfect way get to know him in a less formal setting than town soirees and music recitals. Vanessa was already acquainted with Charlotte Blackthorne, the daughter-in-law of the baronet and a fellow-musician. She'd never met the baronet himself, one of Jamie's relations on his mother's side, but Charlotte's husband Nicholas seemed decent enough. Rather like Jamie, in fact.

Now Jamie's pressure to announce their engagement robbed the outing of its anticipated pleasure. She'd got used to his insistence that she play the pianoforte wherever they went in Bath. That had been bad enough, but this latest ultimatum was much worse.

Meg, Robert, and Ned were already at the hotel when she and Jamie entered. Vanessa couldn't imagine why Ned had decided to impose himself. She wondered how Jamie would handle him.

It turned out Jamie handled him very neatly indeed, separating him from Meg and Robert in order to seat him between Amanda Torrington and a pretty blonde named Lucy Richmond. Vanessa smiled to herself, wondering if Amanda would sink her matchmaking claws into Ned as she already had with half the young men present.

"I had not expected to see you again so soon, Mr. Marston," said Amanda.

Ned's reply was polished enough.

"I could not have hoped for a happier coincidence, ma'am."

Amanda introduced Ned to Lucy, who simpered but said nothing. All through supper Jamie dominated the conversation, albeit with an agreeable smile that made his control seem the most natural thing in the world. The first person he spoke to was Ned.

"Can you forgive my rough manners this evening, Mr. Marston?"

"I saw no such thing, Lord James."

"You will understand my consternation when I entered the ballroom to see my fiancée dancing with a handsome stranger. I heard from every busybody in the room – and there were many – that the two of you were together most of the evening."

Meg's head came up. "Not true, sir. Mr. Marston was most attentive to me while Captain Carpenter had his rubber of whist."

"Only attentive," Ned added, "if that is the proper term for stepping on a young woman's feet."

Lord Jamie laughed. "You do yourself an injustice, sir. Vanessa has now told me your families were intimate in America, and I declare myself content."

Amanda Torrington was listening intently to this exchange, watching Ned's expression. She caught herself, turned, and whispered something to Lucy. In the meantime one of the other guests asked how Jamie and Vanessa had met. Vanessa assumed Jamie would mention Robert Carpenter's introduction, but instead she found herself wincing as he replied.

"When I first saw Vanessa at the pianoforte I knew I should marry her. Such technique, such spirit! They say that Beethoven in his prime was one of the great performers on the instrument and I am told that Miss Wieck in Saxony may soon rival him. But I cannot imagine either as superior to Vanessa. I plan to enlist her in my own projects after we are married."

"And what might those projects be, Lord James?" Robert interposed.

"I am sure, Carpenter, you have heard of my friend Lord Burghersh, son of the Earl of Westmoreland?"

Robert's nod was impassive, or perhaps he was immune to name-dropping. Vanessa saw him catch Ned's eye, smiling as Lord Jamie continued.

"Burghersh founded the Academy of Music ten years ago but at present it is doing little teaching of composition. The best new music is coming out of Germany. I intend to make a British home for these new composers and to encourage them to share their knowledge with our own young people."

Vanessa stared at the tablecloth. Ned had to be wondering how she could bear Jamie's pomposity. He'd already shared a smile with Robert.

Jamie was still talking, used to being the centre of attention. She ate quickly, pleaded fatigue, and was joined in her departure by Meg and Robert. Ned was deep in conversation with Amanda as they left.

CHAPTER X

Sunday morning brought more rain. Vanessa suggested they skip the service at Bath Abbey, but Meg insisted they go, confessing she had invited Ned to share their pew. Vanessa swallowed her annoyance and put on her boots. They were soaked and squelching by the time she'd walked halfway down the hill.

Ned had an umbrella and was waiting in the Abbey churchyard. In spite of the rain he was alternately gaping at the façade of the Pump Room and the adjacent statues of Sts. Peter and Paul on the Abbey front. Meg took Ned's arm and the two women walked him inside, where like any other tourist he gazed back at the largest of the stained-glass windows. He turned to Meg and whispered.

"How can you not be Catholic?"

"Of course I'm Catholic," she hissed. "Is your head altogether away? And so is this church Catholic. Every great church in England was built by Catholics, except maybe St. Paul's in London and that one's so big there's no religion in it."

"Hush," said Vanessa, scanning the pews for any sign of Jamie. When she saw none she took Ned's other arm. Robert was waiting in their usual place, and Vanessa relaxed as the choir entered, singing to the Abbey organist's accompaniment.

Ned insisted on taking them all for a meal after the service.

"We cannot," said Robert. "The clouds are breaking up and the three of us have promised to meet a party of walkers in Batheaston."

"Another of Lord James's?" asked Ned.

"Are you jealous, Ned?" asked Meg.

"Of course not," Ned replied.

"Jamie will be there," said Vanessa. "I'm afraid you're on your own."

Vanessa had intended to sound sarcastic, but she heard a touch of regret in her voice. She wondered if Ned had heard it too.

Ned was turning away as she called to him again. "Megan and I shall take our exercise tomorrow morning at Mrs. Giorgio's studio. Number 3, Westgate Buildings, if you would care to join us. Eight o'clock."

Meg and Robert stared in astonishment, but Ned seemed the most surprised of all.

"I shall be honoured," he said after a moment, bowing.

CHAPTER XI

Ned was in his lodgings that afternoon when a caller arrived.

"In the vestibule, sir," the landlord told Ned, his manner positively deferential.

The caller was a bewigged and liveried servant bearing an invitation to a supper-party at Lord Jamie's that very night, obviously the sequel to the walk Vanessa and her friends were taking that afternoon.

"I am instructed to await your reply, sir," said the servant.

Without thinking Ned found a card and penned his acceptance, but he regretted it as soon as the servant left. Short of running after the man and retrieving his card, there was nothing Ned could do but go.

He spent the afternoon on edge. What motive could Lord Jamie have for including him in this society? He felt like the young aristocrat was gloating, showing off his triumph over Vanessa and rubbing Ned's face in it. But Lord Jamie had no way of knowing that Ned had been in love with Vanessa. And the longer Ned stayed in Bath, the more he realised he still was.

Lord Jamie sensed *something*, of that Ned was certain. He tried to get the younger man out of his mind by taking a late-afternoon walk on the Common. But he couldn't resist going on to Cavendish Crescent, where the supper-party would be held. There he felt like a soldier, reconnoitring in enemy territory.

He was back in his lodgings at nightfall and took his time changing into his dark suit. He knew he'd once again be underdressed, just as he was at the Assembly Rooms.

Cavendish Crescent was one of Bath's later developments, not far from the much grander Royal Crescent. The Cavendish houses were smaller, but still four full storeys high and with splendid views across the Common.

A footman took Ned's overcoat and showed him upstairs, past portraits of handsome women and kilted soldiers adorning the walls above the stairs, generations of Hamiltons, he assumed. Once he was announced in the drawing room there were more liveried servants serving champagne. He helped himself to a glass. Only a couple, he resolved. Two would soothe his nerves; any more would compound his gloom and lead him into trouble.

As he sipped Ned took in his surroundings. At the far end of the room stood a large and obviously new mahogany piano, as yet with no Vanessa to complement it. Above the fireplace hung an enormous Chippendale mirror and as Ned raised his gaze still higher he was drawn to an elaborately moulded ceiling with a central, classically-themed fresco.

"The pattern is Mr. Robert Adam's, I believe," said a female voice behind him. Ned turned, as the voice continued. "And the central panel depicts the story of Cupid and Psyche."

It was his dancing partner Amanda Torrington, very *à la mode* in a dress cut straight across her shoulders and gathered at the waist with a wide belt. She curtsied and Ned bowed.

"How agreeable to see you again, Miss Torrington."

Amanda smiled. "I trust you will find the entire company more agreeable than yester-evening's, sir. I was sorry to see you so awkwardly placed with Miss Horwood."

Ned protested. "It was, I am certain, no fault of hers."

Amanda tossed her mane of chestnut curls. "Doubtless no more her fault, sir" – she gestured at the ceiling fresco – "than Psyche's for bringing down the wrath of Venus."

"It is fine work, is it not?"

"Oh, yes," said Amanda, "but I doubt if anyone else present quite appreciates how immodest the story really is."

A servant interrupted. "I am instructed by Lord James to bring you close by. Miss Horwood is about to play."

Other guests were drawing close to the piano, where servants were rearranging chairs. Lucy Richmond was already seated and Ned was nonplussed to find himself so obviously matched with these two young women he scarcely knew, in places of honour behind Lord Jamie and with a fine view of the bright ivory keyboard. It had to be some kind of set-up. Ned's feeling himself a soldier in enemy territory increased.

Vanessa appeared at the piano, evidently uncomfortable in a stylish dress not so different from Amanda's. She glanced at Lord Jamie – perhaps pleadingly? – Ned could not be sure. Then with sudden resolution she sat down and launched into the beginning of a Mozart sonata.

"I know it," Amanda murmured, "the Sonata Facile. Half the women in the room have played this. It is a staple of the young student's repertory, requiring no feeling and only modest technique."

Ned smiled to himself. Vanessa brought all the technique anyone could wish, expertly negotiating her way through the frothy allegro. But there was none of the passion Ned had seen when Vanessa played Chopin in her own cottage. Tonight's choice of such an anodyne piece was clearly Vanessa's way of declaring her unhappiness at having to sing for her supper. But Lord Jamie was oblivious, caught up in the music and revelling in what Ned had to admit was a fine round tone from his new, seven-octave, "grand forte-piano."

There were sixteen for supper afterwards, at the large dining table on the ground floor. Vanessa sat on Lord Jamie's right while Ned was placed at the far end, once again between Amanda and Lucy.

"I believe we are destined to have a conversation, Miss Richmond," said Ned, holding her chair before taking his own seat.

"Indeed you are, sir," cried Amanda. "I have taken particular pains to arrange it."

Lucy blushed, her colour rising from a quite low bodice, up a shapely neck and into her face. She was distractingly pretty, thought Ned with a surge of lust.

"I know nothing about America, sir," she replied. "I am entirely at a loss."

"May I compliment you on your gown?"

Amanda interrupted before Lucy could reply. "You should not, sir. You may tell in a single glance that she did not purchase it in London, but from that low Irishwoman in Milsom Street."

Ned turned hard eyes upon Amanda, who recoiled, averting her own.

"If you mean Miss Gallagher," he said quietly, "you are seriously mistaken."

"Indeed you are, Amanda," cried Lucy. "Many of the best ladies in Bath go to Miss Gallagher for their gowns."

"Ah," said Amanda, looking complacently from Lucy to Ned. "You agree on everything. It is a match made in heaven."

Ned straightened in his chair. This was getting dangerous.

"I have no plans to marry," he declared.

"Then you are a roué, sir," Amanda replied. "Unsuitable for any society." Before Ned could reply Jamie proposed a toast. From that moment the young lord again dominated the conversation, albeit with his usual elegant manners. Only once did his control slip, when two couples squared off in a debate about North Americans. One side asserted that Americans and Canadians alike had long since fallen under the influence of French Jacobins and that the lot of them were no better than freethinkers and atheists. Voices were raised until Lord Jamie interrupted, flatly denying any such thing and offering Vanessa as proof of Canadian civilisation.

Much of Jamie's discourse was aimed at drawing Vanessa out. He deferred to her observations on music and selectively engaged her in conversation with groups around the table. Ned wondered if she could see how patronising it all was, but he had to admit it was skilfully done, a man grooming his intended wife for high society.

Ned downed his claret in two swallows. He was about to raise the glass for a refill when he caught himself.

He wanted oblivion, but not that kind. Lord Jamie was the best thing that ever happened to Vanessa, probably a happier ending for her than anything she could have had in her own time, with or without Ned. And he had nothing to offer now. He needed to behave himself tonight and get out of town.

He kept his eyes on his plate until halfway through dessert, when Lord Jamie addressed him directly.

"Vanessa tells me you are a bibliophile, Mr. Marston."

"It is a term well-chosen, Lord James," replied Ned. "I love books, but only rarely may I indulge myself in the luxury of collecting them."

"My father," Lord Jamie replied, "was invited to join the bibliophilic club occasioned by the library sale of his friend the Duke of Roxburghe. Perhaps you have heard of it?"

Ned nodded and smiled: more name-dropping. The Roxburghe book-collectors' club remained the most distinguished of its kind in Ned's own time, two centuries later.

Jamie continued. "Have you an area of particular interest?"

Vanessa answered, her first acknowledgment of Ned's presence the entire evening.

"The Elizabethans, I'll warrant, Jamie. Mr. Marston spoke of buying an English Plutarch from Gibbons just the other day."

"North's Plutarch, sir?" asked Lord Jamie.

"The very same," said Ned.

"You may not know, Marston" – Jamie was at his most condescending – "North's Plutarch was a source for Shakespeare himself."

"The Roman plays," Ned shot back.

"The barge she sat in, like a burnished throne,
Knelt on the water. . . ."

"Cleopatra," said Lucy determinedly, with a coy glance at Ned. "And beautifully spoke, if I may say so, Mr. Marston."

Out of the corner of his eye Ned could see Vanessa stifle a giggle.

"Thank you, Miss Richmond," Ned replied. "We are fond of Shakespeare on my side of the Atlantic as well."

"Must have been a fine swordsman, Shakespeare," put in a guest in army uniform. The man spoke rather too loudly, as he held out his empty glass for the servant to refill. "Tremendous battle scenes, and of course the duel at the end of *Hamlet*. Man knew what he wrote, hmm?"

Ned's unhappiness commingled with his painful recollections of Shakespeare himself, the man he'd so recently left behind. A vision of Judith flashed before his eyes. He could have stayed with them, he thought despairingly. Vanessa hadn't needed him at all. He fought to control his voice.

"I doubt it, sir," he said finally, thinking of Shakespeare's own words in the back room of Nicholas Ling's bookshop. "If you've seen a good staging of the *Hamlet* duel it's because it was invented by the acting company. There are no fighting directions in the plays and Shakespeare certainly never got serious training in swordsmanship."

"How can you be so certain, Marston?" asked Jamie. Ned was surprised to see that his host seemed genuinely interested.

"He was a grammar-school boy from Stratford, Lord James, his father a glover. He might have held a broadsword or a pike in the trained bands and learned a few turns with a rapier as an actor, but nothing about real fighting."

"Why, Mr. Marston." Vanessa was the picture of wide-eyed innocence. "One would almost think you had been there."

CHAPTER XII

Ned left the dinner-party as soon as he could, remaining at the table with the men for an obligatory glass of port but making his exit before they rejoined the ladies in the drawing-room. He was in a black mood as he walked back to his lodgings, thinking once again of Shakespeare and Judith. There was no hope of getting back to 1607, no hope of getting anywhere.

His mind groped for answers but found none. Maybe he should go to Bristol, a dozen miles away, and take the first vessel bound for North America. He could do that tomorrow and put Vanessa behind him. But what money he had was in London, along with the rest of his books.

He slept badly that night and when he rose in the morning he remembered his promise to meet Vanessa and Meg at their exercise studio.

"I don't want to *do* this," he said out loud. It was only going to make him feel worse.

But a promise was a promise, and he was at Westgate Buildings shortly before eight, waiting on the stoop when the two women arrived.

"It's as well that I'm here as a chaperone," said Meg. "Leaving the two of you alone again would be most improper."

"Since when have we ever been proper?" Vanessa replied with a grin.

The ladies had loose leggings and heavy blouses, the closest thing possible in this time, Ned imagined, to modern sweat-suits. When he shed his trousers and overcoat, revealing his freshly-laundered Shakespearean breeches and the ragged shirt he'd pulled off the corpse of his dead assailant, Meg stared but made no comment. Vanessa was equally silent, but he could tell she knew exactly where his outfit had come from.

Ned followed the two women in their warm-up exercises, the same ones Vanessa had used in their own time. After fifteen minutes she called a halt.

"I promised Meg you would show us what you're made of."

Meg smiled. "Vanessa tells me you fought with each other as children."

Ned returned the smile. "It was nothing personal. Vanessa was always a tomboy, trying to be better at everything than the rest of us."

"Usually I was, too," Vanessa declared.

Meg backed into a corner of the room while Vanessa and Ned pushed some mats into a rectangle, a bit larger than a boxing ring.

They bowed to each other in the formal face-off that preceded *tae kwon do* combat. Ned smiled, remembering what they'd sometimes said to each other.

"No head shots," he prompted.

"And gentle on the ribs," she replied.

Twenty seconds later Ned was on the mat. Vanessa had come at him slowly and deliberately, arms extended. Ned was still making the mental shift from defending against a swordsman when she flung back her arms and took him on the back of the thighs with a two-footed twirling kick that completely upended him.

Vanessa backed off, bowing again as Ned resumed his ready position. He bowed too. Vanessa took the offensive once more, but this time Ned anticipated she would come at him from the opposite side. He leaped back as her kick flew past his belly. She spun full circle, recovering, but was too late. Ned was upon her with a short, right-footed kick that brought his calf against her ribcage. Now it was Vanessa's turn to hit the mat.

"Too hard! Meg cried. But Vanessa shook her head, saying nothing.

She and Ned went five more falls in similar fashion. Ned took four of them, the last from a spectacular tornado kick delivered to the upper arm, so powerfully that he fell over, as Meg put it, "like a sack of potatoes."

"In real combat," Vanessa said happily, "that one really *would* have been to your head."

"Hands," Ned panted. "I need to use my hands."

Vanessa shrugged. "That's a different sport. I don't do free-style anymore."

"Lord," called Meg from the corner, her face bright with enthusiasm. "As if this weren't sport enough. Could you not teach this in Ireland? We should drive the English into the sea with it."

Vanessa asked the time and Ned checked his watch. "Two more falls," she offered. "Then I have to clean up."

Ned held his own in the first one, parrying two midriff shots and knocking Vanessa to the floor with a straight kick to the shoulder that he managed to deliver from mid-air. Vanessa won the next round, but not before both took several sharp blows.

As Ned scrambled to his feet he saw Vanessa hunched over, seemingly in pain. He was beside her in an instant.

"Don't lift your head too soon," he cautioned. "Are you all right?"

Vanessa held her position. "I'm not used to real fighting," she puffed. "I can't get Meg to put any force behind her kicks, hard as I try, so all we do are the ritual touches."

Meg was with them now, her arm around Vanessa's shoulders. "He had no cause to strike you so," she said indignantly.

All three were touching now, bodies hunched over in tandem. Meg craned her neck to glare at Ned. "You are no gentleman, sir."

Vanessa straightened, pulling the other two up with her. She started to giggle.

"No, Mr. Marston, you are not. No gentleman at all." She turned to Meg. "Thank you, love. I wouldn't trade our workouts for anything, but Ned has given me exactly what I wanted. Don't blame him."

"Very well," said Meg slowly, her face softening. "As long as there is no harm done."

CHAPTER XIII

Jamie was driving a handsome curricle with the hood down, just the kind of dashing conveyance he was bound to have chosen for a sunny afternoon. Vanessa was packed and ready when he arrived. He soon had the horses at a gallop, explaining that their host, Sir Peregrine Blackthorne, dined at the old-fashioned hour of four o'clock, sharp.

Upon their arrival Vanessa's friend Charlotte accompanied her upstairs. Charlotte was slender and very fair. Usually she was quick-witted and outgoing, but today she seemed a little shy. Perhaps, Vanessa thought, she felt overshadowed by her parents-in-law in the rambling brick manor house.

Once in Vanessa's bedroom Charlotte explained that the other couple they'd invited had cancelled. She apologised for the lack of any other guests.

"But I hope you will announce your engagement nevertheless."

Vanessa had avoided the subject on the drive with Jamie, who was intent on speed anyway and disinclined to shout in the open curricle.

"We're not engaged," Vanessa replied. "How did you know, anyway?"

"Jamie told Nicholas most particularly that you had written to him accepting his invitation here."

"So I did," said Vanessa.

"Do you not appreciate what that implied?"

Vanessa considered a moment, realizing that the invitation had been the first note she had received from Jamie that required an answer. The house party had sounded innocuous enough. She had replied immediately, without think-ing about it.

"It implied nothing," she finally said.

"Oh, my dear," said Charlotte softly, taking Vanessa's arm. "Don't you know that an unmarried woman may never, in propriety, accept such an invita-tion from a man to whom she is neither related nor betrothed? Your writing to Jamie bespoke your acceptance of him."

"Damn Jamie," Vanessa said quietly.

Charlotte recoiled. "Surely you and he had an understanding beforehand, did you not? He has spoken of you as his intended for the past month. If only you'd confided in me I could have invited you myself."

"Never mind, Charlotte," said Vanessa, forcing a smile. "Thank you for the instruction in etiquette. I am certain Jamie and I can resolve this somehow."

Charlotte pointed to a carriage clock on the dresser and reminded Vanessa of their dinner hour, fast approaching. A maid arrived with Vanessa's portman-teau, and Charlotte took her leave.

Vanessa cursed as she unpacked. How could she have been so stupid as to write Jamie directly? She'd grown complacent after sixteen years, assuming she knew the ins and outs of this society. And she'd let herself be seduced by her anticipatory notion of the house-party, imagining the kind of gathering familiar to her from Jane Austen's novels: regular meals, country walks, and the men departing *en masse* to go shooting. She figured she'd have a couple of quiet days reading – and, as Jamie had insisted, playing the piano.

But she'd missed the significance of Jamie's invitation. She was furious with herself. She'd lived close to poverty for so long that she never considered the baronet's house party might be a trap. But it was. And she'd walked into it, wide-eyed.

In the dining-room things went from bad to worse. Sir Peregrine was over-weight and overbearing, contemptuous of anyone he perceived as beneath him, which included all foreigners and colonials. A Tory through and through, he was vehemently opposed to any notion of political equality and still bitter about the Whig party's passage of the great Reform Act the year before, in 1832.

"There'll be no end to it, mark my words," he proclaimed. "Enfranchise the God-damned factory and farm-workers and the next thing you know the Catholics will be after the vote. And then, Lord help us, it may be the women."

Vanessa knew she should keep quiet, but she was still seething. She threw caution to the wind.

"And why shouldn't women vote, Sir Peregrine?" she asked mildly.

Sir Peregrine glared at her. "Where did you say you were from, young woman?"

"Canada," Vanessa replied. "But don't let that distract you, sir. I am certain I should remain disenfranchised as a colonist even if you allow suffrage to Englishwomen."

"I allow no such thing," roared her host.

"That was my question, sir," Vanessa repeated. "Why do you not allow it?"

Sir Peregrine ignored her. "Jamie," he said heavily. "I shall not tolerate such insolence from your woman. Take her away."

"You need not direct him, Sir Peregrine," said Vanessa, rising from her chair. "I am perfectly capable of removing myself." She paused and turned back to the table. "And I am nobody's woman. Except my own."

She spent the rest of the evening alone in her room, consoling herself with the thought that Sir Peregrine's outburst had prevented Jamie's mentioning their engagement. Jamie had scarcely spoken at all.

The next morning at breakfast there was no sign of the baronet. Charlotte began to apologise for him, but both Jamie and Charlotte's husband Nicholas interrupted.

"It is Sir Peregrine's house," Jamie said. "He is entitled to his opinions in it."

Vanessa smiled grimly. "A man's home is his castle, Jamie?"

"Just so, my dear."

Vanessa said no more, but her spirits lifted when Charlotte proposed a walk. The weather was promising and Nicholas suggested an outing to Castle Combe. There was a Roman road that led there, now little-used and much overgrown, but it was suitable for pedestrians and Nicholas knew an inn that would serve a mid-day meal.

The four of them walked the five miles through rolling wooded countryside with no further disagreements. Nicholas and Jamie talked about their last visit to London, buying shotguns and practicing wafer shooting at Manton's firearms manufactory in Mayfair. Charlotte asked Vanessa about new piano-music and offered unexpectedly full commentary on recent publications by Chopin and Robert Schumann.

After their meal Charlotte declared herself too tired for the return walk. There were families she knew dining at the inn, and she insisted that Vanessa accompany the men on their walk home.

"Nicholas will send the carriage in time for us all to take tea together."

Vanessa kept behind the men most of the way, avoiding conversation. As they approached Blackthorne Park, their path led through a grove of elms where some ragged gypsy children confronted them, hands extended to beg. Vanessa smiled, thinking of Harriet Smith's gypsy encounter in *Emma*, but her smile faded as Nicholas shoved one of the children out of the way.

"Damned riff-raff," he snarled as the child fell.

Nicholas began pushing his way through the others but as the fallen child started to wail a half-dozen men emerged from the trees. They were mostly young, flamboyant in headscarves and earrings, but the foremost had a large knife in his hand. He nodded at the crying child.

"My boy, 'e is asking for your 'elp, your charity."

"Be off with you, ruffian," said Nicholas Blackthorne. "This is not asking, but highway robbery. The magistrates shall hear of it."

"Hush, Nicholas," said Jamie nervously. He spoke to the man with the knife. "What would you have of us?"

The gypsy's smile was fierce, his teeth brown and uneven.

"What you will, your honour. Our children, they are 'ungry."

"Not a damned farthing," said Nicholas. He stepped forward, but one of the other young men blocked his way. Nicholas struck him, a solid blow that knocked the man sideways.

Vanessa lifted her skirts as the man with the knife intervened. She had a split-second to reflect that the leggings she wore underneath left her not quite as indecent as she might otherwise have been, and then she was upon him, kicking upwards at his knife-hand. His weapon flew into the air, as Vanessa's second kick took him to the ground.

"His knife, Jamie," she shouted, whirling to fell a second gypsy. But Jamie didn't move, and the first man rolled to his feet and recovered his weapon. The children seemed to hold their breath and for a moment everyone in the grove stood still.

The knife-wielding gypsy began to laugh. "She is a fighter, that one." He turned to Jamie. "You should bring 'er to our camp this evening. We 'ave some women fighters too." He paused, looking Vanessa up and down. "Per'aps not so pretty."

Jamie kept sullen silence. The gypsy stared at him for a moment before turning to Vanessa.

"You are wasted on 'im, miss," he said with a shrug. "But you 'ave saved them their money."

A rustling noise from behind made the young gypsy whirl. The man Nicholas struck had unsheathed his own knife.

"Put it away, Constantine. The 'ell-cat might not be as gentle with you as she was with me."

As the two men put away their blades the spokesman looked around the grove, nodding to his comrades. Then he turned to Vanessa, gave a courtly bow, and with a gesture led his party back into the woods.

Vanessa smiled as she watched them go. Then she looked at Nicholas and Jamie. Nicholas was purple with anger – the image of his father the night before – but Jamie was pale and sweating. As Vanessa approached she could smell his fear. She'd caught the scent of him before when they'd danced, but this time it reminded her of curdled milk. Reflexively – she struggled against it – her sensory recollection brought up Ned Marston's scent yesterday in the exercise studio. Fir trees, the same as she remembered from workouts in their own time.

I don't need this, she thought. Leave me alone, Marston. Pulling herself back to the present, she spoke softly.

"Are you all right, Jamie?"

Jamie straightened and stepped back. "Certainly I am." He glared at her. "I was about to take that man's knife when they gave up and decided to run."

Vanessa bit her tongue. She looked at Nicholas, only to see him scowling at her too.

"You'd no business interfering," he said.

"Well," she said brightly. "We mustn't keep Charlotte waiting for her carriage."

Jamie was silent for the rest of the walk. Occasionally he cast a sidelong glance in Vanessa's direction but whenever she tried to meet his eyes he turned away. She knew the symptoms. He'd been humiliated in front of his friend and she had been the cause of it. Better for Jamie's self-esteem if they'd simply been robbed.

Nicholas made it worse when they reached the manor house. He told his father the whole story, including Vanessa's part in it. Sir Peregrine sent the carriage for Charlotte and ordered his steward to ride to the magistrates. At the same time he dispatched some farm-workers to search for the gypsies. But the workers returned empty-handed and the steward reported that the magistrates declined to act, that it appeared to them Nicholas had struck first and in any event there had been no actual robbery.

In the meantime Charlotte returned, glowing with excitement and full of questions. She smiled at Vanessa.

"If only I'd known there would be such a spectacle! I should never have let you leave the inn without me."

"You were tired, Charlotte," said Vanessa.

Charlotte stepped close, dropping her voice. "Tired? I was *bored*."

All the excitement delayed their dinner-hour. Vanessa knew this would further upset Sir Peregrine. She resolved to wear the same modish dress she'd worn to Jamie's dinner-party. She hated it, but it would remind her to keep demure silence.

No sooner were they seated than Sir Peregrine launched into a discourse on the danger of allowing foreigners into the country and the legal system's shocking neglect of innocent landowners.

"Indeed, my love," said Lady Blackthorne. "Nowadays women are not safe out of doors, even to take the air."

Charlotte smiled. "Unless you send Miss Horwood to protect them."

"Be quiet, girl," declared Sir Peregrine. He stared at Vanessa. "I call it damnable insolence that Miss Horwood should interfere with the right of our two gentlemen to offer their own protection."

Vanessa's colour began to rise, but before she could reply Charlotte began to laugh.

"I shan't be quiet, sir," she said, her retiring demeanour of yesterday entirely gone. "Gentlemen's protection indeed! From what Nicholas tells me, Jamie didn't lift a finger."

"That's enough, Charlotte," said Jamie heavily. "I suggest, Peregrine, we take our port and join the ladies later for some music." He looked around the table, carefully avoiding Vanessa's eyes.

The women retired to the drawing room. Vanessa paused at a shelf of novels, pulling out the first volume of a new three-decker called *The Invisible Gentleman*. Wishful thinking? she wondered. Would I like them all to disappear? But the book turned out to be a heavy-handed historical romance set in the twelfth century. She flung it down at the same moment Lady Blackthorne sat at the piano and began to massacre one of the Pleyel sonatinas Vanessa had played for Jane Austen so many years ago.

Ten minutes later the gentlemen joined them, red-faced from their port. Lady Blackthorne's playing limped to a halt and Jamie turned to Vanessa. He seemed ashamed and vulnerable, and she saw the uncertainty in his eyes as he invited her to play. She stepped up without hesitation.

Later she realised what a mistake it had been for her to play a composer as challenging as Chopin. But at the time she was thinking how much it meant to Jamie to see her at her best. So she played the two etudes she had performed when Ned visited the cottage, both of them with scarcely a pause and closing with the tumultuous "Revolutionary."

She rose from the stool knowing she'd played well, a performance that could have brought an audience to its feet. But tonight there was silence, broken only by the sound of her host puffing on his cigar. Jamie had lifted his hands to applaud, but dropped them when he saw Sir Peregrine's expression. The baronet took his cigar out of his mouth.

"Impertinent," he declared.

Vanessa was taken aback. "What, Sir Peregrine?"

Jamie stood up, responding to the warning signal in her voice, but their host blundered on.

"Unspeakable clamour, not music at all. And the one before" – he waved his arm dismissively as Vanessa recalled it as Meg's favourite – "no more than simpering. Composer's Polish, they say, what? No breeding, no taste. What can one expect?"

Vanessa knew she was on thin ice and about to plunge through, on the verge of throwing away her new status in Jamie's society. But she spoke anyway, rising from the piano stool and facing her host.

"I believe, Sir Peregrine, that Chopin expects rather more discernment than he could possibly hope for in someone like you."

"Vanessa!" said Jamie, horrified.

"Quiet, boy!" shouted Sir Peregrine, pushing himself to his feet.

Vanessa stood stock-still, awaiting a fate somewhere between excommunication and firing-squad. But Sir Peregrine surprised her.

"How long have you been in this country, young woman?"

"Sixteen years," she replied.

Sir Peregrine looked at Jamie and spoke mildly.

"Long enough to learn manners, boy. I suggest you find another wife."

He took another, longer draw on his cigar, as though punctuating this last statement. Then he turned on his heel and left the room.

The rest of the group remained in their seats. Lady Blackthorne and Nicholas's faces were hostile, but Charlotte caught Vanessa's eye and smiled.

Jamie spoke. "Perhaps, my dear, you might wish to apologise to the others? I believe our evening's music is at an end."

"I do apologise," Vanessa said immediately. "I shall return to Bath in the morning."

"Join me in our carriage," Charlotte said immediately. "Nicholas is shooting with Jamie tomorrow and has promised me a day's shopping." She stood up. "And now you must come with me to the library. There is a folder of mezzotinto landscapes you should not fail to see before you leave."

She took Vanessa's arm and purposefully walked her from the room.

"We shall see you at breakfast, Jamie," she said as they passed.

Once in the library Charlotte gave a sigh of relief.

"For a moment I was afraid my father-in-law might have come here to cool his temper. I knew you needed some time away. You looked near to exploding."

"Did you mean it about taking me to Bath tomorrow?"

"Of course. We shall drive across Lansdown and deliver you directly to Beckford's Tower."

"I cannot tell you. . ." Vanessa began, but at that moment Jamie entered the room.

"Ah," said Charlotte. "I did not think I could hold him back, although I tried. Goodnight, Vanessa. Our carriage will leave at ten o'clock." She gave Vanessa an enigmatic smile and nodded at Jamie as she left the room.

Jamie hurried over and took Vanessa's hands. "Will you forgive me, dearest? I could not contradict our host."

Vanessa stared at the floor. Why not? she thought. Charlotte could. She tried to find an excuse for him and could not. But she comforted him anyway.

"I understand, Jamie. It must be awkward for you to have to defend a renegade colonial like me."

"You know it is not that." He stepped closer and once again Vanessa caught his scent. She recoiled, speaking more sharply than she'd intended.

"Jamie, this is not the time or the place to discuss your relations or my behaviour."

"But I love you, Vanessa. And I cannot choose my relations."

"No," she agreed. "But you can choose the ones you visit."

Jamie drew himself up. "Not always. I do not believe you understand the demands my position can impose."

"Perhaps I do not. But I shall be better able to discuss your demands in Bath. And we must also discuss *my* family's request that I return to Canada."

"Don't say it, Vanessa," he said, holding her hands tighter. "And you mustn't leave Blackthorne Park tomorrow. It would only confirm all the terrible things Sir Peregrine and Nicholas have said about you."

Vanessa flushed with anger, but her voice was slow and deliberate.

"All the more reason for me to go. I don't doubt that everything they say is true."

Jamie responded in kind. "Very well," he said coldly, taking his hands away. "As you suggest, we shall discuss these matters further in Bath. As long as we may do so without Mr. Marston present."

"On that," she said, "we agree."

Vanessa spent a sleepless night. The violence in the forest, the confrontation with Sir Peregrine, and suppressing her anger towards Jamie all took their toll. She listened obsessively to the irregularity in the movement of the carriage clock on the dresser, longing to stop it. But then she would have no way of knowing the time, or when she could hope to escape with Charlotte Blackthorne.

The moon was low in the sky when it finally occurred to her that she could cover the clock with a pillow. But by then she was too much on edge to try again for sleep. She thought again of the confrontation with the gypsies and the kick she'd used to disarm the man with the knife. A sideways shot, like one she'd used to level Ned Marston yesterday morning. The recollection gave her a smile, what felt like her first smile since she'd arrived at Blackthorne.

A half-hour later Vanessa was grateful that her room faced east, as she watched a slow, radiant sunrise penetrate the morning mist. She read by the light of the sun until, shortly before nine o'clock, there was a commotion outside.

She rose to look out the window. Jamie was shouting at a stable boy who was trying to hold onto a haltered horse, protesting that the steward had ridden it hard yesterday and it needed a rest. Jamie struck the boy who cringed, retreated into the stables, and returned with a bridle and saddle. When the horse was ready Jamie jumped astride, whipping it up to a gallop. Soon he was out of sight.

Jamie had not returned when Vanessa went down for breakfast, nor was Sir Peregrine or Nicholas present. But Charlotte was as good as her word. Vanessa climbed into the carriage at ten o'clock sharp and was home before eleven.

She unpacked slowly, wondering if Meg would close her shop early as she sometimes did on Wednesday afternoons. Then Vanessa tried to practice at the piano, but even in her own cottage she seemed to see Sir Peregrine's cigar smoke and hear the echo of his insults.

She knew he'd called Chopin impertinent for composing the pieces she'd played, but he must also have been referring to her own impertinence as well. And Jamie had not said a word in her defence. Nor – she smiled wryly – had he made any move when the gypsies threatened. He saved his violence for helpless stable boys and horses.

Could she live the rest of her life with such a man? She had felt safe with him before, but she knew that came partly from his often-declared affection for music – a familiar and comforting sentiment – and partly from the material safety of his wealth and family. Both of these now seemed less important.

And so did Jamie himself. As the memory of his milky scent returned Vanessa began to shudder.

At that moment Meg walked through the cottage door. She was at Vanessa's side in an instant, crouching to take her hands as she dropped her parcels by the piano.

"Are you ill, love? I didn't expect you home till Friday."

Vanessa slowly stood, lifted Meg up and held her close. With her head bowed she said, "I thought I was finally safe with Jamie."

Meg held Vanessa's shoulders and took a step back, looking at her carefully and shaking her head.

"I'm making you a toddy and putting you to bed. You can tell me the story afterwards."

Vanessa nodded. "Yes, please. Will you stay with me a while?"

"The day and the night long, love," Meg replied.

While Meg went to the kitchen to heat milk Vanessa shed her travelling clothes, put on a familiar old nightgown, and crawled into bed, propping herself up with pillows. Meg drew a chair close and as Vanessa sipped her drink she told the story of Blackthorne Park, concluding with the same statement as she'd begun.

"I thought I was finally safe with Jamie."

"You poor honey," said Meg, reaching for Vanessa's hand. "Safe isn't in your nature – never has been and never will be. But do you love him?"

Vanessa's shoulders began to shake. She twisted her body away, burying her face in the pillows.

"I don't think so," she whispered. "I don't think I'm capable of love."

"You're daft," Meg said firmly. "Do you think I'd have survived gaol if I hadn't felt your love every morning like sunshine? If you don't love Jamie, give him over. We'll get by."

Vanessa had started to cry. She fought it. Her fists clenched, one of them around Meg's hand, but her eyes and nose were running as she turned back to face her friend.

"Shall we?"

Meg smiled. "Never doubt it. You may even get some help from your mysterious American."

Vanessa's face crumpled. "Not him," she said. "I'm sure I've sent him packing."

Meg's smile grew wider. "I doubt it. Now, love, I have two messages for you. Martha and Frank leave tomorrow on the afternoon coach. She sent a note asking me to visit in the morning and I was about to write that I had no-one to help in the shop. But you can go. She will be so pleased to see you."

"What's the other message," asked Vanessa, pretending not to hope it was from Ned.

"Mrs. Giorgio asks if you could give a piano lesson in her studio tomorrow at noon. A sweet young girl, she says, with very rich parents."

Vanessa tried to hide her disappointment. "It's as well I came back. I'll need some new piano pupils when Jamie's lot goes away." She pushed herself further under the bedclothes and closed her eyes. When she opened them Meg was still looking at her. "Shall we ever be happy, Meg?"

"Of course we shall, poppet."

Vanessa closed her eyes again, but came alert to a noise from under the bed. Katrina the cat emerged, jumped onto Vanessa's feet and padded purposefully along the length of the bedclothes. She gave Vanessa's chin a couple of licks, turned, settled herself on Vanessa's stomach, and began to wash.

Two minutes later Vanessa was asleep. She was still asleep when Meg left for her shop the next morning.

CHAPTER XIV

Ned had felt agreeably battered after Monday's *tae kwon do* in Mrs. Giorgio's studio. He'd said his farewells to Vanessa and Meg knowing that Vanessa was leaving for her house-party that afternoon and that it was time he made some decisions about his own future.

No decisions were forthcoming. He needed a distraction. The Hot Baths would soothe his bruises from the morning's exercise. But the heat wouldn't stop him thinking about Vanessa. He decided to hire a horse, to retrieve what few skills he'd ever had as a horseback-rider.

He got more distraction than he'd bargained for, discovering that everything he'd learned in the United States about riding was useless. The horse bucked, pranced sideways, and did everything except follow what Ned thought were perfectly clear signals. In despair he let the reins go entirely slack and after a few minutes the horse found its own way home, where a sympathetic groom took Ned in hand and showed him the rudiments.

The first thing he learned was that English horses responded to being led with the appropriate rein rather than to pressure on the opposite side of the neck. After that and with a fresh mount, Ned and the groom made good progress, ending a three-hour lesson with a fine gallop in the open country above Widcombe Hill.

The next morning he took a horse from the same stables and rode the twelve miles to Bristol. He spent the night there, and two days in the bookshops, returning to Bath Wednesday evening, stiff, worn-out, and with a saddlebag full of sixteenth and seventeenth-century books.

On Thursday he gave himself a respite, sleeping late before heading to the baths for a morning soak. Just as he'd feared: as soon as he settled into the water the image of Vanessa returned. There were no hot baths to console sore minds.

If Vanessa was at a grand house-party with Lord Jamie it had to mean their engagement was decided. And that, he reminded himself again, was good news. He'd seen how the young lord doted on her: a perfect dance partner, deferential in conversation, even buying her the new piano she'd played in Cavendish Crescent.

After ten minutes he pulled himself from the bath, knowing that this train of thought led nowhere. As he dried off he decided to take another walk. A *long* walk. He wouldn't return to Queen Square until he had a plan.

He reversed the route along the river he'd taken with Vanessa, when they'd talked about Theseus and Ariadne. Then he turned round and went the other way.

No plan emerged. Everywhere he went he saw visions – of Vanessa shocking the tourists at river's edge with her ribald song, at the exercise studio in Westgate Buildings, taking his arm at the Abbey.

It was time for him to leave Bath. He could no longer intrude on her life, or expect her to share her friends.

He entered Meg's shop shortly after noon, ready to say he was taking the afternoon coach to London, that he was returning to America, and that she should say his farewells to Vanessa and Robert.

But Meg spoke first. "Vanessa returned early from the house-party, Ned, angry and unhappy that Lord Jamie hadn't defended her from her host's insults. She left Blackthorne Park without saying goodbye."

Ned felt a shiver of hope, but suppressed it.

"This does not speak well for matrimonial tranquillity."

"No, sir," Meg retorted. "It does not."

"They'll make it up," he said gloomily. "I've seen how much he loves her."

Meg didn't answer. Ned began to wander around the shop, intrigued by all the paraphernalia of 1830s womanhood. He paused in front of a triangular piece of steel, wondering what it was doing among all the laces and frills. Meg looked across at him and started to laugh.

"It's called the 'divorce,' Ned."

"I'm none the wiser."

"Gentlemen aren't meant to be. It goes in a corset to separate the breasts."

Ned blushed as she continued. "Do you not see the drollery in it? It divorces not only the bosom but also the adulterer caught in its snare."

Ned stared at the floor. "I never imagined Englishwomen were so honest."

Meg snorted. "Never trust the English to be honest, sir. For that you must rely on us Irish."

Ned raised his eyes to see Meg's sparkling with affectionate mischief. He wanted to ask more about Vanessa's trouble at the house-party, but he caught himself.

Meg saw his discomfiture. "You're a lost lamb, aren't you?"

"Am I so obvious?"

"Only to a friend," she replied. "Call on Vanessa at Mrs. Giorgio's studio. She has a piano lesson there. If you arrive at one o'clock the lesson will be over. She'll be glad of a walk if the weather holds."

Ned was torn.

"I don't think I should see Vanessa before I leave Bath."

"No, Ned. She needs to see you."

"She *can't* need me. She has Lord Jamie."

"Trust me. Women cannot tolerate sudden disappearances. Or silences."

If Vanessa was in town, leaving without saying goodbye was a coward's way out. He hadn't booked his place on the coach yet, or collected his bag from his lodgings. There was an evening coach that would do just as well. He could spend the night in Reading and be in London tomorrow before the banks closed.

CHAPTER XV

Vanessa also slept late on Thursday morning. When she went downstairs to make tea Meg had left a letter on the dining-table. It was from Jamie, declaring he was returning to Bath and insisting she return with him to Blackthorne Park. She crumpled it up and threw it in the fireplace. Then she dressed for her visit to Martha Austen.

One of the hotel maids accompanied Vanessa to the Austens' room, where she found Martha alone with her needlework. Martha was wearing a plain grey dress that made her look old, but the lines in her face fell away as she smiled. Frank was overseeing transport of their luggage to the coach-house and collecting his boots at the cobbler's. The two women had time for coffee, which the maid undertook to deliver.

"I perceive you have something to tell me," Martha said as Vanessa took a chair opposite. Martha carefully set her needlework on a side table, sat up straighter, and met Vanessa's gaze.

Without hesitation Vanessa recounted Jamie's behaviour at Blackthorne Park, pausing only when the maid returned. By the time Vanessa had finished her story their coffee had gone cold.

"My dear child," said Martha, smiling as she dipped a biscuit in her cup. "I never conceived you would be happy with Lord James. You and he were bred differently, and I do not say this out of deference to the Earl of Arran."

Vanessa smiled ruefully. "Is the aristocracy so determined to breed all kindness out of its men?"

"I am scarcely acquainted with families of such high station, but among my own circle I have known men's kindness all my life. I do not think Frank ever entertained an unkind thought for anyone, even when he fought the Americans and the French. The same was true of his father and brothers."

Martha leaned back in her chair and gave a reminiscent smile.

"When Jane was at her most satirical she contrasted the benevolence of her family to the rest of the world she knew. That is one reason there is so much spirit in her novels, and why I love them so."

"You sound as though she were still with you."

"I believe she is, my dear, watching and smiling. We were husband-hunters together when we were young, you know, the husband-huntingest girls you ever saw. And now that I have the finest husband in the world I feel myself closer to Jane than ever before."

Vanessa smiled. "I only met her three times, but I sometimes feel she is with me too."

"I conceive she is, and that like me she would encourage you to reject a suitor who is inferior to you in all respects other than rank and wealth."

"I can't understand why it took me so long to appreciate his true nature."

Martha shook her head. "Don't blame yourself. On the surface he had everything a young woman could possibly desire. Indeed I expect that to many, perhaps most women his superficial attractions would be so great that the absence of liberality would pass unnoticed."

Vanessa leaned forward, taking Martha's hands. "Thank you," she whispered.

Martha smiled. "And what of your American visitor, Mr. Marston?"

Vanessa pulled her hands away, blushing.

Martha gave a gentle laugh. "Did he not play some part in your new-found understanding of Lord James's character?"

"Oh, Martha, I don't know. I knew Ned Marston so long ago and so much about our lives has changed."

"Perhaps not, my dear. If you were close to him in the past, that may be the best ground for your future happiness. I loved Frank's two sisters from childhood as though they were my own, and so many of his ways now — especially his teasing — remind me of Jane. Our past connections are part of our present."

Vanessa smiled, encouraging Martha to continue.

"You know that Frank was married for many years before he found his way to me. I shared his family's sorrow when his first wife died, and I only hope God will forgive me for taking such joy in his company now."

Vanessa was startled. "Surely you don't believe it's a sin to love your husband?"

Martha shook her head. "I never dreamed I would love him so much. I married him because I admired him and because he had been part of my life for so long. But now our love is different. I wonder if mothers learn something of this kind of love when they have children."

Vanessa saw the tears in her friend's eyes. This time she took Martha's hands and held on.

"So perhaps," Vanessa said softly, "familiarity does not breed contempt?"

"No, my dear. Familiarity breeds understanding. And without familiarity there can never be true love."

Martha withdrew her hands and picked up her needlework. Vanessa took the hint: their moment of intimacy had ended.

"Now," said Martha. "I am certain Frank will return at any moment and insist you take a late breakfast with us before we depart. I can tell from your expression that you would prefer not to, or have another engagement, and I quite understand. Go quickly, and give my love to Megan. I rely on you to visit us in Hampshire."

Vanessa rose. She was about to turn away, but on an impulse she leaned over and threw her arms around her friend, kissing her cheek. She left the room without another word.

Vanessa recovered some of her equanimity on the walk from the York Hotel to Mrs. Giorgio's studio in Westgate Buildings. She was grateful that her employer was away and she had the studio to herself. After her piano lesson Vanessa would have the rest of the afternoon free.

Her new pupil was little more than a beginner, but anxious to please. The hour passed quickly and Vanessa delivered a happy child into the arms of her mother at one o'clock.

She stretched her fingers as she returned to the studio, thinking about changing into her exercise clothes. But her sorrows returned. She sighed and resumed her seat at the piano stool. No sooner had she done so than there came a knock at the door.

CHAPTER XVI

Ned couldn't understand why Vanessa blushed as she answered the studio door. She seemed almost as ill-at-ease as he was.

"I came to say goodbye," he said.

"Oh," said Vanessa, her blush fading as she stared at the floor.

"I went to Meg's shop to leave you a message and she told me you were back from your house-party."

"I am."

"I said I didn't want to bother you, that it would be better if I just left quietly and let you go on with Lord Jamie."

Vanessa finally raised her eyes. Ned was shocked at the pain in them.

"You'd better come in," she said. "There's no-one else here."

Ned followed her into the studio. Vanessa sat on the piano stool.

"Where will you go?"

"America, I guess. I don't want to live in London, even though it's the only other place I've made friends. I never got to see my family's old townhouse in Philadelphia. Maybe it's still there in 1833."

Vanessa was only half-facing Ned, looking across the big studio room and avoiding his eyes. He wondered if she was remembering their *tae kwon do* practice on Monday. After a moment her left hand settled on the piano keys, repeating a short sequence of notes over and over.

"I suppose," she finally said, "you might meet some of your ancestors."

"I might. If I mess things up the way I did in Shakespeare's time I might kill one of them and cease to exist." He paused. "Which might not be such a bad thing."

"Don't be melodramatic, Ned."

"Why not?"

"Because *I* need to be melodramatic right now."

She played the sequence of notes again, this time using both hands. The music was repetitive and gloomy. After the third time Ned said, "What *is* that?"

"Sorry." Vanessa pulled her hands away. "I get things stuck in my head that reflect my moods. When Jamie first started courting me I felt safe, as though I had a future that finally looked bearable. I played Mozart then. Now when I think of him I get tunes like this."

She played it again. "It's one of Rachmaninoff's *dies irae* themes – 'day of wrath, day of terror.' He uses them in his music all the time."

Ned could see the sadness in her eyes as she continued. "I can't normally play things ahead of this time if there's anyone else in earshot. But you're different. It must be because we're both from the future." She looked down. "Or maybe it's just who you are."

She put both hands on the keys and played again. Ned was swept up in the music as she followed the theme through a relentless, surging series of ascending chords. Ned shivered when she stopped.

"What's it called?" he asked reverently.

"It's one of the preludes. B-minor, opus 32."

"You played it at one of your London University recitals. Why did you stop performing there?"

Vanessa became thoughtful. "When I interviewed with Caroline I told her it was because I wanted to wait until my dissertation was finished. But I'm not sure I could have done my final recitals at all. Complete strangers came up and talked to me after my first two. It went on for weeks." She gave a wry smile. "One of the strangers was you, of course, but I didn't know then that you had a different ulterior motive."

She sighed. "Most of the time I couldn't bear it. I couldn't bear the idea of being recognised, so I stopped playing. But here I have no choice."

Ned nodded and touched her arm in sympathy.

She met his eyes. "It's not that bad here, for some reason. The audiences don't bother me the same way."

"They don't presume."

"What?"

"They don't expect that buying tickets to hear you play gives them entry to your social life."

"I suppose that's part of it." She broke their gaze, hesitating. "You've heard about the trouble at Blackthorne Park?"

Ned nodded. "Meg told me."

"I got a note from Jamie this morning, saying he was bringing a carriage to take me back."

"You don't have to go."

"I know I don't. But part of the trouble with Jamie is you."

"He's one of the reasons I'm leaving," Ned replied. "Maybe the only reason."

Vanessa suddenly sounded shy. "Would you have stayed, just for me?"

Ned fought his emotions, regretting he'd come. It was cruel of Vanessa to bait him this way.

"Don't ask me that," he said.

"I *have* to ask. I'm finished with Jamie. It's all over but the disentangling."

"No," Ned cried. "I *never* interfered."

"You didn't have to."

"We're never going to be rescued," he said. "You have a chance for the perfect Jane Austen marriage. Don't throw it away."

Vanessa's face darkened. "I don't intend to marry anyone. I don't belong in this time. I don't belong anywhere. The idea of marrying and having babies seems monstrous, against nature."

"I see," said Ned. But he didn't. How could she have seemed so happy with Jamie if she'd never intended to marry him?

"Never mind," said Vanessa, rising to her feet. "Let's walk."

CHAPTER XVII

Poor Ned, Vanessa thought. Too much talk about feelings and men are lost. But she hoped he'd share her walk, and she had an idea.

As they left Westgate Buildings she turned back, pointing at them. "Speaking of Jane Austen endings, have you finished *Persuasion*?"

"Yes." She could tell he was grateful for the change of subject.

"Anne Elliot's schoolfriend Mrs. Smith lived here as a poor widow. Gives you an idea of my usual social status in Bath, doesn't it?"

He smiled. "Why don't you take me on an Anne Elliot tour?"

His voice was so gentle that Vanessa got a lump in her throat.

"That's what. . . ." She caught her breath and started over. "That's what I was thinking. You've already seen the sights of Milsom Street."

"Let's see them again."

She knew that most of the walk was familiar to Ned, but he didn't seem to mind. In twenty minutes they'd passed Molland's and the Assembly Rooms. As they reached the top of Russell Street she pointed to their left.

"That's Rivers Street, where Lady Russell lived. We're most of the way to Sir Walter Elliot's house in Camden Place now. One way or another Anne would have climbed this hill almost every day."

Ned was next to her on the broad pavement now. She thought of his invocation of Captain Wentworth, Anne's romantic interest in *Persuasion,* when she had first introduced Ned to Frank and Robert. Those two were the true naval officers, of course, but now Vanessa was starting to feel that Ned himself was even more like Captain Wentworth than either of her friends. There was a steadiness about him, something solid and true.

She took his arm, thinking what an odd world it was where she could publicly walk arm-in-arm with a single man, close enough to feel his heartbeat, without too many inferences being made. But if she wrote that man a letter accepting an invitation the whole world would assume they were going to marry.

Fifty yards more and they were in sight of Camden Place, another of Bath's honey-coloured Georgian crescents. They crossed over the road and up some stone steps to the level of the houses. The crescent's far end was shorter than the near one, with the road passing very close to the last house. Beyond that was a steep drop in the hill.

Vanessa anticipated Ned's question. "They built a perfect crescent but the embankment was unstable and the eastern end just fell off. That's probably why it's called Camden Place instead of Camden Crescent. I've wondered whether the collapse didn't make the locals nervous and depress property values. Maybe that's why Sir Walter Elliot, twit that he was, rented his house here. It was the most ostentation he could get for his money."

They continued east beyond the crescent, where they had the pavement to themselves. Vanessa pointed at the little houses on the right.

"These have another floor below street level and are much nicer than they seem. Meg and I almost took one." She dropped her voice. "But I refused to have neighbours so close. It's bad enough having my speech change when people are around, but with neighbours everywhere I would never have been able to play my own piano music."

"Like the Rachmaninoff?" he asked.

She nodded. "At the cottage I can tell if anyone's coming because if I'm playing something written after this time, the music just stops. I don't know whether it's the piano or my brain or what."

When Ned didn't reply she went on. "I don't play the later Romantics much – they're just too heavy – but you'd be surprised how nice Ravel sounds on my little pianoforte." She gave him another look. "Were you fond of twentieth century jazz?"

"Some," said Ned, sounding wary.

"I play it all the time when I'm alone. 'In a Sentimental Mood?'" She gave a sly smile.

Ned grinned. "How about that Leonard Bernstein song from *On the Town?*"

She knew exactly which one he meant and sang softly,

"Where has the time all gone to?
Haven't done half the things we want to,
Oh well, we'll catch up some other time. . . ."

Ned's reply was scarcely audible. "Being here puts a whole new meaning on the words, doesn't it?"

They stopped and faced each other. Vanessa saw the sadness in his eyes and reached out, caressing his cheek with her fingertips.

"*Touché.*"

She tensed as he kissed her, her skin electrified by his touch. The faint smell of fir trees was back. As their bodies drew close together she let her lips melt against his.

A sudden gaggle of voices came from a steep, narrow path below. Vanessa broke their kiss an instant before they were seen.

"You are presumptuous, sir," she whispered.

But she took his hand as she crossed the road towards a flight of steps opposite, feeling as though a great weight had been lifted from her shoulders. She pointed up at a handsome terrace of six houses set directly in front of a cliff. The two middle ones shared a triangular pediment with a coat-of-arms.

"Um," she said slowly, shifting gears. "That's another Camden. Camden Terrace. The poor people who live there have to climb all those steps to their front doors. They're no good to us, those steps. They're a dead-end. We'll go up this footpath to the top and cut back to Lansdown Road. We've seen enough of Anne Elliot's Bath for one day."

She took his arm, tugging him up the steep hill. At the top the path veered to the left and soon entered the shade of a cluster of ancient trees.

Ned finally spoke. "I should have kissed you when I knocked you down in Mrs. Giorgio's studio the other day."

Vanessa smiled, knowing he was remembering the moment in the time-travel laboratory when he'd held her by the shoulders, suspended in mid-air.

"We don't-have to be that gymnastic every time," she said. "And I wasn't ready for you to kiss me on Monday." She looked at him again. "But I am now."

Ned took the hint. Then they sat on some tree-roots, side by side. He reached across, brushing the row of curls across her forehead. Vanessa leaned against him, remembering how the cat had purred as Ned stroked her on his first night at the cottage. After a few moments she made herself sit up and face him.

"I don't know what I was thinking with Jamie."

"You don't have to say a thing."

Vanessa put her finger on his lips, silencing him. "I so wanted to be safe that I made myself get used to being with him. I suppose thousands of women – married women – could tell the same story. And he was my first suitor whose intentions seemed honourable."

She paused, wondering how much more to say. Her heart told her this explanation needed to be short.

"When Jamie first proposed I refused him. I kept on refusing. Then I made the mistake of replying to his invitation to Blackthorne. I found out later that my acceptance in writing implied our engagement."

"Nice girls don't write," Ned said, his eyes brightening.

"Shut up," she replied.

"No, really," Ned protested. "Do you think Jamie was setting a trap when he wrote to you?"

"I don't know," she sighed. "Maybe he sensed I was never really attached to him. And he's the kind of man who's provoked by rejection. It made him want me more."

Ned smiled. "I can't say I blame him. And I can't hate him for trying to make you happy."

Vanessa shook her head. "It wasn't about making me happy. I fed his longing to be – I don't know, an impresario. He never saw who I really was."

"His mistake," Ned murmured.

She stood up, embarassed. Ned stood too, reaching for her hands, but she pulled away.

"I know somewhere else we could go on our walk," she said.

"Good," he replied. "I'm not ready to say good-bye."

"Back down the hill and over to Sydney Place. That's where Jane herself lived."

CHAPTER XVIII

They retraced the path to Camden Road. From there they went directly down the steep hill to the new Cleveland Bridge.

"In Jane's day there was only a ferry," Vanessa said.

At the end of Bathwick Street Vanessa made a detour, bringing Ned into Sydney Gardens at their easternmost point. They walked along sloping lawns and across a stone bridge that spanned a canal, emerging at the western end, closest to town.

Number 4 Sydney Place was on their right. It had little to distinguish it from its neighbours, at least from the outside, and Vanessa said it had housed so many tenants since the Austens left in 1804 that there was no trace of the family on the inside either.

"But it's where she lived."

Ned was looking pensive. "There were only two characters with real titles in *Persuasion*. Viscountess Dalrymple was a harridan and Sir Walter Elliot was — well, you called him a twit. Were all the aristocrats in Jane Austen as dreadful as those two?"

"They were pretty bad. Sir Thomas Bertram in *Mansfield Park* at least had what the novel called a general wish of doing right, but he wasn't much of a prize. Sir Edward Denham in *Sanditon* was another baronet and another twit, a younger version of Sir Walter."

Vanessa paused, gathering her thoughts. "Lady Catherine de Bourgh in *Pride and Prejudice* was probably the worst of them all. And she was a younger child of an earl, just like Jamie."

She met his eyes. "That's what you're getting at, isn't it? That the way Jane Austen wrote her aristocrats should have given me a clue about Jamie?"

Ned nodded. After a moment Vanessa continued.

"It probably wasn't a coincidence that Jane made her aristocrats so awful, but I don't think that was the problem. I was the problem. Jane and her family were so kind to me, so much what I'd dreamed they would be, that when Jamie came along I was sure he had to be Mr. Darcy."

She gave Ned an inquiring glance. "You've read *Pride and Prejudice*, surely?"

"I saw the movie," he said sheepishly.

"So you know who I'm talking about."

Ned nodded again. Vanessa was determined to see her confession through to the end. She rushed on.

"I decided Jamie had Mr. Darcy's arrogance and that I could overcome it. Then he'd be the perfect husband. I didn't really consider that if I went that far I might actually have to marry him. Maybe I was just a gold-digger. I feel so ashamed of myself."

She looked away, fighting tears. Ned touched her arm, but she shrugged him off, turning towards Great Pulteney Street and the centre of town.

Ned matched her stride. "It's lucky for me," he said. "If Jamie had really been like Mr. Darcy I wouldn't have stood a chance."

Vanessa finally smiled, taking his arm. "Oh, I don't know. You might have had to be a little more patient, that's all."

"So I don't have to play second fiddle to the Austens?"

Her smile grew broad. "No. You could never play second fiddle to anyone."

She kept her arm linked with his as they walked contentedly along the level pavement, beneath a grand terrace of uniform, honey-coloured houses. They had nearly reached the bridge when Vanessa spoke again.

"I'm glad I started to love you in our own time."

"I know," said Ned. "It makes this less like – I don't know, I suppose less like clutching at straws. Less like taking solace in each other."

"That's it," said Vanessa. She started to smile up at him, but a voice from behind called her name. She dropped Ned's arm and turned.

It was Jamie, rounding the corner from Henrietta Street. He was dressed for the road in a short jacket and breeches, red-faced and dusty, with his driving gloves in one hand.

"I've been searching the town for you," he panted. He glared at Ned. "And you, sir, are walking alone with my fiancée."

Vanessa answered quickly. "I am not your fiancée, Jamie."

"You may not deny it, Vanessa. I have brought the curricle to take us back to Blackthorne Park, where we have an announcement to make. I requested that you remain at home so I might collect you. Instead I find you in the company of this jackanapes."

"I have no intention of returning to Blackthorne. Nor will I tolerate your insulting my friend."

Ned smiled. "I've been called worse."

"Perhaps I must do so, sir," snapped Jamie. "I intend to speak privately to Miss Horwood. I require your departure."

"That," Ned said flatly, "is up to Miss Horwood."

In an instant Jamie whipped up his gloves, aiming for Ned's face. But Ned was faster, his arm a blur as he gripped Jamie's wrist. With a yelp of pain Jamie dropped the gloves.

"Poor decision, Lord James," said Ned conversationally, still holding Jamie's arm aloft.

"Would you strike me, sir?" Jamie cried.

Ned released the arm, taking a step back. "I should rather say I prevented you from striking *me*."

"Perhaps. But my intention is evident."

Ned began to laugh. "Not again," he almost choked. "It can't be happening again."

"What does this signify?" Jamie was indignant. "Am I insufficiently clear?"

"You are clear enough," Ned replied coldly. "I suggest you leave now and take your intention with you."

Vanessa looked from one man to the other. Lord Jamie was shaking with rage. Ned was calm enough and still amused, but the way he carried himself reminded Vanessa of how dangerous he had seemed when she first met him.

Go, Jamie, she thought. Go now.

Jamie raised his chin. "You fail to understand me, sir. I have offered a challenge to which you must in honour respond. You are required to designate a second, and you will have the choice of weapons."

Now Ned's smile was positively frightening. "I did not hear that, Lord James. Miss Horwood and I are continuing to" – he gave a sideways glance at Vanessa, who said "Milsom Street."

"Milsom Street," Ned repeated.

Jamie's eyes shifted, avoiding Ned's stare.

"I require. . . ."

Vanessa could stand no more. "Not another word, Jamie," she cried angrily.

Jamie began to retreat, his eyes fixed on hers. After a dozen backward steps he turned, disappearing up Henrietta Street.

Vanessa whirled on Ned.

"And you," she said, her voice lower but still furious. "You're as bad as he is. He thinks I'm desperate because I'm poor. *You* think I'm desperate because I'm lost outside our time. I don't need either one of you."

Ned stood his ground. "I know you don't," he replied. "I'm not here because I think you need me."

"Good," she said shortly.

She took his arm and resumed their walk towards Milsom Street, the opposite direction to the one Jamie had taken. Once again Ned matched her stride. Halfway across the bridge he spoke.

"Shall I take that packet to Philadelphia?"

"Not now," she replied. She cocked her head, looking up at him, "Not ever." Then she grinned. "You handled yourself well."

"I learned in Shakespeare's time that fighting can be the easy way out."

Vanessa took his hand, entwining their fingers. "I could get used to spending time with you."

Ned pulled her closer. "It looks like we'll have a lot of it to spend."

Vanessa stiffened. "But don't expect me to marry you. I don't intend to marry *anyone*."

They walked in silence for a few minutes. As they passed Barrett's bookshop in Bond Street Vanessa changed the subject.

"Do you sail, sir?"

"You asked me that. . ." Ned began.

"The day before I time-travelled," she whispered.

"The answer hasn't changed," said Ned. "It's still no. Why?"

"I have plans for you, Mr. Marston." She took her hand away as they came into Milsom Street. "But first," she said, "we have something to tell Meg."

HISTORICAL POSTSCRIPT

*T*he *Perfect Visit*, needless to say, is a work of fiction. It presumes its readers are acquainted with the works of Jane Austen, but I have tried to ensure that those who are not will be able to make sense of my references. The only essential detail not specifically described in my text is that at the end of *Persuasion* its heroine, Anne Elliot, is reunited with her suitor Captain Wentworth after rejecting him eight years earlier.

I have not invented or tampered with important events in the lives of the several historical characters who appear in my novel. In 1817 Jane Austen lived at Chawton until she moved to Winchester to be closer to her doctor, Mr. King Lyford. Martha Lloyd was in near-constant attendance.

Two of Jane's brothers, Francis and Charles, were naval officers. Francis (known in the family as Frank) married Martha Lloyd in 1828 and outlived her, ultimately — as his friend Robert suggests — becoming Admiral of the Fleet. Daguerreotypes of Martha and Frank in later life survive.

Henry Austen was partner in a bank in Alton which failed late in 1815. I am not sure what happened to the premises afterwards, but its becoming a branch of Hoare's suited my story. Henry later took clerical orders and was curate at Bentley at the time I put him there. Edward Austen Knight had to have felt the pinch from his enormous loss (my figure of £20,000 is accurate) resulting from the failure of Henry's bank, but I have not tracked down specific documentation as to when and where he stayed with his family on visits to London in 1818.

Jane Austen was especially close to two of her nieces, Fanny Knight and Anna Austen Lefroy, both mentioned here. I should be surprised, however, if young Anna actually had any correspondents in Ontario.

Judith Shakespeare was one of the bard's two daughters and Nicholas Ling one of his primary publishers. Ben Jonson, George Chapman, and John Marston were historical playwrights. John was generally reckoned a feisty and unpleasant character, quick both to give and take offence. Ben Jonson reported that the two had many quarrels and that on one occasion Jonson "beat him and took his pistol from him." Shakespeare's *Troilus and Cressida* is thought by some to have been performed at one of the Inns of Court in 1607 or 1608, but I doubt that any respectable theatre historian would agree with my account of the performance.

Nicholas Ling was arguably the greatest of the literary booksellers in Shakespeare's time. He was an author as well: his *Politeuphuia, Wits Commonwealth*, a collection of apophthegms first published in 1597, went through three or four editions during his own life and at least a dozen posthumously. Its popularity spawned several imitations, of considerable importance to Shakespeare scholars. I have invented Ling's "Shakespeare cupboard" and his larger proprietary interest in Shakespeare's plays and sonnets, but Ling did publish the specific Shakespeare titles I describe and the two men were certainly acquainted. I also invented Ling's apprentice-boy Thomas Crane, imagining him the son of the poet and scrivener Ralph, whose role in Shakespeare's First Folio remains a subject of scholarly debate.

Elizabeth Fry, active at Newgate prison beginning in 1816, is unlikely to have visited Winchester Gaol as early as 1817, if at all. James Joyce was not at Shakespeare & Co. in Paris on February 2, 1922, making eyes at Caroline or anyone else. Sir Richard Colt Hoare did not hold a position at Hoare's Bank. Nor did William Beckford ever build a Gamekeeper's Cottage to accompany his Tower in Bath, although he was notoriously lecherous, even in later life.

I have tried to be true to the spirits of all my historical characters, however peripherally they appear. It is presumption of a very high order to bring both Jane Austen and William Shakespeare into a single work of fiction, let alone a first novel. Of the two, somehow Jane Austen intimidates me more, even though Shakespeare is perhaps the greater genius. Perhaps, too, it is easier to conjure one's own vision of Shakespeare because so little is known of him. Jane's letters and the memoirs of family members give some idea of her, although there will always be scholarly disagreement about her nature.

I tried to write more of Jane in this book, but I could not. The scenes that remain are those seeming to me most true (or perhaps I should say least false) to her character.

Fanny Dickens, Charles's older sister, did play the piano but I got my dates in a muddle and initially thought the family had moved from Chatham to London in 1817 instead of 1822. By the time I realised my mistake Vanessa had already given her piano lesson and become attached to Fanny, and so had I. When Fanny's parents enrolled her at the Academy of Music in 1823, her nominator was the piano-maker Thomas Tomkisson. By then, as Charles Dickens's biographer Peter Ackroyd puts it, she "was already a talented pianist." Her father worked for the Navy and Fanny might have heard "Oh, Shenandoah" on a dockside walk with him. The song is generally reckoned to have originated as an American sea-shanty at least as early as the 1820s.

If I have tinkered a little with history, I have done my best not to tinker with bibliography. The working title of this book was "A Bibliographical Romance" and I have tried to be strictly true to that descriptive science. Every reference to books, authorship, texts, publisher's imprints, and prices is, as far as I know, accurate, except where Vanessa and Ned's ownership is concerned. The texts of the Jane Austen poems transcribed herein are the standard versions and I hope I have not misquoted any of the lines from her novels. My only intentional textual fabrication is the supposedly-earlier version of a single Shakespeare sonnet, but of course that entire manuscript, including its binding and inscription, is my own invention.

Vanessa's verses and book-titles, as well as her surname, are appropriated from a real author named Caroline Horwood. If I have made my Miss Horwood a character of whom the real Caroline Horwood, afterwards Mrs. Baker, would disapprove, I apologise to her and any descendants she may have, wherever they may be. Caroline's books were published by the female booksellers Dean & Munday and I believe my description of their premises is accurate as far as it goes. The other booksellers Vanessa visits were also real, both the named Darton and Harris, and the unnamed couple on Skinner Street, whom one or two readers may recognise as Mary Jane Godwin and her indigent husband William, the latter of whom constantly importuned his son-in-law, Percy Bysshe Shelley, for loans.

Richard Heber had a fabulous collection of Shakespeare. His 1594 quarto of *Taming of the Shrew* was described as "unique" in his 1834 auction catalogue and it fetched £94, then the highest price ever paid at auction for a single play. He had a baker's dozen other first edition Shakespeare plays in quarto, more than twenty pre-1660 later quarto editions, and a passel of doubtful, spurious, and associated plays. He was the obvious man to buy Ned's manuscript, although I am not sure whether the real Heber would have overcome his scruples to pay Ned's astronomical price for it.

John Payne Collier, Alexander Dyce, and others from the Society of Antiquaries, excepting Dr. Walcot, are also historical figures, as is "Mr. Perkins," whom I modelled on Francis Douce, changing his surname to avoid confusion with Dyce. Collier was later proved an active forger and a rogue on other counts, but in all fairness there is no indication that the historical Collier ever commissioned outright robbery. I have described the Society and the general nature of its proceedings as accurately as I could, but I should say that its real meetings were on Thursdays and rarely if ever in September.

ACKNOWLEDGMENTS

This book would never have been written without the encouragement, support, and editorial expertise of my wife, Valerie Andrews. It is dedicated to her with love. Friends and family read variously sprawling drafts and offered advice, pretty much all of which I adopted. Among them were Adrian Bennett, Clare Claydon, Barbara Cowart, John Crichton, Janet Freeman, Charles George, Katy Homans, Noel King, Harvey Klinger and associates, Howard Lakin, David Lesser, Kevin MacCormack, Stephen Orgel, Rocky Stensrud, and John Varriano. My agents Jane Judd in London and Jennifer Unter in New York gave more of their time and energy than I had any reason to expect. I can't thank either of them enough.

ABOUT THE AUTHOR

Stuart Bennett was an auctioneer at Christie's in London before starting his own rare book business. He is author of the Christie's Collectors' Guide *How to Buy Photographs* (1987), *Trade Bookbinding in the British Isles* (2004) which the London *Times Literary Supplement* called "a bold and welcome step forward" in the history of bookbinding, and many publications on early photography, auctions and auctioneers, and rare books.

14549192R00200

Made in the USA
Charleston, SC
18 September 2012